HER AVENGING ANGEL
HER ANGEL: ETERNAL WARRIORS
BOOK 4

FELICITY HEATON

Copyright © 2014 Felicity Heaton

All rights reserved. No part of this publication may be reproduced, stored in a retrieval system, or transmitted, in any form or by any means mechanical, electronic, photocopying, recording or otherwise without the prior written consent of the publisher, nor be otherwise circulated in any form of binding or cover other than that in which it is published and without a similar condition being imposed on the subsequent purchaser.

The right of Felicity Heaton to be identified as the Author of the Work has been asserted by her in accordance with the Copyright, Designs and Patents Act 1988.

First printed August 2019

Second Edition

Layout and design by Felicity Heaton

All characters in this publication are purely fictitious and any resemblance to real persons, living or dead, is purely coincidental.

THE HER ANGEL WORLD

HER ANGEL: BOUND WARRIORS
Book 1: Dark Angel
Book 2: Fallen Angel
Book 3: Warrior Angel
Book 4: Bound Angel

HER ANGEL: ETERNAL WARRIORS
Book 1: Her Guardian Angel
Book 2: Her Demonic Angel
Book 3: Her Wicked Angel
Book 4: Her Avenging Angel
Book 5: Her Sinful Angel

Discover more available paranormal romance books at:
http://www.felicityheaton.com

Or sign up to my mailing list to receive a FREE vampire romance ebook, learn about new titles, be eligible for special subscriber-only giveaways, and read exclusive content including short stories:
http://ml.felicityheaton.com/mailinglist

CHAPTER 1

It had been twenty-seven days, give or take a few, since Nevar's master had bothered to show up for his duty and relieve him, taking his place outside the crystal chamber in which the Great Destroyer slumbered, deep in the bowels of the Devil's fortress in Hell.

A destroyer that Nevar had awoken by spilling Asmodeus's and Liora's blood in the very chamber he now guarded, and had become the creature's master, much to the annoyance of the Devil.

Twenty-seven days of mind-numbing silence and boredom.

Nevar was going out of his head.

Or at least more out of it than normal.

He was feeling honest enough with himself today to admit that he might have been out of his head before the guard duty had started, but doing such a thing was dangerous.

The darkness within him spread tendrils outwards, filling his mind with vicious hissed words that goaded him into finding Asmodeus, the wretched angel who had turned him into a monster, and satisfying his soul-deep hunger to make the bastard pay.

Nevar closed his eyes and practiced his breathing, filling his lungs from the bottom up and counting slowly to five on each long inhale through his nose and five again on each exhale out of his mouth. Liora had taught him it as a method of regaining control of himself and quashing his darker urges whenever they came upon him. It had been step one in his rehabilitation programme—taking control. He was still working on step two—taking responsibility.

He drew another deep breath and shut out the coaxing voice and the other one that liked to mock him.

Once a proud guardian angel serving Heaven and the protector of Erin.

Now a loathsome creature forced into a contract with an evil angel, filled with darkness and an endless unstoppable hunger for violence, and cursed with an unquenchable thirst for blood.

Euphoria addict.

Recovering alcoholic.

Whore.

Bastard.

The worst part was that he couldn't even bring himself to lay the blame squarely on Asmodeus's shoulders. Some of it kept slipping off and landing back on his. He had been the one who had sought the sorceress and asked her to inscribe the spell on his shoulders that gave him control over his wings, and more control over his own body, making it difficult for Asmodeus to command him and force his compliance.

He had been the one to repay that sorceress by fulfilling the dark urge to kill her.

And she had repaid him by cursing him with her dying breath to feel an overpowering, never-ending craving for blood.

He had been the one who had sought a way of escaping the haunting memories of all the mortals and angels he had brutally slain whenever the darkness growing within him had seized control.

That escape had come in the form of sweet oblivion, delivered to him by Euphoria, a potent cocktail of alcohol, demon toxin and blood designed with enslaving mortals in mind and giving them a high that would make them forget every wicked thing they did while temporarily under its influence.

Demon toxin was fatal to angels.

When it had only made him high, giving him the beautiful escape he had craved and couldn't find in alcohol alone, he had realised that he was no longer an angel.

And he had thrown himself head first into a downward spiral of Euphoria, screwing every demon female who offered it to him in exchange for sex. In hurling himself into that addiction, he had blurred the line between the evil and the good within him. He had embraced the darkness and bore the evidence of it on his body in the form of permanent claws and black skin up to his elbows and his knees, a sliver of his other side shining through.

Oh how the mighty had fallen.

He hadn't quite hit rock bottom at that point though. No. He had stepped a little closer to rock bottom when Veiron, a Hell's angel now married to Nevar's former ward, Erin, had found him in a grotty bathroom banging a demon in exchange for a fix, and had taken it upon himself to save him. When Nevar had found himself pinned to the floor of that bathroom, in a pool of the demon bitch's blood, he hadn't been able to stop himself from licking it off the grimy tiles.

He had finally hit rock bottom when he had decided to discover Asmodeus's weakness and exploit it, and had abducted the woman his master had been falling in love with, Liora, and handed the witch over to the Devil. No questions asked.

And then when Asmodeus had been about to save her from the very chamber at Nevar's back, he had snuck in like a shadow and tried to kill the bastard.

Liora had attempted to shield Asmodeus. Nevar had skewered both of them on the sword.

Their combined blood spilling in the chamber and soaking into the crystal had been the key to unlocking the prison of the Great Destroyer, and because his hand had spilled it, Nevar was now the creature's master.

He sighed and pinched the bridge of his nose.

Liora would be proud of him.

Seven months of rehab and he had finally admitted that Asmodeus had started the ball rolling when he had forced a contract between them, but Nevar had kept on pushing the damn thing until it had picked up enough speed to do some real damage.

Damage being a nice way of saying that he had probably brought about the end of the world.

Nevar tipped his head back and stared into the darkness. Golden light from the two torches on the wall behind him, one either side of the broad door, held by gilded dragon bones, flickered across the ceiling. How many times had he lost himself in following the shifting ribbons of light? It was up there with his other favourite form of entertainment.

He turned around to face the huge black stone door.

His jade gaze slowly took in every inch of the carved surface that was now imprinted on his memory. It depicted dragons roaming the landscape of Hell in the upper portion of the door and a monster far larger than they were ravaging lands in the central section. That gigantic beast devoured mortal, demon and angel alike.

He ran his fingers over the beast to the figure of an angel being crushed under its front left foot and then drifted them back up to the other figure it clutched in the claws of its right.

The Great Destroyer.

He wasn't sure what would happen when it finally rose from its slumber, or what his role was when it emerged, but he was sure it would be a hell of a lot more interesting than his current situation.

Would it be such a bad thing if it awakened?

The thought of standing guard in the cramped black antechamber for decades, centuries or more was an unwelcome one. He would rather the world went to Hell now than he be put through another month of loitering outside the chamber, alone and bored.

And tired.

Unlike his master, Hell wasn't his home, and when an angel wasn't in their natural environment, they had to eat and sleep.

Asmodeus never seemed to take that into account, or perhaps he did. Perhaps his wretched master was in his fortress halfway across Hell laughing about the fact that he was here starving to death and about ready to gnaw his arm off. Nevar resisted the urge to sink his fangs into his lower lip. It wouldn't appease his hunger or do him any good. He couldn't survive on his own blood. He had been living for the past seven months on regular doses of Asmodeus's blood.

Saliva pooled in his mouth at just the thought of sinking his fangs into his master's arm and sucking down his rich, thick blood.

Wonderful. Asmodeus and Liora's fantastic rehab plan had now turned him into some sort of Pavlov's dog, salivating at only the idea of being allowed to drink from his master.

He sighed again and traced his fingers down the ridged back of the beast carved on the door.

Maybe there was a reason Asmodeus had left him here alone for almost a full month.

Liora had told Nevar that now he had been weaned off demon blood, the next step was to wean him off blood entirely.

It would be typical of the bastard angel to decide the best way to do that was to ditch him here at the chamber and leave him for a month, knowing he was under orders not to leave it unguarded.

Did Liora know what her male was doing? He doubted the pretty little witch would approve of such a move.

Whenever Nevar had been at their fortress, watching her and Asmodeus attempting to rebuild it, she had stuffed him full of mortal food, telling him that he needed to keep his strength up. Of course, Asmodeus glared at him whenever the witch fussed over him, and Nevar had repaid him by drinking up her attention and coaxing her into giving him more of it, stealing it away from Asmodeus.

The mark on his chest pulsed, fire flashing over it, and his fingers tensed against the hindquarters of the beast on the door.

He growled and mentally commanded the breastplate and back plate of his violet-edged black armour to disappear, revealing his bare chest. Purple light traced over the circular mark directly over his heart. The size of his palm, it depicted a serpentine beast with a reptilian head armed with sharp fangs and six curved horns. Wings followed the sweeping arc of its scaly body and its barbed tail. In the centre of the mark, clutched in the dragon's claws, was a perfect replica of Liora's pentagram—the one he had destroyed.

The dragon's wings shifted and he ground his teeth against the fiery pain that blazed like lightning across his pectorals in response. He pressed his hand to the mark, breathing through the agony, using the same technique he employed when trying to retain control.

The beast settled and his heart settled with it, slowing back to a normal rhythm.

It wasn't the first time the mark had shifted. It moved from time to time, as if it was as restless as he was.

Nevar kept his hand over the mark and placed his other one on the carving on the door that was a perfect match. The Great Destroyer.

Would it be such a bad thing if it awakened?

He could fight it or control it or something as its master.

It would beat the hell out of guard duty.

Nevar shoved the heavy stone door open and entered the bright crystal chamber. The jagged walls were brightest, blinding white that reminded him of Heaven and stung his eyes. They adjusted gradually, allowing him to see more of the room. In the centre stood a raised oblong dais of pure clear crystal. To the left of it on the floor of the chamber was a dull patch where he had spilled Asmodeus's and Liora's blood and it had soaked into the crystal.

He moved deeper into the room and came to stand over that spot, looking down at it and his booted feet.

Red still swirled within the layers of crystal.

It was further from the surface now. He had made a habit of entering the chamber each day to see if the blood was sinking deeper into the crystal and always ended up wondering if it was heading towards a certain point far beyond his vision, slowly working its way down each crack and layer to the Great Destroyer.

The Devil had been his usual cryptic self when Nevar and Asmodeus had asked him for more details about the destroyer, giving answers that provided no illumination. Nevar still didn't know if the destroyer was actually beneath all the layers of crystal below him, or whether it was linked to this place from one far away that only the Devil knew about.

Nevar sat on the raised slab, swung his legs up and lay down on it, staring at the glowing ceiling.

Light danced across the crystal shards, reflecting rainbow colours like an aurora. Whenever he grew restless, he came to this spot and lay for a while. It was peaceful and soothing, and a much-needed distraction from his heavy thoughts.

Whenever he was in this room, he felt different. He could never put his finger on the why of it though. The only way he could explain it was that he no longer felt alone. There was a presence in this room that calmed him and filled a hole in his chest, one that gnawed at him when he was beyond the chamber walls.

His eyes slipped shut and he forced them open again, stifling a yawn at the same time.

Nevar rested his hands on his chest, over the mark there, and tried to track the brighter spots of light as they slowly danced over the crystals like fireflies. His eyelids drooped again, heavier this time. He struggled to lift them and drowsily stared at the ceiling as it spun out of focus, blurring and whirling together.

His eyes closed.

Pain skittered across his chest.

Nevar frowned and rubbed the mark. Damned thing.

He grimaced and then opened his eyes. The crystal chamber came back into focus. He had fallen asleep.

"Fuck," he growled and sat up, swinging his legs over the edge of the dais, and quickly looked off to his left, expecting Asmodeus to be there in the doorway, glowering.

It was empty.

Nevar huffed, planted his hands on the edge of the dais next to his bare thighs, and looked down at his knees.

The part of him that was glad his lazy master hadn't caught him sleeping on the job warred with the part that snarled it was typical of Asmodeus not to show up to relieve him.

He could die down here and it would be decades before Asmodeus realised it.

The bastard was so wrapped up in teaching Liora how to read his magic books, and so wrapped up in her too, that he didn't care about anything else, not even the duty the Devil had given to him as one of his servants.

Well, Nevar didn't care about anything other than getting something to drink.

Deep breath in, and out.

He didn't need to drink.

His stomach growled and his fangs itched, one baying for booze and the other for blood. He ignored both of them and slid off the dais, landing on his feet. He looked down at his violet-edged black greaves that protected his shins and his black leather boots. The crystal beneath them shimmered, light pulsing outwards from his feet.

His head swam and sent the room spinning.

Nevar leaned back against the crystal bench for support.

He didn't need to drink, but he did need to eat. If he didn't eat soon, he would pass out, and what use would he be as a guard then?

He needed to get out of this place and get out of Hell, away from the Devil who had made it his pet project to drive Nevar insane over the past month by taunting him in his head.

Away from his bastard master Asmodeus.

He needed some freedom and air.

He needed to fly.

He needed a break.

Just a small one.

Maybe it would make Asmodeus sit up and take his duty more seriously too. The Devil had banned Asmodeus from leaving Hell without his permission, and that meant the angel would have to ask his master for said permission in order to come after Nevar and would have to explain what had happened. The Devil would probably punish Asmodeus.

Asmodeus would definitely punish Nevar, but it would be worth it.

No punishment Asmodeus or the Devil could inflict would be worse than what he was already suffering.

He was starving, parched for blood, and unable to shake the quiet craving for a fix of Euphoria that had been riding him for what felt like forever. It drove him mad and he feared he would snap if he stayed down here alone much longer, and would end up in the mortal world hunting down a demon bitch.

He would deny both hungers, was strong enough right now, but he couldn't deny the hungers for a drink and some food.

He strode to the door of the crystal chamber, cast one look back into it, and then pulled the door closed, shutting out the light.

He threw his free hand out in front of him, calling a portal. Black smoke curled out of the air and swirled like a maelstrom, growing denser as the portal enlarged to match his six-foot frame and widened enough to allow him through.

He released the door and focused on himself, using a fraction of his power to first reinstate his back and chest plate of his armour, and then cast a glamour that would change his appearance to mortal eyes. He dressed himself in black jeans, a charcoal t-shirt, and army boots, and masked the obsidian skin that reached past his elbows and the black claws that tipped his fingers.

He ran those fingers through the messy jagged strands of his silver-white hair, preening it back to ensure it concealed his small horns from immortal eyes. He hated it when people at Cloud Nine stared at them and whispered about him behind his back, and more often than not it was the horns that got them talking. The last thing he needed tonight was someone pushing his buttons when his fuse was shorter than usual because of the overwhelming combination of hunger for booze, blood, Euphoria and food.

He had the angel equivalent of low blood sugar right now and was liable to rip the head off anyone who merely looked at him funnily.

Nevar stepped into the portal and out into the wide alley in London.

The neon sign above the burly skinhead bouncer shone down on him like a light from Heaven.

Cloud Nine.

One drink, some food, and then he would head straight back down to Hell. Cross his heart. The chamber wouldn't miss him. His master definitely wouldn't.

Nevar grinned, flashing his short fangs.

Let the good times roll.

CHAPTER 2

It was cold. Dark. She ached, a thousand lacerations and bruises burning on her tired limbs, the result of the battle she had survived.

Noise blurred around her, loud and piercing, a din of unfamiliar sounds.

It drove her to move.

She was vulnerable here, out in the open. Exposed.

Her stomach growled.

Hungry.

Lysia shoved her bloodstained hands against the green earth and pushed herself up into a sitting position. Verdant nature closed in on her from all sides, and beyond it pricks of bright yellow lights. Where was she?

She tried to remember how she had come to this place.

Sharp pain stabbed behind her eyes and she screwed them shut, unable to bite back the whimper that slipped from her lips. The fierce fiery ache subsided and fragments of memories of the battle took its place, speeding through her mind, distorted and bringing their own form of pain as her head throbbed and her body throbbed with it. Each blow she recalled echoed on her body, pain that burned in her limbs and seared every healing gash anew.

She forced her eyes back open and scanned the area around her, focusing on it to push the memories to the back of her mind. No sign of the battle she had taken part in. It hadn't happened here.

Lysia thought back to it again and pain blazed through her bones, setting them on fire, and she cried out as it seared her mind. She collapsed against the grass, breathing hard, each inhale filling her senses with the smell of it and the sweet coolness of the dew that clung to each blade.

The memories ended with the darkness of sleep.

She could only surmise that she had stumbled here from the battlefield and had passed out.

Lysia pushed herself up again and studied her surroundings. They were unfamiliar, noisy and strange. She could see great stone buildings beyond the trees and odd colourful growling creatures that roamed beyond the boundaries of the patch of nature. Their bright eyes swung her way at times and she shrank back, her heart pounding, fearing they would come for her while she was weak.

She needed a haven. Somewhere warm that would provide her with sustenance so she could restore her strength.

She stumbled onto her feet and closed her eyes, tipping her head back and her face to the inky sky.

Deep within her, she felt a familiar stirring. Demons were nearby. She would be safe with them.

She followed the sensation, using it to lead her to them. When she reached the edge of the trees, she hovered in the shadows, watching the growling boxy beasts as they rumbled past, seemingly patrolling the area but not acknowledging each other. Thankfully, they didn't seem to notice her.

There were a few mortals on the path ahead of her, between one set of the great buildings.

She was in their world.

She waited for them to disappear from view before scurrying across the black smooth rock surface to one of the buildings. From there, she stayed close to it, hurrying along the paved path, tracking the demons. She was closing in.

The sensation led her down narrower paths into darker areas, and she slowed her pace, sensing mortals ahead of her. Where the demons were.

Why were the demons with mortals? Were they feeding?

Her stomach growled again, the noise loud in the quieter air.

In the distance, she could hear the distinct chatter of voices, and a heavy tribal beat. A gathering?

Perhaps there was a sort of feast happening.

Her stomach made a stretched out series of gurgles, whistles and peeps at that. She rubbed it and hurried forwards, stopping only when she came upon the mortals. She lingered in the shadows of a building, hidden behind the corner of it, and peeked around to view the feast and gauge whether it was safe.

A string of mortals were lined up against a wall, a large demon ushering them one by one into the building. He eyed them all closely and turned some away. Was he in charge of picking the best from the worst? He flashed a toothy grin at two females and raked dark eyes over them as they entered.

Lysia had the impression he had earmarked them for himself.

A bright colourful sign hung on the wall above the door, the language unfamiliar.

She studied it until her eyes hurt and the words were burned onto her retinas, trying to make sense of it, and then shrugged. It didn't matter. She would enter this place and there she would find sustenance. She needed to be inside, out of the cold and safe. She would be safe inside. She felt sure of it.

Lysia scurried across the flat cool expanse of stone to the door. The big demon looked her way and his eyes widened.

She smiled and he staggered backwards, his eyes dropping to her body and widening further. Pleased that he was allowing her entrance, she hurried inside and immediately clapped her hands over her ears. The noise she had heard from outside was even louder inside, pounding at an ear-splitting volume. She growled beneath her breath and searched for food.

And paused.

The demons in their human forms were not eating the mortals.

This was not a feast.

Many of the demons were occupied in dancing with the mortals, grinding against them and almost fornicating in front of everyone.

She hovered by the entrance, unsure whether to enter or leave. Her stomach gurgled again, making her decision for her. She had to stay. There were colourful glass bottles lining the wall to her right and demons there were serving drinks to people who lined a long black bar. If they had mead and other liquids then perhaps they had food for her.

She moved deeper into the room and everyone turned to stare at her, their eyes wide. She frowned at them all. Why did they stare? She thought them all strange but she wasn't being rude by staring at them. If she hadn't been so hungry, she would have asked them, or forced them to tell her the reason.

She pushed through a group of male demons, all of which were wearing their human forms, and they turned on her. Their growls died as their eyes fell on her and they parted, staring as she passed.

Lysia leaned against the tacky black bar top.

A man walked over to her, tossed a rag over his shoulder, and smiled.

"What'll it be?"

"I require sustenance."

He frowned, a puzzled edge to his dark eyes, and shook his head.

Lysia tried again. "I must eat."

He waved his right hand and another man joined him, a blond with pale eyes.

"Problem?" the blond said.

"Not getting this one," the brunet responded.

The blond raked his eyes over her, his right brow quirking. "Taking things a bit far, aren't we? You want something?"

She nodded. "I need sustenance."

He looked at his friend and shrugged. "I don't understand her."

What was there to understand? She only wanted food.

Blood.

The two men walked away, serving others who seemed to have no problem ordering what they desired and receiving it. She cursed them and everyone who communicated with them with ease. While she could understand many languages, she could write and speak only one. Without being able to speak to the serving staff, she had no chance of getting blood.

A woman beside her cast a glance her way, looked down at herself, and slipped off her seat and walked away, disappearing into the heavy crowd.

Lysia sighed, perched herself on the seat, and leaned on the bar with her forehead resting on her arms. She was warmer inside this noisy inn but still hungry, and still tired. She needed to feed. How?

A male stopped to her left.

She turned her head towards him and ran her eyes up from the waist of his impeccable crisp black suit to his shoulders and then his face. Vampire. She knew his kind and could see through his façade to the wretched monster beneath. He smiled, his fangs on show to her and his pale blue eyes swirling with ill intentions.

"Having trouble?" The dark-haired vampire leaned his left elbow on the bar beside her and she sat up.

She nodded. "I need to order blood."

He frowned at her and her heart sank. He didn't understand her either.

"What language is that? I'm afraid I'm not familiar with it. Can you mime what you want?" He shifted closer and she focused hard on every word he said, listening closely so she could grasp the words he used and use them too.

He smiled a little wider, and shifted a little closer. His gaze drifted down to her chest and back up again.

"Mime?" He made a show of using his hands to make shapes.

She was about to do as he asked when he danced his fingers over her left shoulder.

A cold shiver ran over her flesh and skated down her spine.

Lysia flicked her right wrist and hurled him across the room, scattering the crowd and ripping a few shocked gasps from them.

A male further along the bar looked her way.

She froze as her eyes met his, heat pulsing through her, a visceral throb that reached right down to her bones.

The male was handsome, but darkness clung to him, danger that called to her and lured her to him. There was evil in him.

He would know her tongue.

He raised a glass filled with green liquid and tipped his head, causing threads of his silver-white hair to fall and brush his brow. He swept them back and she caught a brief glimpse of tiny horns above his ears. Her belly flipped and heated.

"Kudos for giving Villandry hell," he said above the thumping music, his deep rumbling voice doing funny things to her insides and turning her knees to rubber.

She presumed Villandry was the name of the vampire now picking himself up off the floor across the busy room. She wasn't sure what kudos meant though.

Lysia swallowed her trembling heart, slipped off her seat and approached the pale-haired male with all the confidence she could muster when he was staring at her, his jade eyes burning into her body and setting her aflame.

Rousing strange feelings within her.

She halted beside him.

He swivelled to face her, set his drink down on the bar but kept his left hand on the stem of the elegant glass, and raised an eyebrow.

"Why are you naked?"

He held his right hand out and black material appeared in it. He offered it to her.

Lysia took it and stared at it, unsure what to do with it.

The male huffed, released his drink and stood, managing to tower over her despite the fact she was taller than the other females present. He moved closer to her and took the material back, but she didn't notice it leaving her hands. The heat radiating from his big body washed over her, cocooning her in warmth and strengthening the feelings stirring in the pit of her belly.

She stared down at the strip of cut, hard muscles visible between the armoured plates around his hips and his breastplate. A warrior. Her heart accelerated. Her breathing quickened. She dragged her eyes back up to his face and found he wasn't looking at her. He busied himself with slipping her arms into the garment he had made for her and she busied herself with memorising every sculpted plane of his face, from his straight nose and strong jaw, to his firm lips as they compressed into a mulish line.

She inched her gaze up higher, to the stunning jade eyes that were focused on their work with an intensity that made her ache inside with a desire to have them locked on hers with the same ferocity.

They shifted to meet hers and then dropped, a fascinating glimmer of shyness in them that lasted only a heartbeat before coldness swept in to wash it away.

He tugged the material closed over her front and tied a belt around her waist, fastening the garment in place.

"There," he murmured, "now people will stop looking at you funnily, and you can stop looking at me funnily."

He stepped back, a scowl darkening his striking eyes. She hadn't been looking at him strangely. She was merely fascinated by him. Now that she was close to him, she could sense the depth of the darkness within him but something else countered it, something she could only describe as good. There was more to the male before her than she had anticipated, and it made the pull she felt towards him grow stronger.

She looked herself over. The sleeves were too long, concealing her hands, and the material reached her ankles. The garment covered all of her, leaving nothing on show. Had that been his intention?

"What do you want?" he said, bringing her focus back to him.

She lifted her eyes to meet his. "Blood."

He back peddled, almost falling over his seat, a flicker of something dark crossing his handsome face. His eyes shone pure violet.

He had eyes like hers.

And he understood her.

"Leave me alone," he barked and snatched up his drink with a shaky hand. He downed it, slammed the glass back onto the bar top, and shoved it forwards, away from him. "I'm not interested."

Lysia frowned and shrank back. Why was he rejecting her company? He had given her something to wear, had seemed concerned about her, and now he was pushing her away. She clutched the robe over her chest in both hands and risked a step closer to him instead.

"I only desire blood… but I cannot order it."

His violet gaze darted to her and away again. A shadow settled on his troubled features, turning them grim. He looked down into her eyes for long seconds, stealing all of her attention, sucking it away from the room and her surroundings.

He raised his hand and she flinched away, anticipating the strike.

It didn't happen.

She squinted, remaining held away from him, and looked up into his eyes.

He cocked a single pale eyebrow and waved his left hand. The brunet male behind the bar came to them. He had been signalling the serving staff.

Lysia grimaced.

She had much to learn about this realm.

"Blood, straight up," the white-haired male said.

The servant's expression turned wary and he shifted foot to foot. "I'm not allowed to serve you blood, remember? You made me promise."

He had? She canted her head, studying both men. Why had the man asked the servant not to give him blood? Did he drink it as she did?

The pale-haired warrior scrubbed a hand down his face and sighed. He pressed both hands into the bar, digging his black claws into the wood, and leaned forwards, closer to the man.

"It is not for me. It is for the woman."

The brunet shrugged. "She has to order it then."

The warrior tipped his head back, screwed his eyes shut and sighed, and she felt he was searching for calm. He drew several slow deep breaths before opening his eyes again and fixing them back on the barman.

"I do not think she knows how," he said.

"I tried, but the man didn't understand me." That brought his gaze back to her and she shivered under the intensity of it.

"That would be because you are speaking a language this man doesn't know... one I don't have a fucking clue about either but for some godforsaken reason I can understand you." He shoved his fingers through his hair, clawing it back until it tugged at his forehead, smoothing the skin, and ground his teeth. He released his head, dropped his hands to his sides, and huffed as he leaned over, bringing his face close to hers. "Repeat after me if you desire... blood."

She nodded, noting that it had taken a lot of effort for him to speak that final word. Why?

She leaned closer to him, trying to shut out the noise of the room so she could hear every syllable that left his lips.

She watched how they moved as he spoke. How his tongue moved. How his teeth moved.

Her focus shattered.

He had fangs.

Made for drinking blood.

Yet he had asked the man not to serve it to him.

And she had asked him to speak of it, something which had evidently pained him.

She stepped back and his pale eyebrows dipped low above his now-green eyes.

"I'm sorry. I have troubled you with my request." She went to turn away but he caught her arm in a vice-like grip, holding her firm. She looked down at his black fingers around her and the claws that blended into the robe he had given her, and then up into his eyes.

He shook his head and spoke again, slower this time. "A glass of blood, please."

Lysia swallowed to wet her parched throat and spoke the sounds he had made, repeating them several times over and growing in confidence when he smiled, making her heart flutter in her chest. He nodded and jerked his head towards the brunet behind the bar.

She turned to face him. "A glass of blood, puh-leeese."

"We'll work on that last bit," the warrior muttered beside her, a touch of warmth in his deep voice.

The man nodded. "That's ten quid."

Ten quid?

What was a quid and where did she find ten of them?

"Money," the brunet said.

She looked down at herself. As the warrior had clearly mentioned, and this man knew, she had come here naked. She had no coin.

The warrior huffed and slammed two pieces of reddish paper down on the bar top. "It's on me. Plus my usual."

The bartender looked displeased and Lysia feared he wouldn't give her the blood because the warrior was paying for it, and had requested this man not serve him blood.

She bared her fangs and growled at the brunet, preparing to attack.

"Down girl." The white-haired warrior caught hold of her arm again, wrapping long fingers around it, and heat blazed through her.

She looked across at him, her eyes wide. He glared at the bartender.

The man heaved a sigh, swiped the money off the bar, and walked away. A sharp spear shot through her heart and she tried to pull away from the warrior to follow the man, afraid he wouldn't return.

The warrior's grip on her arm tightened and he pulled her closer, until her backside bumped against his thighs. An achy shiver bolted through her and she spun to face him, catching the shock in his eyes before he covered it. He had felt it too.

"He will be back with your drink and then you can leave me alone," he said in a gruff tone, released her and sat back on his seat, turning his profile to her.

Lysia's heartbeat began to climb, awareness of the people around her creeping back in. The vampire was on his feet again and glaring at her. Others stared her way too. Some of them not mortal. She didn't like how they watched her, not when she was weak.

Only the warrior felt as if he wasn't a threat to her and that he would protect her rather than seek to harm her.

She didn't want to leave his side.

The brunet returned as the warrior had said, bringing an elegant glass of green liquid for him and one filled with dark liquid. He set that one down in front of her and moved off to serve another patron.

The warrior eyed her expectantly.

He wanted her to leave.

Lysia sucked down a breath for courage and reminded herself that she was a warrior too and as powerful as any of these beings on her best day. Today was not her best day though and it was wreaking havoc on her courage, leaving her feeling vulnerable. She was injured, starving, and everything around her felt so alien and unfamiliar.

Except for him.

He made her feel safe.

She made sure she had all of his attention before she whispered, "Allow me to stay. The men here mean me harm."

His face darkened, his jade eyes swirling into blazing violet, and he slid his deadly gaze towards those staring at her.

She felt their eyes leave her.

"Sit," he growled, more a command than a request, and she obeyed.

She took the stool beside him, swivelled to face the bar and picked up her glass. She sipped the blood, her gums itching and fangs aching to descend. She wanted to gulp it down but it was such a small quantity and she didn't think the warrior would buy her more.

It wasn't enough to appease her hunger. It would only take the edge off it.

She would need more and her heart said she knew where she wanted her next meal to come from.

Her gaze slid to the warrior, settling on his strong neck and the pulse hammering there, powerful and steady, a beat that called to her.

She wanted to bite him.

CHAPTER 3

Nevar silently cursed the black-haired beauty for the millionth time and followed it up with a prayer for control and patience. He downed his drink, keeping him one step away from sober for the next minute at least. It constantly chased on the heels of each drink, his angelic constitution making it difficult for him to get tipsy, let alone drunk. The boss of Cloud Nine had made it the law that the bartenders were to cut him off if he made it past tipsy. She hadn't appreciated him setting up home in her club and drinking her dry in order to remain drunk, chasing her patrons away.

He needed another drink, if only to cope with the head fuck that was the woman beside him.

He had intended to leave the packed noisy club after his previous drink, having already downed twenty glasses rather than the one he had sworn he would have.

She had chosen that moment to walk into his life, drawing the eyes of everyone in the room, including his.

He could lie and say that the first thing he had noticed as the crowd had parted to reveal her was that she wasn't a mortal, but he was still feeling honest with himself, despite his best attempts to kill that part of his brain with alcohol.

The first thing he had noticed? That was how beautiful she was, with rich hazel eyes and sleek black hair. The second thing he had noticed was how that black hair reached down to her navel, two thick streams of it covering her breasts, but not concealing their dusky peaks.

The third thing had been that she had curves in all the best places, and that he had gone too long without a woman, because just the sight of her had had him steel-hard beneath his loincloth and armour.

That she wasn't a mortal had been the fifth thing he had noticed about her. The fourth?

It had been the purity that shone from her, a touch of innocence that showed in how she reacted at times to the men around her and to him. Whether it was a stolen glance or a blush from her, it had him enthralled. Completely enchanted.

Utterly bewitched.

He had noticed many things since then, including that appearances were deceiving and she was powerful beneath that slender feminine exterior. The latest thing he had noticed was that she brought out a dangerous side of himself, one he had never realised the depth and strength of before tonight.

Since her confession that she felt the men here wanted to hurt her, he had found himself wanting to kill any male who so much as looked at her. He couldn't stop himself from contemplating tearing their heads off or gouging their eyes out with his thumbs. He wanted them all away from her, wanted to take them all down, all to ensure one thing.

That she would feel safe.

Somewhere in the middle of the rollercoaster ride of feelings that had started the second he had set eyes on her and had been sending him hurtling up and down and throwing him for a loop ever since, he had realised something.

He could understand her and no one else in the bar could.

That disturbed him.

It unsettled him almost as much as the feel of her gaze boring into his throat and the need it stirred, a deep consuming desire to feel her teeth pressing into his flesh.

Blood.

He was hungry and that was the only reason he was fantasising about letting the female take a bite out of him. He wanted to do the same thing to her. He wanted to devour her.

He pushed that wicked tempting thought out of his head, replacing it with ones about her language. He was one hundred percent certain that he didn't have a clue what she was saying and didn't know her language, but it seemed to filter into English in his head. It wasn't a power she held, because no one else could understand her.

Was it a power he held?

He was still discovering ones that Asmodeus had passed to him when they had formed a master-servant bond.

Maybe he would ask the bastard about it later, when he returned.

Whenever that would be.

He wasn't in a hurry. He didn't give a flying fuck about his duty right now, when in the presence of the immortal beauty beside him. Hell seemed like a million miles away, nothing more than a distant memory, and he liked it that way. For the first time in what felt like forever, the weight of the world and his sins wasn't resting heavily on his shoulders. What was it about her that chased all his cares away?

Was it just because he was so absorbed in studying her, had all of his focus pinned on her and turned away from himself, or was it something else at work?

The female was taking her time with her glass of blood. Savouring it. Fuck, how he would do the same. He would treat it like ambrosia, manna, a gift from the highest power. He would taste every drop, savour every molecule, and relish every trickle of heat that would flow through his veins as his body absorbed it.

Nevar growled and closed his eyes, fighting the urge to swipe the glass away from her and down its contents.

He wouldn't touch the blood. He was stronger than the curse the sorceress had placed on him. He would overcome it.

The little beauty next to him shifted on her seat, stealing his focus away from himself again and back to her. He opened his eyes and slid them towards her, studying her as she leaned on the bar and sipped her drink, her eyes pinned on the dark surface now.

Her black hair had fallen forwards with her, revealing a dark streak on her skin that cut down under the collar of the robe.

He reached out with his right hand and brushed the black material aside, revealing her creamy shoulder. He traced his fingertips lightly over the deep healing wound on her left shoulder.

A dark rosy hue climbed her cheeks and she shied away from his touch, bringing her right hand up to catch her robe.

Enthralling.

She had walked in here naked as the day she had been born, brazen and bold, yet him seeing her bare shoulder had turned her shy.

She had tossed Villandry across the room when he had attempted to touch her, yet him laying his fingers on her caused her to blush.

"Who did this to you?" Whoever it had been, he wanted to kill them and avenge her. That dark urge swirled in his chest, malevolent and powerful, a force that felt as if it was strong enough to seize control of him by spreading through his limbs, twining tendrils around each bone, and hijacking command of his body.

Although, this time he would willingly hand control over to his darkness, embracing it in order to strike down whoever had harmed her.

He studied the healing mark that looked as if it had been done with a blade, his mood darkening as he recalled that it wasn't the only one her body bore. Someone had hurt her, lacerating her pale smooth skin, and they would pay for it.

A brief shadow of panic crossed her hazel eyes and she looked away. "I cannot remember. I woke not far from here."

"Naked?" he offered.

She nodded, but didn't seem concerned by it. It concerned him.

He looked her over and the darkness stirred within him, roused by the insidious words whispering through his mind.

"You were not touched there?" His anger spiked at the thought that such a pure female might have been sullied in such a fashion.

That her fear of the males in the bar might stem from such a horrific act of abuse.

His claws elongated as the black writhed up his arms, gaining ground, his darker self pushing for freedom. His fangs punched long from his gums and he had to fight hard to tamp down the urge to call one of his black blades to him.

She didn't seem to understand.

He looked down at her hips.

Her blush deepened. "No. It was a battle."

That drew a frown from him. "You were naked though."

She nodded.

His frown hardened. "How did you come to be naked?"

She looked into his eyes, hers as flat and emotionless as her face, and said, "I never had robes on."

She touched the one she wore, glancing down at it and then back at him.

A smile curved her rosy lips. "It's beautiful."

It wasn't. It was plain and black, but she treated it as if it was precious, stroking her fingers over the material, a smile on her face and a sparkle in her hazel eyes.

It made him wish he had manifested her something worthy of being called beautiful just so he could see how she would react to it.

So she was wearing something worthy of her.

She raised her eyes back to his and he knew he was about to sound like an idiot, but he needed to be sure he understood her.

"You fight naked?" He waited for a reaction to that, sure she would laugh at him.

She nodded. He looked her over again, recalling her curves and how they had inflamed him. Still inflamed him.

Fighting naked would certainly give her an advantage over a male opponent, but it provided no protection for her too.

"I can highly recommend armour." He regretted it the moment it left his lips and she looked down at his, making it clear that she could see straight through his glamour to his real appearance. Her eyes danced over every piece of it, studying it so closely that he squirmed under the scrutiny.

He had loved his armour once, when it had been blue edged with silver, the colours of a guardian angel, and his wings had been stunning silvery-blue.

His contract with Asmodeus had turned it obsidian edged with violet and had corrupted his wings, turning them as black as Hell.

He could do nothing about either of them, no matter how deeply he wished he could.

So he kept his wings hidden so he didn't have to see them and did his best not to look at his armour. He had once considered giving it up and disposing of it somehow, but it provided protection, and he didn't think he could fight like the delicate-looking female currently staring in absorbed fascination at him.

Naked.

Maybe he could fight naked with her.

His body stirred at that wicked thought and he shifted on his stool, hoping she wouldn't notice. She would probably toss him across the room if she did.

Telekinesis.

He would give anything to have that power.

Where did she come from? She wasn't mortal. She wasn't angelic. He didn't think she was demonic either.

She was something else.

And she was beautiful.

And he was sober again.

He didn't care. Not right now. She had all of his focus, fascinating him with every little thing she did.

She sipped her blood.

Except that.

His stomach cramped, his fangs itched, and his hunger rose like a demon within him.

He breathed through it. In for five. Out for five. He didn't need blood. In for five. Out for five. He was stronger than his hunger. The cramps subsided. He exhaled slowly, silently congratulating himself for successfully working through another attack, just as Liora had made him promise he would do. Some ridiculous thing she had called positive affirmation.

The female lifted the glass back to her lips and took another slow sip that painted them red and made him hunger to kiss her.

The darker needs lurking within him gave positive affirmation the finger and seized control, crushing his will to resist before he could muster it.

He tried to back off before he jumped on the female and stole the blood on her lips. The backs of his thighs snagged on the leather of the stool seat, and he fumbled in an attempt to remain upright. His left arm shot out, catching all the glasses on the bar and sending them flying as he fought for balance.

The female stared at him and cocked her head to one side.

He growled at her, dug his claws into the bar and dragged himself up, leaving deep grooves in the black wooden top. The shadows swirled higher, curling over his biceps and twisting around his thighs. His fangs lengthened and he ground his teeth, desperately seeking some calm so he could centre himself or whatever the fuck Liora had called it. His eyes blazed violet, burning in his skull as the skin around them bled into darkness.

His shoulder blades itched, his wings pushing for freedom.

Nevar snarled and buried his claws deeper into the bar top, clinging to it as he fought the change, refusing to give into it. It would pass. He just had to breathe.

What he really needed to do was let this hippy shit go and rip the heads off everyone who was now staring at him as if he was a one man freak show.

Including her.

He fixed his gaze on her.

Not including her.

Calm came over him like a cooling balm as his eyes met hers, washing through him and chasing back the darkness enough for him to get a grip on it and shove it back in its place, under his control. He breathed slowly and steadily, willing to try the hippy shit again because he had to admit it did work most of the time, and mentally apologising to Liora for doubting her methods, and everyone in the bar for wanting to tear their heads off and drink from their gushing necks.

The woman stood studying him still, her head canted to one side, a curious edge to her gaze.

"You have a sickness," she said.

He nodded. "I brought it upon myself... and so I must conquer it myself too."

She hopped back up onto her stool. "Why do you deny what will make you better?"

She held the glass out to him and he shot backwards, hit the stool, lost his balance and toppled over it. To add injury to insult, he landed hard on his knees and cracked his chin on the seat, and a few people nearby snickered at him, including Villandry.

Nevar shot Villandry a glare filled with intent that he knew the vampire would clearly read. One more laugh out of him and Nevar would make him intimately acquainted with something wooden and pointy.

"I'm sorry." The woman drew the glass back to her, clutching it to her chest between her breasts.

He grimaced, clawed his way back onto his feet, and huffed as he sat down. "Blood only makes it worse. Vicious cycle."

She drank the rest of the glass in one go, set it on the bar and pushed it behind her, where he couldn't see it. He appreciated that. It was better than shoving it in his face and taunting him with it as she had a minute ago. She toyed with the belt of her robe, an awkward edge to her body language, and Nevar surmised that he wasn't the only one having trouble not making an idiot of himself tonight.

Her head jerked up, her eyes leaping to his, and she blurted, "What are you?"

Nevar leaned back, caught off guard by her question and unsure how to respond. "I was wondering the same thing about you."

Her smile bewitched him. There was a touch of innocence in it. Purity that he found alluring, as if she could cleanse him and make him good again. Impossible. The only way he could be good again was to die and be reborn as an angel of Heaven, and he had no intention of letting that happen. Heaven had tampered with his memories, controlling his actions. They had taken his free will from him. He would never return to that place and that life, under their control and unaware of how they played their angels like pawns, erasing memories when it suited them, keeping them in order.

"I don't know what I am. Perhaps I am like you," she said, luring him back to her, and he frowned at what she had said.

He shook his head. "Impossible. I was an angel, and now I am a demon, and not by choice."

She played with the belt of the robe again, her black eyebrows dipping low and darkening her hazel eyes. "If you had a choice, would you still be an angel?"

He pondered that. "I would want to be an angel again to extinguish the evil inside me, but I have no desire to serve Heaven again. I want to serve no master."

She stared at her knees, her gaze distant and her fingers paused against the material. She was still for so long that he grew concerned and leaned towards her without thinking, reaching one hand out.

She spoke before he could lay it over hers, her tone solemn and edged with pain, and he froze.

"I despise angels."

He sat back and settled his hand on his bare knee instead. "Why?"

She frowned and he expected her to bite out something, and then her expression turned troubled and he sensed the panic rising within her. Her eyes slowly widened, her eyebrows creeping upwards, and she shook her head.

"I cannot remember." Her gaze leaped to his and her breathing quickened. "I cannot remember."

He could sympathise. He had been there himself, unable to recall events that people told him had happened and he had been involved in. He reached out and touched the robe covering her shoulder, his focus on the wound beneath.

"Did angels do this?"

She snarled and smacked his hand away, and shot to her bare feet. She shoved him in the chest and backed off, her eyes wild, filled with fear that flowed over him together with her power. It rose, growing stronger and pressing down on him. The colourful lights in the club flickered.

"I don't remember," she whispered on repeat and clawed at her hair, drawing the long black strands back from her face, tugging at them. "I want to remember."

A light above the bar shattered, raining blue glass down on the black top.

Everyone stopped to look at her and she shook her head, curling into a ball.

Nevar did the only thing he could to get their eyes off her.

He caught her right wrist, pulled her between his thighs and wrapped his arms around her. He cupped her head with his left hand and rubbed the small of her back with his right.

"Breathe," he murmured into her hair, closing his eyes as he felt her trembling. She smelled like dew, fresh and clean and earthy. Pure. The scent of a cool summer morning.

She sucked down one breath and then another.

"Slower." He stroked her back, cursing himself for enjoying the feel of her pressing against him. "In through your nose and out through your mouth. Breathe like you're filling your lungs up from the bottom. Nice and slow."

He couldn't quite believe he was spouting Liora's hippy shit to his beautiful stranger.

She seemed to be embracing it though, and it seemed to work for her just as it did for him. Each slow breath she took had her power falling, the weight of it lifting from his shoulders. She released her head and pressed her palms to his breastplate, and a foolish part of him wished he wasn't wearing his armour so he could feel her delicate hands on his flesh. Her breath skated across his arm.

"I know a little about forgetting things," he said in a low voice destined for her ears only and kept stroking her back. He couldn't stop himself now. She was soft and warm beneath his calloused palm. Tempting. "It can get a little too much to handle at times. You just have to breathe."

She nodded, exhaled, and pushed back from him. A sense of loss immediately engulfed him as she slipped from his arms, placing some distance between them, and straightened her robe.

He lowered his hands to his knees and searched for something to say, trying to come up with something that would make him look good. Something reassuring. Women liked that sort of thing.

She swept her hair out of her face and lifted her chin, looking him straight in the eye. "What do they call you?"

"They call me many things, and most of them not complimentary." He smiled at her formal way of asking. She leapt between antiquated and modern so much that he was going in circles trying to figure out how old she was. He held his hand out to her. "But you can call me Nevar."

"Nevar," she whispered and he liked how his name sounded when it fell from her lips, spoken in her soft voice, edged with warmth.

She reached out to take his hand.

A black vortex appeared off to his right. Asmodeus stepped out of it, his expression stormy and dark, relaying his anger, and his golden eyes locked on Nevar like a hawk's on prey. The portal shrank and Asmodeus advanced, the crowd parting for him. Every demon here knew of his master. It was impossible to mistake him for anyone else as he towered above them, his short black hair and golden eyes matching the Devil's, and his partial gold-edged black armour in place, protecting his hips and shins, and leaving his chest bare.

"The King of Demons," the woman whispered with the same reverence as she had used to speak Nevar's name and stared at Asmodeus with wide eyes that were a little too adoring for Nevar's liking.

Asmodeus paid her no heed, which spared him from Nevar's wrath.

He seized Nevar's wrist and dragged him off the stool, and Nevar fought him, clawing at his hand to get it off him. He was damned if the bastard angel was going to drag him around and command him in front of the female, belittling him.

"You will return to Hell, Nevar," Asmodeus said, the compulsion behind the words sinking claws into Nevar and dragging him downwards, towards that realm.

He wasn't strong enough to fight Asmodeus or his commands when he was weak with hunger, but that wasn't going to stop him from trying.

He attempted to pull his arm free of his master's grip but Asmodeus tightened it, digging claws into his flesh and spilling his blood. He fought him every step of the way as they headed towards the exit. The female left the bar and followed, her gaze darkening by degrees.

"I will not go with you," Nevar snapped. "I will not return. It is time you did your duty."

Asmodeus yanked on his arm and sent him barrelling through the open door. He hit the damp tarmac and snarled over his shoulder at Asmodeus. The wretched angel would pay for that.

Asmodeus loomed over him.

The female stopped a short distance away, hovering near the entrance to Cloud Nine.

Nevar fought the change that threatened to come over him and the need to fight Asmodeus burning inside him. A need that would never die. He growled and flashed his fangs at Asmodeus. The male stood his ground and glared at him, his lips compressed into a thin line and his arms folded across his bare chest, as Nevar rose to his feet.

"You will return to Hell, Nevar." Asmodeus's deep voice echoed around the walls, drawing a few glances from the mortals in the queue for Cloud Nine.

Nevar shook his head, but he wasn't answering his master. He was answering the dark hunger inside him, the vile need to surrender to his urges and act on his impulses. He refused. He wouldn't give in to them, not while the female was watching him.

He hated that part of him and how he felt when it emerged.

Not just the way he changed psychologically, craving violence and bloodshed despite not wanting to feel such things. It was the physical changes he underwent that really sickened him. The claws and the fangs, and how his skin turned the colour of shadows, and most of all the horns that made his skull feel as if it would explode as they emerged.

Asmodeus cast a black portal and the female's eyes darkened and she bared her fangs, her deadly gaze pinned on his master now.

Was she going to attack him?

Asmodeus didn't give Nevar the chance to find out. He shoved Nevar into the swirling vortex and he landed in Hell, on the black plateau on which Asmodeus's ruined fortress stood, high above the rest of the barren basalt wasteland.

He landed hard but was on his feet in an instant, rushing back to the portal, a sliver of him filled with hope that the female would step through the vortex too.

It shimmered.

He waited.

Asmodeus stepped through it and the swirling black ribbons evaporated.

Nevar growled and cursed him in the demon tongue.

His master gave him an unamused look. "You are drunk. I have a way to sober you up."

Nevar straightened, forgetting his desire to correct his master and point out that he wasn't drunk, at least not on alcohol. Perhaps he was drunk on the female, intoxicated by her beauty and innocence. All of that fell away though, drowned out by what Asmodeus had said and his overwhelming reaction to it.

All angels suffered from intense curiosity and he was no exception.

Asmodeus folded his arms across his broad chest and crimson bled into the edges of his golden irises, a sign of the anger that laced the incredible wave of power that swept over Nevar, battering him fiercely enough that he had to plant one foot behind him to keep himself steady.

"I sensed you leave Hell and went to the chamber after dealing with the Devil on your behalf."

Nevar took a step towards him, a trickle of dread running through his veins. "What of the chamber?"

Had something happened to it while he had been absent? The look in his master's crimson eyes said that it had, and that the Devil would be punishing both of them.

Asmodeus flashed his fangs on a black snarl. "The chamber is dark."

Nevar's heart plummeted into his stomach.

"The destroyer has awoken."

CHAPTER 4

Nevar beat his black wings and swooped lower over the inhospitable obsidian basalt fields. Heat rose from the glowing orange cracks where lava had broken through, creating a pattern of deadly veins across the land. As far as he could see all around him, it was the same, an endless grim plain that would be impossible to traverse on foot.

Had the destroyer come this way?

He rubbed his jaw as he flew. It still ached from the blow the Devil had personally delivered. A punch that had sent him flying across the black courtyard of the Devil's formidable fortress and crashing into the obsidian spires of rock that formed a sweeping curve around it.

His leg burned with the memory too. The damned spires were still repairing themselves after the battle that had taken place there several months ago, spewing lava from their broken tips and slowly climbing high into the thick acrid air. When he had struck the wall, his impact had created a fissure and lava had bled through, singeing his right thigh before he could escape it.

He growled, grinding his teeth, his head filled with black thoughts, dark desires to head back to the fortress and punish every Hell's angel who had been present for his humiliation. The minions of the Devil had paused at their work to repair the courtyard flagstones and had laughed as he had suffered. His fangs lengthened as he pictured tearing into them with claw and tooth before silencing them with his blade and sending them back to Heaven to be reborn as angels of that realm.

They would learn not to laugh at him.

Nevar beat his wings and huffed, giving up the pleasing images and tempting thoughts. If he returned to the fortress, the Devil would kill him. He had threatened to do as much when he had banished Nevar from his sight for a period of seven days.

He wasn't sure the Devil would come good on the threat to kill him, since he had warned Asmodeus and his cohorts to keep him alive at all costs as he was now the Great Destroyer's master, but he wasn't willing to risk it. The Devil had a temper and was liable to lose his head and butcher him, and then regret it afterwards. He had seen the powerful male kill the commander of the First Battalion, the best of the Hell's angels under his command and a male the Devil had treated like a son, all because he had lost his temper over a bet the commander had won.

What made the whole thing more stupid in Nevar's eyes was that the bet had been the birth date of Erin's son, the Devil's grandson.

The Devil had lost, and had taken his commander's head for it, and had clearly regretted it afterwards when golden light had engulfed the angel's body, taking him back to Heaven to be reborn. Nevar had been glad that he hadn't been included in the bet, and Asmodeus had smiled smugly. The bastard had chosen a date weeks beyond the one his master had selected, ensuring he couldn't possibly win the bet.

Nevar definitely wasn't willing to risk his neck by returning to the fortress in order to dish out some vengeance on the Hell's angels.

Hot air buffeted him and he swerved right, away from the broad expanse of lava river ahead of him. He would have to go around it. His gaze tracked the snaking glowing ribbon in both directions. Impossible. It stretched as far as his eyes could see, illuminating the darkness far into the distance.

He sighed and beat his wings to keep himself steady in the warm thick air.

His stomach growled, reminding him once again that he had forgotten to get something to eat when in the mortal realm.

He couldn't fly for much longer without feeding and he was damned if he was going to plummet into a pool of lava and get himself killed and sent back to Heaven.

They had scoured Hell for the beast. There was no sign of it.

Had it hidden itself in one of the thousands of caves that dotted the immense landscape of Hell?

He opened a line of telepathic communication with Asmodeus. *No sign of it in this direction.*

None in this one either. Came the reply.

It was still strange being able to do this with Asmodeus. He had always been able to communicate with other angels of Heaven via telepathy, but had lost that talent when Asmodeus had contracted with him. He had thought the talent gone forever, until recently, when he had been cursing Asmodeus in his head and the angel had heard it and responded.

Asmodeus had never experienced telepathy before that point.

To say it had freaked his master out a little was an understatement.

Any idea at all where it might have gone? Nevar said and heard Asmodeus huff in his head.

The angel wasn't pleased with his master, the Devil. The Devil had been vague when they had questioned him, eventually admitting that he had no information on where the beast might go.

Yet he'd had the audacity to punish Nevar and Asmodeus for not finding it the first time they had scoured Hell and had sent them back out to look for it again.

His stomach gurgled again, twisting in on itself so hard that he grimaced and rubbed it. He couldn't concentrate, not with the constant pressing presence of his hunger. It was a weight in his gut that he could no longer ignore.

Maybe we should check the mortal world. It was worth a try.

No response.

I am starving. I am liable to drop into a boiling pit of lava or expire from lack of sustenance alone. You have orders to keep me alive.

Asmodeus grunted in response to that. *Very well. Scour the mortal world for the beast and I will send word to Apollyon, and he can alert the others to the situation. Eat while you are there.*

Nevar grinned, threw his hand out and cast a portal directly in front of him. He flew through the swirling black vortex, unwilling to linger for even a second in case his master changed his mind. He had a pass and he was taking it.

He landed in the middle of London, on a quiet broad street that bustled with mortals during the day. The rain-soaked pavements and road reflected the lights from the closed stores that lined the road. He stretched and focused to put his wings away. They shrank into his back, aching as they went, slow to do his bidding tonight. It had been weeks since he had used them and it had felt good to fly again. Their reluctance to disappear was his reluctance to see them gone for once. If his stomach had been full, he would have kept flying, taking in the mortal world from the air.

It was as empty as his master's heart though and he needed to fill it and refuel before he could fly anywhere.

The mark on his chest pulsed, sending fire sweeping over the curve of the beast. He pressed his hand to his breastplate and grimaced, waiting for the pain to subside. When it did, he felt a glimmer of something that distinctly felt like fear.

Fear?

He frowned at that. Perhaps it was his fear. Fear that Asmodeus would come for him again. Fear that he would spend forever trapped in Hell. Fear that the Devil would kill him and send him back to Heaven, to his worst nightmare. Although, he wouldn't remember what a nightmare it was to him. He would forget everything the moment he died and was reborn as an angel of Heaven. He would forget how Heaven had used him.

He drew in a deep breath and focused on the mark on his chest. Where was the destroyer? If it was awake now, could it sense him? Did it know he was its master? If he stayed in one place for long enough, would it find him and save him from having to search for it?

He still wasn't sure how such a gigantic beast could elude him and Asmodeus, and the Hell's angels the Devil had dispatched to hunt for it too.

Unless it wasn't in Hell.

He had goaded his master into letting him come to the mortal world so he could escape the constant torment and stench of Hell, feeding him a lie about the possibility of it being in this realm. What if it was here though?

There were many remote places on the planet where it could hide.

And it was a big fucking planet.

Nevar groaned. Was he doomed to spend the rest of his life flying around trying to locate the damned thing before it destroyed the world?

If he had to cover an entire planet, he was going to need a serious amount of fuel.

He kept his hand over the mark and pondered where the destroyer might be as he walked the familiar path down the warren of alleys towards Cloud Nine. Despite its grotty and often grim appearance, the club served some of the best food he had eaten in centuries. Full fat, full flavour, bad food. The sort mortals viewed as a future heart attack in the making.

Angels viewed it as superfood.

Fuck those greens and shoots and berries.

Meat oozing with flavour and fat was angelic superfood.

He knew angels who swung the other way when it came to their choice of superfood, preferring the high sugar content of cakes and sweets. Asmodeus was definitely one of those angels. The male could devour a whole chocolate gateaux in one sitting, and he had heard Liora mention in passing that his twin, Apollyon, could do the same.

Nevar could devour a whole spit-roasted pig.

His hand dropped to the bare patch of stomach between the edge of his chest plate and the slats of armour that protected his hips and he rubbed it, his mouth filling with saliva at the thought of the pulled pork buns and chicken wings that the club served.

Fuel up and head out. Do not linger. Do not drink. Understood?

Nevar growled at Asmodeus's voice in his head and mentally flipped him off.

His master had no faith in him.

That was the plan... and it still is the plan. He severed the connection between them before Asmodeus could respond and turned down the alley that would bring him to Cloud Nine.

He stopped and frowned. The sign was off and there was no queue of mortals, but the club was open. What was going on? Only one way to find out. He walked towards the door.

The bouncer acknowledged him with a jerk of his chin and he pushed past the huge demon male and stepped into the club.

The lights were on inside, the colourful ones above the bar bathing the area and the demons milling around along its length. No music though.

No mortals.

His gaze sought the female he had met before, although he wasn't sure why. It had been days since his last visit. She would be long gone, and it was stupid of him to hope that she would still be around, or remotely interested in him.

He headed for the bar, his eyes still scanning the demons for the woman even when he told himself to let her go and shove her out of his head.

A blonde cut into his path, her hands firmly planted on her hips, pale against her red jeans. A flicker of darkness danced in her eyes. Her stance caused her chest to jut upwards, showing off ample cleavage in her low cut black camisole. She narrowed her gaze on him and looked as if she was about to lose her pretty façade, revealing the hideous monster that lurked beneath her skin.

The boss.

And she was pissed about something.

He scanned the club again, frowning as he noticed that the demons present were jittery too, disturbed for some reason. Had something happened?

If it had, he wasn't sure why the boss was holding him responsible, and the intense glare she was giving him said she definitely thought it was his fault.

"Do something," she snapped, sharp teeth flashing between her glossy red lips, and flicked her short hair away from her face.

He arched an eyebrow down at her. "I don't follow. What is your problem?"

She turned and pointed, and the crowd parted.

Nevar's jaw almost dropped.

The female was there, curled up and sleeping on the grimy black bar top, naked again.

But not exposed.

Dark leathery wings wrapped around her slender form, cocooning her.

His feet moved of their own accord, carrying him across the room to her, unable to resist the powerful pull he felt towards her. The demons stepped back, making more room and allowing him and the boss to pass and approach the female.

What was she?

He cocked his head and his eyes darted over her before settling on her face. She was even more beautiful in sleep, her face soft and peaceful.

"She's been sleeping there since the other night and she's ruining my business. I can't let mortals in when there's a demon asleep on the bar." The bite in the boss's tone caused several demons nearby to edge further away and exchange nervous glances. "Do something."

The blonde had a reputation as a hard-ass bitch with a temper, but he was damned if she was going to order him around. He had enough bosses in his life already.

"Tell her to leave then." He cast her a glance as he folded his arms across his chest and shrugged. "It's not my problem."

She flashed twin rows of deadly sharp teeth on a hiss. "I tried that... and the bitch attacked me and started ranting. None of us could understand her."

Nevar struggled to hold back the grin that tried to curve his lips as he thought about the boss getting a taste of her own medicine, served to her by such a delicate looking female. It was probably long past due and was definitely time someone had the balls to stand up to the demon owner of Cloud Nine.

He looked back at the woman sleeping on the bar and drew closer to her, feeling light and hazy as he approached her, as if he wasn't quite with the world.

She had refused to leave the club. Why?

He had his answer when her eyelids fluttered and slowly opened, revealing sleep-filled hazel eyes that brightened as they settled on him.

She sat up, her black wings falling away from her body to drape across the bar top.

Her Avenging Angel

"I waited for you."

He felt strange on hearing those words leaving her soft lips, as if they had cast a spell on him all over again and pulled him deep under it, leaving him suffused with warmth and peace.

"Can you understand the bitch like the bartenders said you could?" the boss said from beside his elbow and he nodded.

"I can. I don't speak her language but I know what she's saying, and she understands English."

The blonde snarled, "Tell her to leave then or things will get ugly."

Nevar had no doubt that things would only get ugly for the boss. The little female on the bar could probably lay the whole club to waste without breaking a sweat. What was she?

"I shall ask her nicely for you." Nevar smirked at the boss and then turned his attention back to the female. "You have to leave."

Her face lit up, she hopped down from the bar, landing close to him, her bare body almost brushing his, and smiled. "I will leave with you."

Not quite what he had said and far from what he had intended, but he didn't have the heart to tell her. He stared down into her eyes, picking out all the flecks of gold amongst green, lost in her all over again.

She stretched, raising her arms high above her head and flashing the entire room. Several of the male demons suddenly looked less nervous and more as if they might risk their balls by pouncing on her.

Nevar growled at them all and used his powers to produce jeans and a top.

He shoved them at her. "Dress."

She took them and stared down at them, and he began to wonder if she had any concept of clothing and dressing herself.

He snarled at her. "Put them on or I swear I will break your wings off and dress you myself."

She shrank back against the bar and curled her wings behind her, shielding them with her body as she eyed him with a flicker of fear colouring her face and her feelings.

Nevar sighed, pinched the bridge of his nose and breathed slowly. Utter bastard. Maybe he was better off in Hell, stuck in a room on guard duty, away from the world. He wasn't fit to be near other people, and definitely not her.

He drew in another slow breath, exhaled it and lowered his hand to his side.

"You cannot walk around naked," he said, trying a gentler approach, one worthy of such a beautiful female. "You must dress."

She nodded, turned her back on him and set the clothes down on the bar. When she grabbed the jeans and bent forwards to put them on, flashing her bare backside at every male in the bar, Nevar growled and called his wings. They burst from his back, knocking a few of the demon males away, and he used them to shield her from their hungry eyes.

She shimmied into the black jeans and then held the silver-grey halter-top up, staring at it for so long that he realised she wasn't sure how it worked and was trying to figure it out.

"Here." He caught hold of her left wrist and spun her to face him, doing his best to keep her shielded by his black feathered wings and keep his eyes off her bare breasts. He took the top from her and eyed her leathery wings. "Can you make them go away?"

She shook her head. "Not right now. I am hungry. Weak. I require sustenance."

"Same here." But he didn't think he was going to get his order of pulled pork buns and chicken wings now. The boss would kick him out as soon as the female was dressed and ready to leave.

He sighed again and pushed the image of delicious food from his mind. He could find somewhere to eat once he had lured her out of the club and ditched her.

He crouched in front of her and opened the tube of material that formed the lower half of the halter-top. "We will do this the hard way then. Step into it."

She did as instructed and he slowly tugged the top up her long legs, biting back a groan as the feel of her thighs against his hands and his position had him instantly rock hard in his loincloth. No one would notice with his armour in place, but he didn't like how quickly his body responded to her, or that they might see the effect she had on him.

She might see.

Was it because she was a demon and he was subconsciously thinking about her giving him Euphoria? Was his body hard-wired to see a female demon now and automatically prepare for sex?

He ground his teeth and cursed himself.

If it was, then it was his own damned fault.

He would ditch her as soon as he could and continue his mission, and forget all about Euphoria. He didn't need it. He wouldn't go back to whoring himself for a fix. It wasn't worth the pain and humiliation.

If he wanted pain and humiliation, he could just return to Hell.

"Pull it up over your chest." Nevar averted his gaze and rose to his feet.

She wriggled in the corner of his vision and then grumbled something as her arms moved. She waved the two lengths of fabric that were designed to hold the top up.

"What do these do?"

Nevar took them and placed them around her neck, and slowed as her silken hair brushed his skin and the heat of her washed over him, becoming painfully aware of how close she was to him, the bar at her back stopping her from being able to move away.

He breathed in her sweet dewy fragrance and savoured the soft warmth of her skin as his thumbs brushed her neck. He drank in her beauty as she tilted her head back, bringing her eyes up to his, and listened to her breathing as it hitched with each sweep of his skin across hers. She filled all of his senses, stealing his awareness of the world from him and narrowing it down to only her. He stared down into her eyes, mesmerised by the way they widened and overflowed with dark allure, and how her lips parted, tempting him to taste her and making him hunger for her.

He swallowed hard, forgetting what he was meant to be doing, transfixed by her and lost in the moment.

"I told you not to linger." Asmodeus's deep voice rumbled through the silent room and shattered the spell she had cast on Nevar. "I should have known you would."

Nevar drew back and looked over his right shoulder, towards his dark master.

Asmodeus's golden eyes fell on the female and widened. "What is she?"

Nevar kept asking himself the same thing. She shrank back as Asmodeus advanced, casting her gaze downwards and shifting behind Nevar.

"I do not know what she is." He moved in front of her, blocking Asmodeus's path and earning a glare for his chivalry. "But I have to get her out of this place before the boss loses her temper."

He quickly snagged her wrist and pulled her with him, making a break for it. A hot jolt ran up his arm at the feel of her soft flesh giving beneath his bruising grip and she gasped, as if she had felt it too. He tugged her towards the door.

Asmodeus stepped into his path. "Is she demonic?"

Nevar growled. "I do not know."

"I have never seen a demon like her." The dark angel pressed his palm to Nevar's breastplate, holding him in place, and peered around him. "She is powerful."

He nodded. He could feel just how powerful she was now that he had his hand on her and it was far beyond the level that he had previously thought.

It sent him back to his initial thoughts about her.

"I do not think she is a demon."

Asmodeus drew back and studied him. "If not a demon, then what is she?"

"I do not know." Nevar rubbed his thumb across the inside of her wrist as she emerged from behind him, her free hand clutching the two pieces of silver material to hold her top up and her leathery wings curled around her shoulders in a protective way. He looked down at her. "What are you?"

"Born of Hell." She looked certain about that, but he still wasn't sure she was a demon.

There were other beings born of Hell that weren't demon. Asmodeus was one of them. He was all that was evil in his angelic twin, Apollyon. The Devil had tortured Apollyon until he had lost all good and had then used his blood to create Asmodeus, his own powerful angel of destruction.

Nevar took the two lengths of material from her and tied them behind her neck, afraid he would lose his temper if the top fell down and exposed her to Asmodeus's golden eyes. He wasn't strong enough to fight his master right now, but he wouldn't be able to stop himself.

"Interesting, but we are leaving. Did you eat?" Asmodeus said and he shook his head.

"I was rather preoccupied. The boss of this place told me to make her leave."

Asmodeus's black eyebrows met in a hard frown and his gaze drilled into him. "Why you?"

Nevar shrugged but could see his master wouldn't take it as an answer. He scrubbed his hand over the jagged back of his white hair and flicked a glance at the female. Her hazel eyes flitted between him and Asmodeus, the glimmer of curiosity back in them.

"Apparently, only I can understand the language she is speaking, although I do not know how."

"I can understand her." Those words leaving Asmodeus's lips gave him pause. The angel had understood her when she had informed them she was born of Hell.

He looked back at Asmodeus. "How?"

Asmodeus lifted his huge black wings in a shrug. "I did not question it. I understand many languages. Hers is as old as the Earth."

"It is still spoken?" Nevar said and the dark-haired male shook his head.

"I have not heard it in millennia."

Nevar's gaze drifted back down to her and she smiled, a beautiful one that struck him hard in his chest and knocked the wind from him. "How old are you?"

She looked little more than thirty to his eyes, but then he was beyond two thousand years old and didn't appear much older than she did.

Her black eyebrows pinched together and she mimicked his master, lifting her slender pale shoulders and shifting the clawed tips of her wings. "I do not know. Ancient. I recall the birth of the King of Demons."

Asmodeus choked. "Excuse me?"

She beamed at him. "I remember your creation, although I did not witness it."

Nevar stared at her. "Just how old are you and how can you recall the birth of Asmodeus but not the battle you survived?"

Her hazel eyes turned troubled and she lowered her head, her smile falling away. "I do not know. It hurts when I try to remember it."

Asmodeus moved closer, studying her in a manner Nevar didn't like. He wanted the male's eyes off her.

"Erin told me that when Heaven tampered with Veiron, he experienced great pain when attempting to recall events from his true past," Asmodeus said and Nevar growled at the casual mention of his ward. His master knew that when he was weak and tired, just the sound of her name was enough to cause him pain, stirring all the terrible things he had done.

Things he hoped she never found out about.

Things he regretted with every drop of his blood.

Asmodeus slid him a warning look and then turned back to the female. "Perhaps Veiron can assist you in regaining your memories, and he may know of your species."

"No," Nevar barked, a knee-jerk reaction to the idea of heading to the island where Erin lived. "You said yourself that we have a mission that needs our focus. We shall escort the female away from this place and then continue that mission."

"You are leaving me?" she snapped and shot between him and Asmodeus. Her power rose so swiftly that Nevar's knees almost buckled under the sudden pressure of it on his body. Her eyes darkened, blazing violet and her pupils stretched thin in the centres of her irises. "I will not let you leave me again."

She snarled and claws curled from her fingertips, as black as night, and the tips of her sleek dark hair fluttered as if a breeze played with them.

Asmodeus's left eyebrow shot up and then he grinned at Nevar, flashing his short fangs. "It would appear you have an admirer."

His smile dropped from his face when she turned on him.

"What are you?" he said and Nevar knew he had seen her eyes too.

He had never seen eyes like them.

They matched the colour of his, and Asmodeus's, when he lost his temper, but her pupils were elliptical.

"It is time we found out." Because Nevar had the dreadful feeling that her origins were more than merely born of Hell. "But we will not ask Veiron. We shall seek the advice of another."

Their presence wouldn't go down well, but it was the only choice he had and his only shot at discovering what the female was without taking her to Veiron.

And Erin.

But not because he feared seeing his ward and seeing the pity in her eyes.

The female's power began to lower, the weight of it lifting from his shoulders. She was dangerous and he wouldn't take her to Veiron for that reason. He wouldn't place Erin in danger, or her infant son. He would protect her. Them.

Asmodeus looked over the female's head to him. "Where are we taking her?"

Nevar stared straight back at him.

"To the half-demon. Taylor."

CHAPTER 5

Lysia stared up at the huge white building that stretched wide in front of her, dotted with rectangles, some of which shone yellow while others were dark. The third row of them on the section of building before her were all yellow, as if a fire burned within.

Nevar tugged on her wrist, pulling her along the path towards the building and a broad dark door up some steps beneath a columned porch. The King of Demons followed behind her and she could feel his shrewd gaze on her. It hadn't left her since they had departed the place that Nevar had informed her was called Cloud Nine. The wily king did not trust her, although she didn't know why.

Perhaps because she felt attached to his servant?

It hadn't taken her more than a few seconds to realise that Nevar was just that—the sole servant of the King of Demons, bound to him by contract. Asmodeus had been the one who had turned Nevar demonic, and it seemed her warrior desired to make him pay for that. Because he believed it would bring back the good in him?

She felt sorry for him, because she knew deep inside her that on some level, unconscious to him, he truly believed that, and it wouldn't work.

Even if he slayed the King of Demons, it wouldn't free him from the darker side of his soul.

She looked down at his hand on her wrist, at the black fingers tipped with claws. He despised what had happened to him and yet half of his arms and up to his knees was darkness, a sign that he was merging with another form. One locked within him? She had heard tales that the King of Demons could wear another form, one closer to the dark beast the Devil held hidden beneath his charming façade. Nevar had such a form too, but he had given it free reign, allowing both forms to become blurred and altered.

Why had he done such a thing when he wanted the evil gone from his soul?

By allowing it, he had made it impossible for him to purge that evil.

She lifted her other hand and stroked the line of his fingers, from his knuckles to the points of his black claws. He looked down at her, his jade eyes fixed on his hand too, watching her. His black skin was smooth beneath the pads of her fingers and warm too, not as rough or cold as she had expected. He held such heat and strength, and countered it with softness that she could only surmise came from his angelic side.

He flitted between violent and aggressive, and gentle and tender with her.

Asmodeus moved past him, his enormous glossy black wings furled against his bare back, and knocked on the dark door.

In the club, the black-haired male had declared her an admirer of Nevar's and had spoken it with a mocking edge to his voice, one that had made her feel he believed no one could admire his servant.

She did.

He was strong, whether he felt it or not. She could see his strength in his eyes and it came not from his body but his heart. It was born of the gentle side of him, the one that battled the darkness and craved the light.

The door swung open and Lysia looked there.

A tawny-haired large male stood in the opening.

An angel.

She shrank behind Nevar, pressing her free hand to the back plate of his armour, between the two vertical slots where his wings should be. He had hidden them back at the club, forcing them away with a trace of disgust colouring his eyes. He despised them too.

He hated much, and she could sympathise. She hated many things too.

At the top of that list were angels.

She bared her fangs at the male in warning. If he dared to attack, she would kill him. She wouldn't allow him near her or Nevar.

"Einar will not hurt you." Nevar gave an expectant look to the angel. "Will you, Einar?"

The big male shrugged thickly hewn shoulders beneath his tight black t-shirt. "Not unless she gives me a reason to hurt her."

She growled at that.

His full lips quirked at the corners and an amused glimmer shone in his rich brown eyes. "It was a joke."

"Not a very funny one," Nevar said and walked forwards.

She stayed put, refusing to move, even when Nevar stopped and tugged on her wrist. She unleashed a fraction of her power, enough to keep her bare feet rooted to the spot.

"He means me harm," she whispered when Nevar looked over his wide shoulders at her.

He sighed and smiled, melting her insides. He was gorgeous when he smiled and it reached his jade eyes, brightening them and chasing away the shadows. "He won't hurt you. If he does, I will kill him. Okay?"

She considered that and then nodded. "Okay."

Einar turned to Asmodeus. "Did your boy just threaten to kill me?"

Asmodeus grinned wickedly. "It has become apparent that he has a possessive streak."

The tawny-haired male shifted his dark eyes back to her. "Who is she anyway?"

When she stepped out from behind Nevar, his eyes widened just as Asmodeus's had on first seeing her wings. She wasn't sure why they all looked at them that way, as if they had never seen such a thing. She felt certain there were other females in Hell who had wings.

She knew of one female who definitely did.

"Why do you all stare so? The original angel had wings and none stared at her."

All three men turned stunned gazes on her.

It was the angel who spoke. "What the hell did she just say?"

Neither Asmodeus nor Nevar acknowledged him.

Nevar turned back to face her and dipped his head, bringing his eyes down to level with hers. "You know Amelia?"

Amelia?

She shook her head. "I know no such female."

"Amelia is the original angel," Nevar said and she shook her head again.

"She is not called Amelia." Lysia searched her memories for the name of the original angel, the one who had provided much amusement for the Devil over the millennia. "I do not recall her name but it was not Amelia. I recall that she died. Was another born?"

He nodded. "She survived this time, with the help of the Hell's angel and the angel of Heaven."

"Interesting. What else has happened?" She wanted to know. The world had changed from how she remembered it and the balance of power had changed with it.

"Maybe you should all come inside and tell me why you both can understand her and I can't," Einar said and she glared at him. He shot one back at her and shifted into the shadows inside the building.

Asmodeus followed him inside and she trailed along behind Nevar.

"What is the last thing you can remember before the battle?" he said in a low voice that she felt was meant for her ears only.

She racked her brain, working forwards from the furthest point she could recall until she reached the memories that hurt her head.

A beautiful scene played out in her mind, golden sand stretching as far as the eye could see, broken only by the wide dark swath of the Nile and the palms that dotted its banks. Beyond it stood the most incredible thing she had seen.

"Thebes."

Nevar stopped dead and she bumped into his back. He looked over his shoulder, his jade eyes filled with incredulity.

"You remember Thebes?"

She nodded.

"Not Thebes like a ruin… like it is today… but like a city?"

She nodded again. "I recall the people coming and going, and how they would speak of their lives. I spent the whole day basking in the sun and watching them, learning about them."

"You understood their language?" He turned back to face her. "As you understand mine?"

"I understand all languages… but I cannot speak them."

He stared at her as if he hadn't understood her and she was on the verge of repeating herself, afraid that he might have lost the talent to hear her words in a language he knew, when he moved closer, coming to tower over her, his expression holding a cold edge that she didn't like, one that unsettled her.

"Thebes has not been a city in over two thousand years."

Her eyes widened. Two thousand years.

"But I recall it as if it was only yesterday and it was the last memory that is clear to me. How is that possible?" Her heart pounded hard against her chest, a shiver going through her as she stared up into his eyes, searching them for the answer even when she knew he didn't have it for her.

He hesitated and then lifted his right hand and settled it against her cheek, his palm resting softly on her skin and his fingertips touching the line of her jaw. "We will find out, but first we must see if Taylor knows of your kind."

She looked beyond him to the dark entrance of the building. A half-demon. Nevar had explained that Taylor often worked with people he knew, helping them with their problems. She hoped the female warrior could help her.

Nevar took her hand in his and the world and her worries melted away as she looked down at them, at his long black fingers pressing into the back of her hand. She liked the feel of it and the heat that rushed through her whenever they touched.

She liked his heat.

It was there in his eyes whenever he looked at her, a palpable hunger that echoed within her and called to her, luring her into stepping nearer to him and closing the gap between them.

She climbed the twisting wooden staircase with him, heading high into the building, towards the level where she had seen the golden light. It shone ahead of her now, illuminating the corridor, and voices drifted to her ears, among them a soft feminine one that carried warmth and possibly a teasing note.

"This is who was at the door, and you let them in, Romeo?"

"They have someone with them and it seemed rude to turn them away."

The angel. The female had called him by another name, speaking it in a voice laced with affection.

The angel was the half-demon's mate.

Strange.

She had never thought she would see a union between two creatures of the opposing realms.

Nevar reached the top step and looked back at her. "Don't flip out. Einar will not lay a finger on you."

She nodded and followed him into the brightly lit room. Old paintings in gilded frames hung on the deep red walls and furniture cluttered it despite the expansive size. A fire burned in the grate directly across from her and two long dark sofas formed a line to her with a wooden table between them. Weapons covered almost every inch of the furniture, including half of one of the couches, and one resided in the dark-haired woman's hand.

She was beautiful, her elegant figure clad in tight black trousers similar to the ones Lysia wore and an even tighter black t-shirt that accentuated the size of her breasts. The woman's blue eyes found her and she smiled.

"Nice wings," Taylor said and came forwards, brushing past her mate and stopping very close to Lysia.

The woman ran a hand down Lysia's left wing and she couldn't stop the giggle that bubbled up her throat.

Nevar raised a silver-white eyebrow at her, as if he had been expecting a different reaction. She frowned at him. She had no reason to attack the half-demon. The woman hadn't meant her any harm by touching her wings. She had merely been curious.

"Do you know of her kind?" he said.

Taylor pinned him with a cold stare. "*Her*? Does she not have a name?"

He looked down at Lysia and a flicker of guilt crossed his handsome face. "I had meant to ask her when I first met her but Asmodeus interrupted. It slipped my mind today. What is your name?"

"Lysia."

He released her hand and looked her over, his jade eyes taking her in from head to toe, heating her down to her marrow. They roamed back up her body to her face and locked with hers.

"I should have guessed you would have a beautiful name," he murmured in a low voice with a half-smile that reached his eyes.

Taylor made a retching noise.

Lysia gasped. "Are you unwell?"

Taylor stared at her blankly.

Nevar sighed. "She asked if you were sick."

The dark-haired beauty laughed. "No. Just… I've only met Nevar a couple of times and didn't have him pegged as a poet."

He snarled and flashed his emerging fangs at the woman, the skin around his eyes turning black as they switched to violet.

Lysia preferred them like that. They made her feel they were kindred spirits, connected somehow.

"So what's her name?" Taylor looked across at Nevar. "Because Einar was right and I haven't a clue what she said. It sounded like gobbledygook."

"Lysia," Nevar said.

"So, Lysia, how does it feel to be lumped with two blokes who don't even bother to ask you your name?" Taylor caught Lysia's arm and pulled her further into the room. "Bet it charmed the pants off you. Come on. Take a pew and let's get a good look at you."

Lysia stumbled along behind her, struggling to comprehend half of what the woman was saying. She threw Nevar a pleading look and he sighed again.

"Less slang, more words from a dictionary," he said and followed her.

Taylor made a rude gesture to him and sat on one of the long dark couches. Nevar took hold of Lysia's shoulders and guided her down onto the one opposite the half-demon, and sat to her right. The seat was comfortable. Perhaps a little soft for her taste. She felt as if she might sink into it.

The half-demon scrutinised her, her blue eyes slowly narrowing as her perusal went on, flicking over every inch of her and leaving no part unstudied.

"Where are you from?" Taylor said.

"She said she was born of Hell, but the last thing she remembers is Thebes... as a bustling city." Nevar slumped back into the couch, the action causing his legs to relax and part further.

His left knee brushed hers.

She burned where they touched and couldn't stop herself from looking at him.

He screwed his eyes shut and tight lines bracketed his sensual mouth.

"Are you unwell?" She took hold of his left shoulder and tensed. His arm was like a rock beneath her hand, his powerful muscles speaking to a deeply feminine part of her and stirring wanton thoughts.

She snatched her hand back and blinked, unsure how to handle the way she reacted to him but certain that she couldn't allow it to get the better of her and act on her impulses.

He rubbed a spot on his black armour over his heart. "Oh, I could not be better. I have the Devil mad at me, a beast on the loose, and a woman who cannot communicate with the majority of the world dumped on me."

She glared at him for that, crossed her arms over her chest and wished him pain.

He growled and curled into a ball, clutching his chest with both hands. His lips peeled back off his fangs and the darkness crawled over his skin, gaining ground as it twined up his arms and snaked over his thighs.

"Fucking son of a bitch," he barked and clawed at his black armour.

Asmodeus rubbed the same spot over his heart. "The beast?"

Einar took hold of the dark angel's arm and spun the male to face him. "This beast on the loose... wouldn't go by the name of the Great Destroyer, would it?"

The King of Demons nodded. "I was coming to warn the others while Nevar attempted to locate it. We could not find it in Hell."

The angel paled. The half-demon paled with him.

"You all fear the destroyer?" Lysia said, looking between them all, including Nevar.

He snarled and sweat dotted his brow. "Right now, I just want to kill the fucking thing to stop it from hurting me."

Lysia pressed her left hand to his cheek and closed her eyes, focusing on him and his pain. She pushed past the surface layers of it, heading deeper into him, forging a connection between them that would allow her to steal it away.

There was so much pain inside him, most of it not born from whatever connection he shared with the destroyer. His deepest suffering stemmed from the things he had done and she couldn't take that pain away for him. Only he could heal it.

She snipped away the pain his link to the destroyer caused him, severing the ties that bound them. It would be a temporary reprieve, a mere weakening of whatever part of their connection transferred pain from one to the other. It would restore itself before long.

Her heart ached as his settled, the hurt in it eating away at her, leaving her trembling inside.

She drew her hand away from his face when he opened his eyes and looked at her, his jade ones overflowing with astonishment and gratitude.

Lysia schooled her features so he wouldn't see the pain she now held within her, hurt that stemmed from both her and from him, blended together into a deep ache that throbbed within her breast.

"I think I will just go ahead and admit right now that I do not have a Scooby Doo what she is," Taylor said with a wide smile. "But she is made of all kinds of awesome. Erin is going to love her."

Nevar growled at the half-demon.

"Get over it." She made another rude gesture to him.

Erin. That name had been mentioned by everyone several times now and each time Nevar had reacted adversely.

"Who is Erin?" she said to Nevar and he ignored her.

He shifted to the edge of the couch and leaned forwards, resting his elbows on his bare knees. "You have never seen anything like her, or heard of anything like her?"

Taylor shook her head, causing her glossy black hair to bounce against her shoulders. "Nope. Hasn't Asmodeus? He's as old as the hills and spent his whole life in Hell."

The King of Demons shook his head too.

"Not in my lifetime. Hell is vast and there are many parts where I never venture." His piercing golden gaze dropped to Lysia and narrowed. "I hope you are not from the area where the demons prefer the taste of mortal flesh."

Lysia's eyes widened and she came close to growling at him. "I feed on blood, not flesh."

He lifted his broad shoulders in an easy shrug. "It is almost the same thing."

Lysia shot to her feet and Nevar caught her wrist.

"Lay off her." His voice was little more than a deep rumble and she looked back at him, catching the violet in his eyes before they melted back to cool green.

"I take only blood," she whispered.

His beautiful eyes shifted to her and he nodded. "I know you take only blood, and now everyone knows."

"Like a vampire." That snapped her attention back to Taylor.

Lysia shook her head. "Not like the pervert at the bar."

Nevar relayed that for her. The big tawny-haired angel smiled grimly, his dark eyes sparking with golden flecks of fire.

Taylor laughed. "I see you met my ex."

"She threw him across the bar with a telekinetic blast." Nevar smiled and Lysia couldn't help smiling too. Her power had impressed him, and that was only a tiny fraction of what she could do.

"Nice." Taylor grinned. "Erin will love her. She does love a Hell raiser."

"She is a Hell raiser," Einar said and everyone nodded in agreement.

Lysia wasn't sure whether they meant that as a good thing. She looked back down at Nevar, seeking the answer from him. When his firm lips curved into a smile that stirred heat in her belly, she took it that it was a compliment, and that he liked it about her, just as the half-demon did.

And the mysterious Erin would.

"Then it is settled that we should take Lysia to Veiron and Erin and see if they can help her," Asmodeus said but there was only darkness in his voice and his expression, and she felt his power rising, coming to press against hers. She held her ground, uncertain what the dark angel intended, but unwilling to show him any fear. His golden gaze slid to her and crimson bled into the edges of his golden irises. "If you try anything... if you raise a hand to harm anyone on the island... I will kill you."

Nevar was on his feet in an instant, pulling her behind him so quickly that her head spun from the swift jarring movement. He growled and flashed his fangs at the angel he called master, his eyes blazing violet and the skin around them turning to inky shadow.

"You dare lay a hand on her and I will kill Liora," he snarled, the vicious growl more beast than man, and she felt the evil within him, the intent to spill blood and the pleasure that thought gave to him.

He desired to make his master suffer.

Such desires only gave the evil he wanted to purge more hold over him.

Lysia laid her hand on the back plate of his violet-edged black armour again, between the vertical slits, a need to soothe him compelling her to touch him and make him aware of her presence and that she knew his pain.

His tremendous suffering.

Some of his anger abated, draining from the air around them, and the thundering beat of his heart in her ears began to slow.

"Do not try me, Nevar, and do not threaten Liora," Asmodeus growled and rose to his full height, using it to tower over Nevar. The black-haired male glared down at him and folded his arms across his bare chest. "You have hurt her enough. It will be your death if you attempt anything like that again."

His furled obsidian wings arched higher on his back, and she mentally cursed him for using such an intimidation tactic, making him appear larger to his opponent. Angels had done such a thing to her. She remembered it. She remembered them towering above her while she lay on the ground, their wings held aloft and haughty expressions on their victorious faces.

She breathed harder as her throat closed and her head ached, a trickle of panic making her fingers tingle. She twitched them and shook her head, squeezing her eyes shut in an attempt to rid herself of the image of the angels.

They raised their blades.

Blades meant to strike her down.

Asmodeus's power pushed at hers, buffeting her and making her wobble on her bare feet. Hers rose to meet it, instinct driving her to protect herself from the angel who meant her harm.

No, not only her.

She desired to protect the warrior shielding her too.

He stood between her and the angel, bearing the brunt of his malice, weakening its effect on her. He shook beneath her hand, straining to remain standing under the full force of his master's power. Such pride. Such strength. In a battle of wills, she had no doubt he would win, but this was not a battle of wills.

He was losing, slowly and surely, his body faltering despite his efforts to remain strong and his deep desire to withstand this assault and shield her.

Lysia shoved the fingers of her free hand into her long black hair, clutching her head, and something snapped inside her.

"Leave him alone!" Her entire body jerked as her power blasted from her of its own will, too much for her to contain in her weakened state.

The shockwave tore through the room, sending not only the furniture but the occupants flying. It hit the centre of her focus with the most force, tossing

Asmodeus hard across the room and into the wall. His impact created a crater, splintering the coloured wall and knocking several of the paintings down.

Only Nevar remained unaffected, held within the circle of her power, safe from harm.

Just as she had wanted him to be.

She breathed harder, struggling to regain control.

Nevar turned to face her, causing her hand on his back to slip to his waist and settle on his warm bare skin. He gently clasped her upper arms and rubbed his thumbs across her flesh, eliciting warm shivers that danced across her skin.

"Look at me," he whispered and she lifted her head, releasing it as she brought her eyes up to meet his. "You're making my chivalry thing a little difficult when you keep showing me up by flashing killer moves... but... I appreciate the back up, even if it is a little emasculating."

She wasn't sure what to say to that. Was he angry with her because she had used her power to protect him or was he teasing her?

"Are you good now?" His violet eyes followed his fingers as he lifted his right hand and brushed her black hair behind her ear.

"I do not think I was ever good." A smile trembled on her lips and he smirked.

"That makes two of us, but you know what I meant."

She did, and she didn't think he had never been good, because there was still good within him, a light that he couldn't see through all the darkness. She wanted to guide him back to that light.

"I am in control," she said, and realised that she was. She had regained control the moment he had touched her and she had seen that he was unharmed.

He nodded in approval and stroked his fingers down the curve of her jaw, his gaze still following them, distant yet focused.

"We need to find a way to help you remember," he murmured and she was no longer sure she wanted to remember what had happened to her or anything else she might have forgotten.

She had more power than she had realised, a terrible force locked within her that she had little control over, and she feared if she discovered the true depth of it, that it would overwhelm her.

Nevar's fingers slipped from her face and she grew aware of the gazes fixed on her and the wariness of their owners.

Even the King of Demons was looking at her differently, with more respect in his golden eyes. The touch of malice remained though, directed at her. He thought her dangerous and a threat to those he loved.

She would prove him wrong about that.

Lysia stepped out from Nevar's shadow and faced Asmodeus. "I swear to you, King of Demons, that I shall not harm anyone on the isle, but in return you must swear you will not harm Nevar."

One black eyebrow shot up and then he sighed. "Why you desire to protect him is beyond me. If you knew the things he had done, if you knew the truth about him, you would think differently of him."

Lysia held his gaze, unflinching even when it narrowed on her, filled with darkness and cruelty. He meant to make her feel differently about his servant, but his words had only made her feel closer to him.

Because if the people knew of the things she had done, if they knew the truth about her, they would think differently of her too.

They would think her a monster.

They would rise up to strike her down.

CHAPTER 6

Nevar kept hold of Lysia's hand as they stepped out of Asmodeus's swirling black portal and onto the white sand of the tropical island. The heat hit him hard and he squinted against the early morning light, cursing the sun. Lysia gasped and her grip on his hand tightened. He looked across his shoulder at her to find her staring at the sand.

Her wide hazel eyes darted up to his and then swept across the island, taking in the turquoise water of the curved bay to their right and then the leafy green canopy of the forest that filled the centre of the island to their left.

She went to move off and he held her firm, keeping her in place beside him. He wasn't sure how the others would react to them bringing a stranger to this place of sanctuary. Asmodeus had warned that he had been greeted with violence when he had first dared to come here, and he'd had Apollyon with him at the time. Apollyon was adored by the entire group, except for Asmodeus, who had a love-hate relationship with his doppelganger.

Einar and Taylor went on ahead, crossing the white sand to the fire pit where the others waited. Einar had contacted Marcus through telepathy, a gift all angels of Heaven shared and Einar had retained even though he was currently without wings, and his fallen status was pending investigation. The jury was still out on whether Taylor should be counted as demon or human. If the verdict came back human, then Einar could have his wings and status restored. Nevar wasn't sure the angel would desire to serve Heaven again, after everything he had witnessed since falling.

Marcus had sent a message back that they would allow them to visit the island, but that Einar and Taylor had to meet with them first and explain what was happening.

Nevar waited, watching them interacting with the group, hoping they wouldn't turn them away and would be able to take Lysia in. Asmodeus had made it clear that they needed to continue their mission as soon as Lysia was settled on the island and they had informed the others that the Great Destroyer had awoken.

"I will retrieve Liora," Asmodeus said and threw his right hand forwards. The air there darkened and black ribbons formed, shifting slowly at first but gaining speed, gradually beginning to spin together into a vortex.

When it was large enough, his wretched master cast him a look that he couldn't fail to understand and then stepped through the portal. It closed behind him.

Nevar would do as ordered. He would ensure that the female didn't harm anyone on the island, keeping her promise. Despite the fact these people didn't trust him, part of him cared about them, no matter how hard he tried to convince himself otherwise.

He kept his eyes on Lysia, avoiding looking at the group as another figure emerged from one of the small huts built beneath the towering palms.

Erin.

He felt the weight of her gaze on him and closed his eyes, steeling himself against it and the darkness that swirled through him in response, filling his mind with a replay of every terrible thing he had done. He tried to shut out the images but they only came faster, a rapid succession of bloodshed, violence, sex, and death. Every transgression he had committed.

Every demon bitch he had fucked before killing, chasing a high that had damned him to darkness.

He released Lysia's hand and turned his back on her, struggling to breathe as it all overwhelmed him and afraid he would taint her with his impurity, passing all of his black sins on to her somehow.

"Nevar?" she whispered, her voice a soft soothing melody that reached out to him, bathing him in warmth that chased the chill from his skin. "You are unwell again."

He nodded and dug his fingers into his white hair, hanging his head in shame. He hated her seeing him like this, a weak and despicable creature. A mess. A man destroyed by his own stupid actions and his own weak nature.

Her warm fingers caressed the bare strip of skin between the back plate of his armour and his hip pieces, stroking across his spine as she moved around him. They drifted over his hip, stealing all of his focus without him knowing it, drawing it all to her and away from himself.

She floated into view, an ethereal thing, more fantasy than reality to him. Her head tilted, causing the sleek fall of her black hair to clear her shoulder as she dipped lower, bringing her face into his field of vision. Her hazel eyes found his and she smiled, her rosy lips curving sweetly. There was no curiosity in her gaze this time. No distance held between them. She wasn't looking at him from afar, studying him as if he were nothing more than a stranger to her, one with an affliction that interested her.

She was looking at him as if he meant something and she desired to help him.

As if she knew her touch was black magic and stole his suffering away.

She lifted her hands to his face and cupped both cheeks. "Tell me what plagues you."

He shook his head. He would never tell her such dreadful things. Asmodeus had been right. If she knew his bloody history, she would view him with different eyes, ones devoid of the light he was coming to crave seeing in them.

Her smile faltered but she rallied. "I only want to help you."

He knew that but he still couldn't bring himself to confess his sins to her.

"Erin." A deep male voice boomed across the island, a note of warning in the low growl.

"I want to see her," a lighter female voice replied and his heart jerked in his chest and he shot back, away from Lysia, and swiftly turned to face the owner of it.

Erin strode across the white sand, her black summer dress fluttering around her thighs and her bare feet eating up the distance between them. Her short black bob bounced with every determined stride, the red stripe down the right hand side shining brightly in the morning light.

Her formidable husband followed her, the ex-Hell's angel growling as his eyes blazed gold edged with crimson, a sign he was on the verge of unleashing his other side and his anger on the world. His long legs gave him an advantage over Erin, carrying him faster across the sand, but it wasn't quick enough for the angel's liking. He beat crimson wings, the sudden blast of wind sending sand in all directions and tousling his overlong scarlet hair, and closed the distance between him and Erin.

Erin disappeared and reappeared further ahead of him.

"Goddammit, Sweetheart, will you give it a rest?" the immense male growled and beat his wings again, catching up with her.

Erin smiled wickedly, clearly enjoying annoying her husband, and her amber gaze met Nevar's.

He shrank back and cast his gaze down at his boots.

She huffed and only stopped walking when she was practically toe-to-toe with him. "Are you still refusing to look at me?"

He closed his eyes.

"You don't even want to see the baby?"

That gave him pause. He hadn't seen the child yet, had thought he wouldn't be welcome near it. She wanted him to meet the tiny babe?

She trusted him near it?

He opened his eyes and sought the answer in hers. She smiled at him and looked to her left.

Veiron stood there, towering several inches taller than Nevar, his broad chest bare and his thickly muscled arms held closed over it. Nevar frowned. Not closed over it. Closed protectively over a black swathed bundle.

The bundle wriggled.

"You know he gives me hell when you teleport," Veiron grumbled and gently rocked the bundle.

His son.

Nevar swallowed hard.

The Devil's grandson.

"Play nice," Veiron said and Nevar wasn't sure whether the angel was speaking to him or the baby as he uncurled his arms, revealing a chubby little face.

The black cloth fell away from the baby's head, so he could see the boy's thick black hair and tiny dark horns.

"Thankfully, Dante didn't have those when he decided to say hi to the world." Erin lovingly stroked the small horns, still beaming.

The baby wriggled and opened his eyes. Golden irises swirled brightly, flecked with black.

Nevar tried to stop himself from saying it but his mouth overrode his brain. "He looks like Asmodeus."

Veiron scowled at him. "He's my kid, and there's proof of it."

Nevar hadn't been suggesting that Erin had produced the child with Asmodeus's help but the similarities between the two were striking. Dante had horns.

Veiron carefully shifted the squirming boy in his arms, lifting him by his armpits. The black blanket fell down, revealing the proof Veiron had mentioned.

Tiny clusters of puffy red feathers on the baby's shoulders.

"Aren't they to die for?" Erin brushed her fingers over them and the boy giggled, kicking his legs and bouncing up and down. "He loves it, just like his daddy does."

Nevar nodded dumbly, astounded by the little miracle of life. It was Erin's DNA that had allowed her to have a child with Veiron. As the Devil's daughter, she shared her father's powers, including the ability to make life even when her mate, Veiron, was an angel and therefore sterile.

Veiron grinned at his son, lifting him higher into the air. "She loves your wings right now, Little Fella, but she will hate them when you start using them. We can all imagine the trouble you're gonna be."

Nevar had to agree with that. The thought of a child, too young to know the dangers of the world, having wings that could carry him high into the air or out over the sea, sent a shudder through him.

Erin was his ward and when he had discovered she was pregnant, he had extended his protection to her son.

"I think we can handle him between the thirteen of us," Erin said, still smiling.

"Thirteen?" Nevar frowned at that.

She nodded. "Veiron, me... Amelia and Marcus of course... and Apollyon and Serenity come all the time now. Plus Einar and Taylor when they can make it to the island with a little lift, and Lukas and Annelie are due to visit any day now. Even Liora visits and I think Asmodeus is a sucker for punishment or something because he insists on bringing her and gets himself into trouble with my father every time."

"That's twelve." Nevar looked at the boy. "Does Dante make thirteen?"

How could the boy look after himself?

"You're lucky number thirteen." Veiron bounced Dante in his arms, grinning like a madman at the infant, eliciting a high squeal from him and more wriggling.

Nevar just stared at him, reeling and sure he had heard him wrong.

"Oh, don't give him that look, as if he's gone mental." Erin slapped Nevar on the arm and he staggered from the force of the blow, his bones aching and nerves stinging. "Shit, sorry. Since giving birth my power has grown because it's no longer split between protecting him and protecting me. I don't know my own strength."

"It was Erin's decision." Veiron settled the boy, holding him in the curve of his left arm while he covered him with his right hand, tugging the blanket up and tucking it around his tiny form. "I'm not saying we didn't duke it out because of it, but the missus always gets her way."

Erin smiled and placed her hands on Veiron's right biceps, her fingertips tracing one curved spike of the black and red tribal tattoo that swept around it and over his shoulder, matching the one on his left arm. She tiptoed. The huge male dipped towards her and she kissed him. When she pulled away, Veiron settled his free arm around her shoulder, pulling her into the shelter of his embrace.

"This the girl?" Veiron jerked his chin towards Lysia.

She was staring at Dante, her hazel eyes wide, barely blinking.

Nevar nodded. "What's wrong?"

She jumped and her gaze leaped to his. "He's of the Devil. Do they know?"

"They know. Erin is the Devil's daughter."

Her eyes went even wider and she grabbed his arm, her small hand grasping his right vambrace that protected his forearm. "The Devil has produced offspring? How many?"

"Just the one." He refused to look back at Erin when he said that.

Lysia looked at her, and then at Veiron and the baby, and then beyond them and her eyes darkened. "There are angels here."

"I know." He placed his hand over hers on his arm to reassure her. "They are friends though, not foes."

She nodded, but didn't look fully convinced that the angels wouldn't harm her. She didn't need to worry. He would never let them lay a finger on her.

"Fascinating language, although it must be a right pain for her. How does she understand you, and how the hell are you understanding her?" Erin eyed both of them.

"She understands all languages, but only speaks the one. Both myself and Asmodeus can understand her. Do not ask me how I understand her, but Asmodeus is familiar with the language." Nevar placed his arm around Lysia's shoulders, careful to avoid knocking her wings, and drew her to him. "This is Lysia, and she needs your help. Will you help her?"

Erin nodded.

"It's what I do."

CHAPTER 7

Nevar stood at the periphery of the group, listening to them as they discussed Lysia and went over everything he had told them about her. Asmodeus had returned with Liora and was acting as Lysia's interpreter, relaying her answers to every question the group posed. Erin had the most, but Veiron came a close second, with Apollyon in third. The dark angel stood opposite his twin, Asmodeus, making it easy to see the striking similarities and the differences between them.

They appeared the same, with the exception that Asmodeus wore his black hair shorter, shorn around the sides and left wild on top, much like Nevar now wore his hair, and Apollyon wore his hair long, tied at the nape of his neck with a blue thong that matched his eyes. Their eyes were the biggest difference between the two. Apollyon had eyes like the endless blue skies. Asmodeus's matched the Devil's golden fiery ones.

Apollyon's petite blonde witch stood off to one side, deep in conversation with her dark-haired cousin Liora. Lysia constantly studied the two of them, her gaze leaving them only when someone posed her a question and she relayed her answer to Asmodeus.

The original angel, Amelia, stood guard at her sister Erin's side, her silver hair tied in a high ponytail that was all business, much like her choice of clothing today. Rather than wearing one of her usual pale summer dresses, she had donned her chrome armour and had her wings out. Silvery feathers covered the top half of them, but the lower half were leathery and dragon-like, a sign of her part-demonic blood.

At Amelia's side, her lover and servant Marcus stood sentinel, his matching wings on display as his silver-blue eyes closely watched Lysia. At least he had chosen not to replace his long black shorts with his armour, opting for a more casual approach to his safeguarding of Erin.

Einar and Taylor stood close to Apollyon, forming a bridge between the powerful former angel of death and destruction and his twin.

Lysia turned away from the group, wandering towards the shore. Nevar sighed and trudged after her, caught her arm and brought her back to the discussion. It wasn't the first time she had drifted away from them. It was happening with increasing frequency. Maybe she was as bored of this conversation as he was. They were getting nowhere.

Veiron didn't have a clue what she was and neither did Apollyon.

Asmodeus glanced at Nevar and he received the silent message loud and clear. Now that they had revealed that the Great Destroyer had awoken, it was time for them to leave Lysia with the others and go in search of it again.

Fine with him.

He needed some distance and space. He needed to be alone for a while.

Erin and the others were more comfortable with dealing with the sort of situation Lysia had found herself in and they would figure out what had happened to her and help her. He couldn't. He wasn't any good at that sort of thing and wasn't fit to help, not when he was finding it increasingly difficult to concentrate.

His ward had given him a plate of leftover food to devour but it hadn't been enough to begin restoring his strength. It had only been enough to keep him ticking over for a short time and now he was starving again, and with the hunger for food came a different sort of craving.

One for blood.

He needed to get a meal in his stomach, half a cow at least, and get on with his mission. If they delayed much longer, the Devil would find out and would send his minions after them, and he didn't want the Hell's angels anywhere near Erin and her son.

Besides, he wasn't fit to look after Lysia. He wasn't fit to look after anyone.

He couldn't even look after himself.

He growled under his breath and tamped down the voice that had said that, mocking him with his weakness, before it could conjure the memories of what he had done and batter him into submission with them, giving his darker self a chance to seize control.

A darker self that he insisted on viewing as a separate being, even when he acknowledged deep in a small recess of his black heart that it was his true form now. He was the darkness, playing at being the light.

He felt Asmodeus's glare burning into him and lifted his head to meet his fierce gaze.

Someone was missing from the group.

Lysia had wandered off again.

He huffed and stomped after her, and was about to grab her wrist and haul her back to the others when she spoke.

"I prefer this place," she whispered, her back to him and black hair fluttering in the light warm breeze that stirred the white sand. She wrapped her arms around herself and kept walking, luring him with her towards the waves that lapped gently at the shore. "I feel comfortable here."

That made him want to leave her here even more. She was happy here and safe. She didn't need his protection anymore. He could continue with his mission, away from these people, alone again.

"The other place is too loud and new."

That gave him pause. "New?"

She nodded and walked forwards, until the jewel-blue water washed over her feet and soaked into the hem of her black jeans.

Her last clear memory had been of Thebes, and that had surprised him, but he hadn't considered that London might have felt alien to her and filled with unfamiliar things. Angels watched over the Earth from Heaven, able to see the world developing through the ages even if they never ventured there. Creatures of Hell had no such path open to them. They lived in that realm of darkness and fire, unable to see the mortal world above them, and uninformed of the changes that took place there.

Liora had told him that Asmodeus had been shocked when he had first visited the mortal world, and the angel had had the advantage of seeing the pool in Hell in which the history of that world was recorded. He had known of the buildings and vehicles and everything the mortals had created.

Something told him Lysia had not been so fortunate.

No wonder she had felt vulnerable in Cloud Nine, surrounded by things she couldn't comprehend.

He moved closer to her, unable to ignore the powerful compulsion to protect her. It was so strong that it overrode his desire to return to the shade of the palms, escaping the fierce sunlight that felt as if it was burning his skin away like acid.

"You are not used to the mortal world as it is now?" he said and she shook her head, her black hair swaying across her silver halter-top and her hazel eyes remaining fixed on the distant horizon. "You are unfamiliar with it and things like cars."

Her brow crinkled. "Cars?"

He nodded and shifted another step closer. A small wave rolled over his boots but he didn't care. The only thing that mattered to him right now was understanding more about Lysia. Everything else had fallen away again, leaving only her.

"Large metal conveyances with lights and glass windows, and black round tyres that carry them." Describing a car in such a fashion made him feel as if he were speaking to a child and he hoped she didn't think he was treating her as if she were one.

She was definitely not a child.

His gaze betrayed him, hungrily dropping to her sensual curves and devouring them.

She was all woman.

His fangs itched for a taste of her.

He dragged his eyes away and fixed them on the water. There was a fish dancing among the shallow waves.

"Do they growl?" Lysia said.

He shook his head. "I do not think fish make any noise."

She moved and snagged his attention, and he found her frowning at him. "Fish?"

"Sorry. I was distracted by the fish." He pointed to the water, hoping she would see the fish and not think he had lost his mind and couldn't do something as simple as keeping up with a thread of conversation.

She peered into the water. "There are many fish, but I was speaking of cars."

"Do cars growl?" He pondered that. "I suppose they do in a fashion. They have engines, a mechanical heart that gives them motion. Some are loud and some are silent."

"I believe I saw some of these monsters." She waded into the water.

"They are cars, not monsters... and what are you doing?" He went to go after her and the water washed across his greaves.

He stepped back and frowned down at the black plates moulded over his shins and sent them away, leaving his legs and feet bare. She had advanced while he had been distracted with keeping his armour untarnished and was thigh-deep in the water.

"I want to see the fish." She looked back at him, her smile disarming him and making his step falter.

He had never seen her so at ease. She was even more beautiful, an angel in form with the wings of a demon. Those wings dragged through the water behind her as she waded deeper.

"You will spook the fish," Nevar said when she scowled at the water. "Come out and they will return."

He held his hand out to her and she looked back at him. A jolt went through him when her eyes met his, a hot bolt of awareness that made his skin prickle and his blood burn. She reached out to him and he held his breath, anticipating the lightning that would zing through him when they touched.

Her fingers brushed his palm and he hadn't anticipated enough voltage.

He twitched with the fierce current that went through him, lighting every inch of him up inside and dragging every drop of his focus to her. Her cheeks coloured and her eyes darkened, the deep flicker of desire in them awakening the hunger he felt for her and goading him into surrendering to it.

"I like it here," she whispered, her voice barely there, distant to his ears and her own judging by her lost expression.

With you.

He felt the words she didn't say beating within him, filling his mind and taunting him. She liked it here with him and he meant to leave her. How would she react to that? She had reacted with violence when he had tried to leave her before. Would she do such a thing again now that she had found a place that made her feel safe?

She no longer needed him to make her feel that way.

She now had people around her who were more able to protect her than he was.

And he had a mission to complete.

She blushed and looked beyond him, towards the others. "Everything here is familiar."

He looked back at the camp. Small huts made from materials sourced from the island. A fire pit. There were only a handful of modern conveniences, including a generator that rumbled away at the other end of the island, set at a distance from the huts in the shadow of the palms, used to power the refrigerator in a shelter next to it.

Everything else was basic and simple.

As basic as the dwellings in Hell.

"How long were you in Hell before you ended up in the mortal world a few days ago?" Nevar looked back at her.

She paled, released his hand and clutched her hair. A startled cry left her lips, tearing at his heart, and she shook her head. Her hands trembled as they tangled in her black hair and her pain washed over him, stronger than he had ever felt it.

"I cannot remember." She threw him a look filled with fear and her knees gave out.

Nevar caught her before she could hit the water and scooped her up into his arms, carrying her back to the shore. She muttered things beneath her breath, her entire body shaking against his.

"I shouldn't have asked." He held her closer, cursing himself for questioning her without thinking about the consequences and the pain he would cause her.

She looked up at him, her hazel eyes swimming with that pain. Tears lined her dark lashes and spilled onto her ashen cheeks.

"I'm sorry," he whispered and kneeled with her on the sand, resting her backside on his thighs.

Her dark leathery wings draped across his stomach and the sand beyond his knees, the grains sticking to their damp skin.

Her trembling began to subside as he held her and smoothed her hair from her sweat-slicked brow.

"Is she sick?" Veiron's deep voice drew his gaze to the large male as he approached, jogging across the sand, causing threads of his scarlet hair to come loose from the thong that held it at the nape of his neck.

The Hell's angel crouched beside them, genuine worry in his near-black eyes.

Nevar shook his head. "She experiences pain whenever she tries to remember events from a specific timeframe. Her last clear memory is of Thebes as a city, more than two thousand years ago."

Veiron's expression turned grave and dark. "Do you think Heaven had something to do with it?"

"I do not know." Nevar looked back down at her, glad she was settling again, the pain in her subsiding. "But she doesn't trust angels and can't tell me why."

"Hurt me," she whispered, her eyes darting between his. "They struck me down."

He growled, his lips peeling back from his emerging fangs, and his wings burst free, called by a dark desire to fly to Heaven and tear it down as payment for what it had done to her.

A bright shaft of golden light shot down from the endless blue sky, stinging his eyes. The bolt struck the sand between him and the group near the fire pit, spraying it everywhere, and weapons appeared in the hands of Marcus, Einar, Apollyon and Asmodeus.

It appeared Heaven had come to him instead.

He rose to his feet, set Lysia on hers, and recalled his greaves, completing his armour. He pushed her behind him and shielded her with his black wings as he called his obsidian blades to him. Beside him, Veiron growled and grew, his muscles expanding as he changed into his demonic form. His skin turned black and his eyes blazed gold and red, and his armour covered him, the red-edged black plates protecting his upper torso, hips, forearms and shins.

Veiron growled, flashing twin deadly rows of crimson teeth, and the scarlet dripped from his wings like blood, turning them black before the feathers fell away, revealing the leathery dragon-like wings beneath.

The angel who had travelled within the Heavenly beam of light straightened and as the golden shaft faded and died, Nevar saw a male he had hoped he would never set eyes on again.

Fury flashed like lightning in the depths of the blond angel's ice-blue eyes, a shadow crossing his face that was dark and unholy as he furled huge wings against his black armour.

Lysander.

Nevar would never forget the time they had met in Hell on the plateau where the pool that recorded the world's history stood, protected by the angels of Heaven. He had been at his lowest point, filled with a need for vengeance and bloodshed, despising himself and his master because of it. Blaming Asmodeus for everything he had done. Every innocent life he had taken. Every bitch he had screwed for a shot of Euphoria. Every inch lower he had sunk into depravity.

He had been there to use the pool, but Lysander had blocked his path.

He would never forget that he had promised this very male that he would halt his quest to seek out Asmodeus's weakness in exchange for him revealing the location of that male's fortress, something that had eluded him. He had made a pact with Lysander, swearing he would go directly to Asmodeus's castle and battle him. It would have been a suicide mission, and the angel had known it. Lysander had wanted him dead and had thought to play him for a fool, so Nevar had played the bastard too.

Mere days after swearing to give up his quest, Nevar had tasked a sorceress with finding his master's weakness and had discovered it in the form of Liora.

He had exploited that weakness.

He had broken that pact.

Lysander had come to deal out the punishment he had sworn he would inflict if Nevar betrayed his trust.

He had come to take Nevar's head.

CHAPTER 8

"Wretch." Lysander strode towards Nevar and four more shafts of golden light shot down behind the angel, throwing sand in all directions.

Four more angels dressed in black armour rose behind Lysander, each of them taller than the slender golden-haired male, but none of them as formidable as they cast curious gazes around the island.

All five radiated power that didn't just press down on Nevar's shoulders, it crushed his body, as if it was forcing his bones inwards, and his knees threatened to give out under the pressure.

Nevar struggled to remain standing and fought for air, his throat closing as Lysander stared at him, his eyes swirling like ice and filled with malice and intent.

"I warned you not to betray me," Lysander snarled and the shadow crossed his face again, a dark phantom of some sort that settled on his skin for a moment before it disappeared.

The four immense angels behind Lysander grinned at each other, evidently excited by the prospect of watching their comrade paint the white sand red with his blood. There was darkness in their eyes now, a shadow of something similar to what showed in Lysander's at times, as if they all held a blackness in their souls, the same as Nevar did. These angels were capable of evil and if someone gave it a push, they would turn as easily as he had.

They were not normal angels. Their power, bearing and behaviour warned that they were warriors, bred for a purpose, one that Nevar wanted to know as he watched them eyeing everyone on the island in turn, a cold and clinical edge to their eyes. They were calculating every outcome of everything that might go down as a result of their appearance and Lysander's fury.

Nevar had never seen anything like them.

Angels in Heaven worked together, but these four seemed closer than mere allies on the same side. They acted as a unit and Nevar had a feeling that Lysander was their fifth member, and while they were happy to stand back and not interfere in Lysander's crusade, they would step in should their comrade need them.

They reminded him of his allies gathered here on the island, a powerful unit that wouldn't stop in their pursuit of victory against all who opposed them. Only these angels wouldn't stop in their pursuit of carrying out their orders. He could see it in their eyes, recognising the hard edge to them as they scanned everyone present. He had seen that look in Marcus's eyes once, back when the angel had been a member of the guardian corps and devoted to his duty. Marcus would have done whatever it had taken to fulfil his mission, and these angels were the same.

But different.

Several things set them apart from regular angels of Heaven. The most prominent was their armour. They wore the same armour as Lysander did and Nevar had never seen anything like it. The pieces matched the ones all angels wore, but theirs was covered with finely tooled black leather, and each bore different images engraved onto them. He had never seen wings the colours of some of theirs either.

Lysander's were no longer black.

They were as golden as his hair.

The other four angels' wings all matched their hair colour too. The largest male who stood directly behind Lysander had the strangest colour—a pale shade of jade. He wore his hair overlong, tied at the nape of his neck with sections that had escaped the thong and curled beneath his ears.

The other three were barely an inch shorter than his six and a half foot frame, and just as broadly built. The one to his right had pure long white hair, worn with the top half tied back and the rest left the flow down his back, and white wings, and the one to his left had short crimson hair and red wings like a Hell's angel. The fourth angel had wild black hair and wings.

Their hair, wings and armour wasn't the only thing that warned him these were no normal angels. The power they possessed was far beyond any angel, including Apollyon, and they had something else that set them apart from their brethren.

Ink.

Not a curse, or a spell like the wings he bore tattooed on his back.

Some of the tattoos these men wore were not the sort of ones Heaven would condone—naked women.

The one that drew his attention the most was on the one with short red hair.

It curved beneath his navel, spanning his stomach, visible just above the armoured plates that protected his hips.

It read 'VICTORY' in big black serif letters.

Lysander closed in, the incredible pressure of his power reminding Nevar that it was unwise to take his focus off the angel, especially when the male had evidently come to fight him, and had brought back up.

"Did I not warn you?" The blond's sharp gaze bore into him but Nevar didn't answer. He flexed his fingers around the violet hilt of his black blade, preparing himself. A golden curved blade appeared in Lysander's hand. "I told you not to go after Asmodeus's weakness and now the Great Destroyer has risen and the proof of that stands at my back. With the destroyer's awakening, came the awakening of these angels of the apocalypse."

Veiron grumbled, or he might have chortled, it was hard to tell when he was fully demonic, standing three feet taller than usual and far wider.

"You royally fucked up this time." The big Hell's angel grinned at him. It might have been a grimace though, because the pressure of the power the five angels were emitting grew stronger at that moment, driving Nevar to his knees.

"Did you know someone was stealing your gig?" Erin said, standing near the fire with her eyes on Apollyon where he knelt on the sand with the others, fighting the crushing force of the power flowing over them.

She bounced Dante in her arms, completely unaffected.

Apollyon grunted. "I was. I trained the bastard."

Lysander looked over his shoulder in their direction. "Six centuries under your wing, Old Man. Never once did you tell me my true purpose."

Someone was bitter.

Nevar chuckled.

Lysander swung deadly ice-blue eyes his way and held his free hand out, unleashing more of his power in Nevar's direction. He ground his teeth and fought it, unwilling to be driven into the sand. The Devil had held him pinned flat on his stomach on the ground before him once and he had sworn it would never happen again.

Lysia curled behind him, tucked safely against the shield of his black wings, and he willed her to stay there, hidden from view. He wasn't sure what Lysander would do if he saw a demon on the island, a creature so clearly born of Hell. Angels had a tendency to send demons to Heaven for questioning rather than asking the questions themselves and finding out whether the demon deserved to end up incarcerated and tortured.

"When I awakened to my true purpose, I sought to stop you Nevar, and you lied to me. You betrayed my trust, and you will pay for it." Lysander pointed his golden blade at him.

Erin appeared next to Lysander's band of angels, her short black dress fluttering around her thighs from the act of teleporting, and looked at each in turn, her fine black eyebrows raising high on her forehead so they disappeared beneath the fringe of her bob.

Curiosity shone in her amber eyes. "So, you're like the four horsemen or something? You've come to destroy the world?"

They all looked at her.

Dante burped.

Their eyes flashed in unison and fell to the baby, and Erin backed off a step.

"But there are only *four* horsemen. What does that make you?" She looked straight at Lysander, not flinching when he turned his glare on her.

Some of the weight of his power lifted from Nevar's shoulders, allowing him to breathe normally. She was drawing the focus of the angels, giving everyone a chance to recover. She was placing herself and her son in danger for him.

"Ward," Nevar whispered and shook his head when she looked at him. He wouldn't let her risk herself.

She patted her black bundle on the back and he belched again. "Who's a good boy?"

"Boy?" Lysander sneered. "It is an abomination."

Her face darkened at the same time as her eyes brightened to gold. "Need I remind you whose island you're on? You're just sore because you're some sort of apocalypse fifth wheel."

Lysander turned fully to face her and more of his power lifted from Nevar. More of it directed at Erin. She didn't seem to feel it at all.

Near the fire, Asmodeus and Liora linked hands and rose to their feet. Apollyon joined them, helping Serenity onto hers.

Veiron staggered a few steps towards Erin before stopping and breathing hard. While standing was now comparatively easy, moving clearly took its toll. Nevar needed more of the angels' power off him if he was going to fight Lysander, but that meant more directed at Erin and her child.

"I am no fifth wheel," Lysander snapped and jerked his chin up. "I am their leader, the angel of destruction, created to defeat the destroyer as my brethren were created to stop the plagues, end the wars, heal the land and beasts, and save the mortals."

Erin eyed them all again, her golden irises beginning to glow. Shadows fluttered on her shoulder blades, small wisps of smoke that danced against the breeze. She had wings like her father's.

"So you haven't come to destroy the world... you're all about saving it." She smiled at that. "Cool. I thought we were going to have a problem."

"We have a problem, Devil Spawn," the big white-haired one said and his blue eyes flashed with fire. "You and that abomination are a problem."

Her face darkened again.

Veiron growled and staggered forwards, his immense body shaking from the exertion, and almost reached Erin before he collapsed.

"Do not touch her," he snarled, his black claws churning up the sand as he glared at the angels, his eyes swirling red and gold, filled with impotent rage.

Nevar knew his fury and frustration. They weren't strong enough to contend with the power of these angels when they worked together. Only Erin and Dante could withstand it. The two they all wanted to protect were the only ones strong enough to protect themselves and stand their ground against these angels.

Erin went to Veiron, crouched beside him and placed a kiss on his black forehead. He seemed to recover within the sphere of her power, shielded by her, and managed to sit up on his knees and breathe easier. She handed him Dante and he wrapped his huge black arms around the tiny bundle, and then his leathery dragon-like wings around him too, cocooning him completely.

"Daddy will protect you," she said to Dante and stroked his cheek before standing and facing the five angels again. "I really wanted to be nice to you all."

They exchanged glances and the white-haired one called a burning white sword to his hand.

Erin sighed dramatically. "You just had to go there."

"We will deal with you first, Demon." He pointed the flaming blade at her.

Veiron definitely chuckled this time and whispered to Dante, "Watch mummy do her thing."

"What was that? You want me to crush you like a bug?" She approached the group, fearless with her head held high and shadows flowing from her back, becoming wings.

The male laughed.

Erin's expression went blank, she raised her left hand, and all five men dropped to their knees, grunting in unison.

"I really do hate it when people laugh at me." Erin pinned each angel with a glare. "It's so hard to get anyone to take me seriously at times."

Veiron chuckled again. Erin gave him a pointed look and he fell silent.

She turned back to the five angels and walked in a circle around them, her hands behind her back and her gaze constantly on them. The shadows fluttered and flowed from her back, and tendrils curled around her arms, black where they emerged from her hands but turning red near their tips.

The five angels' shoulders shook, trembling under the weight of her power. The pressure on Nevar disappeared as the angels withdrew their power, using it to combat Erin's instead. It didn't seem to help.

Nevar wished he possessed Erin's power.

She was incredible.

"I think you should leave now." Erin stopped in front of Lysander. "Before I really lose my temper."

He edged his blue eyes up to her face. Sweat beaded on his brow and darkened his wild blond hair.

He managed to nod.

"Good." Erin waved her hand again and walked back to Veiron.

The five angels stumbled onto their feet.

Lysander grinned wickedly and launched himself at Nevar.

Before Nevar could respond, Lysia was in front of him, blocking Lysander's sword arm with her bare hand and driving him backwards. The male didn't seem to know what to make of her as she fought him, slashing at him with long black talons and catching him at times, drawing lines of bright scarlet on his flesh.

The other four angels called their weapons and Lysia threw her hands forwards, hitting them with a telekinetic blast that only made them stagger back a few steps. Either she was growing weaker and so were her attacks, or the angels were powerful enough to withstand the full force of her abilities.

All five angels stopped and stared at her in stunned silence.

Why?

"I like this chick. She rocks," Erin said, shattering the tension in the air for a heartbeat.

Lysander sneered. "This chick? This is no mere female."

He raked cold icy eyes over Lysia and Nevar growled, warning the male away from her. He was about to step in front of her to shield her again when Lysander spoke, stunning everyone into silence this time.

"She is the Great Destroyer."

CHAPTER 9

Nevar stared at the back of Lysia's head, his hand slowly coming up to rest on the centre of the violet-edged black breastplate of his armour. Beneath it, the mark on his chest pulsed, a steady rhythm that felt like a heartbeat, out of sync with his own but just as fast.

She slowly turned her head and looked over her slender shoulder at him, her fall of black hair obscuring part of her face. Her eyebrows furrowed and her hazel eyes implored him, filled with a combination of hope and fear, and incredible hurt.

Hurt that he felt sure was beating in his own chest through the mark there.

Her mark.

She was the Great Destroyer.

He had been looking for a beast, bigger than one of the dragons that resided in Hell, a gigantic creature with six horns, spikes down its back, a vicious barbed tail and enormous wings.

His gaze briefly dropped from hers to her wings and they drew closer to her back, no doubt responding to the pulse of fear that had shot through her when his eyes had shifted to them. She wanted to hide them from him, but she didn't need to feel such a thing or be ashamed of them.

She had the wings and the talons of the creature carved on the door of her chamber, but she wasn't a monster.

She was beautiful.

But he couldn't move past one thought that stuck in his mind, sending fear in crushing waves through his body.

Was the attraction he felt for her and the electric rush of tingles he experienced with every brush of their skin, no matter how innocent the touch was, purely because they were bound to each other?

He was her master. He wasn't sure what that made her though. Not a servant. She was so much more than that to him.

That revelation hit him hard, knocking him back a step.

She was more than a servant. More than an animal or an abomination. She was filled with light and shone so brightly it hurt his eyes at times. She was incredible. She was Lysia.

Part of him wanted to bark out a laugh at the suggestion that the delicate, pure and ethereal woman standing before him was the Great Destroyer, a beast that would ravage Hell, Earth and Heaven and bring about the end of the world.

Everything she had said to him rushed through his mind, making him dizzy as he lifted his eyes up to meet her hazel ones.

Angels had struck her down.

Her last clear memory before a battle was Thebes in all its glory.

A shiver trickled down his spine and his thighs and crawled over his scalp.

She didn't know the modern world and all its inventions because she had been locked in Hell, held in a dormant state, waiting for the combined blood of the angelic destroyer and a witch that was a key to spill and awaken her.

"Say something," she whispered, her striking eyes pleading him.

Eyes that matched Liora's.

Hair that matched Asmodeus's.

She had been made in their image.

He pulled in a deep breath through his nose and exhaled it just as slowly, seeking some calm amongst the raging storm of his thoughts and fighting to get the words he wanted to say, and she needed to hear, to line up on his tongue.

"I will take the creature to Heaven, into our custody where it will be safe." Lysander stepped forwards.

Nevar's eyes blazed violet and he snarled at the blond male through his fangs as they dropped. "No one is taking Lysia anywhere… especially not angels."

A gust of wind battered him and suddenly Amelia was between Lysia and Lysander, shielding her with her half-feather half-leather silver wings. The sunlight reflected off her chrome armour and highlighted her silver ponytail, and glinted off her sword as she swept it in a sharp arc at her side.

"You won't do to her what you did to me," Amelia snapped and spread her wings, her power rising as she began to unleash it. "I won't let you take her to Heaven just so you can kill her, you bastard."

Amelia kicked off and barrelled into Lysander's stomach, taking the angel down. He hit the sand hard, his blade almost falling from his grip. His fingers closed around the hilt of the curved golden sword and he brought his hand up hard, cracking Amelia across the side of her head. She grunted and fell sideways, and Lysander scrambled free.

Marcus was there before the angel could launch his own attack, shoving him backwards into the four angels of the apocalypse. The men parted to allow him and Lysander through and Marcus flicked his curved blade out at his side, extending the silver engraved handle into a staff that rivalled his six-foot-plus frame. He beat his silver wings to match Lysander as the angel shot backwards, his golden wings working frantically as he attempted to gather himself and gain some space. Marcus didn't give him a chance and neither did Amelia.

She kicked off the sand, launching high into the air, and held her hands out before her. A swirling blue orb materialised between her palms, growing as it began to spin faster and faster, the different shades in it blurring together. When it was the size of a basketball, she moved her hands behind it and beat her silver wings hard as she shoved forwards with her hands. She jerked backwards and the orb shot forwards, heading straight for Marcus as he kept Lysander busy dodging swift stabs of his spear.

As if sensing the approach of the blue orb, Marcus dropped flat on his face and covered his head.

Lysander looked up, straight at Amelia.

The blue swirling ball struck him hard in the chest plate and exploded, the blast rocking the island as it created a crater in the sand and hurled Lysander through the air. The angel spun heels over head and lost his blade. It disappeared. He spread his golden wings, twirling two more times before he finally righted himself.

Lysander pressed a hand to his head and shook it.

Nevar snarled and dragged Lysia behind him, darkness rushing through his veins as he thought about what the angel had suggested. Amelia was right and he couldn't allow Lysander to take Lysia to Heaven. Heaven would seek to destroy her in order to protect its realm, even if Lysia wasn't liable to go nuclear and unleash hell on the three realms. It wouldn't care, not even if the only pool in Heaven that recorded the future showed that she would live forever without raising a hand against any of the realms. It would view her as a threat regardless and would kill her.

Nevar would never allow that to happen. His life wasn't worth much, but he swore on it anyway. He would keep Lysia safe. He would fight the forces of Heaven and Hell, and any army the mortal world could throw at him. He would never relent and never surrender. They would have to kill him if they wanted to get to her.

He snarled and darkness crawled over his skin, encroaching like shadows at nightfall, devouring the golden tone of his flesh as it gained ground.

He tried to fight it and hold it back, fearing how Lysia would look at him if she saw the form he despised, the one that shamed him and made him feel like a wretched monster. He had embraced it though, had allowed it to merge with him and had become the darkness, and now it was quick to come whenever he faltered, allowing the black part of his heart to dictate his actions.

That part screamed at him to protect Lysia and that he was strongest in his other form, when he was one with the darkness and unleashed it. Used it.

He snarled through his fangs and they grew longer, his lower canines beginning to sharpen too and cut into his gums.

His black wings took on a violet shimmer that matched the raised edges of his armour, and the skin around his eyes burned into darkness as they switched to purple. He growled, pain tearing through him as his skull ached, his horns growing despite his best efforts to contain them.

He felt Asmodeus's gaze on him and Liora's too, sensed her desire to come to him. He shook his head, warning her away, and snapped at Asmodeus, torn between fighting Lysander and attacking him. He wanted the bitter tang of blood on his tongue. He wanted to gorge himself on the powerful life force of his master and then take down Lysander in the most gruesome way imaginable to satisfy his dark hunger to see the male pay for daring to take Lysia from him.

To her death.

Nevar clawed his hair back and breathed hard, redoubling his fight against himself. He couldn't go all out. If he unleashed that side of himself, there was a chance that he wouldn't stop at killing Lysander and sending him back to Heaven with his tail between his legs. He would want to continue the fight, wouldn't be able to resist the sick craving for more blood and violence, for the feel of blows battering his bones and flesh, and the sounds of the anguished cries of his enemies in his ears.

Calm yourself. Asmodeus's voice rang in his head and he screwed his face up.

You think I am not trying? Nevar snarled back at him and wished the bastard could see the wicked things his mind was throwing at him, images of him taking down the King of Demons and finally having the vengeance that had driven him for so long now that he didn't know anything else or any other way of living.

"You try to interfere, Nevar, and I swear I have an orb with your name on it." Amelia's voice, edged with all the dark rage lacing her incredible power, snapped his focus to her.

She glared down at him, her wings beating hard to keep her steady a few metres above him, closer to the fire. Her silver eyes swirled like mercury and he read her intent in them. She would follow through with that threat.

"Protect Lysia," she said and turned her focus back to Marcus and Lysander where they were battling, both blocking more blows than they landed, carving up the sand with their weapons and their powerful wings.

Nevar focused on Lysia behind him and placed his hand on her arm, using the feel and the sense of her to calm himself. He had to protect her and that meant he had to keep his head and not go off the rails. She wouldn't like the other side of him, but her dislike of it would be nothing compared with how she would feel if she saw him attacking people she believed to be his friends. She would never trust him if she witnessed that.

Amelia began forming another orb of energy.

The four larger angels who had come with Lysander armed themselves with weapons that blazed with white fire and turned their focus on her.

Erin tsked and shook her head, her black bob swaying as her golden eyes brightened and red edged them. "Why don't we keep this a fair grudge match between Team Amelia and Lysander, and you all fuck off."

She held her hand out, palm facing them, and the four males' eyes widened just before they disappeared. She laughed.

Veiron snickered too, bouncing Dante in his arms as he began to change back from his demonic form, his skin turning from black to tanned golden and his body shrinking back to his normal build.

Lysia drifted past Nevar without him realising she had moved out from behind him, her hazel eyes locked on the fight unfolding before them.

Nevar moved forwards and wrapped his fingers around Lysia's wrist. She gasped and shot to face him, and then blushed when she saw it was him. He drew her to him, tucking her against his side and clutching his sword in his free hand. If Lysander dared to come after her, he would deal with the male as best he could while retaining his normal appearance and he wouldn't be alone. Something told him everyone on the island would fight to protect Lysia.

"Where did you send them?" Apollyon asked Erin, watching the fight between Lysander and Amelia with interest, and an intriguing amount of satisfaction. Evidently, Lysander had no friends on the island who would fight on his side, not even the angel who had trained him for six centuries. Everyone seemed to want to see him punished.

Nevar hadn't been present for whatever had taken place between Amelia, Marcus and Lysander, but if the angel had been responsible for taking her to Heaven to kill her, then he hoped the bastard got what he deserved.

"I sent them to Hell," Erin said with a wide smile. "More precisely, to my father's fortress."

Nevar couldn't stop himself from smiling too as he pictured how shocked the four angels would be to suddenly find themselves not only in Hell and most likely surrounded by the Hell's angels working on repairing the Devil's courtyard, but in the presence of the prince of darkness himself.

"He will not be pleased," Asmodeus said and Apollyon nodded in agreement and looked across at his twin.

"I take it you recognised one of them too?"

Asmodeus dipped his chin. "The white-haired one who threatened Erin. Mihail... my master despises him."

"Why?" Nevar found it impossible to hold that question in. He had never heard of the angel before, or of the Devil hating anyone other than Apollyon.

"While I have to fight the Devil at intervals to decide whether he may leave Hell or will spend the next few centuries trapped in that realm, I cannot kill him. No one can... except Mihail." Apollyon flinched as Lysander landed a hard blow on Marcus's jaw, driving the dark-haired former angel into the sand, and Amelia cursed him and unleashed another blue orb that sent Lysander blasting into the water. Apollyon glanced at Nevar. "Mihail and the Devil came to blows many thousands of years ago and Mihail came close to killing him. The Devil will not be pleased to see the angel again, even if this incarnation of him does not remember what he did or that he has such a power."

"He will be pissed at you," Asmodeus said to Erin.

She shrugged and took Dante from Veiron. The little boy squirmed in her arms and latched onto her neck, sucking furiously.

"Someone is hungry again. I swear he has your appetite," she muttered in Veiron's direction and then looked at Asmodeus and Apollyon. "I don't care if he kills my father... score one for us. Dante is safe then and I can rule Hell in his place. I am a perfect female replica of him after all."

It was true, and she could ascend the throne and rule Hell, but Nevar didn't think she would be up to the task. As tough as Erin was, she wasn't strong enough to do the things that were necessary as the ruler of Hell. She was born of a human mother and had a softness about her because of it. She had heart and cared deeply about people.

As the ruler of Hell, she would have to deal out punishment to mortals who were sent there. It would destroy her.

Asmodeus grimaced, pressed a hand to his bare chest, and shot Erin a black look. "Pissed may have been putting it too lightly."

"Asmodeus?" Liora took his hand, her hazel eyes flooded with concern.

"I will be back. Remain with your cousin while I help my master deal with a certain angel infestation." He dropped a kiss on her brow, stepped back and looked over at Nevar.

Nevar sighed and released Lysia, knowing what the angel was going to say. It was time to go.

Asmodeus shook his head. "Remain here with Liora and the others. Keep her safe... both of them."

Nevar nodded, unable to do anything else while he processed what Asmodeus had asked of him. He had asked Nevar to protect his precious Liora, the woman he had tried to kill in order to strike a blow at Asmodeus. He trusted him with her, and with handling Lysia.

Asmodeus cast a portal and Apollyon caught his arm.

"I will go with you. I cannot fight the Devil, but I can fight angels," Apollyon said and the other male nodded, a glimmer of gratitude in his golden eyes.

They stepped through the black vortex together and when it disappeared, Serenity moved to stand beside Liora.

They formed a line as they watched the spectacle unfolding on the island, spectators in an arena. It appeared Lysander was losing against his two opponents, the patches of skin between the pieces of his black leather armour stained with blood. He beat his golden wings and readied his blade as he shot towards Marcus, dark intent and hunger in his icy eyes and the shadow settling across his features again.

Marcus grinned and casually twirled his spear.

Amelia created another blue orb where she hovered a few metres above the white sand, her silver wings keeping a leisurely pace that held her stationary.

Lysander roared as he swung his blade.

A bright beam of light shot down from the sky, encasing him, and disappeared just as quickly, taking him with it.

Veiron grunted. "I hate it when Heaven cheats like that."

It seemed the show was over but no winner had been declared.

Amelia unleashed a barrage of curses at the sky and began flying upwards. Marcus caught up with her, grabbing her from behind and taking several blows from her wings as he fought to contain her.

"Let me go. I want to kill the bastard." She battered Marcus with her wings but he didn't release her.

"You will have your chance… but if you leave, Erin will be vulnerable."

That seemed to get through to her and she instantly stilled in his arms, allowing him to gently drift downwards with her. The silver-haired female was breathing hard as they landed softly on the white sand. Lysander hadn't been the only one to take a few blows. Amelia had a long gash across her thigh and one on her arm, and Marcus had cuts on his stomach and arms.

Veiron and Einar trudged across the sand to them and began using their two very different powers to heal their wounds, one born of Hell and the other of Heaven. Erin trailed after them, Dante still mouthing her neck as she rubbed his back, and Taylor followed.

Nevar looked at his new wards. Three of them. Serenity and Liora were deep in conversation and he allowed them to wander a short distance away, drifting towards the group, but kept an eye on them.

Lysia remained with him.

He shifted his gaze to her and let everything slowly sink in. He had thought her a demon, one born of Hell, and he supposed she was in a way, but she was so much more than he had thought her to be. This was the beast he had awoken and was now his responsibility. She was made of Asmodeus and Liora, built in their image, and that made the feelings he felt towards her even stranger to him. He was attracted to her, a woman who was in a way their progeny. A woman who was bound to him.

He couldn't stop thinking about what he had done as he looked at her, wondering whether she had risen because of his foolish thoughts about her awakening and giving him something to do rather than his boring guard duty. He had contemplated terrible things and had left her chamber, and she had awoken.

Another monumental fuck up to add to his tally?

If he hadn't thought those things, would she have remained dormant?

He now suspected she had appeared in the mortal world on waking because he had been there. She had found herself in the middle of a strange city because of him, had been frightened by the loud and confusing surroundings because of him, and now she was destined to herald the end of days.

Because of him.

And angels were after her, wanting to take her to Heaven and no doubt kill her, all because of him.

He couldn't bear the thought of her suffering at the hands of angels again or knowing it was his fault. This was all his fault. He had been weak, taking the easy route in all things, when he should have been strong. He should have fought harder—against Asmodeus, against the darkness, against himself. He couldn't undo what he had done, and couldn't change the past, but he could change the future.

He could change her future and the future of the world. He could save her from the destiny others had set out for her and protect her from those who meant her harm.

He didn't see a weapon of destruction standing before him.

He saw a woman, one who had shown fear and vulnerability, who had been hurt and afraid, and one who had fought to protect those she cared about. She wasn't a heartless creature bent on destroying the world and everything in it. She was a woman who marvelled at the world, delighted in the smallest things, and wanted to save others.

She was good, not evil.

He would stop at nothing to do what was right and good and fight to become a stronger male, one who could right his wrongs and set everything straight again.

One worthy of the beautiful woman standing before him.

CHAPTER 10

Lysia didn't like the way the others were looking at her now and how they held themselves at a distance. Only Nevar remained close by her side. It had comforted her at first, but over the hours that had passed since the angels had left the island, she had begun to feel differently about his presence because of his behaviour.

She had studied his reactions to the group as they had posed questions and she had answered them, and he had relayed her answers to them in a language that they could understand.

He acted strangely whenever he had to speak with the King of Demons, who had returned from Hell with his twin, Apollyon, declaring that Heaven had reclaimed the four angels just as everything had been going in the Devil's favour.

He also acted strangely whenever he had to speak with the Devil's daughter, Erin.

The female in question eyed her closely, a sharp edge to her golden irises.

"She doesn't look like the beast we saw on the chamber door," the black-haired woman said and gently rocked her son in her arms.

The father, an enormous red-haired brute that she had discovered was formerly a Hell's angel, cooed over her shoulder at the boy and tickled his cheek, his other arm slung possessively around the waist of his female.

It was a protective stance, and Nevar didn't seem to like it. His gaze kept falling to the large hand softly gripping Erin's hip through her black dress and it darkened whenever it did.

Why?

Lysia had a terrible feeling she knew the answer to that question but pretended that she was wrong. He didn't harbour feelings for the Devil's daughter.

"Why don't you look like the beast?" Erin said to her and she looked away, casting her eyes down at the white sand and scrunching it between her toes.

"We have been through this. She does not remember," Nevar replied for her, a biting edge to his tone that he seemed to immediately regret. His voice softened. "I mean… ask her something else. It is pointless going in circles like this."

Lysia risked lifting her eyes to his face and wished that she hadn't when she caught him looking at Erin with a gentleness in his eyes that she had never seen before.

A dark urge rose within her and she squashed it, knowing that she couldn't obey it. She had tried to leave the group twice already, and both times Nevar had guided her back to them, his grip on her wrist unrelenting. Each time the others had looked at her with more suspicion.

Did they think she meant them harm?

She supposed she couldn't blame them if they did. Lysander had revealed the truth she had wanted to remain hidden, locked inside her and unknown to even her. Before he had announced it, she had known she had done terrible things and had been aware of the battle that had taken place and that angels had brought her down, but she hadn't known exactly what she was.

It had come as a shock to her too.

She had believed herself a monster, but hadn't been prepared for just what sort of monster she truly was—a creature that would destroy the world.

She didn't want to destroy this world.

She looked around the island at the verdant green of the palm trees, the crisp white of the sand, and the clear jewel blue of the sea. It gently lapped at the shore, a steady rhythm that she found soothing. She breathed in time with it, soaking up everything about this place.

Including the people here.

They looked upon her with wary and cold eyes at times, but they were still trying to help her. They had been kind and had protected her from the angels. She didn't want to end their lives. She wanted to see them live long and happy ones, together as they were now.

"You said angels struck you down. Were you a beast at the time or woman?" Apollyon said, his blue eyes holding hers, cold and clinical.

The male was a born leader and seemed to be the one everyone turned to whenever they were unsure of how to proceed. Even Erin would turn to him for guidance.

Erin who Nevar was staring at again, a flicker of warmth in his jade eyes and tenderness in his heart. She could feel it in hers and it sickened her, filling her mind with dark things that tormented her.

Lysia closed her eyes and shut him out, focusing on what Apollyon had asked her and seeking the answer.

She bit down on her tongue when a sharp hot lance pierced her skull above her right eye, trying to hide her pain from everyone as they stared at her in silence. The weight of their expectation pressed down on her and she pushed past the agony searing her mind and searched deeper, trying to grasp hold of the elusive answer for them. If she could answer them, perhaps they would trust her and she could stay in this peaceful place with them. She would be safe from the angels here—both those of Heaven and those of Hell. If she could give these people reason to believe in her, then they would protect her as they had before.

She reached deeper, stretching for it now, seeing shadowy images of the battle in her head.

Another hot bolt of lightning struck her mind and she couldn't stop herself from crying out and clutching her forehead.

"Enough." It was Asmodeus's deep voice that broke the silence and shattered her attempt to find an answer.

She opened her eyes and blinked them to clear the tears away, and found him standing before her, his golden eyes dark but not with malice or intent. He placed his hand on her right shoulder.

"Do not push yourself," he said and she wished it had been Nevar who had intervened and had spoken those words to her.

But Nevar was too busy looking at Erin again, that strange glimmer of hope mixed with guilt back in his heart.

Lysia's claws extended and she turned her back on him and the group, struggling for control. What was wrong with her? She didn't understand what was happening to her or why she was unable to stop herself from feeling angry towards Erin when the woman had done nothing wrong.

She feared that if she remained with the group much longer that she would end up harming the woman and that would turn the entire group against her.

Shadowy memories surged into her mind, a flood of them that swept her away, distorted and fragmented and impossible to see.

She could feel them though.

She could remember a sensation that everyone was against her.

That she was alone.

Her heart clenched, gripped in icy claws, and she breathed harder, trying to combat the crushing fear that seized hold of her and refused to let her go.

She could remember feeling alone, and that had terrified her.

She never wanted to feel that way again.

"Lysia?" Nevar said and she jerked away from him when he reached for her arm. His hand fell to his side and he was silent for long seconds before he sighed. "Take a break. Go to the water or something."

She closed her eyes on hearing that.

He wanted her to go away.

He hadn't offered to go with her, to escort her in case the angels returned and keep her safe.

He wanted her to go alone.

She wrapped her arms around herself and curled her wings around herself too. She didn't want to be alone. She had a horrible feeling she had been alone ever since the angels had defeated her. Nevar had spoken of her being dormant, but she wasn't sure that she had been in a sleep state, not as everyone thought it to be anyway, a peaceful darkness where she wasn't aware of anything.

"Who were the angels with Lysander?" Einar asked, his voice as deep and smooth as a calm ocean.

She had hated the tawny-haired angel when she had first met him, but now she liked him the most out of all the angels. He was kind and gentle, and had been the only one who hadn't looked at her with ice in his deep brown eyes. He hadn't changed from the way he had been when they had first met, and had been the one to tell everyone to give her a minute to rest when they had first started questioning her. He had enforced several breaks in questioning since then, giving her a moment to recover.

"I knew of their existence. They were created after me. There was a rumour among the other angels at the time that they were the second incarnation. I remember that no matter how many times I am reborn." Apollyon's voice gained a cold edge as he spoke. "I do not know what happened to the first incarnation. I was given the duty of training Lysander after he had been reborn around two millennia ago."

"Did you know what his true purpose was?" Marcus said.

"I was informed, but did not link him with the angels we met today until Lukas came to me."

"Lukas?" Marcus's voice took on an incredulous note and Lysia couldn't stop herself from turning back to face the group. The look on his face matched his tone and his pale blue eyes searched Apollyon's darker ones. "What does he have to do with anything?"

Apollyon looked upwards, to the endless blue sky. "Lukas was responsible for the training of the former mediator... the one we know as Mihail. Lukas came to me when he discovered the angel was different and he wanted to know more. I warned him to leave it be... to not ask questions and train the male as instructed."

Marcus's expression darkened.

"Two millennia ago... you argued with Lukas then. I remember it. The whole sky turned black. Shortly after that, Lukas died in a battle in the mortal world." Marcus's blue eyes widened and the silver in them swirled brighter. "Heaven killed him off and reset him because he found out about Mihail's true purpose."

Apollyon's handsome face turned grim and his power rose, as dark as midnight and edged with a hunger for violence that shocked her. Asmodeus truly had been born of this male, of everything dark and malevolent he held within him.

"I did not realise that at the time." Apollyon ran a hand over his long black hair, smoothing his ponytail, as if that action would also smooth his anger away. "But yes, I believe they reset him in order to keep knowledge of their angels of the apocalypse hidden from others. Even the angels themselves were unaware of their true purpose."

"Until someone woke her." Veiron looked towards Lysia and she stood her ground, refusing to let the large male intimidate her. His dark eyes slid across to Nevar. "I hope to the Devil your rehab is going swimmingly and you've got your shit together now... because I have a feeling you might need to step up to the plate and stop the whole world from going to Hell in a hand-basket."

Nevar turned on the scarlet-haired Hell's angel with a snarl, his eyes flashing violet, and she felt his pain beating within her, sharp and fierce. It was destroying him.

She reached out to him and he instantly turned on her instead and smacked her hand away, the force of his blow sending a thousand hot needles stabbing up her arm from her wrist to her elbow. She recoiled and clutched her arm to her chest, her eyebrows furrowing as she gritted her teeth against the pain.

Asmodeus was there before she could blink, shoving Nevar in his black breastplate and pushing him away from her.

Nevar bared his fangs at his master and the skin around his violet eyes turned black.

Asmodeus rose to his full height. "Calm down and consider what you just did, or I will calm you down."

Nevar's purple eyes flickered to her and widened. He blinked, shock written across every line of his handsome face, and his gaze slowly fell to her wrist where she still held it to her chest.

He shook his head and a bolt of fear struck her heart.

He was going to leave her.

CHAPTER 11

Nevar wrestled with the dark urges running rampant through him, flooding his mouth with saliva as his fangs itched to taste blood. Whether it was the blood of his enemies or his own, he didn't care. He craved the coppery tang on his tongue. Hungered for the sweet flow of it down his throat.

With the rising need for blood came a rising need for the violence that would spill that precious liquid.

He faced off against Asmodeus, anger curling through his veins and eating away at them like hot acid as the male stood in a protective stance between him and Lysia.

The darker part of his heart told him to leave her with Asmodeus and the others. He didn't care that he had awoken her and was her master. He wasn't fit for that role. It would be better for everyone involved if he turned his back on her right now and left her with this motley band of warriors. They would know what to do and would no doubt save the day, triumphing over anything and everything that stood in their way and protecting the world.

They could deal with Lysia and take care of her for him.

He had just proven that he was not the person for that job.

He had struck her.

"Clearly the rehab isn't going well," someone muttered, just within range of his sensitive hearing.

Nevar cursed them and the way they spoke about him in front of Lysia, and cursed Asmodeus for protecting her.

His master believed him capable of hurting her.

Nevar wasn't sure what to believe.

He had struck without thinking, only meaning to stop her from touching him when he was losing himself to the darkness. He hadn't meant to hit her with such force that it would hurt her.

He had sworn to protect her and had been incapable of protecting her from himself. What hope was there for him? The only hope for her was him leaving her with these people, with his master. He could have laughed at that had his heart not felt as if it was breaking apart in his chest, ripped into pieces by the knowledge that the man he had cursed to Hell and believed to be pure evil was more capable of taking care of Lysia than he was.

He was the evil one now.

Asmodeus had good in him and more of it shone through his dark exterior every day.

The more of it that Nevar saw, the less he felt there was any left in him. He had become more evil than his master, more wretched and despicable, quick to violence and forever hungry to spill blood.

What hope indeed?

Lysia would see it too in time. She would come to realise that he was no good for her and that these other men were far more capable of protecting her, far more powerful than he could ever be, and far more good than he could dare hope to become.

He growled at his despairing thoughts, a manifestation of the weakness living within him now. Perhaps he had always been this weak but had refused to see it. He had clung to his duty like a fool, even after Asmodeus had forced the contract between them. He had clutched it to him as if it could redeem him.

As if Erin would ever desire him as her protector when she had a man far more capable of that role.

She had a whole family who were more capable than he was and had protected her countless times already.

He looked across at her and snarled a black curse when he saw the pity colouring her amber irises. She thought him weak too, a wretched creature without hope.

Veiron shifted in front of her. "We going to have a problem, Nevar?"

He wanted to shake his head and vow he would never harm Erin, but hadn't he vowed the same thing to Lysia?

Asmodeus offered his bare forearm. "Feed."

Nevar's stomach clenched, coaxing him into taking his master's blood. He was starving, out of his mind with hunger, but he forced himself to shake his head at the same time as he cursed himself for refusing the one thing that could help him claw back his sanity.

He wouldn't take Asmodeus's blood in front of everyone, with them staring at him, as if he was an animal. What would they think of him then? They would see how truly wretched he had become. These people who had known him before he had fallen so far. These people who had seen him at his best and now saw him at his worst, but couldn't see how hard he fought to pull himself out of the abyss and find some solid ground again, a balance between the good and evil within him.

They would never see it.

They would always view him with suspicion and lack trust in him.

He shoved Asmodeus away from him, snarled at everyone as they stared, and unleashed his black wings and took off with a single hard beat of them.

Come back. Asmodeus spoke in his head and Nevar shut him out, refusing to return.

He kept flying, heading high into the darkening sky, needing the cold air in his lungs and the space from everyone. He wasn't strong enough right now to deal with everything. He was drowning and there was no hope of saving himself, and he couldn't bear how the others had been looking at him. He despised them for it.

The further he flew, the calmer he felt, until he could breathe again and the dark urges began to subside. He had to keep flying. He felt sure that if he could just keep flying away from everything that he could escape what he had done and the expectations everyone had placed on him, setting him up to fail.

He couldn't do this.

His heart clenched.

But he couldn't bring himself to leave Lysia behind either.

He halted in the cool night air, beating his broad black wings to keep him steady, and looked down at the island far below him, watching everyone around the bright glow of the fire. He felt certain they were talking about him, filling Lysia's head with poisonous words and making her believe he was weak and evil, and no good for her.

Which he was, but he couldn't bear the thought of her believing that about him.

He couldn't bear the thought that the others might do such a thing either.

He didn't belong in the group and had proven himself unworthy of a position within it more than once, but a small piece of his heart wanted them to welcome him, rather than look upon him with distrust and hold him at a distance.

He hovered in the cool air, breathing deep of it, fighting the darkness beginning to rise inside him again, born of his emotions this time. The ferocity of his need to protect Lysia warred with his need to leave and gain some space, seeking a place where he could rediscover his strength. She would be safe on the island, but that thought only made the darkness rise swifter and grow blacker, flooding him with a terrible urge to attack every male who would dare to protect her in his stead.

Nevar closed his eyes and fought to smooth the turbulent waves of his emotions, trying to grasp hold of them and centre himself again. It was impossible.

The thought of the other angels on the island protecting Lysia twisted his stomach and filled his heart with darkness, a dangerous hunger to force them all away from her. That hunger only grew worse when he recalled how Lysia had looked at Asmodeus with awe in her beautiful eyes and he thought about how his master was more suited to protecting her.

Jealousy caught his heart in a tight grip, crushing it in his chest, and his lungs constricted. He couldn't breathe through it. The idea that Asmodeus would now take care of her, that he would do a better job than Nevar ever could, and would secure her admiration and affection, tore at him like claws, savaging his heart until he was bleeding inside.

Dying.

A dark, possessive need rose within him, obliterating everything else he felt, spawning a compelling hunger that demanded he returned to her and protected her, keeping her away from all the other males on the island.

He wanted to be the only male she needed.

He wanted to be the only man she could see.

Was that possible?

Could he make her need him as much as he needed her?

Nevar placed his hand on his chest, resting his palm on the cold metal of his violet-edged obsidian breastplate over the spot where the mark existed on his skin, and focused on it.

Something akin to hurt flowed through their link, mingled with fear.

A tiny figure broke away from the group and drifted across the sand, heading into the darkness.

Lysia.

His gaze tracked her, following her progress and how her feelings deepened as the distance between her and the group grew, beating stronger within his heart.

His claws scraped over his black armour as he tightened his fingers against it, trying to reach through to the mark and comfort her somehow. He couldn't do such a thing from where he was now and he couldn't bring himself to leave and sever the link either.

He beat his wings and gently flew downwards, unable to stop himself from returning to her.

He couldn't leave her.

He needed her too much.

CHAPTER 12

Lysia headed away from the fire and into the shadows, leaving the group behind as they discussed Nevar, unwilling to listen to them speaking about him in such an ill manner. She wasn't sure what he had done to deserve such harsh words, although she did wish he had chosen to stay rather than leaving her.

With him gone, she now feared the others. Asmodeus had protected her, but she didn't like the coldness that entered his eyes at times and didn't believe he would protect her from the others if they turned on her. She could protect herself, but she didn't want to hurt them, and fighting them would only give them even more reason to push her away and lash out at her.

Or worse.

They could end up doing what the five angels had wanted to do—kill her.

In her weakened state, she was no match for their combined power. She needed to feed. The sip of blood she'd had at the club in the city had been far from enough and it had been days since she'd had that scant amount. When Asmodeus had offered his arm to Nevar, demanding that he feed, she had felt a deep compelling urge to seize him and take him up on that offer. Her fangs had itched with the hunger gnawing away at her stomach, weakening her.

She wasn't sure how Nevar had managed to refuse his master, not when she had seen in his eyes and felt in their bond that he hungered for the blood as fiercely as she did. Why did he refuse what he needed? At the bar, she had offered him blood and he had refused to feed. It had provoked a startling reaction from him, a violent response that had shocked her and had left her feeling that he craved the taste of blood yet despised what it did to him. As far as she could tell, it would only make him stronger, as it did with her, providing necessary sustenance.

Did it do something else to him?

Something to do with that deadly and beautiful side of himself that he had tried to contain when the wretched angel had threatened to take her to Heaven?

She had seen the darkness rising within him, colouring more of his skin with its inky shadows and causing his small horns to grow, jutting out of his tousled white hair. He seemed to despise it, but she couldn't understand why. That side of himself was his strength, not his weakness.

If he had allowed the change to come over him, he would have been strong enough to battle Lysander, just as he had desired.

But he fought the change whenever it happened.

She wanted to know why, but he had left her before she could dare ask him, and now she feared he would never return.

Lysia pressed her hand to her chest, between the two triangles of grey material that formed the upper half of the top that Nevar had given her. Her skin there glowed faintly purple and then began to brighten and reveal a shape. The same mark that she knew Nevar bore on his chest. A mark he had touched more than once in her presence. A mark she had become aware of after the blond angel had announced she was the Great Destroyer, servant of Nevar. As soon as it had sunk in and she had acknowledged it was true, she had felt the tingling between her breasts and had known that she bore a mark concealed beneath her skin.

A mark that linked her to Nevar.

Their link grew stronger and she could sense his pain. Where did it stem from?

She had caught the look he had thrown at Erin before leaving. There had been so much regret in his violet eyes and guilt in the feelings she could sense in him. There had been hope too, and a deep desire for something she couldn't decipher.

Something she didn't want to decipher.

Her heart leaped into her throat when a shadowy figure landed hard on the sand before her in a crouch, spraying the white grains over her jeans-clad legs, his huge feathered wings spread wide and one hand pressing into the ground.

Nevar rose to his full height and furled his black wings against his back, his chest heaving with each deep breath he drew. Breaths that shifted the muscles of his stomach in an alluring symphony that she found hard to ignore.

She looked away from him and dropped her hand to her side, her heart stinging in her chest as she recalled how he had acted around Erin.

Whatever she was feeling towards him, the intense pull that she couldn't shake or ignore and that she felt certain stemmed from more than their bond, it was one sided. He didn't feel the same about her.

"It is not safe for you to be alone." His deep voice curled around her, offering her comfort that she wanted to take, no matter how much it hurt her.

He had seen her alone and had returned to her.

It should have been the balm her heart needed to heal but it didn't soothe her in the slightest. The anger she had felt at times returned, so fierce and swift that it shocked her.

"It might not be safe for you to be alone either," she snapped and kept her cheek to him, her eyes on the fringes of the palm trees that filled the centre of the island. "And I am always alone."

"What do you mean by that?" He moved a step closer and it was hard to stop herself from taking one backwards, keeping the distance between them steady.

What was wrong with her?

He had come back and it should have been comforting, but instead she wanted to rail at him, wanted to strike his chest and push him away. A confusing part of her whispered that she wanted to force a reaction from him. She wanted him to fight to contain her and pull her into his arms. She needed to feel them around her and have all of his focus on her, just for a heartbeat of time.

A stupid notion.

It didn't make any sense at all. Why would she want to hit him and push him away if she wanted to be close to him?

She shrugged. "It's how I feel. I feel I've always been alone and will always be alone. I remember that much. I remember that everyone was against me and none stood with me."

She went to turn her back on him but he closed the distance between them and his heat wrapped around her, his masculine scent filling her senses and commanding all of her focus, keeping it locked on him and beckoning her closer.

"That isn't the case anymore." He lifted his right hand towards her. She stepped back and he sighed. "It won't happen again. I am on your side now and I will not let anything happen to you. You are no longer alone."

She wanted to believe him, but she couldn't face the thought of doing such a thing and then having him turn against her. She would sooner remain alone than allow him inside, where he could do more damage when he pulled away and left her.

She glanced at him, easily seeing him despite the darkness, and then looked off to her left, at the water steadily lapping at the shore, a mesmerising rhythm that she lost herself in as she fought to understand the maelstrom of feelings swirling within her.

The words flowed from her. "I will end up alone again."

There was a growl in his deep voice when he spoke. "Why do you say such a thing when I have just sworn you will no longer be alone?"

Lysia hesitated, her heart in her mouth, feeling certain that he was going to break it. She remembered being alone. Always alone. She didn't know how to process her feelings and couldn't understand them because she had never experienced them before. She had never felt desire for someone. She had never needed someone as she needed him.

It was a weakness.

It made her feel vulnerable and afraid.

She was the Great Destroyer, a creature formed to extinguish all three realms, powerful and dangerous, and yet he made her feel weak and uncertain, defenceless against him and his dark allure.

If she could be the destroyer she was born to be, the ruthless and powerful woman locked within her, held back by foolish fear, perhaps he would desire her too.

She knew that he found strength and power alluring, and incredible calm in the face of great danger, and the ability to do whatever was necessary to protect others.

Lysia swallowed her heart, lifted her chin and looked him right in the eye.

"Do you desire the female?" she said without allowing the tremble in her limbs to show in her voice.

Her heart beat harder as she waited for his reply.

He frowned, confusion colouring his beautiful jade eyes. Eyes that had studied the female in question, lingering on her with a myriad of emotions showing in them.

"What female?" He moved a step closer.

She backed off another one, keeping necessary distance between them, knowing she would crumble and give in to her need to touch him and have him holding her if he came within reach. His jaw tensed in response, the frustration he felt trickling through their link. She looked back over her shoulder towards the fire.

"That female." Those two words came out quiet, lacking courage and strength.

He looked there and his eyes widened and darted back to her. "No."

"No?" she said, certain she had heard him wrong or he had mistaken her target for another woman. "You do not desire Erin?"

He shook his head and looked as if he might have laughed if the weight of hurt in his eyes hadn't been dragging him down. "Erin was my ward, when I was an angel of Heaven. I was her guardian. I was meant to protect her. I tried to do just that and events happened that drove a wedge between me and Heaven. They tampered with my memories. Apparently, it seems to be an everyday occurrence up there. The moment we deviate from their plan, they either fuck with our heads and replace our memories, or they kill us and reset us."

Pain beat in his heart and shone in his eyes and she went to step towards him, driven to comfort him, but he spoke again and she froze down to her marrow.

"Erin is not the woman I desire."

Her heart sank. "There is a woman you want then?"

He nodded and she couldn't bring herself to keep looking at him.

He moved closer, demanding her attention, and her gaze swung back up to meet his. There was darkness in it, a hunger that she felt echoing within her. A hunger that had been a constant presence since she had first set eyes on him.

He stepped into her and slid his right hand along her jaw, tipping her head back, and she couldn't breathe as she stared into his eyes, lost in them and the feel of his warm hand on her face. His gentle touch and the softness in his gaze lured her deeper under his spell and she was powerless to resist, could no longer fight her feelings for the warrior standing before her, claiming every ounce of her attention.

"I want you," he whispered and dipped his head.

The first brush of his lips across hers sent a thunderbolt zinging straight through her, electricity that crackled along every nerve and set her on fire.

He angled his head and laid claim to her mouth with a hard demanding kiss that turned the fire into an inferno that threatened to consume her and burn her to ashes.

It was too much.

Lysia beat her wings and shot backwards, away from him. Her hand trembled against her lips, her heart beating so fast that she felt sick as she shook all over, unsure how to respond to every feeling colliding inside her.

She stared at Nevar through wide eyes.

His hand slowly fell to his side and he straightened, the darkness of passion in his eyes giving way to pain.

"I am sorry... I should not have done that." He backed off a step and the distance yawned between them like a vast crevasse, filling her with fear as she realised she had hurt him and he was going to leave her again.

"Why?" she whispered, struggling to find her voice as her heart continued to race and her lips tingled from his kiss.

A kiss that had felt too good.

A kiss she wanted to taste again.

"Because you did not like it." He went to look away and then clenched his jaw and stared at her instead, a hardness in his eyes that she didn't like. It masked his pain but it couldn't hide it from her, not when they were linked.

She hesitated before taking a step towards him, dragging her courage back up and holding on to it this time.

"I did." She was surprised by the strength in those two words and the reaction they caused in him. The hardness in his eyes lifted, leaving soft jade behind, and his pain eased. "You surprised me. I was not prepared... but I am now... so will you do it again?"

He swallowed hard and looked as if he might refuse.

She was on the verge of kissing him instead when he spoke, the deep raspy huskiness of his voice stirring heat in her belly.

"Would you like that?" His smile was wicked, causing her heart to flutter like a timid butterfly in her chest.

How did he make her feel so weak? With just a look or a smile, or even a few words, he reduced her to a state where she felt strangely weak, a nervous little thing with no strength left in her, unsure whether she was coming or going.

He made her want to surrender to him, and she had never surrendered to any man, angel or demon in her entire existence.

She nodded to answer him, couldn't express in words how much she wanted him to kiss her again. They all seemed so inadequate.

She braced herself when his smile widened, reaching his eyes and darkening them with the passion that had faded when she had pulled away. It came back stronger than before and it grew within her too, filling her with an all-consuming need to feel his hands on her flesh and his mouth against hers.

She needed to surrender to him.

Felt she couldn't survive another second without knowing his touch and his kiss, without knowing what it was to be with him.

He stalked towards her across the sand, his gaze locked with intent on hers, holding her prisoner. Her heart began to accelerate again, driven by the heady and intoxicating anticipation that grew within her, filling her mind with thoughts of how it would be.

His palms claimed her cheeks and his mouth descended on hers, a hot fierce press of his lips that had her legs shaking beneath her. She couldn't hold back the moan that shot up her throat when his tongue teased the seam of her lips, demanding entrance. She surrendered to him and gasped as he angled his head and hers, and brought them together in a harder union. His tongue grazed hers, wickedly commanding, and she clutched his arms, groaning over both the dance of their tongues and the feel of his hard muscles beneath her hands.

He dropped one hand to her waist and tugged her against him, bringing the full delicious hard length of his body into contact with hers. She heated wherever they touched, burning for more. His other hand tangled in her hair at the nape of her neck, pinning her mouth against his as he devoured her, taking her higher out of her mind.

She pressed her claws into his arms and began to kiss him back, unable to stop herself from making clumsy sweeps of her lips across his and trying to master his tongue with her own. He went to pull back and fear shot through her, making her dig her claws in deeper and keep him with her. He growled and she silenced him by stroking her tongue down one of his fangs. It ended on a deep rumbling groan that sent a bolt of heat straight to her belly.

She liked the masculine sound of his desire and satisfaction. She wanted to hear it again.

She shoved him hard and knocked him down onto his back on the sand, landing on top of him. She straddled his hips and kissed him harder, stroking his other fang, tearing another delicious moan from him. His hand on her hip roamed lower, coming to cup her backside, pulling her forwards. She settled herself on top of him, her body plastered to his, and he deepened the kiss again, mastering her once more.

She squeaked when he rolled them, pinning her wings beneath her and her back to the sand, and ending up with his hips wedged between her thighs. His weight pressed down on her, a heaviness that she liked despite the coldness of his armour against her breasts.

Lysia stroked over his shoulders, cursing the thick metal that hindered her. She wanted it gone. She ached to feel his naked flesh against hers and beneath her fingers, hungered to boldly explore it with her lips.

Nevar drew back and she seized his shoulders.

"Not going anywhere," he murmured against her lips between kisses. "I know what you want and I need it too."

She released him, trusting he would keep his word, and he smiled as he came into focus above her. His pale hair was bright in the darkness and his black wings rested on either side of her, cocooning her in a way that she liked, one that made her feel he intended to keep her beneath him and wouldn't let her escape him now.

She didn't want to escape.

She wanted to keep plunging headlong into whatever was happening between them.

Nevar looked down, drawing her gaze down to his chest, and his armour disappeared, revealing hard cut muscles that sent a hot thrill through her and had her fingers itching to explore. Not only his breastplate and back plate vanished. His vambraces disappeared from her peripheral vision and she felt the coolness of his hip armour disappear too.

Heart lodged in her throat, she looked down between them, unsure what she would see.

A glimmer of disappointment went through her when she discovered he wasn't naked. His black loincloth remained in place, providing a barrier between them that she wanted to strip away, together with her own clothing.

She reached up and tugged at the ties on her grey top and Nevar's smile disappeared as he stared down at her, following her every move. His eyes darkened as she took hold of the two long lengths of material she had untied and drew them downwards. Her pulse doubled as she found the courage to keep going, shifting her hands down to her waist and pulling the triangles of cloth away from her breasts.

Nevar groaned, his hungry gaze gobbling up what she offered.

His eyes flickered between hers and her breasts, and she waited to see what he would do, silently willing him to touch her.

He scrubbed a hand over his mouth, drawing his lower lip down and revealing that his fangs were extending.

Another hot shivery ache went through her and she couldn't stop herself from imagining him placing his mouth on her body, scraping his fangs over her sensitive flesh and teasing her with them.

He groaned, as if he had sensed her wicked thoughts and approved of them, but still didn't move.

Lysia lifted her left hand, wrapped it around the nape of his neck and drew him down, arching her breasts up to meet him halfway.

He closed his eyes, shuttering his beautiful irises from her view, and wrapped his lips around her right nipple. She bit back the gasp that tried to escape her and sank into the sand as he sucked it into his mouth, tugging on the tight bead and sending fire sweeping over her skin. He moaned and sank against her, his warm bare flesh pressing against her stomach as he clutched her to him and suckled her nipple.

His wings arched higher, blocking out some of the stars that twinkled against the velvet darkness of the sky. She couldn't resist laying her hands on them. She had never felt feathers before, had always feared them and associated them with angels, but Nevar's wings were beautiful, cast with a violet sheen that caught the moonlight.

Lysia gently stroked her left palm down the arch of his wing and he grunted against her breast and then growled, sucking harder. She felt the arousal that bolted through him and smiled. He liked this. She caressed both wings this time, following their strong curves and feeling the softness of his feathers. They tickled her fingertips, making them tingle in the same way that Nevar's suckling made her tingle at the apex of her thighs.

When she wrapped her hands over the muscular ridge of his wings, he growled and jerked his head up.

"Lysia," he husked, his voice deeper than ever, scraping low enough that she was left in no doubt of the desire her touch had stirred.

If she had doubted it, he would have shown her the depth of it when he kissed her, claiming her and sending her out of her mind.

His lips clashed fiercely with hers and their tongues tangled, his fighting her for dominance that she refused to give to him. She liked the battle, a duel of strength and passion, and wouldn't surrender so easily to him. It thrilled her together with how he responded, kissing her harder and bringing his body down against hers, so their chests pressed together.

The mark on hers blazed violet.

Not only hers, she realised as he pulled back again and stared down at them, his white hair hanging forwards and coming away from his horns.

Lysia made them her next target for exploration and reached for them as the mark on her chest faded again, sinking back under her skin.

"I did not realise you had a mark to—" He cut himself off with a deep grunt when she wrapped her fingers around his horns and his jaw clenched.

His big body shuddered and he unleashed a rumbling groan. She brushed her fingers over the hard protrusions and his lips parted, his eyes screwing shut as his eyebrows met hard above them.

"Fuck," he uttered and shook again, one of his arms giving out this time, sending him back down against her.

His heart thundered against her chest.

She smiled mischievously and stroked his horns again, running her fingers up to their pointed tips this time. They grew in response, flaring back from behind his ears, and he bucked against her.

Lysia froze, her heart beating wildly now, all of her awareness locked on the steel length rubbing between her thighs. She quivered in response and tried to hold back her moan, but it was impossible. It slipped from her lips and Nevar's eyes opened. His wicked smile beat the one she had given him as he ground against her, tearing another breathless gasp from her.

"I can play with the best of them," he murmured and lowered his mouth back to hers. "Just remember that."

She would. She would remember that if she wanted to drive him to the brink of madness, the point where he would surrender to his desire for her, all she had to do was stroke his horns.

He kissed her again, swallowing her moan as every inch of her came alive and clamoured for more. She needed more than this rubbing and teasing.

She rocked against him and he uttered a black curse.

"Need you naked," he said between kisses and she nodded in agreement. Naked sounded good.

Perfect in fact.

She gasped when her clothes disappeared in the same fashion as his armour had, and then groaned when he shifted against her and his naked flesh glided across hers. His response was a guttural moan, a sound of pure male satisfaction that lit her up inside and made her rock against him, wanting to hear it again.

She opened to him, allowing him closer, moaning as he moved against her, rubbing her with his hot hard shaft.

"Nevar." She tangled her fingers in his hair, brushed his horns with her thumbs, tried to keep on kissing him, but every part of her felt as if it was overloading and all of her actions became jerky and desperate.

He seemed more in control, better able to cope with the feel of their flesh meeting, and she cursed him for it. She was beyond kisses and gentle rocking now. She needed more.

"Please," she whispered, her desperation overwhelming her and the tightness in her belly, the fierce need for release, demanding she surrender to him now.

She needed him inside her.

He moaned and raised his hips away from hers, and she came close to cursing him for it, but then he reached between them, taking hold of his shaft, and she lost her ability to breathe.

She struggled to keep kissing him as he rubbed the crown over her, guiding it downwards. Anticipation coiled within her, driving back the fear, and she waited, eager to feel him completing her in the most primal of ways.

The blunt head nudged inside her and she barely had time to gasp before he drove his full length home.

Lysia bit down on her tongue to stop herself from crying out from the pain of the invasion.

Nevar froze above her, his lips resting against hers.

He stayed there for long seconds in which she wasn't sure what to do but knew that he was upset with her for some reason.

The silence grew thick and oppressive.

He snarled.

"Dammit, Lysia," he growled against her lips and then drew back, his eyes searching hers in the low light from the moon. He stroked the strands of her hair from her face, smoothing them back into place, and settled his hand against her cheek. His expression softened, matching his gentle tone. "Why didn't you tell me?"

She only had one answer to that question.

"Because I didn't think it would matter."

He frowned and shifted, resting all of his weight on his elbows. The action moved him inside her and her eyes widened when tingles shot through her belly in response, fire the magnitude of which astounded her. He felt thick and long inside her, filling her in a way that was beginning to feel more delicious than painful.

"It matters," he snapped and closed his eyes, turning his face away from her. "It matters because I am not worthy of this."

Lysia caught both of his cheeks in her hands and gently drew him back to her, hating the pain that flowed through him, the self-reproach that seemed ingrained in him for some reason. Whatever the reason was, she wanted to destroy it. She wanted to show him that he was wrong about himself.

She lured him down to her and kissed him, softly brushing her lips across his, hoping it would make him see that what she was about to say was the truth and what she felt in her heart.

She rested her forehead against his so their noses touched and whispered, "There has never been anyone more worthy of me than you, Nevar."

He opened his eyes and pulled back, his gaze questioning hers. She let him see into her, leaving nothing hidden from him and allowing him inside.

"That is why my body is untouched. I have never desired anyone before you. I have never felt a tender caress or a heated stroke of a hand across my flesh. I have never known such feelings as you awaken in me." She held his gaze and kept hold of his cheeks, ensuring he stayed with her and didn't try to pull away again. She could feel the discomfort her words caused and could see it in his eyes too. A touch of colour climbed his cheeks and she brushed them with her thumbs. "Speak to me."

He sighed and closed his eyes, hanging his head between her hands. "Is this real?"

It wasn't quite what she had expected him to say and it hurt her a little that he doubted what was happening between them, even when she could understand his uncertainty.

"I think so," she said, unafraid of putting voice to that feeling. If he doubted the feelings between them because of the bond that existed, then she would show him that they were real and wouldn't give up until he believed her.

He opened his eyes and looked back into hers. "I hope it is... because I've wanted you since I first set eyes on you."

She couldn't stop the blush that burned her cheeks on hearing that soft confession after he had declared himself unworthy of her. His expression turned uncomfortable again and she kissed him to soothe him and make him see that he had no reason to be embarrassed, because she had liked what he had said to her.

He deepened the kiss, seizing control of it again, and settled his body back against hers. She moaned as he moved inside her, still hard and hot, reawakening the needful ache she felt for him.

"This is real," she murmured against his lips. "I know it is... because I have never felt anything like this before."

Never.

She hoped he understood that and everything she wasn't saying. It wasn't the bond between them that made her desire him, because she'd had masters before him, and had known only hatred for them. She had never desired anyone before meeting him, had never craved knowledge of a man's touch or had wanted to allow someone to see beyond the barriers and let them inside.

He kissed her softly as he began to move inside her, gentle thrusts that tore breathless moans from her lips and had her clutching his shoulders. He gathered her to him, into the circle of his strong arms, and covered them with his wings, blocking out the world, as if he wanted her to know only him in this moment.

He was all she knew.

He was all she could feel as his kiss drugged her and his body moved within hers, claiming all of her.

His fingers curled around her shoulders and he kissed her harder as he began to rock deeper, building a different tempo between them, one that felt it would take her out of her mind, if not her body.

She couldn't stop herself from wrapping her legs around him and delighting in stroking his back, feeling his powerful muscles shifting beneath his skin with each deep thrust of his cock into her body. She moaned and nipped at his lower lip, tearing a groan from him and a jerk of his length that struck deeper within her, sending sparks skittering over her flesh.

He lowered one hand to her hip and drew it up to him, and she gasped, her eyes flying wide when he plunged back into her and she felt every inch of him as he filled her, far deeper than before, leaving no part of her untouched.

She dug her claws into his backside and he chuckled against her lips as she drove him into her, unable to stop herself from satisfying her deep need to feel him taking her and making love with her.

His lips played across hers and over her cheek and she lifted her eyelids and stared at the column of his throat. Her mouth watered. Her fangs itched.

The hunger for release collided with a hunger for his blood, swirling together into one fierce need that would not be denied.

Her fangs dropped and she kissed her way down his throat, her body heating to a thousand degrees as she felt his pulse kicking beneath her lips. He moaned as she suckled a point above his vein and pumped harder, each powerful commanding thrust driving her into the sand.

"Nevar," she moaned, more a plea for permission than an outburst of pleasure.

He rocked harder, the deep plunge of his steel hard length into her ripping a different sort of moan from her throat as sparks shot through her and her belly tightened. The primitive voice within her told her to drive him harder and push him to keep thrusting like that until she fell apart and the bliss of release took her.

She clutched his backside, her mouth working furiously against his throat, losing herself for a moment in the hunger to feel him joining with her, giving her the pleasure she craved from him.

Her other hunger rose again, fighting and gaining ground once more, until she came close to sinking her fangs into his flesh and drinking her fill of him. She held herself back with her fangs poised to strike, part of her lucid and aware that he would be angry with her if she bit him without permission.

"Do it." Those two words, spoken in such a dark and hungry voice, one made of pure black magic, made her shiver from head to toe. He lowered his mouth to her neck and whispered into her ear. "I want it... bite me, Lysia... God only knows I will go fucking insane if you don't. Just thinking about it has me so hard that it hurts. Do it... feed from me."

She sank her fangs into his throat and he moaned and shuddered against her, ramming his cock deep into her body. He grunted with her first pull on his blood and she cried out against his neck as it flowed down her throat, his strength instantly washing through her. She clutched his head with one hand and drank deeply, each mouthful only making her hunger for more of his intoxicating taste. He moaned and mouthed her neck, kissing and devouring her with blunt teeth, and it was on the tip of her tongue to beg him to bite her too, but she silenced that need.

It would push him too far.

He grasped her hip, his claws digging into her flesh, and pumped faster, each long stroke hitting her as deep as he could go and his pelvis slamming against her sensitive flesh. She couldn't take much more. Her belly felt so tight she thought she might explode.

She moaned and pulled down another mouthful of his blood. It combined with the pleasure ricocheting through her, heightening it until she felt she was floating high above the world, up in the stars.

Nevar growled against her throat and gave another powerful thrust, and the entire universe exploded, every star in the sky detonating in a colourful burst. Tingly heat blazed through her, making her thighs tremble against him, and she convulsed in his arms, releasing her grip on his neck as she cried out her bliss.

He swooped on her mouth and kissed her hard, his tongue lapping at the blood on her fangs and thrilling her as she gave herself over to him, surrendering completely. He thrust harder, his actions turning rougher, and grunted with each powerful meeting of their bodies. She clenched him inside her, the last ripples of her pleasure making her quiver around him, and he jerked to a halt and growled as he shot hot pulses of his seed inside her, his length throbbing and sending aftershocks of bliss through her.

When his climax subsided, he slowly sank down against her, pinning her to the sand, and his kiss gentled.

Lysia let everything wash over her, piecing herself back together as she kissed him and savoured the feel of him inside her. It had been far more powerful than she had imagined it would be, leaving her changed forever and awakening a hunger within her that she felt sure would never die, an eternal need to have this beautiful warrior at her side.

He rolled onto his back, bringing her with him, his soft feathered black wings folding around her at the same time. They tickled her bare flesh but she liked the feel of them wrapped around her, shielding and protecting her from the world.

She liked the feel of him beneath her, their bodies still joined, and the way he looked at her as she pushed herself up, breaking their kiss.

There was tenderness in his gaze that she had never seen before, feelings that she had seen in the eyes of the other men when they looked at their women. He was looking at her with that same deep affection and she knew his eyes were a mirror of hers. They both felt something, and they both feared it.

He for reasons unknown to her.

She because part of her heart felt that there would be no happy ending for them as the others shared. She tried to shut out that poisonous voice but it refuse to be quiet, playing on repeat in her mind and threatening to ruin the moment.

He lazily brushed her hair from her face, tucking it behind her ear, and slid his hand around the nape of her neck and chased away the voice in her heart.

He kissed her and she moaned when she felt him growing hard within her, rousing her own passion as she thought about losing herself in him all over again.

With his blood flowing through her and restoring her strength, and the way he looked at her with hunger flaring in his jade eyes, she felt more confident.

This time, she wanted to be in control.

He would surrender to her.

CHAPTER 13

Nevar woke alone in the small hut and unleashed a string of the foulest curses available in the demonic tongue, all of them directed at himself, a berating he deserved for what he had done.

Kissing Lysia had been bad enough, but taking her virginity cast him right down there with the Devil in the despicable and evil stakes.

He should have stopped before, when she had been kissing him and he'd had a passing glimmer of suspicion. It had easily fled him, driven out by the need he had felt for her, a powerful urge to lose himself in her and just forget the world and their positions in it. He had wanted to devour her and all that was good in her, everything that was pure and beautiful, and somehow take it into him. He had needed her with an urgency and desperation he had never felt before, not even when he had been in the deepest throes of his addiction to Euphoria.

He cursed himself again for good measure when he thought about that time in his life and the horrendous things he had done. He raised his black clawed hands above him and stared at them. Hands that had groped countless nameless demon bitches and had killed them after they had given him his high and his release.

Hands he had dared to lay on beautiful Lysia.

These tainted hands didn't belong anywhere near her and he should have been aware of that last night. He should have stopped himself from kissing her, let alone what had come afterwards. He hadn't only placed his filthy hands on her, but he had been all too eager to get inside her and spoil her that way too. He hadn't only taken her virginity from her, something that he didn't deserve, but he had fouled her with his touch and his cock.

He growled and covered his eyes with his hands, digging the heels in deep as he pressed his claws into his scalp.

What had he done?

He had been so drugged by the thought of being with her, by the taste of her sweet kiss, that he hadn't been thinking clearly but he no longer had that problem or that excuse. Hindsight was a bitch.

He couldn't deny that he wanted her, craved her with an intensity that startled him at times and made him feel weak, aching for her smile or an innocent touch, or that his feelings for her had changed, growing stronger.

He couldn't even really get himself to regret what he had done, because it had been incredible and he had found the purest source of an addictive new high, and the name of his drug was Lysia.

But he could admit that it had been wrong of him on more levels than he could count and that he wasn't sure how to face her or what to say when he saw her.

He placed his hand over the mark on his bare chest and focused on it.

A trickle of fear ran through him.

Lysia.

He was on his feet and out of the door of the hut in a heartbeat, his gaze scouring the island for her as he called a pair of loose black cargo shorts and covered himself. The second the blazing sun touched him, he hissed and recoiled back into the shade of the towering palms. His eyes watered from the brief assault and he rubbed them, waiting for them to stop stinging while he cursed the sun.

Lysia's voice drifted across the hot white sand to him and he frowned as he listened to her stumbling along in English interspersed with her own language. Her fear stemmed not from the reappearance of angels as he had expected, but from her attempting to communicate with someone in their language.

He gave his eyes one last rub and then looked for her, finding her standing a short distance away near the blackened fire pit with Erin.

Nevar gaped at the sight of her.

She had cut away the lower half of her silver halter-top, turning it into a sort of bikini top and revealing her midriff, and had cut her black jeans into a small pair of shorts that made him want to growl in appreciation of her long toned legs while snarling at any male who was in the vicinity.

Thankfully, there was only Erin and Dante, and the boy wasn't old enough to care about any woman other than his mother.

Erin waved a pair of scissors around in one hand and cradled Dante in her other arm. "Now you're equipped for island life."

Lysia nodded and then looked at Dante, a flicker of fear in her eyes. She frowned, opened and closed her mouth a few times, and her gaze darted to Erin.

"Baby," Erin offered. "Bay-bee."

Lysia took a deep breath. "Bay-bee."

Erin nodded.

Lysia drew a few more deep breaths and Nevar found himself fixated on her breasts and struggling to get his eyes off them. She caught his attention by speaking again.

"Your bay-bee is bee-you-tee-full."

Erin grinned and bounced Dante in her arm. The little boy frowned, yawned and opened his eyes, squinting up at Lysia.

"He has his daddy's good looks," Erin said.

Lysia bent over and offered her finger to the infant, and her hazel eyes shot wide when he took it, curling tiny fingers around it and holding it. He drew it down to him and pulled it into his mouth. Erin laughed. Lysia looked as if she wasn't sure what to do.

Nevar found himself relaxing as he watched her interacting with Erin and the boy. Erin pointed out more things on the island, slowly naming them so Lysia could hear the words, and Nevar was grateful to her for being so understanding and accepting of Lysia, and was glad that Lysia felt more comfortable around her now.

If there was anyone on this island capable of protecting Lysia against any foe, it was Erin. Lysia would need her in the fight that he felt sure lay ahead of them.

He leaned against the hut and folded his arms across his bare chest, lurking in the shadows and able to watch Erin without feeling guilt or remorse when she was unaware of him. No matter what happened or how long he went without seeing her, he still felt a pull to protect her, and today he was feeling strong enough to admit to himself that it was because there was a part of him that desired to be the angel he had been when that duty had been his.

He wanted to go back to that life, but didn't at the same time.

He didn't want Heaven to tamper with his head or go back to a point when he had been unaware of the things they did to their angels. He now understood what had driven Veiron to war with both realms. He wanted what the Hell's angel had back when they had first met—he wanted to be free and able to live his life.

How long would he have though?

His steady gaze studied Lysia as she stumbled her way through naming things on the island in English, her finger still grasped in Dante's tiny fist.

How long would they have?

Lysander would return. The angel wouldn't stay away. Nevar was certain of that. Heaven would send the bastard and his band of angels back down to complete their mission to take her into custody and Nevar was going to be ready for them.

He would find a way to keep Lysia safe.

She looked over at him and smiled, and it struck him hard in his chest, making his heart kick. She appeared so normal today with her wings gone, and so much more beautiful with her black hair tied in a messy twisted knot at the back of her head and her hazel eyes bright and shining with warmth.

Or perhaps it had been last night that had put that sparkle in her smile and that rosy hue on her cheeks.

He could easily fool himself into believing that it was responsible for the light glowing inside her today—a light that brought out his own smile in response and chased away the dark clouds that often filled his mind.

She was stronger today too and he knew it was because he had allowed her to feed from him. Hell, he had practically begged her, even though he had vowed to himself that she wouldn't touch his blood. He hadn't really been thinking last night at all. He had been feeling. That was all. Thinking had gone completely out of the window and his feelings had driven his actions, and had come close to driving him into biting her too. He knew she had wanted it, just as he had craved the feel of her fangs in his throat.

Part of him was glad that she hadn't asked, hadn't pleaded him in that way he couldn't resist, when every fibre and instinct would respond by demanding he give her whatever she desired.

His fangs itched, threatening to descend if he kept on this topic, quietly imagining just how incredible it would have been if he had gone through with it and had bitten her.

How many women had he bitten in the throes of passion when he was hunting for a fix?

He closed his eyes, shutting her out. Too many. Lysia deserved better than that. She deserved better than him.

Yet he couldn't bring himself to actually believe that. It was beginning to seem as if it was something he felt he should feel but no longer really felt it. She had told him that she had wanted him and that the feelings that existed between them, the deep attraction, was real.

She had told him so much more than that too.

She remembered her life and she had never been with a man, and he knew she'd had a master before him or possibly even more than one. He didn't know how many times she had been awoken and then sent back to her dormant state. He placed his hand over the circular purple mark on his chest, crushing the voice of fear that still insisted this passion between them, the fierce need, was a product of their bond, and opened his eyes and looked across the dazzling white sand to her.

She was speaking to Erin again, her sweet lips permanently curled into an enchanting smile that made his heart beat a little quicker. She wasn't only stronger today. She was happy.

Not only because Erin wasn't pressing her for information, or the others were occupied in various tasks and not around her.

What they had shared had made her happy.

And since he was on a roll of admitting things, he was going to put it out there that it had made him happy too.

Erin glanced across at him and smiled.

Nevar averted his gaze to his boots.

She sighed and said to Lysia, "I wish we could get along but he has such a problem with me."

He wanted to refute that and explain that he didn't have a problem with her. He had a problem with himself. He huffed and walked away, leaving Lysia to her lesson with Erin. He trailed around the fringe of the palm forest in the centre of the island, sticking to the shadows.

Amelia and Marcus were off fishing from the spit of rocks that protected the far left hand side of the curved bay, assisted by Einar and Veiron while Taylor lounged on a boulder and watched them. Apollyon and Serenity were in the water, her laughter ringing out at times as they played together and bringing a rare smile to her lover's face.

Asmodeus and Liora were ahead of him on the white sand, near the other spur of rocks that curved around the bay from the right side, both of them dressed casually for the weather, with Asmodeus in a pair of black jeans shorts and Liora in a small black bikini top and tight black shorts. His master had been back to Hell while he had been asleep. Romulus and Remus, Asmodeus's two pet hellhounds, bounded around them. Each almost as tall as Liora, the gigantic sleek black beasts resembled Great Danes on steroids. They were pure muscle and menace, their red eyes almost glowing as they played rough with each other, attempting to sink black fangs into the other's nape.

Liora laughed as she watched them and Asmodeus gathered a log the length and thickness of his leg from the white sand. He spun on his heel and hurled it back along the beach, and the two hellhounds took off after it. Remus barked, the thunderous sound echoing across the island, and jostled for position with his brother, barging his shoulder against him.

It didn't slow Romulus or deter him. He beat Remus to the stick and went to pick it up, but Remus grabbed the other end and began a tug of war.

Asmodeus curled his arm around Liora's shoulders and tucked her against his bare chest. She laughed at the antics of the hellhounds and looked up into her lover's eyes, her smile widening as she met his gaze.

Nevar envied them.

He hated admitting that one, but it slipped out of him before he could deny it.

He envied them as they smiled and laughed, and exchanged tender glances. He envied how easy they were around each other and how they would touch at times or rest close to each other as they were now, with Liora held in the shelter of Asmodeus's protective embrace.

He tried to ignore them and move on unnoticed, but Liora spotted him and waved. She slipped out from under Asmodeus's arms, caught his hand, and led him across the sand with her, towards Nevar.

As she drew closer, he noticed something different about her.

Something wrong with her.

There was darkness within her.

He turned a black glare on Asmodeus. "You have planted a seed of evil within her... I can feel it. How could you?"

How could he have done such a thing to Liora? She was light and good, and cared about Nevar, always seeking to help him and ensure he was well.

Her face flushed.

Asmodeus turned on him. "You speak lies. I have not harmed Liora. I would never."

Nevar growled. "I can feel it within her. There is a seed of darkness."

The gold in Asmodeus's eyes swirled with crimson and his power rose, coming to press against Nevar.

His master snarled, flashing fangs. "Lies."

Asmodeus shifted his deadly crimson glare to Liora.

"Confess that nothing is wrong with you," he demanded and then the hardness left his expression and uncertainty flickered in his eyes. "Is there something wrong with you? Are you sick? You are sick aren't you? I have done as he said..."

He turned on Nevar with a growl.

"Tell me what you feel... is there darkness within her? I swear I did not place it there. Did you place it there?"

Nevar bared his fangs. "I would never harm her. There is darkness within her and you placed it there."

Asmodeus's strength faltered and Nevar saw the panic as it flooded him, felt the fear swamping his power and washing over him.

"No. I feel no evil in her. You lie," Asmodeus snapped and shadows curled from his fingers, twining around his hands and crawling up his arms. His eyes began to switch to violet and his horns grew from the sides of his head above his ears, his black hair fluttering back to reveal them. He turned imploring eyes on Liora. "Tell me it is not so... you are not sick... there is not a seed of evil within you."

Nevar opened his mouth to say that there was.

Liora shot him a glare and stole his voice with nothing more than a wave of her hand, silencing him with her magic.

She took hold of Asmodeus's black clawed hand and drew in a deep breath as her eyes searched his violet ones.

"You did plant a seed within me," she whispered and shook her head when he went to speak. "But it isn't evil."

Nevar felt as confused as Asmodeus looked.

Liora lowered her hand, bringing Asmodeus's down to her stomach, and pressed it there.

"It isn't evil," she whispered, her eyes holding Asmodeus's, tears lining her lashes. "I know it in my soul."

Nevar blinked as the meaning of her words sank in.

Asmodeus seemed to have more difficulty understanding her.

He stared blankly at their joined hands where they pressed against her bare stomach. "What are you saying?"

She smiled.

"I'm saying we're going to have a baby."

CHAPTER 14

Nevar couldn't quite believe what he was hearing and it seemed neither could Asmodeus. The black-haired angel pressed his hand harder against Liora's bare stomach and stared deep into her eyes, his own wide with disbelief and the shock that rippled through Nevar too.

"It isn't possible," Asmodeus said and searched her eyes.

"I assure you that it is." Liora linked her fingers with Asmodeus's as they began to transform back to their normal state, the inky shadows slipping from his skin. "It seems you have more of the Devil's powers than you thought. Just as Erin got pregnant from Veiron when he's sterile, I'm pregnant from you. Clearly, you're far from sterile."

Asmodeus blinked. "We are having a baby?"

She smiled and her hazel eyes lit up as she nodded.

Asmodeus grinned down at her.

The sight of his master so happy brought Nevar's darker urges rushing to the surface, unleashing every cruel and evil impulse he possessed.

His gaze slowly dropped to Liora's stomach, boring into it, as if he could see through it to her unborn child if he looked hard enough.

Asmodeus's unborn child.

A weakness.

His fangs began to drop and his claws extended at the thought of snuffing out that tiny life, striking a blow at Asmodeus in the most painful way imaginable.

Nevar recoiled as that thought hit him and he stumbled away from them, not stopping when Liora called after him. He couldn't be around them, not when the hunger for vengeance that refused to die was riding him, filling his head with thoughts that were both tempting and terrifying.

He would never hurt Liora, not again. She had been kind to him and he could see how much this child meant to her, and to Asmodeus. He would never hurt either of them. The part of him that had craved such a thing was dead to him now and he felt sure that if he could only go long enough without succumbing to its wicked suggestions that he could purge it completely. He didn't want to be that person anymore. He wanted to be a better man, and he would be.

He would be.

No matter how long it took him to claw himself out of the abyss and rid himself of his dark impulses, he would keep at it and keep fighting. He wouldn't give up.

Nevar headed around the island, moving from palm to palm, using their rough trunks for support as he forced himself to move away from Asmodeus and Liora. Romulus and Remus trotted up to him with the stick and he shooed them away, not in the mood to play with them.

When he was around the opposite side of the island and alone at last, he stopped and stared out across the reef-enclosed shallow lagoon that stretched almost as far as he could see. The pale turquoise water sparkled at him in the strong sunlight, both tempting and mocking him. He wanted to walk into it and wash away his cares by floating on the surface for a while, staring into the endless blue above and letting his thoughts drift away on the gentle waves. He couldn't. Not with the sun beating fiercely down on the island.

He held his hand out, slowly pushing it towards the edge of the shadows and the start of the light.

"There you are." Lysia's bright voice cut through the silence and he snatched his hand back and swiftly turned to face her.

She approached from the direction he had come, her hands linked behind her back and a bounce in her step as she crossed the white sand.

Nevar seated himself on the sand in the shade and she stopped in front of him.

"I want to try to swim," she said and he waved towards the lagoon.

"Go ahead. It's shallow enough and only small creatures come into it."

She frowned down at him. "I would like to swim with you."

Nevar scooped up some sand and stared at the grains as he allowed them to flow through his fingers. "It is too bright."

She stepped backwards into the sunshine and shielded her eyes with her hand as she tipped her head back and looked at the sky.

Beautiful.

He had thought her beautiful when he had seen her with Erin, but she was even more so now as she stood bathed in warm light with a smile on her face.

That smile faded as she brought her gaze back down to him.

"You are not well?"

He shrugged. "I do not like the sun."

She raised an eyebrow at that. "But it feels nice on my skin. Warm and soothing."

"It doesn't feel nice to me," he barked and threw sand across the patch of ground between them. Some of it scattered over her bare feet. "Just leave me alone."

Her face fell and the light in her eyes died. "You want me to leave?"

He glared at her, all bathed in sunshine, unaffected by it, and spat out, "That is what it means when someone asks you to leave them alone."

She looked down at her feet and pain pulsed in the mark on his chest. He cursed himself for snapping at her when she had done nothing wrong. She had done everything right. She had sought him out because she had wanted to swim, not alone but with him, sharing a moment as the others did with their lovers.

Her pretty face darkened and her lips compressed.

The messy ends of her hair fluttered in the chilly breeze that blew in off the lagoon.

Clouds gathered over the ocean beyond it, as black as night, boiling as they rapidly expanded and rolled towards the island.

Her breathing quickened, her breasts straining against her makeshift bikini with each hard inhalation.

"You want me to leave," she whispered, violet beginning to fill her hazel irises and her pupils stretching in their centres, turning elliptical. "You want to be... alone."

Nevar cursed himself all over again as he recalled the things she had told him last night and the pain he had felt in her at the time, agony that was beginning to surface again. He hadn't meant it like that and hadn't meant to make her feel that he was rejecting her company.

Her eyes burned violet and her fangs flashed between her lips as she muttered to herself.

The raging black clouds swept across the island, blotting out the sunlight and plunging it into darkness. The sea grew violent, great waves battering the reef that edged the lagoon, and the wind caught the water as it crashed against the rocks and blasted it against him together with sand.

Thunder rolled in the distance and white-purple lightning blazed trails across the clouds.

The ground shook.

Nevar got to his feet. "Calm down."

She shook her head, her purple eyes narrowing on him. "I thought... I thought..."

He knew what she had thought and she was right.

Nevar grasped her shoulders and pulled her into his arms as the skies opened, fat drops of rain hammering the island and spraying off him. It was cold, instantly chilling his skin. He unleashed his wings and covered her with them, not caring that his feathers would take hours to dry.

He only cared about keeping her warm and safe.

"Lysia," he murmured against her hair as he held her tucked close to him, her hands pressing against his bare chest. "I did not mean it like that. I do not wish you to leave me or I to leave you... I am sorry. I was upset and I took it out on you. What you thought is right... I will never leave you alone."

She pressed her tiny claws into his pectorals and the rain fell harder.

"You must calm down now." He stroked her soaked hair and smiled. "Unless you intend to flood the island in order to learn how to swim."

She gasped and drew back, her eyes raised to the sky even though his wings remained above her, shielding her from the rain.

It began to ease and the wind dropped.

"I'm sorry," she said and he furled his wings against his back, giving her some air, but didn't release her. He kept his arms locked around her waist, pinning her against his body. He couldn't convince himself to let her go. Her focus dropped back to him. "I didn't mean to lose my temper."

He shrugged and shook his wings, trying to get some of the water out of them before it soaked in, and forced them away.

"It's probably not the first time the island has felt some divine wrath. I heard that when Erin was having the baby, the whole place was in danger of going under the waves."

That made her smile and he was glad to see it and to feel she was no longer angry with him because of his thoughtless words.

He raised a hand to her cheek and brushed his knuckles across it, holding her gaze as he watched her eyes slowly changing back to hazel.

"I am sorry I snapped at you," he said, needing to know that she had heard that part and knew that he regretted it. "I just don't like the sunlight."

Sunlight which had been returning as the clouds dissipated but faded away again as they thickened once more, shutting out its bright rays. Lysia could control the weather. It didn't just respond to her emotions as it did with angels, turning stormy whenever their moods blackened. She had control over it. What other powers did she hold?

He wanted to ask her, but he didn't want her to hurt herself by trying to remember things.

"Why don't you like the sunshine?" she said and he stared off into the distance, where there were no clouds and the sky was blue, shafts of sunlight streaming down, visible in the water vapour lingering in the air after the storm.

He sighed and tried to find a way of explaining that one.

"I don't really understand it myself." He let her slip from his arms and looked down at her hands as she linked them in front of her stomach. An urge struck him, a voice whispered against it, stating that he would taint her, and he found himself saying the most ridiculously boyish thing that had ever left his lips in his two thousand years of existence. "Can I hold your hand?"

Lysia blushed and held her right one out to him.

Nevar felt like an idiot as he hesitated in taking it. It was just a hand. He had done things far more wicked with her. It was a little late to begin asking for permission and being embarrassed when she granted it.

He seized her hand and started walking with her, fast at first, as if he could outrun how idiotic he had been. He slowed when he realised he was dragging her along behind him and fell into line with her, matching his pace with hers.

She stared down at their joined hands the whole time as they headed across the island towards the shallow water of the lagoon. It was murky now, the sand stirred by the storm, and far less inviting. He preferred to be able to see what was swimming with him beneath the water.

He stopped at the water's edge with her and let it lap over his bare feet. It was still warm.

Heated by the sunshine he hated so much.

"I really don't understand it," he muttered and she looked up at him. "Asmodeus has no problem with the sunlight. Liora thinks it's psychological."

"Psychological?" Lysia said with a frown.

He nodded and pondered how to explain that to her. He would have to tell her where his problem had begun, and he wasn't sure he wanted her to know about the person he had been before, the one he despised because it embodied his weakness.

"I told you when we met that I was an angel once and that I wasn't given a choice when I became what I am now, remember?" He moved a few steps back from the water and sat down on the sand.

Lysia joined him, sitting close to his side, her knees together and turned at an angle towards him, so she was almost facing him.

"The King of Demons is your master." She brushed her fingers over the sand. "He is the one who gave you no choice."

He kept his eyes on the water, letting the steady rhythm of the small waves soothe him.

"Yes. Asmodeus is my master now…"

"And that is why you desire to kill him." She said it without inflection, a statement of fact, and he looked across at her. "I have seen how you act around him. I know desire to kill when I see it because I hold that desire within me too."

"The angels," he whispered and she nodded. He placed his hand over hers, curled his fingers around and held it. "I will not let them hurt you."

"Angels hurt you," she said and he shook his head.

"Not angels. No. Heaven hurt me. They played with my memories and made me do things. They took away my free will. I had gone to Hell to see what they had done to me… there is a pool there that records events that occur in the mortal realm… and I saw… I saw it all." He frowned down at her hand beneath his, held in his, a slender and delicate little thing that belied her incredible strength and power. It was easy to forget that she held such power within her whenever he looked at her and saw her purity and the depth of her innocence.

But she was innocent only in part.

She had seen so much evil and horror, and had been put through so much pain and loneliness.

She hadn't had enough light in her life to balance all that darkness.

He was her opposite.

He'd had so much good in his life that when the darkness had swallowed him it had been too much for him to handle and bear. He had crumbled in a matter of moments, before he could muster his strength to stand against it and find his balance.

He wanted to give her all the light she needed, the joyful moments and the shared memories. He wanted to give her life balance because he couldn't find his own.

"When I was in Hell, reeling from what I had seen, Asmodeus found me. Under his master's order, he attacked me and drove me to the edge of despair, and then deviated from the Devil's plan."

"He forced a contract upon you, and changed your appearance." She turned her hand beneath his and linked their fingers, and warmth flowed up his arm and seeped into his cold heart.

"But not who I was." He kept his eyes on their hands, absorbing her warmth and how gently she held him, silently offering her strength to him. "I thought he had made me evil... but others were right and he had only given what already lived within me a push."

It was hard to admit that and he would never allow Asmodeus hear him say such a thing.

"I am not a good man, Lysia." He took his hand from hers, rested his forearms on his bent knees, and let his hands dangle above his bare feet. "I did terrible things... unforgivable things."

"Things that did this?" She leaned towards him and ran her fingers over his shoulders, tracing the wings inked onto his back.

"Things I did after this."

"There is magic in this mark." She followed the arch of the wing on his left shoulder blade down towards his spine, bringing her whole body closer to him as she stretched. "Was it done by Liora?"

He shook his head and closed his eyes. "No. I killed the sorceress who gave it to me and she cursed me with her dying breath, damning me to an eternity of craving blood in exchange for spilling hers."

She frowned and pulled away from him, coming back to sit beside him. "That's why you hate blood and your need to feed?"

He went to shake his head and then nodded. "In part... I do not want to say the rest."

She canted her head and her hazel eyes darted between his, as if she could see the answer in them if she looked hard enough.

He closed them. "I have done terrible things, Lysia. I have killed many I shouldn't have... for no other reason than they reminded me of the terrible thing I did with them."

He heaved a sigh and flopped onto his back on the sand, landing with his arms spread wide, and opened his eyes, staring up at the clouds.

"I have done things I do not want you to know about. Can we leave it at that?"

She appeared above him, strands of her black hair falling down to caress her neck and cheeks. "But these things hurt you... why?"

"Because if you knew them, you would see me for what I am... I am not good, Lysia... I do not think I am evil, either... but I am a monster."

"These people you speak of were women. You slept with them..."

He spat out a curse, wishing she had kept that to herself, because he honestly believed she would hate him if she knew and he would be alone again. He didn't want to be alone. When she had told him about how she had always been alone, it had made him realise that he was alone now in a way. Everyone held him at a distance. No one trusted him. He was worse than alone. He was on the outside looking in, without hope of ever being accepted by the people he cared about.

"I fucked them," he snapped and didn't stop when she flinched. "You push to know me and you won't like what you find out... I warned you... but you want to know and I will tell you."

He sat up and she shook her head, but he refused to be quiet now. He was going to put it all out there.

"I wanted to rid myself of the evil part of me, the side that found sick satisfaction in killing mortals... angels... demons. I couldn't live with the memories of the things I did when I gave in to the darker part of myself... the other side of me." He caught her jaw and forced her to keep looking at him, so she would see the real him, the ugly truth that would come out eventually whether he liked it or not. Better to put it out there now and watch her walk away before he fell for her and she destroyed him when she left him. "I found the oblivion I craved in Euphoria. You know what Euphoria is?"

She tried to shake her head.

"It's blood and toxin from a demon, mixed with booze. The demons give it to mortals to kill their inhibitions and they have a little fun with them. Demon toxin doesn't hurt the mortal. They get one heck of a hangover and that's all. It's fatal to angels."

"But you're an angel." Her eyes widened.

"Funny... that's what I thought when I realised what I had drunk in my desperate search for some kind of release from the things I did and what was happening to me. But it didn't kill me... and when I realised that meant I was no longer an angel... I went looking for the next fix to kill the pain... and then the next." He tightened his grip on her jaw when she tried to look away, tears lining her lashes and her hurt beating in the mark on his chest, echoing in his heart. "When the demon bitches demanded I fuck them as payment for my fix, I fucked them... and when I was done with them and I had the high I craved, I killed them so I didn't have to see what I had done and see how far I had fallen."

"Nevar," she whispered.

"I'm not done... it gets better." He grinned at her, flashing his emerging fangs. "So the vampire you threw across the club... Villandry. He's the vampire who got me hooked and the bastard had the audacity to bring Veiron in to clean up his mess. I didn't want to go cold turkey, because I had hit rock bottom and by embracing oblivion in the form of Euphoria, I had ended up embracing the darker part of myself."

He held his free hand up and stared at the black skin that covered it and spread down his arm, permanent now, no matter what he did in an attempt to reverse it.

"They should have left me alone and maybe I would have killed myself eventually," he said. "Or someone would have put me out of my misery."

"How can you say such a thing?" She shoved his hand from her face and scowled at him.

"Because it would have been better than what happened." He held her gaze and refused to look away. "Lysander was right... I vowed not to go after Asmodeus's weakness and then I went after it anyway. Hunger for revenge was all I knew. I pinned the blame for everything on my master and I thought if I could just strike him down, it would somehow make everything right again. I was weak... a fool. I wanted to hurt him as he had hurt me. I wanted to take everything good from his life and watch him suffer. I found a sorceress who told me that Asmodeus's weakness was a woman and I plotted to take that woman from him in the most painful way possible."

"Liora." Her hazel gaze turned solemn.

And now she was coming to understand just how evil he had become and she was already beginning to look at him differently.

The warmth was leaving her eyes.

"I waited until Asmodeus had fallen for her and then I handed her over to the Devil. He sent her to sleep in your chamber. Asmodeus went charging in like a white knight to save her and I saw my chance to kill him while he was weak." Nevar dragged his eyes away from her, not wanting to see all the light leave hers when he confessed this next part. "Liora tried to block me and my sword went through her and Asmodeus. I almost killed her."

"You spilled their blood and because of that you're my master."

"I'm the reason you woke up."

He dug his claws into the sand.

"And I'm sorry... I am sorry for everything I have done... but no matter how many times I say it, it doesn't change that I did it. I did it... I did it all and now the world is going to pay for it. So you see, Lysia... it would have been better if everyone had given up on me and let me die, because there is nothing good left in me. I am not worth saving."

He closed his eyes.

"How am I meant to save the world if I cannot save myself?"

CHAPTER 15

Lysia didn't have the answer to that question, even when she wished that she did, because she could see it was one that pained Nevar and played on his mind. After everything he had told her, and all she had felt in him through their link, she wasn't sure he would ever be able to save himself, because he didn't want to be saved.

He couldn't see the good that remained locked deep within him, tempering the evil that now existed inside him too.

It had been that darkness, that dangerous, violent and unpredictable edge, that had drawn her to him when they had first met.

But it was this side of himself that had made her fall in love with him.

It was his fight against that darker nature, and his desire and battle to be good despite the evil he held within him, and it was how he never failed to place himself between her and danger, even though she was powerful enough to defend herself.

It was the fact that he had protected her from the angels who had tried to take her away.

That touched her most of all because she now understood how he felt about his demonic self, but that side of himself had come forth, ready for him to use it if he needed it to give him the strength to keep her safe from harm. He had fought it, but she had no doubt he would have embraced it if she had been in immediate danger.

He had come back for her too, after the others had upset him and he had left. Asmodeus had warned her that he wouldn't return, and her heart had hurt on hearing that. She had left the group and he had come back to her. He had come back for her.

There was good in him.

He couldn't see it but she could.

He was noble, and perhaps a little broken by the things he had done while despair had gripped him, and he was beautiful in his hunger to be good again and purge the evil.

If he could only see that side of himself as clearly as she could, the good part of him that still existed and knew right from wrong, felt remorse because of the things he had done and strived to change so he wouldn't commit the same atrocities and mistakes. If he could see it, she felt sure he would believe he was worth saving.

He would finally find the strength to save himself.

She slipped her hand into his and linked their fingers, losing herself in the beautiful contrast of his inky black skin against her pale.

He hated this visible sign of the darkness within him and how it provided a constant reminder of his other form, but she couldn't understand why. She had seen his horns and his fangs, his black wings with their violet shimmer, and the shadows that had swirled across his skin. She knew that if he embraced that side of himself and the strength it gave him, that his skin would change to all black, just as it did with the Hell's angels.

She would still think him beautiful.

He had wanted to push her away by telling her everything he had done, choosing the most shocking and vivid language to paint a terrible picture of himself.

It had only pulled her closer to him.

It had only made her want to fight for him.

She knew his doubts and his fears, and they were unfounded. She wouldn't let him deny her or push her away. His behaviour had hurt her a little after everything they had shared, but she refused to do as he wanted and give up on him. She would fight him every step of the way until he finally believed that someone in this world was capable of loving him and that she wasn't going to hurt him, not as others had.

He could be as cruel as he wanted to be, could try to drive a wedge between them with his callous behaviour and coldness, but she would stand firm and not waver in her feelings for him. She would endure it because she knew deep inside he was doing it because everything that had happened to him had hurt him, leaving scars on his heart and his soul. She would find a way to show him that she was here for him and would kiss away those scars if she could. She would prove to him that they could be together and that it was okay. He had no reason to fear. She needed him as much as he needed her.

"Say something," he croaked and his pain beat within her heart through the mark, calling to her.

"You're wrong."

He frowned.

She toyed with his fingers and ran the pads of hers over his short black claws. "You are worth saving, Nevar, and that is why Asmodeus and the others try."

He laughed at that and it was her turn to frown at him.

"They only saved me because I'm your master and the Devil threatened them and told them to keep me safe." He tried to take his hand from hers but she tightened her grip, until her nails dug into the back of his hand and she felt sure she was hurting him.

He relented, his hand going limp in hers, and she wanted to pick him up on his behaviour. Just because she had refused to release him, he now refused to hold her hand, leaving his as dead in her grip, as if he had cut it off. She wondered how Asmodeus had the patience to deal with him at times. Perhaps the dark angel didn't know how to deal with him, and that was why he had been allowed to continue on his path with so much despair in his heart.

No one had said the right things to him.

She had zero experience of helping others, but she felt compelled to help him and wouldn't allow her fear of making a fool of herself and messing things up deter her. Nevar needed her. He needed someone to share his burden and understand him. He needed someone on his side.

She placed her other hand over the one she held and stared down at it.

"Is that really true?" She felt his gaze shift to her, the intensity of it sending heat rippling through her veins and making her want to look at him. She would lose her nerve if she did. "Did they only try to help you after they had been ordered to do it?"

His eyes left her and he was silent for long seconds.

"No," he whispered and she felt it had taken a lot of strength for him to admit that to her. "No... after I had tried to kill Asmodeus, they brought me to this island. They held me in a cage."

She growled at that, flashing her fangs as they punched long from her gums, and her eyes changed as they leaped to him, needing to see his face and see he was speaking the truth and the others had caged him like an animal.

He smiled, as if her reaction had pleased him, although she didn't understand why it would, and curled his fingers around her hand, holding it again.

Was it because she had wanted to avenge him for the cruel way he had been treated? He had attempted to kill his master as an act of retribution and had almost killed Liora in the process, and she couldn't approve of what he had done, but after everything he had been through because of Asmodeus, the male should have shown him more compassion.

Nevar thought himself evil, but he was nothing compared with the King of Demons.

"Liora saw what Asmodeus had done to me and demanded he help me, and she pledged to help me too." He dropped his jade gaze to their hands and brushed his thumb along the length of hers, a flicker of a smile on his lips. He liked this. She liked it too. It was a simple sort of thing, but it gave her comfort and made her feel she wasn't alone. He was with her, and she was with him. They were together. "It was after that the Devil revealed what I had done."

"Awakened me," she said and regret coloured his eyes and his feelings. "I am glad you did."

His white eyebrows dipped low. "Why? Because of this?"

He held their hands up.

"Not only that." She tried to stifle the pain in her heart but it was too strong as the memories came back to her.

"What's wrong?" He placed his hand over hers, completing the tangle, his grip firm and speaking of his strength. Strength she wanted to draw into herself as hers began to crumble again. He squeezed her hand. "Tell me."

She sighed and looked away, needing a moment to regain her composure. She stared at the white sand and the gentle rolling waves. The memories pressed down on her and she struggled against them, trying to keep them at a distance so she would no longer experience the pain they brought whenever they played out in her mind.

"Lysia," Nevar whispered softly and lifted his other hand to her face, gently cupping her cheek. "Speak to me."

She glanced into his eyes, catching the concern in them and the tenderness.

"I remember everything." She pulled her knees up to her chest and tightened her grip on his hand, needing the comfort now more than ever. He squeezed her hand and moved closer, placing his arm around her shoulders and tucking her against his bare chest. She closed her eyes and settled her head on his shoulder. "I dream of my past. I experience all of my deaths every time I sleep. I realised that at the bar where I met you. I slept so I could wait for you without wasting my strength, hoping you would return, and the nightmares came on repeat, fragmented but slowly coming together. I know I have died once already. Last night, when I slept in your arms, it all became clear. I saw it all."

"What happened?"

"There was hell in this realm, a great battle between angels and the demons, and it drew me to it. I remember standing on a hill watching it... I remember feeling great sorrow in my heart... and the next thing I recall is the forces of Heaven and Hell joined to defeat me in a battle in that same location in this world, and then the Devil trapped me in Hell, but I wasn't dormant."

"What?" Nevar's hand on her shoulder tightened and she felt his anger sweep through her. "What are you saying? I thought you were held in a sort of stasis."

She shook her head and curled closer to him, needing his heat. She was cold, right down to her bones, had felt that way since waking after discovering what had been done to her and what Nevar had saved her from. She had done her best to shake it off, to continue as if it had never happened, not wanting to spoil this time she had on the island with him, but it haunted her.

"I was asleep... reliving my last death over and over again." It terrified her. She had spent millennia constantly experiencing a replay of her death. Every blow that had broken bone and sliced flesh. Every face of every angel who had struck her. Every face of every demon who had sneered at her. "I don't want to go back to a place where I will see that on endless repeat. There was no peace there, Nevar. There was only horror and pain... and I'm afraid I can't escape my past to have the future I desire."

He pulled her closer, wrapping both of his strong arms around her, and pressed a kiss to her hair. He inhaled slowly, his muscular chest expanding against her, and sighed, and she knew it was because she felt how he did—unable to escape the things that she had done in order to seize the future she truly wanted for herself.

"What happened to awaken you?" he murmured against her hair.

"I do not understand."

He drew back and clutched her shoulders, holding her away from him, his expression more serious and grim than she had ever seen it. "Something must have happened between you seeing the battle and the forces of Heaven and Hell fighting you... because the woman sitting in front of me isn't capable of destroying this world. You care too deeply and take pleasure from the smallest things, like the sun on your skin. You take more joy from this world than anyone else I know. I don't think you would want to annihilate all that without a fucking good reason."

He was right, and she didn't want to destroy this world. In her memory of Thebes, before the great battle, she had delighted in how beautiful the stone had looked in the fading sunlight, and how intricately carved the statues were, and had been fascinated by how the mortals had gone about their lives in the shadow of the great city and their gods.

"I don't remember what happened between the battle between the angels and the demons, and them fighting me." That frightened her. She had thought nothing of it until Nevar had mentioned it. She had gone from feeling great sorrow to being filled with tremendous rage, fury that had controlled her.

"We need to find out somehow, so we can avoid it." He took hold of her hand and stood, pulling her onto her feet with him. "We need to find a way to see your past… but you're not an angel, so you couldn't control the pool in Hell… but maybe I could or someone else, Asmodeus maybe, he is older than everyone else and powerful. He might be able to do it."

"Or we need to see the future and that way we can avoid it."

He stared at her with wide eyes. "The future."

She nodded.

His jaw clenched and his eyes turned steely, edged with violet, a reflection of the dark hungers springing to life inside him, trickling through their link.

Lysia had a terrible feeling he was about to suggest something dangerous.

The right corner of his mouth tugged into a wicked smile that flashed the tip of his fang.

"There is a pool in Heaven that records it."

CHAPTER 16

Lysia threw her arms around his neck and kissed him with such frantic passion that Nevar was powerless to resist sliding his arms around her waist, pulling her flush against him and kissing her back. He growled as he seized control of the kiss, claiming her mouth and driving her into submission. One hand left her waist and tangled in the messy knot of her black hair, pinning her against him and ensuring she didn't break away before he was ready to let her go.

She moaned, the soft breathless sound drenched with the desire she poured into the kiss.

His little destroyer was no longer the meek and tentative creature she had been with him last night on the beach. She was confident and courageous, battling him for dominance as he kissed her.

She was enthralling.

And up to something.

He dropped both hands to her hips and set her away from him.

It took her a moment to open her eyes, but when she did, he knew he had been right.

"Don't," she whispered and he frowned at her.

"Don't what?"

She swallowed hard and pressed her palms against his bare chest. The mark on it, her mark, tingled in response to her touch and pulsed with the hunger and desire racing through his veins. An echo of the passion that lit hers up too.

"Don't go to Heaven…"

His frown melted away on hearing the fearful note in her voice. It laced her feelings too and shone in her eyes.

"But we need to see what will happen in the future. I have to see it so I can keep you safe."

She dropped her gaze to his chest. "But they will fight you... there are too many angels there... if you go, then they will—"

He pressed a finger to her lips to silence her and she looked up at him again. "I will not go alone."

She lifted her right hand, gently circled his wrist with it, and lowered his hand away from her mouth. "I will go with you."

"No," he barked, the thought of her going to Heaven with him rousing a dark beast within his heart that demanded he protect her. "I might as well just deliver you to them gift wrapped."

She cocked her head at that one.

"It means I should just hand you over to them. It's what they want and it is not going to happen. You have to stay here with the others. They will protect you."

She shook her head. "There has to be another way. What if we tell the others about your plan and see what they have to say?"

Nevar considered that. There was a chance that Asmodeus or Apollyon might know of a better way to find out what the future held for them. He needed to speak with everyone anyway and tell them what Lysia had told him.

She had been in mortal form before her last awakening, enjoying the world. It had been a war between angels and demons that had awoken her as the destroyer. Heaven and Hell were still messing with the world. He had always imagined that the Great Destroyer would rise in response to a war between men, roused by the violence and bloodshed, or had been ordered to bring about the apocalypse by her master. He hadn't even contemplated that it would happen as a result of angels and demons battling in the mortal realm.

He shouldn't have been surprised though.

Now that he knew what had happened to her, he couldn't help thinking how typical it was of the two realms to war between themselves, uncaring of how it affected the mortal realm. It had only been Lysia awakening as the Great Destroyer and threatening to end their realms too that had brought them together to stop her, ending their own war.

It was the same now.

When they had discovered that his actions had awakened her from her slumber, both Heaven and Hell had pledged their angels to the cause of containing her. They wanted to send her back to sleep.

Both sides were probably coming up with a plan to do just that right now.

Nevar wouldn't let it happen.

In her current form, Lysia wasn't a threat to anyone, just as she hadn't been a threat to the world the last time she had been free in it either. Something had triggered a change in her, one that had set her on the path of war against the angels and demons, and mankind.

He just needed to find out what that trigger had been, or what it would be this time.

But she was right and rushing to Heaven was a suicide mission, one that had been tempting at the time he had thought of it but was now looking less appealing. He had fought angels in Heaven before and barely survived, thanks to his darker side emerging and gifting him with its strength. He had been stronger at the time too, not weakened by addiction and hunger. He was in no position to head to Heaven right now, when they were on high alert. Lysander and the other angels would have informed their superiors of what had happened here on the island and what they had discovered. The fortress of Heaven would have immediately issued orders to protect the walls and all points of entry. Flying into it now would mean flying through legions of angels.

There had to be another way.

He just didn't know what that way was.

He could risk taking her to Hell and attempting to see the past in the pool there, but that route would also mean a battle. Heaven controlled the pool and it was often protected by angels from the division of death. If Heaven and Hell were working together, there was a chance both angels and Hell's angels would be protecting it now, aware that he would want to view it.

He growled and shoved his fingers through his white hair.

There had to be a way. He had to see the future if he was going to save Lysia.

He looked down into her beautiful hazel eyes. He had to save her.

She was the one good thing in his dark world. She had brought light into it.

She had stayed with him when he had tried to push her away.

She had continued to look at him with warmth when he had told her the weight of his sins.

She was becoming everything to him—his reason to fight, his balance, and his hope.

For the first time in what felt like forever, he was looking forwards, towards a future that now felt brighter than his past, and he knew it was because he wanted a future with her.

She placed her palms against his cheeks and looked deep into his eyes, hers filled with affection and tenderness that had his heart beating a little quicker. He couldn't remember the last time anyone had looked at him in the way she did, as if he was the centre of her universe and it would mean nothing without him in it.

He felt sure he was looking at her the same way too and he was thankful there was no one around to witness this side of him. If Asmodeus or the others saw him looking at her like a lovesick fool, he wouldn't hear the end of it. They would mercilessly tease him. He had witnessed them do the same thing to Asmodeus. He didn't think he could play it cool and keep his head on straight as his master had.

"We should speak with the others," he whispered, not really wanting to do that but feeling it was the right thing to say.

The sense of urgency he had felt was fading by the second though, drifting away on the warm breeze that played with the ends of Lysia's black hair.

She tiptoed, bringing her mouth close to his, and his mind said to push her away and not let her kiss him again, because he didn't understand how she could still want to do such a thing after everything he had told her. His hands tensed against her hips and she faltered, pausing just inches from his lips.

Her hazel eyes darted between his.

"I feel you," she said in a low voice, one edged with a teasing note. "Don't hold me at arm's length when you really want to pull me closer. Don't let what you think you should do stand in the way of what you want to do. I'm here, Nevar… I heard everything you said and know what you did, and I know you want to push me away because you think you're protecting me from you, but it isn't what I want."

He swallowed hard and pressed his fingertips into her soft skin, his heart thundering against his ribs. "What do you want?"

She smiled and stole his breath with it. "I want you."

Nevar tugged her against him, dipped his head and captured her lips in an unhurried kiss that he felt sure would reveal the feelings growing inside his heart, emotions he hadn't believed himself capable of feeling anymore. He gathered her in his arms, cupped her backside and raised her up his body, his lips never leaving hers.

She moaned softly into his mouth and wrapped her legs around his waist, and her arms around his neck. Her fingers pushed into the shorter hair at the back of his head, twined around the longer lengths on top, and pinned him to her. He groaned and deepened the kiss, showing her without words that he wasn't going to pull away this time.

He needed this too much.

He wanted to take everything she was willing to give him and drown in her, forgetting the world and the things he had done, and whatever might lay ahead for them.

All that mattered was this moment with her in his arms, held close to him where she belonged.

She broke away from his lips and kissed along his jaw, her fingers tugging his head back. He went willingly, a deeper groan escaping him when she tongued the marks she had placed on his throat, making them tingle and his cock throb. He wanted to feel it again but he wasn't strong enough to feed her, not when he was still starving himself. The need to have her fangs in him and that incredible connection it forged between them, strengthening their bond, was strong though and drove him to find someone to feed on so he could then feed her.

He shut out that dangerous thought and focused on her instead, on each soft swirl and swipe of her tongue across his flesh.

He palmed her bottom and she tightened her legs around him, drawing his steel hard length against the apex of her thighs and pressing it between them. A little gasp escaped her and she rocked against him, rubbing him through his shorts. He couldn't take that.

He carried her towards the shelter of the palms and the shade there, afraid she would lose her control over the clouds and they would dissipate. He wanted nothing to spoil this moment. He wanted to show Lysia that he could be gentle for her and could be the tender lover and devoted male she deserved.

When he reached the fringe of the forest, he kneeled and laid her down on the soft white sand, and sat back to admire her.

She stretched her arms out to him, her hazel eyes imploring him to come to her, and he refused, instead running his hands over her bare legs, from her knees down to her thighs. They fell open, inviting and luring him, and he frowned and groaned as he caressed the inside of her thighs, feeling their softness against his calloused fingers.

"Nevar," she whispered and he sensed her desperation, the urgency that she still hadn't become accustomed to or knew how to handle.

He leaned over her, pressing his knuckles into the sand on either side of her hips, and dropped his mouth to her bare stomach.

She half-gasped half-moaned as his lips brushed across her pale skin, her stomach tensing and rippling beneath his questing mouth. He closed his eyes and explored her, seeking out every patch of skin that made her shiver and moan. She arched against him when he swirled his tongue around the sensual dip of her navel and clutched his head, twisting his hair in her fingers and raising her backside off the sand.

He produced a blanket between her and the sand, a soft span of black velvet fit for his beautiful destroyer.

Before she could sink back onto it, he moved his hands to her backside and held it, a low growl leaving him at the feel of her tiny shorts. He would have to have words with Erin about their length and how revealing they were. He felt certain that his ward had done it on purpose, teasing and testing him where Lysia was concerned. She was playing matchmaker and he didn't appreciate it.

Lysia relaxed into his hands as he kissed down her stomach and slowly shifted his grip, so he clutched her hips. He reached the waist of her shorts and lowered her backside onto the blanket before sliding the button free and gently tugging the zipper down.

Her gaze bore into him, intent and focused, her heart beating wildly in his sensitive ears.

Her hands trembled in his hair.

She had no reason to be nervous but he wasn't going to let the trickle of fear flowing through their bond deter him. He wanted everything to be different with her and he wanted all of her, and that meant introducing her to wicked new acts that he was sure she would enjoy once she overcame her initial fear.

He sat up and held her gaze as he tugged her shorts down her long slender legs. She placed her bare feet on his thighs and raised her bottom to help him with his task. He groaned and couldn't stop his eyes from drifting down the luscious plane of her stomach to the neat thatch of dark hair at the apex of her thighs.

Another groan escaped him, this one more of a guttural growl as he thought about spreading her thighs and delving his tongue between her sweet folds.

His cock jerked against his shorts.

He grunted and tossed her tiny shorts, eased her thighs apart and wedged his shoulders between them.

She tensed, her legs locking against his shoulders.

"Relax," he murmured and looked up the length of her as he kissed his way down her right thigh, heading towards heaven.

Her throat worked on a hard swallow and her eyes grew darker as he approached his target, desire and arousal overwhelming her fear.

He held her gaze as he slowly parted her petals and delved his tongue between them, sweeping it over her nub. She gasped and threw her head back, her following moan like music to his ears. He stroked her again, harder this time, eliciting an equally addictive response. She jerked her hips up, pressing herself against his mouth.

Nevar growled at the taste of her, sweet and drugging, everything he had expected from his new addiction. He couldn't get enough of her.

He flicked his tongue around her and then swirled it, using her moans and the way her thighs fluttered beneath his hands as his guide. When he delved lower, probing her entrance, she snatched hold of his head with one hand and cried his name. He did it again and again, thrusting his tongue inside her and lapping at her honey, devouring all of her and driving her right to the edge before he pulled back. She growled.

Nevar smiled as she blushed.

"Growl all you want, Baby," he murmured and her blush darkened. "I love it."

He dropped his mouth back to his wicked work and stroked his tongue over her pert nub, feeling it pulse in response. She moaned and undulated her hips, rocking against his tongue, and he gave her what she wanted. He circled her entrance with two fingers and then gently eased them inside. Her heat scalded him, the wetness of her tearing a low possessive growl from him and making his length kick in his shorts. He wanted to be inside her and feel her around him again, milking him.

Nevar forced himself to focus on her instead and slowly pumped her with his fingers as he swirled his tongue around her, teasing her back towards the edge, letting her think he would give her release this time. He was too greedy to do such a thing, too needful of her and selfish. He wanted to feel her climax on him again.

"Nevar," she moaned, her body stiffening, and he relented again. She growled and tried to thrust his fingers into her, and he took them away. The snarl that left her lips drew a smile from him and he lifted his head, looking up the beautiful length of her body and meeting her eyes.

She swayed her hips beneath him, rubbing her thighs against his shoulders, and smiled, a siren's call that he couldn't resist.

He pushed himself up onto all fours and crawled up the length of her.

When he went to kiss her, she stopped him dead by fumbling with the buttons of his shorts. She had three free before he could even look down and he was in her hand before he had a chance to steel himself for her touch.

He groaned and squeezed his eyes shut as she palmed him, stroking up and down his length, and then rubbed her thumb over the sensitive head.

"Lysia," he whispered, more a warning than a plea for more. He wouldn't last if she kept stroking him like that, pushing him towards the edge just as he had pushed her.

He cracked his eyes open and grabbed her wrist to stop her.

She pouted.

"I wish to play with you too," she said, the innocence and bluntness in her words making him smile.

"Later," he murmured and she released him. "I thought you wanted this?"

He took hold of his cock, lowered his hips and rubbed the head down between her folds, over her sensitive flesh. She moaned and rocked her hips upwards and he gave her more, teasing her by stroking up and down before almost nudging inside her.

"Nevar," she whispered and tangled her hands in her hair, tugging it free from the pins that held it. "Please."

He couldn't deny her. He didn't think he ever would be able to when she asked him so sweetly.

He dropped his hips and groaned as he eased into her hot wet sheath inch by inch, refusing to rush this joining. He wanted to savour it this time and the way she reacted, her body flexing around his, drawing him in deeper. When he reached as deep as he could go, he leaned above her on one elbow and clutched her right hip, pulling it off the velvet blanket, and slid deeper still.

She moaned and trembled beneath his fingers.

He would do things right this time.

He kissed her as he slowly rocked into her, keeping the pace between them even and steady, long strokes that had him almost coming free of her before he drove back inside as deep as he could go, his pelvis brushing her sensitive flesh. She moaned and clutched his shoulders, her short claws digging into his skin, leaving marks for him to remember this moment by.

She tried to shift her hips and he held her firm, keeping her at his mercy but increasing his pace to give her what she needed. She moaned into his mouth, the sweet sound encouraging him to go faster, and he resisted the temptation to do what she wanted this time. He curled his hand around her shoulder and maintained his pace, until she was moaning with each long slide of his cock into her and each meeting of their bodies and he was too.

His balls tightened, drawing up as shivers raced down his length each time he reached as deep as he could go. She arched into him, pressing her breasts against his chest, and clawed at his shoulders.

"Nevar."

He obeyed her, could feel how close she was as she clenched and unclenched him, desperation flowing from her and into him. He kissed down her jaw to her throat and buried his face against her neck, licking and kissing it as he finally quickened his pace. She tilted her head to one side and he fought the change that came over him, keeping his fangs at bay as he kissed her throat, feeling her pulse hammering against his lips.

Her claws sliced into his back and the scent of blood filled the air.

Nevar grunted and his fangs dropped.

He closed his mouth and pulled away from her throat, pressing his forehead against her temple as he thrust harder. Release coiled at the base of his length and he groaned as he felt the beginnings of her climax.

She moaned into his ear, a beautiful sound drenched with pleasure, and her body convulsed against his, her sheath fluttering and pulsing around his length, drawing him deeper into her. He growled against her cheek and screwed his eyes shut as he joined her, his cock throbbing and spilling his seed inside her as her body continued to milk him.

She slowly relaxed beneath him and he sagged against her, breathing hard against her face as he fought to slow his racing heart and hot shivers tripped through him, making his knees shake.

Lysia tilted her head and pressed kisses to his cheek, moving towards his mouth. He eased himself up and kissed her, savouring the softness of it and the warm glow running through every inch of him, and the feel of her beneath him, satisfied because of him.

She was right and he had needed this more than he had needed to speak with everyone. He had needed a moment alone with her, lost in her, and seeing that she wasn't going to turn her back on him because of what he had told her. He had shown her the darkest part of himself and she had stayed with him, her feelings constant and unswerving.

He couldn't thank her enough for that.

He had felt that he had lost everything, but she had given him back something.

She had given him hope.

He hadn't realised how much he had needed it, but he knew how much he needed her.

Let Heaven and Hell come.

He would never let them take her from him.

She belonged to him now and he was going to fight for their future.

CHAPTER 17

It was getting dark by the time Nevar reappeared with Lysia in tow. Erin finished closing the snaps on Dante's black modified romper suit that allowed his tufts of wing feathers to stick out of the back and bounced him in her arms as he gurgled. She tried to contain her smile as she watched Nevar approaching the fire where everyone sat discussing the woman firmly attached to his hand. It appeared her former guardian angel had been busy today, picking up where he had left off last night if she had to guess.

She wasn't the only one who had noticed that the relationship between Nevar and Lysia had definitely altered overnight, or the only one who had been subjected to a little TMI moment when settling Dante down for the night.

Veiron had muttered things about keeping the noise down, a touch of jealousy in his tone and gruff behaviour as he had tidied their small home on the island. Erin had caught her big oaf around his waist and shown him that he had zero reason to be jealous of Nevar, because she was still playing catch up in the down and dirty stakes after the last few months of her pregnancy and the early days of Dante being around.

She let her smile out when she thought about how they had probably given every other couple on the island a little TMI moment last night too.

Well, it was more like three TMI moments, but who was counting?

She had the sneaking suspicion Veiron was as he eyed the couple heading towards them, his dark scarlet eyebrows meeting above near-black eyes edged with a corona of fire. She knew that look and heated to a thousand degrees as he slid his gaze towards her and narrowed it on her, slowly raking it down the length of her body and setting her on fire. Her smile turned wicked.

Dante threw up on her shoulder and she grimaced as it ran down her back.

It hadn't taken long after finally getting him out into the world for her to realise that her son had a jealous streak as wide and deep as his father.

She had figured it out when he had cried every single time she had started kissing Veiron, and had shut up whenever she had stopped.

"Who's a little mummy's boy?" she murmured to him as Veiron came over to her, produced a cloth out of thin air and wiped the sick off her shoulder.

Dante giggled.

"Laugh all you want, Kiddo… won't change a thing… it's still bed time for you, and mummy time for me." Veiron grinned as Dante's laughter died and then grimaced as he unleashed a high-pitched wail.

"Gee, thanks for that." Erin struggled to contain Dante as he wriggled and kicked, crying at the top of his lungs, which was about the same volume and pitch required to burst eardrums.

Apollyon muttered something to Serenity about a spell to block his ears.

Erin shot him a glare. "You want to hold him, Uncle Apollyon? It can be arranged."

The dark angel's face paled, his blue eyes round and filled with fear as he eyed her squirming child. It was rare to see him afraid of something, and that it was her kid who had inspired fear in him had her torn between feeling affronted and laughing.

"Can I?" Asmodeus stood and she stared at him blankly, unsure how to respond to that or whether she had even heard him correctly.

Veiron stared at him too, his hand paused with the cloth resting against her back.

Erin shook herself. "Um… if you really want to… I mean, if you think your brain can handle the noise."

She wasn't sure how Dante would react to being held by a person other than her, Veiron or Amelia. No one else had dared to pick him up or give him a cuddle.

Asmodeus approached with confidence that faltered the moment he held his hands out and she planted Dante into them. He stared down at the wailing boy, holding him at arm's length in front of him.

Erin waited to see how Dante would react, her breath lodged in her throat.

"Hello," Asmodeus said, a quaver in his deep voice, and finally drew Dante closer to him, holding him higher in the air at the same time, so they were face to face and just inches apart.

Erin really hoped that Dante didn't throw up on him. She wasn't sure how the angel would react to it if he did. She was still struggling to process the fact that Asmodeus had been the first to actually ask to hold her baby. She had never given Amelia a choice. She had forced Dante upon her just a few days after his birth so she could get a picture of them to send to their father. Well, Amelia's father and her adoptive father. The man who deserved that title more than the Devil did because he had raised and protected her.

She moved a little closer, just in case Dante did something that made Asmodeus react badly, hovering to the side of them.

Dante opened his eyes and instantly quieted as he stared up into Asmodeus's golden ones.

They looked so alike that it was uncanny, but then she supposed she looked a lot like Asmodeus too, because they both looked like her real father, the Devil.

Dante laughed and bounced, kicking his legs with enthusiasm. His little hands reached for Asmodeus.

"Holy hell!" Erin looked around to make sure everyone was seeing this. Dante had never reacted like this to Amelia. He normally kicked up a royal fuss whenever Amelia held him. Her little tyke had a thing for the so-called King of Demons, an angel born of evil. She probably should have guessed the two of them would get along like a house on fire. "You are so babysitting when we need a break from him. Sucker."

Asmodeus's eyes widened and he looked as if he wanted to hand Dante back to her.

"Nu-huh. No way." Erin stepped backwards. "You walked into this one and you have to deal with it. Look at how much he loves his Uncle Asmodeus!"

Dante bounced harder, frantically kicking and reaching for Asmodeus.

"Give him a cuddle," Veiron said, all darkness and menace, and the picture of fatherhood.

She smiled at him, catching the glower in his crimson-edged eyes.

He would probably tear Asmodeus a new one if he refused.

Asmodeus drew the boy into the cradle of his arms, holding him in the curve of his left one, tucked against his bare chest. He stared down at Dante, a look of absorbed fascination on his face. When he offered Dante his right hand, the boy took it and played with his fingers. Asmodeus lifted his gaze and smiled at Erin.

She had never seen him so happy.

Why?

His focus shifted to Liora where she sat beside Serenity on a log in front of the fire. Liora smiled, her hazel eyes bright with it, stood and came to him. She held her hand up near Dante and ribbons of purple swirled around her fingers, illuminating his face and Asmodeus as she formed them into animal shapes with her magic.

They were definitely on babysitting duty the moment she needed some adult time with Veiron.

Veiron finished cleaning her back for her, dipped his head to her ear and stepped into her, so his front pressed to her back, his bare chest warm against the patches of skin exposed by her tank top.

"You should probably change," he husked and she shivered in response, aching all over at the thought of taking him back to their hut.

She was on the verge of agreeing when Nevar reached them and tossed Asmodeus a strange look. What did he know that she didn't? It was on the tip of her tongue to ask him but he spoke before she could get her question out.

"Lysia remembered part of what happened to her."

Everyone stood and looked at the woman in question, and she stood her ground, not faltering under the intense stares of everyone present.

"It was a war between Heaven and Hell on the mortal plane. Something happened and she awakened." Nevar slid his jade gaze towards Amelia. "I think Lysia is like you were. She hasn't awakened yet… something will happen to trigger her into awakening."

"Like her death?" Amelia said with a flicker of concern in her silver eyes.

He shrugged his bare shoulders, drawing Erin's attention to them and the long red marks that now streaked them from his back to the tops of his shoulders. His focus darted back to her and she looked away, giving Dante her attention as he gurgled in Asmodeus's arms, his golden eyes still watching the animals Liora was forming and controlling with her magic.

Erin had to bite down hard on her tongue to stop herself from letting out every teasing remark that sprang to the tip of it. She had noticed the bite mark on Nevar's neck when she had been with Lysia this morning, but these new marks were something else. As tempting as it was to mention them, she resisted. Nevar was already sensitive enough about his appearance, especially when it came to her opinion about it. If she dared mention the trophies of his broad daylight down and dirty session with Lysia, he would probably flip and leave again.

Although, she wasn't sure he could bring himself to leave. The way he was holding on to Lysia's hand, his fingers linked with hers, and hadn't let her stray more than a few inches from his side, spoke of protectiveness, a trait that seemed to run deep in all angels where their women were concerned.

She only had to look around the island to see the proof of their passion for protecting their women.

Asmodeus and Liora were practically hip-to-hip as they entertained Dante, and Asmodeus's golden gaze kept flickering to her, warming whenever it did and he studied her playing with Dante.

Apollyon had Serenity tucked beneath his arm, her head resting against his bare chest. Amelia and Marcus held hands beside them. Einar and Taylor were nestled close to each other too, his arm around her waist and her back against his front.

Veiron stood in the same position with her, his hands on her waist and his chin resting on her shoulder.

Erin was glad that Nevar had found someone to protect. She hoped that it would give him a reason to remain strong and keep on track with his recovery, and that Lysia would encourage him whenever he faltered and help him along the way. He already seemed different to Erin, more like the man she had first met all those long months ago in London. A touch of pride was back in his eyes, confidence he had lacked over the last few times she had seen him.

"Maybe she can be awakened like I was by my father?" Erin offered and Nevar looked at her.

That was another change in him. He flinched less on looking at her now. He was becoming more comfortable being around her and was less changeable, no longer flitting between looking at her with pleading eyes one second and growling at her the next. It was good to see him finally becoming comfortable with himself as he was now and being around her and the others. There was a chance he would finally fit into their group where he belonged, their motley crew of outcasts.

Veiron squeezed her waist. "But that would mean Nevar would have to hurt someone she loved to awaken her and that would be suicide since she obviously cares the most about him."

Lysia blushed. Nevar growled and flashed his fangs.

"It's the truth, Mate. Deal with it." Veiron was no doubt grinning at the poor man.

Here she was trying not to tease him so he would be more relaxed around them and would feel as if he fitted into the group, and her husband went and teased him about his love life instead.

"Veiron," she whispered and placed her hands over his on her waist. "Play nice."

He shrugged, the action causing his chest to shift against her back and stir more naughty thoughts. She forced herself to focus. Nevar had important information and had come to them for a reason, not just to tell them about what Lysia had remembered. There was more to it than that.

She stared hard at him, seeing if she could figure it out.

His jade gaze flickered to her again and then dropped to his boots.

Erin gave him a moment, knowing it was still difficult for him to see her and not wanting to push him. She checked on Dante and found him still smiling at the purple floating animals. The sight of him warmed her and she couldn't stop herself from smiling too. Her little man. He was already powerful. She hadn't realised his strength until Lysander had brought the four angels to the island and she had handed Dante to Veiron. It had become apparent then that Dante could withstand the full force of the angels' power just as she could, and had provided Veiron with protection from it. She had thought she had been protecting Dante, but Dante was as powerful as she was.

As powerful as the Devil.

She closed her eyes and shut out the niggling fears that surfaced whenever she thought about her father. He wanted Dante for himself. She would never let it happen. Dante would never be her father's vessel.

"Hey," Veiron husked and wrapped his arms around her waist, drawing her back against him. He pressed a kiss to her shoulder and she leaned her head against his cheek, taking every scrap of comfort he offered her. "I'd kill the snide little fucker before he could set his filthy claws on Dante. Okay?"

She nodded. "I know."

She knew because she would kill her father too.

She would do anything to ensure the safety of her child and her family.

"I need to go to Heaven," Nevar said and snapped her focus back to him.

"What?" She didn't want to believe what she had just heard. Everyone on this island was her family, Nevar included, and she wasn't about to let him go off to Heaven where they would probably kill him to reset him. "That's a suicide mission and you know it, Nevar. If they kill you, you won't remember a thing. Is that what you want?"

"No," he barked and his expression darkened, his silver-white eyebrows dipping low above jade eyes rapidly turning violet. "But I must see the future. If I can see the future, then I can stop it from happening. I have to reach the pool."

"You will never make it that far." Apollyon moved closer, coming to stand beside Asmodeus. "The forces of Heaven are too strong for you right now. They are too strong for us. If we go there, we risk everything."

"I'm not asking you to risk yourselves." Nevar looked at them each in turn. "I would never."

"You do not need to ask us," Asmodeus said and Nevar stared at him, incredulity shining in his half-jade half-violet eyes. The dark angel sighed and rocked Dante in his arms. "We would not let you go alone, Nevar."

Amelia and Marcus both nodded in agreement, and Nevar looked as if he wasn't sure how to respond to what everyone had just told him. He wasn't alone. He was part of this family whether he liked it or not, and they took care of each other and had each other's backs.

"There might be another way to see the future." Erin felt Veiron's hands tense against her and rubbed them, trying to soothe the anger and fear she could sense rising inside him.

Nevar swung his gaze to her. "How? There is rumour that the Devil has his own pool in which he can see the future. Do you mean to ask him if we can use it? I do not think he would consent to that."

She shook her head. "I mean that I'll sleep without Veiron holding me and I'll have a vision. It might be of the future, it might not be… but I will do it until I see what we need—"

"No," Veiron interjected and spun her to face him. Darkness reigned around his crimson and gold swirling eyes. "I will not allow it. You suffer with these visions. They upset you. I won't put you through that. We'll ask your father."

She smiled and captured his cheeks in her palms, touched by his desire to protect her and keep her safe from harm. "You know he'll say no, or he'll dream up some clause involving Dante… I won't hand our son over to him when I can help. Let me try."

He looked as if he would say no again.

"You'll be there to wake me, okay? You'll stay with me and I'll know you're there and when it looks as if it's getting too much for me, you'll wake me." She searched his eyes but they only swirled brighter, a sign he was on the verge of unleashing his demonic side.

She tiptoed and kissed him, hoping to soothe away his fear and calm him down. He gathered her against him, his arms steel bands around her that held her a little too tightly. It hurt but she didn't have the heart to tell him, not when he needed to feel her in his arms and know she was safe.

"It's just a vision. I had them all my life until I met you and you kept them at bay. No more nasty dreams for me… just wonderful ones," she whispered against his ear and stroked her fingers through his crimson hair, loosening it from the thong at the nape of his neck.

It was still shorter than it had been when they had first met in Hell, but she still loved the vibrant colour of it and she had grown used to it being shorter. Temporarily. He was growing it back for her, and that touched her too.

"I'll watch over you," he murmured against her shoulder. "No beasties will come near you... not in your visions and not out here. I'll keep them all away."

He had vowed such a thing to her all those months ago when she had told him about her nightmares, and had confessed that she hadn't experienced one when she had fallen asleep in his arms. Since then, he had always slept with her, somehow managing to keep skin-contact between them at all times so she never had a nightmare. She only had good dreams.

"I love you." She pressed a soft kiss to his cheek.

He nuzzled her neck. "Love you too, Sweetheart."

Someone cleared their throat. Erin looked up and smiled at her sister, Amelia. Some of the darkness in her silver eyes lifted and she sighed.

"Just be careful." Amelia shook her head, causing her silver ponytail to sway across her shoulders, brushing the straps of her colourful summer dress. "I used to worry about you every night... your nightmare-free sleep is the only reason I'm glad you met Veiron."

Veiron growled. Amelia grinned.

"I'm just kidding... Dante is another reason." Amelia ignored Veiron's indignant snarl, her smile mischievous as she went to Asmodeus and took the boy from him. "I'll get him settled."

Erin nodded and watched her sister go before drawing in a deep breath to steady her nerves and looking at the group, her gaze leaping between each of them before coming to rest on Nevar and Lysia, and finally Veiron.

The love and concern in his gaze warmed her heart and she took hold of his hand, using the feel of it clutching hers to drive away the last remnants of her fear.

She looked up into his dark crimson-edged eyes.

"Let's do this."

CHAPTER 18

Fire.

It blazed everywhere as far as Erin could see, spewing from fissures in the black scorched land.

Hell.

She squinted as shadows moved in amidst the flickering flames, their shapes distorted by the incredible heat. No matter how hard she tried to bring them into focus, they remained as shimmering black shapes, thousands of them, like a swarm of insects.

The ground beneath her feet trembled and rocked, sending basalt stones tumbling down the blackened slope before her. Hot wind swirled around her, scorching her flesh, carrying the acrid scent of smoke, burning flesh and sulphur.

It had to be Hell.

But the more she looked at it, the less it appeared like the realm she knew existed deep within the Earth.

Dotted around the inhospitable landscape stretching below her were patches of towering spiked poles, all of them ablaze. Trees.

She unfurled her black shadow wings and stepped forwards, onto the steep slope that flowed down into the valley. She skidded down it, using her wings to steady her, unwilling to trust them to carry her over the harsh terrain when the wind was picking up, the heat growing in intensity until she felt sure her skin would blister from it alone.

The shimmering black shapes in the distance moved more frantically and the sound of metal weapons clashing reached her ears as the wind turned towards her, blasting against her front. It cut through her wings and she stumbled. She focused to strengthen them and keep them with her.

Ahead of her, a river of lava snaked around the base of the hill, the edges glowing red against the black land.

Her eyes widened in horror as she skidded closer.

It wasn't the lava glowing red.

It was blood.

A river of boiling blood.

On the banks were the fallen, thousands of them. Angels. Demons. Even animals. They littered the ground from as far as she could see clearly beyond the grim river to halfway up the hill.

Her eyes widened further as she saw she was approaching the charred bodies and she beat her wings, carrying herself above them just seconds before she hit the first wave of the fallen.

Bile burned her throat as she flew above the hideous scene, her eyes darting around as she tried to take in the gravity of what she was seeing and calculate the number of blackened and broken bodies.

So many dead.

Too many for her to number.

She crossed the river, heading towards the shapes moving in the distance, drawn to seeing what they were but fearing what she would see at the same time.

Lava erupted from several vents below her and she rolled left to avoid the magma as it shot high into the air. She beat her wings harder to pick up speed, using the thermals to dart across the endless fields of the dead.

The shapes began to come into focus as the heat haze between her and them lessened.

The ground shook and the air trembled, a mighty roar rising above the sounds of weapons clashing.

A shiver shot down her back.

Warning bells jangled in her head.

Erin dived, plummeting towards the scorched earth and narrowly avoiding the immense clawed foot that swiped through the air where she had been. She hit the ground hard, kicking off a bare patch of land, and flapped her wings, shooting towards the shadows battling ahead of her.

The ground rocked beneath her in time with a heavy beat that steadily picked up speed. Wind slammed against her back in hard waves.

She glanced back at the beast following her.

Green eyes the size of car windshields locked on her, the vertical slit pupils narrowed with intent. Gigantic leathery wings supported the great black dragon as it flew after her. The spikes down its back rippled as it opened its mouth and gold blazed at the back of its throat, illuminating the vicious fangs that were each longer than she was tall.

It roared and unleashed a stream of fire.

Erin shut her eyes and teleported before it could hit her.

She reappeared hundreds of feet ahead of it, close to the battle.

It was worse than she had anticipated.

Angels and demons warred before her. Not Hell's angels. Demons. Huge, scaly, winged beasts.

In amidst the fray were the four angels she had seen with Lysander on the island, a wicked glint in their eyes and a cruel twist to their lips as they attacked with weapons forged of white fire.

What the hell?

They were attacking the angels.

The one Apollyon had named Mihail turned to face her, his icy blue eyes void of any feeling as they locked on her.

He hissed, revealing jagged fangs, and pointed to her.

The biggest one with the pale hair and green eyes swung her way, grinned and licked his fangs as he twirled two curved white flaming blades that resembled sickles at his sides.

Erin didn't wait for him to attack her. She hurled her hands forwards, unleashing a golden orb of energy that tore through the demons between them, filling the stifling air with their cries. The angel evaded it and beat his greenish wings, shooting towards her.

Erin sensed the dragon looming behind her and teleported again, leaving the angel to fly straight at it.

She appeared beyond the battle, above a patch of burning trees.

The war raged on but it was different now.

More black dragons had appeared and in the midst of them stood a gigantic beast twice their size, with enormous leathery wings and six curved horns that flared back from above its violet blazing eyes.

The Great Destroyer.

A shiver went through her, racing down her spine and arms and making her thighs tingle.

The forces of Heaven and Hell were attacking the dragons and the four Lysander had brought with him to the island were nowhere to be seen. Neither were all the demons. The blackened and charred landscape was the same but the players had changed.

She went to fly across the fields of the fallen to get a closer look.

Sharp pain went through her stomach.

"Don't move, Baby." A deep voice curled around her and she realised she was laying on her back, across Veiron's lap.

She looked up at him and her eyes widened as she saw all the blood on him. He clutched her to him, tears lining his swirling golden eyes, and she went cold.

It was her blood.

The pain came again, fiercer this time, burning her to ashes, and she cried out.

"Baby... don't leave me." Veiron pulled her closer, his voice hoarse and his agony tearing at her. "I can't lose both of you."

She froze.

Hot tears formed and spilled down her cheeks, scalding her.

Her eyes dropped to her stomach.

She wasn't holding it as she had thought.

Dante lay cradled in her arms and in Veiron's. Silent. Unmoving.

Dead.

Erin screamed.

The vision shattered but she didn't stop shrieking. The pale blue sky above her swirled into darkness and she kept screaming, unleashing every drop of the fury and agony eating her alive as she saw her little boy dead in her arms over and over again. Wind lashed at the island, driving the rain down so hard that it ravaged the sand, causing a million pockmarks across the normally smooth white surface. Lightning forked across the sky and slammed into the shore, each strike leaving sizzling lava behind.

She kept screaming until she was hoarse and couldn't breathe, and then she broke down in tears.

The storm turned wild, the lightning striking closer to the camp and the wind howling as it blasted the island with icy cold rain.

Above the din, she heard a soft cry.

Dante.

She shoved out of Veiron's arms and stumbled blindly, searching for him.

"Calm down, Sweetheart," Veiron hollered above the noise of the storm and caught hold of her wrist, drawing her back against him, into the shelter of his embrace.

She couldn't.

She grabbed Veiron's arms and dug her black claws into his biceps.

"I need to see Dante," she said and turned wild eyes on Veiron.

He stilled, the colour draining from his face.

"What did you see?" he whispered, the fear in his eyes an echo of what was running through her. Tears burned her eyes and she fought for breath, wanting to answer him but unable to find her voice. "You saw me die again, didn't you?"

Erin shook her head, the wet strands of her black hair sticking to her cheeks and getting in her eyes.

"No." She kept shaking her head, spilling hot tears down her freezing cheeks. "Not this time. This time I will die... and our son with me."

Veiron snarled. "*No*. I won't let that happen. It will *never* happen, you hear me?"

She wished that she believed him but her heart was falling to pieces inside her, breaking apart at the thought of what the future held for her and their son, and the thought of leaving Veiron alone in this world.

He dragged her against him, pinning her head to his rain-slicked chest with one hand and pressing the other into her lower back.

"I swear to you, Erin, it will never happen. The future is never constant. Remember? The slightest thing can change it."

She nodded, forcing herself to believe him because if she kept thinking all was lost, then she felt sure it would be. She would make that future she had seen happen.

Amelia hurried across the wet sand to them, shielding Dante with her silvery half-feather half-leather wings. Erin drew in a deep breath to calm herself and the storm began to relent, the rain lightening to a gentle patter and the wind dropping. She took Dante from her sister and rocked him in her arms, staring down at his peaceful sleeping face.

It will never happen, Daughter. I will not allow it. Her father's voice echoed in her head, suffusing her with warmth and leaving her feeling hazy. He must have felt her pain and heard her fearful thoughts.

Her heart steadied.

Is there a way to stop Lysia from awakening? She sent that question back to him through their link. Normally, she spoke aloud to him, upholding a promise she had made to Veiron so he would always know when the Devil was communicating with her, but she kept their conversation to herself this time, wary of everyone watching her.

Deliver the Great Destroyer to me. I will send her to sleep as I did with Liora. I will seal her back in her chamber.

Erin wasn't sure whether to believe him. Part of her said that he would kill Lysia, and that would kill Nevar because he harboured feelings for her. Erin couldn't bring herself to cause him pain when he had already suffered so much and she didn't want to see Lysia dead, but she was too shaken by what she had witnessed in her vision to think clearly right now.

She stared down at Dante where he lay in her arms, unharmed and safe, and kept seeing him as he had been in her nightmare, covered in both of their blood, unmoving and cold. Dead.

She trembled and clutched him closer, icy claws sinking into her heart and squeezing it tightly in her chest.

She shut out her father's tempting words, afraid she would succumb to them, or worse, would do the deed herself in order to protect her son.

Veiron wrapped his arms around her and she nestled against him, breathing slowly as she fought her fear.

"I won't let it happen," she whispered to Dante and Veiron, swearing on her heart that she would do everything in her power to keep her family safe.

She lifted her head, her heart steadying and her fear fading as she pulled herself together. She was stronger than this. Veiron was right and a vision was just one version of the future, one possible outcome. The smallest thing could change it.

"I will do whatever it takes to protect my son and my husband."

She slid her gaze towards Lysia and Nevar pulled the black-haired woman closer to him. Erin knew why. All the fires of Hell burned in her eyes and shadows fluttered from her shoulder blades and twined around her arms and around Dante too.

"I'm sorry," Erin said to Nevar. "I want to help, but I won't let anything happen to my family."

Veiron shifted behind her and she could feel him growing, transforming into his demonic state, a sign he was in her corner and willing to fight anyone who went against her decision. His black clawed hands curled protectively around her and Dante. Resolve flowed through her, obliterating her fear, and she slid her fiery golden gaze back to Lysia.

"I want you off this island or I will do the one thing guaranteed to stop you from awakening."

Everyone stared at her in disbelief and she cradled her boy closer to her breast.

"I will hand you over to my father."

CHAPTER 19

Nevar stepped out of the swirling vortex and onto the black courtyard of Asmodeus's fortress, his curved black blade held in one hand and Lysia's hand clutched in the other. He scanned the paved area and then the towering building ahead of him, his senses sharpening as he checked every crevice and crack, and then scoured the area surrounding the fortress. No enemies present. He tugged on Lysia's hand and she emerged from the portal and looked around at the grim landscape surrounding them.

It was hardly the tropical paradise of the island they had just left, but it was going to be their home for now.

Asmodeus's once imposing fortress stood mostly in ruin now, but he and Liora had made progress on repairing the damage that had been done to it when the Devil had sent a dragon after them. It stood proudly on a spire of rock hundreds of feet above a wide bowl-like plain. Asmodeus had used the plain to supply him with the rock needed to build his fortress, turning it into a quarry and ending up with the land around the fortress courtyard carved away to what it was now—a valley.

Nevar looked down at Lysia's bare feet and materialised a pair of black sandals for her, so she would be more comfortable walking on the harsher terrain of Hell. She dropped her gaze to her feet as they appeared and then lifted her eyes back to his, a solemn edge to them, before she cast them away again. He gently squeezed her hand, offering her comfort and hoping it would alleviate some of her hurt. It wasn't her fault that they had been forced to leave the island.

His master stepped out of another portal with Liora, his black beach shorts disappearing as he strode towards Nevar, replaced by the slats of worn gold-edged black armour that protected his hips and his greaves and boots, the only pieces of armour that the angel owned now. His two hellhounds bounded through the portal before it closed and snarled and jostled with each other as they trotted up to Asmodeus.

"Check the castle," Asmodeus said to them in the demon tongue and they wagged their long whip-like tails, their tongues lolling over their sharp black teeth and their red eyes alert, and raced off towards the building.

"I'm sorry you had to leave your friends," Lysia said and Asmodeus shook his head at the same time as Nevar did, wanting to reassure her that it was fine. "You cannot hand me over to the Devil."

Nevar drew her closer to him and she looked across her shoulder at him, a solemn edge to her expression that tugged at his heart and told him to offer her comfort. "We would never do such a thing."

He wanted to say something better, something that would erase the fear from her beautiful hazel eyes and reassure her that there was no way he was letting either the Devil or Heaven get their hands on her. He would find a way to ensure she was safe from being triggered into becoming the Great Destroyer.

He only wished that Erin had told them details about what she had witnessed in her vision before asking them to leave. He needed to know whether she had seen Lysia and more about the battle, but he hadn't had the heart to press her when she had been so distraught and disturbed by the vision. A vision she had seen for his sake.

He clenched the grip of his black blade and ground his teeth, hating himself for what she had gone through for his sake. He should have stood with Veiron and told her he wouldn't allow her to risk seeing something scarring in her vision. He should have protected her.

He hadn't been thinking straight though. He hadn't even tried to imagine what she might see and she had seen the worst scenario possible. He couldn't begin to grasp how much it had shaken her and hurt her to witness her son dying and knowing she was soon to follow him.

The need to go back and apologise to her, or somehow find a way to get a message to her, made him restless. He needed her to know that he was sorry and that he would do all in his power to change the future she had witnessed. He wouldn't let anything happen to her and her family either.

He would fix all his mistakes somehow.

"The Devil cannot send you back to sleep and Erin knows it. That is why she asked you to leave. She did it to protect you from him," Asmodeus said and Nevar nodded in agreement, dragging himself away from his heavy thoughts.

He had seen Erin communicating telepathically with the Devil enough times to know when it was happening now. Her father had no doubt tried to tempt her into handing over Lysia as a way of protecting Dante. Erin had done the only thing she could to stop herself from succumbing to that offer or hurting people she cared about. She had made them leave her island.

He wasn't angry with her. He had been on the verge of suggesting they part company at the time she had voiced her decision. He would never place her and her family at risk, not when he knew how much they meant to her. If he could protect her by taking Lysia away and finding another way of seeing the future so he could know how to stop her from awakening, then he would do it no matter what the cost was to him.

His only choice now was to go to Heaven and see the pool there.

He couldn't ask the Devil to see the future for them. Not now that he knew the bastard wanted Lysia.

Lysia stared at her feet, her pain beating through the mark on his chest that linked them. He squeezed her hand but she didn't respond this time. He sighed, shifted closer to her and sent his black blade away.

Nevar lifted his free hand to her cheek and swept the backs of his fingers across it. "Erin wasn't angry with you and she didn't only want to protect her son and her family. She wanted to protect you too. She is your friend now. Everyone on the island is your friend now. You are part of the group, another misfit, and I am sure they are trying to think of a way to help you at the same time as trying to stop whatever Erin saw from happening."

Lysia slowly raised her hazel eyes up to meet his. "But I hurt her."

"Not you. If anyone hurt her, it was me, because I went along with her when I should have stopped her from risking seeing such a terrible thing." Nevar opened his hand and cupped her cheek, resting his fingers along her jaw and holding her head up so she kept her eyes on his. "I promise you, Lysia, we will find a way through this and then we can all be together again."

Her eyes brightened at the same time as her pain faded, and he was glad that she had taken some comfort from his words. She had only been on the island for a few days, but he knew everyone there had come to mean a lot to her in that short time.

"We should separate," Asmodeus said and Nevar caught the momentary flicker of concern in his golden gaze before he masked it and it hit him like a punch in the gut as he realised the source of it. "My master can command me to bring Lysia to him. I am not sure whether he would employ such a tactic, but it is better not to risk it."

Nevar had wanted to remain here with Asmodeus and Liora. They were both powerful enough to protect Lysia should the Devil send forces to take her, or should Heaven risk sending their angels into Hell. He hadn't considered that Asmodeus himself could be used as a weapon against her.

"Agreed." Nevar knew the Devil well enough to know that he would employ such a tactic and that it would hurt Asmodeus.

He had heard the tales of Amelia's awakening and how Heaven had forced Apollyon to turn on Marcus and kill her. It had scarred Apollyon and still pained him to this day, the guilt of what he had done weighing heavily on his heart.

Nevar hated Asmodeus at times, but he didn't wish that sort of pain upon him, not anymore.

He would have to find somewhere else in Hell to hide with Lysia until he was strong enough to head to Heaven.

There were a few places he had frequented during his times in Hell when he had been stalking Asmodeus and searching for his fortress. One of them was a cave deep in the wasteland, far from all the villages of the demons and the Hell's angels, where no one ventured.

"Send a message if you need me." Asmodeus placed his hand on Nevar's shoulder and squeezed it.

Nevar mirrored him, clutching Asmodeus's opposite shoulder. "I will, and you call if you need me or… can you get word to Erin to apologise for what happened and ask her to offer us any information she might have on the future she saw? I don't want to hurt her by asking, but it might help us."

Liora stepped forwards, twisting her chestnut hair up into a knot at the back of her head. "I'll go. Asmodeus can open a portal for me and I'll ask Erin about the vision."

Asmodeus's black eyebrows dipped low above his golden eyes and he curled his arm protectively around Liora's waist, pressing his fingers into her bare skin. "I want you to take Remus with you. He can protect you and he can communicate with Romulus. Tell him when you want to return."

She smiled up at Asmodeus and ran her right hand over his bare chest. "I won't be long. I'll be back before you know it. You don't have to fret about me."

His expression soured. "Who says I am worried?"

Liora tiptoed and pressed a kiss to his cheek. "I do."

His master shrugged that off but Nevar knew she was right and the male was concerned about parting from Liora. Nevar could understand why, but

Liora was a powerful witch, far more so than her cousin Serenity. She would be able to protect herself while she was away from Asmodeus.

Nevar's gaze drifted to Lysia where she stood beside him still clutching his hand and he supposed that he would act the same way as Asmodeus if she were leaving him, even for a short time. She was powerful enough to take care of herself, but he wanted to be the one to do that for her. He wanted to take care of her and protect her, so she didn't have to use her powers.

"I will message you when Liora returns." Asmodeus cast his hand out and a swirling black portal appeared a short distance from it, the ribbons of smoke spinning outwards until the vortex was large enough to accommodate Liora and the hellhound.

Nevar nodded and called his own portal. He formed an image of the place he wanted to go in his head, an outcrop of rocks high on a hill above an immense plain of black basalt streaked with lava rivers in the wasteland, and stepped into the vortex with Lysia in tow.

His gaze scanned the cragged landscape of the hill as he emerged from the portal, the black pebbles crunching beneath his boots as he called his armour to him. The violet-edged black greaves formed over his boots and his loincloth replaced his shorts. The pointed strips of his hip armour covered it and then his breastplate and back plate formed over his upper chest, each moulded to mimic the muscles beneath. Finally, his vambraces appeared around his forearms.

He kept his wings hidden, unwilling to allow them out when he was unsure whether any demons had moved into the vicinity since he had last been there. It had been many long months since he had set foot in this area, since before he had awakened Lysia. He had spent days, possibly weeks in this place plotting Asmodeus's downfall and how to use his weakness against him.

He shook his head as he thought about how he had been in those darker days, ashamed that he had allowed himself to fall so far and resort to such cruel and despicable methods of revenge.

Looking back now, he wished he could change everything he had done from the moment he had been forced into a contract with Asmodeus. He had allowed his hunger for vengeance to consume him, blinded by it and unable to see what he was doing to himself, his actions inviting the darkness within him to grow stronger and take root. Asmodeus had only made a contract with him. Nevar had embraced the darkness and given himself over to it.

He couldn't bring himself to regret everything though.

His foolish actions had brought Lysia into his life.

He had been his own downfall, but she would be his salvation.

He felt sure of it as he led her across the uneven terrain, towards the point where the hill rose even higher ahead of them. The darkness of Hell in this area concealed the entrance of the cave he knew to be there, blending it in with the rest of the black rock that formed the hill.

She would be safe there.

He would bide his time and wait for Liora to speak with Erin about what she had seen, in case his ward could offer him something vital that would help him protect Lysia and stop her from awakening. If everything that Asmodeus relayed to him didn't give him a way of helping Lysia, then he would do what was necessary in order to get that information himself.

He didn't want to leave Lysia here in Hell, alone and uncertain whether he would return, but he couldn't go blindly into the future with her, waiting for something to happen that might end with her awakening as the Great Destroyer if he couldn't protect her from it.

Lysia moved closer to him as the path narrowed and gasped as small rocks at the edge of the track crumbled away and tumbled down the sheer slope to the lava strewn valley below.

The thought of her slipping on the loose path and falling down into the valley sent sharp claws slicing into his heart and squeezing it.

He tightened his grip on her hand, unable to shake the fear that she might fall and master it. When another series of pebbles clattered down the slope, he stopped, turned to face her and scooped her up into his arms. She settled against him, her heart beating wildly in his ears and her palms warm against his neck as she held on to him.

He turned with her and kept walking, his eyes locked on the small flat area ahead of them where the cave opened out onto the side of the hill.

His heart steadied, the resolve flowing through him bringing strength with it.

Lysia would be safe with him here.

They would wait to hear from Asmodeus.

If his master offered no useful information, then he would do the only thing he could do to ensure Lysia was safe.

He would return to a place he had vowed he would never set foot in again.

He would go to Heaven.

A place where he would have to unleash his darker side if he was to have any hope of surviving the assault of the angels who would be awaiting him.

Nevar clutched Lysia closer to him and stared down into her eyes, warmed to his core by the soft tender look in them.

He would use the side of himself that part of him feared and the rest of him despised. He would embrace all the darkness he held within him and he would use the strength it gave him.

He would do that for her.

He would do that so he could come back to her.

CHAPTER 20

Lysia sat on the long padded cushion that Nevar had produced for them in the cave and he slumped next to her, rested his back against the black rough wall and sighed out his breath. He closed his eyes and tipped his head back, and stretched his legs out in front of him.

"What happens now?" Her voice seemed loud in the dark cave, echoing around the curved walls.

Nevar had assured her this area of Hell was safe, and she couldn't sense any demons nearby, but it didn't reassure her. She had been caught up in a whirlwind of new emotions from the moment Nevar had mentioned going to Heaven, and she feared that he still intended to head out on what his friends had called a suicide mission.

Now he was alone too, an army of one, and she knew he would refuse her offer if she said she would go with him.

"We sit and wait to hear what Erin has to say." The weary edge to his deep voice stirred a feeling in her chest, something akin to fear.

She pressed her hand to her chest, trying to decipher it. Concern. The reason for it seemed ten-fold. She worried that he would leave her and head to Heaven without her. She worried that he wouldn't return. She worried what Erin would say. She worried that Erin was still upset and that something would happen to the little boy. She worried that Nevar seemed tired, drained of his strength. It was fading away right before her eyes.

"What happens after that?" she whispered and he cracked his eyes open and stared at his boots.

"I do whatever I have to do."

She wanted to rail at him for that and for speaking only of himself. They would do whatever they had to do. She placed her hand over his where it rested on his thigh and his jade eyes shifted to it.

"You look tired." She stroked her thumb over the back of his hand and he heaved a sigh.

"Because I am tired. Hell is not my home. I still have to sleep when I am here."

"And eat," she said, filling in the blank he had left hanging in the air and had refused to mention. "You haven't fed since I met you. You refused Asmodeus. You have only taken mortal food… and you know it isn't what you really need to restore your strength."

He took his hand from under hers and glared at her. "And what do I need?"

"Blood." She frowned at him and he looked away from her.

"If I have blood, I will just crave more blood. It's a vicious cycle. I told you that." The weary edge to his voice invaded his handsome face, etching it with lines that turned it grim. He pinched the bridge of his nose and closed his eyes. "It doesn't help."

"But neither does not drinking blood. You still crave it. At least if you're drinking it, you are stronger."

His lips compressed into a thin hard line.

"Do not snap at me," she said, feeling what was coming and unwilling to take the brunt of his anger or back down to stop him from turning on her. She caught hold of his hand and brought it away from his face. "You are hungry, Nevar. I sense it constantly in here."

She lowered her other hand to her chest and the mark beneath her skin shimmered to the surface, casting a purple glow over them both.

"I have felt it from the moment I took blood from you. It made our connection stronger, and now I can feel you more clearly, but it's fading." She traced her fingers over the six-horned beast circling the pentagram.

A beast she would become.

Memories flashed through her mind, a vision of gigantic clawed paws covered in black scales and blood, lashing out at the angels that swarmed around her. The tips of dark leathery wings appeared at the corners of her vision as she fought. Her wings. Her claws.

She dropped Nevar's hand and breathed hard, fighting for air as the cave closed in on her and the memories rushing through her head became more violent. Each blow the angels landed on her paws and her chest echoed on her body.

"Lysia." Nevar grabbed her shoulders and shook her gently. "Breathe. In for five. Out for five."

She tried to do as he instructed but her throat tightened and she gasped as an angel drove a white spear straight through her chest and cried out as fire seared her heart.

"Lysia." Nevar pulled her against his hard breastplate and wrapped his arms around her. The feel of his hands skimming up and down her back and his warm breath puffing against her bare shoulder soothed her a little. She pressed her hands to his armour and burrowed closer to him, seeking the comfort of his embrace.

She wasn't there.

It was only a memory.

It would never happen again.

She wouldn't allow it to happen again.

Nothing would take her from Nevar.

She ran her hands up his breastplate and curled her fingers over the raised edge around his neck. She tugged at it, wanting it gone, needing to get closer to him. She needed him to make her memories go away. She needed to fill all of her senses with him and leave no chink where the past could seep through and taint the present.

"Make this go away," she whispered, frantically pulling on the piece of armour. It disappeared and she swept her hands over his bare chest, the growl her touch elicited thrilling her and boosting her confidence.

She worked her way across the broad flat slabs of his pectorals, her gaze devouring his delicious body as she explored every inch of it. Her fingers drifted lower, roaming down the line between his pectorals. She carefully traced each line of the mark on his chest, emblazoned above his heart, watching the violet ink ripple beneath her caress. He loosed another moan, the husky sound of it sending a hot achy shiver through her bones, and she dropped her head and kissed the mark that connected them.

His hand came up and he ploughed his fingers into her hair, holding her lips against his flesh. She swept them over the mark and darted her tongue out, stroking it over his warm skin and tearing another deep rumbling groan from him.

Lysia lowered her hands to the start of his stomach. His muscles tensed beneath her touch and she drew back, Nevar's fingers still tangled in her hair. Her gaze devoured each ridge of honed muscle on his torso as his gaze bore into her. She moaned and lightly raked her short nails over the peaks and valleys of his stomach.

Nevar moaned again and his grip on her loosened. He leaned back against the wall, giving her more access to him, and she ventured onwards, her gaze dropping to her next destination as the dark memories began to disappear, replaced by an all-consuming and driving need of Nevar.

She ran her fingers across the waist of his hip armour.

"And this… make this go away too," she murmured, breathless with anticipation and the desire rising to new dizzying heights within her.

His gaze darkened, his pupils gobbling up the soft jade of his irises.

The armour around his waist disappeared.

Her fingers touched soft cloth and she moaned at the thought of him removing that item next, revealing him to her. She wanted to lick and stroke him as he had her, giving him the same incredible pleasure she had experienced back on the island.

She placed her right hand on his bare shoulder and lifted her right leg over his, settling herself on his thighs. His hands instantly dropped to clutch her backside and he tried to draw her closer as his gaze fell to her lips, a hungry edge to it. She would kiss him, but not yet. Not until she had satisfied a commanding urge stealing through her.

She lowered her left hand and cupped him through his loincloth. A husky moan escaped him at the same time as she loosed a groan of her own. He was hard beneath the black material, as solid as stone. The feel of him had heat pooling in her belly and swirling lower, towards the apex of her thighs. She bit her lip and rubbed him through the material, unable to stop herself from stroking his steely length, wanting to feel every inch of him and know that he would be inside her again before long, filling her and intimately connecting them once more.

She wanted to rush to the finish line but found the strength to hold herself back. Patience was apparently a virtue. She wasn't sure she had ever been big on virtues but she could learn to embrace them if it would draw out the pleasure of this moment with him.

Lysia palmed him one more time before tearing herself away and shifting closer to him. He groaned as they came into contact and tilted his head back, exposing the strong curve of his neck and his Adam's apple. It bobbed as he swallowed and she couldn't resist dropping her head and licking it, tearing another moan from him.

"Lysia," he husked, raw need edging his deep voice, and she gave in to him, rocking her hips against his hard length to give them both a brief burst of pleasure.

His fingers pressed into her backside and he growled. "Time to make these go away."

Her shorts, sandals and top disappeared. She gasped and then moaned as he growled again, a deep rumble of appreciation as he raked his hot gaze over her body. The hunger and need swirling in his violet-edged green eyes sent heat coursing through her body and left her feeling empowered.

She leaned back, giving him a better view of her bare body. He sank his fangs into his lower lip, a ravenous look settling on his handsome face, and frowned as he tugged her hips towards him. She threw her head back and moaned as her bare flesh came into contact with his, the barriers between them gone.

He rubbed her against him, rocking her core up and down his hard length, and she arched her back, thrusting her bare breasts up into the air as she tangled her hands in her hair and gave herself over to his command. A feral snarl filled the cave and a thrill chased through her, the wicked and raw sound of his hunger stoking her desire and making her burn at a thousand degrees, until she felt sure she would melt in the intense heat blazing between them.

The first sweep of his moist tongue across her stomach tore a gasp from her. The second had her moaning his name and on the verge of begging for more. He kissed a path over her flesh, rocking her against him the whole time, driving her out of her mind with need.

She wanted to tell him to go slow, to let her stroke him with her tongue and learn more about his body and the pleasure she could wring from it, but she couldn't find her voice as he sucked her left nipple into his mouth. Sparks skittered over her skin from the centre of her breast. Each swirl of this tongue or scrape of his fangs across her sensitive flesh had her squirming against him, hot all over and slick with need.

She couldn't take any more.

She grabbed his shoulders, shoved him hard against the cave wall, and rose off him. His gaze devoured hers, all violet now and filled with fire and hunger, need that she knew she could satisfy and that burned within her too.

Lysia swooped on his mouth, determined to master him this time. His hands tightened against her hips and he tried to bring her back into contact with him. She tensed, denying him and making him wait. He growled and she swept her tongue across his lips, so the snarl ended on a moan. He opened for her and she delved her tongue inside, tangling it with his as she fought him for dominance.

Claws pressed into her bare buttocks.

Her own had emerged the moment she had kissed him, brought out by the depth of her need and her desire to keep him where he was, trapped beneath her and at her mercy.

She kissed him and threaded the fingers of her left hand into his white hair, holding him in place against her mouth as she skimmed her right hand to his chest and his stomach. He tensed, his hips jerking upwards off the padded mattress as she wrapped her fingers around his velvet and steel length.

"Lysia," he moaned and she echoed him, her body crying out for her to take this to the next level.

She needed him inside her again, one with her.

She needed it with a desperation that astounded her, as if she would die if she didn't get him inside her soon.

She palmed his length, ripping another moan from him that had him tilting his head back and flashing clenched fangs.

He looked beautiful like that, feral and dangerous, as desperate for her as she was for him.

She rubbed the sensitive crown of his cock down her to her core and slowly seated herself on him, taking him into her at an excruciating pace that had him pressing the back of his head into the black cave wall and growling as he dug his claws into her backside.

Every inch of him tensed and the sight of her powerful warrior in all his glory stirred her desire, sending it swirling higher, until she could no longer control herself and surrendered to her feelings and her needs.

She sank down onto him and rose again, and he guided her on him, moaning in time with her and each long stroke. Divine. She grasped his hair and tugged his mouth back to hers, pouring out her passion as she rode him, increasing her pace until he was thrusting into her on each down stroke, sending her soaring higher into the stratosphere, shooting towards the stars.

He grunted with each hard meeting of their hips, each deep thrust of his cock forcing a moan from her throat, one that he swallowed in a kiss that left her feeling there was no place where they weren't connected.

The mark on her chest surfaced and his mirrored it, shining brightly and washing them with purple light.

She clutched his head and screwed her face up as her belly tightened, her thighs trembling against his as she bounced on him and he thrust into her, a wild coupling that she couldn't bring back under control. Need drove her and she was a slave to it, searching for the push she needed to tumble over the edge into bliss.

Nevar growled as she ran her tongue down his left fang and shoved her away. She didn't let him make her stop, not as she knew he wanted to. She grabbed his shoulders, slammed him back against the wall and kissed him again, licking his fangs. They grew longer, sharp daggers that stirred a fierce ache inside her, a dark hunger to feel them penetrating her flesh, joining them in the ultimate way.

She wanted to bite him too. She wanted his rich blood flowing into her body and strengthening their connection.

His fangs grew longer and his guttural groan told her everything he would never voice. He wanted to bite her too. He hungered for it with the same intensity that she did.

His fight ended here and now.

He wanted to bite her and she would show him that it was all right. He was allowed to want it. He was allowed to do it. She would never deny him anything, and he should never deny himself anything either.

She kissed along his jaw on his left side and he stilled, his hands tensing against her bottom. She kept rocking on him, riding his rigid length, as she swept her lips over his earlobe and sucked it into her mouth.

She released it with a 'pop' and whispered into his ear, "It's okay, Nevar… if you want to bite me… because I want it… and I want to bite you too."

He groaned and banged the back of his head against the wall.

She placed her hand behind his head to cushion it and stop him, and kissed down his neck.

"I'm not forcing you… but if you want to feed, you can… just a sip." She nicked his throat with her fang and licked the bead of blood that blossomed there. "It only takes a sip to strengthen our connection. See?"

She wrapped her lips around the cut and gently sucked it, drawing a small amount from him. He shuddered and groaned, his hips thrusting frantically, driving him into her and sending tingly shivers blasting through her. Their connection deepened, growing stronger. It was in their blood. It had to be. She had never been sure how she was linked to him but she was now. They were connected through blood. It was the reason their bond grew stronger when she drank from his vein.

"Lysia," he whispered and clutched her closer. "I don't want to hurt you."

She smiled against his throat, sensing the fear locked deep within his heart, glad that she could chase this one away for him, and the one he refused to voice.

"It will feel good to me. You won't spoil me with your bite, Nevar… you could never spoil me. I don't care what you did in the past… what is happening between us is different. I want you to bite me… I want to make you stronger."

He groaned and pushed her back, away from his throat, and stared deep into her eyes. The myriad of emotions colliding in his made her stop moving on him and she cupped his cheeks in her palms. Her powerful warrior. He looked as if he was breaking inside. Why?

"I don't deserve this." Those four words brought pain to the surface of his violet eyes and she shook her head to deny him.

"I told you before. There has never been anyone more worthy of me than you, Nevar."

He closed his eyes and she cursed him. She wasn't going to let him argue with her about this. He wanted to bite her and feed from her vein, and wanted to strengthen the connection between them. She wanted him to bite her and wanted to make him stronger.

She wasn't above using devious tactics to lure him into surrendering to her either.

Lysia ran her hands upwards, over his cheekbones, and into his mussed silver-white hair. He frowned at her and opened his mouth as if to speak.

It snapped shut on a groan as she feathered her fingertips over the two small horns protruding from just above his ears.

When she stroked them harder, he grunted, growled, grabbed her hips and slammed into her, tearing a gasp from her.

"Give me what I want," she husked and his violet eyes shot open, zeroing in on hers. His firm lips parted to reveal his long fangs. She moaned and rocked on him, slowly rising off his length before shoving back down and taking him as deep as he could go. "Take what you want."

His violet gaze leaped to her throat and the cave swept past her in a blur as he twisted with her, taking her down onto the padded cushion, and she cried out as he sank his fangs into her throat. Exquisite pain arced down her shoulder and up over her head as his teeth sank deeper. He grasped her left shoulder in one hand and her hip in the other and drove home, thrusting wildly as he sucked down the first mouthful of her blood.

Lysia threw her head back and moaned as she surrendered to him, hazy bliss running through her veins and threatening to take her far out of her mind. Out of her body.

She tunnelled her fingers into his hair and held on to him as he drank from her, each pull on her blood sending fire shooting through her body that collided with the heat swirling in her tightening belly. She wriggled frantically, clenching him as he thrust into her, aching with a fierce need to find release before she completely lost her mind.

He drew another mouthful of her blood that had her feeling as if it was all rushing through her veins to him and plunged into her, bringing their bodies back into contact, and she cried out as the tight knot in her stomach unravelled, sending heat flashing through her and her thighs tingling and quivering. Her core clenched him, the hot shivers rushing outwards from it as she trembled around him.

He grunted into her neck and grasped her hip, digging his claws in, and thrust home. His cock throbbed, each pulse discordant to the quivering of her body, his hot seed flowing into her. He pulled his fangs from her throat and lapped at the wound, breathing hard against her moist skin.

Lysia trembled from head to toe, feeling as if she was floating as bliss danced through her veins and the connection between her and Nevar grew stronger.

He settled on top of her, kissing her throat and murmuring quiet things to her in the demon tongue, words she understood because she felt them in her heart too. What he felt was more than the result of their bond with each other. It ran deeper in his veins than blood. It consumed all of him as it consumed her and neither of them could live without it now.

Neither of them could live without the other.

Somehow, he had become a part of her, as vital as the organ thundering against her breast, trying to break free and leap to him, and she knew that she had become vital to him too.

Lysia stroked his sweat-slicked back, her fingers trembling as much as he was beneath their touch, and cradled him to her, her gaze on the ceiling but her sight turned inwards towards her heart and the feelings growing inside it.

Feelings she had never experienced before.

One question echoed in her mind. One question she wasn't brave enough to voice and hear his answer.

Was this love?

CHAPTER 21

Lysia kissed down Nevar's spine as he lay on his front on the dark padded mat in the cave, his handsome face softened in sleep. She stroked the tangled threads of his white-silver hair from his brow and studied his face, absorbing his masculine beauty. She hadn't been able to sleep. The nightmares had returned and she had awoken in a cold sweat, afraid that the angels would find them and take her while she was vulnerable.

With her other hand, she caressed the marks he had placed on her throat, and looked at the ones she had placed on his. They had exchanged blood after making love and she had told him her theory about their bond. He had agreed with her and also believed that their connection was somehow in their blood, and they were more than master and servant. He thought that they were more like partners, two halves of one whole, each tempering the other. She liked that theory, and the way he had looked at her as he had said it, with something akin to affection in his green eyes.

She leaned over him again and traced the intricate swirls of the wings inked onto his back.

They were large, covering both of his shoulders, including the vertical twin ridges of scar tissue where his wings hid. She could feel the magic in them, laced with great sorrow and regret. The two emotions were Nevar's, carried on his back for eternity, woven into the spell. He hated himself for what he had done to the witch who had given him this spell.

Lysia wished she could ease that pain for him, but all she could do was stand by his side and slowly show him that he was still the good man he wanted to be. He just couldn't see it right now. He was too close to the events that had turned him against himself, his eyes clouded by the things he had done. It would change in time, the dark haze clearing to reveal that era of his life was over and he was stronger now. It would never happen again.

He had come through the darkness and was determined to keep striding onwards into the light.

Lysia pressed a long kiss to his left shoulder. Her warrior. He was beautiful in his desire to be good again, to be a man worthy of her and to right his wrongs.

"Tickles," he mumbled into the cushion and his silvery eyebrows met in a frown.

His jade eyes slowly opened and sought her. She smiled and brushed her fingers across his back.

"You were meant to be resting." She drew away to give him more room and he rolled onto his back, gloriously naked and delicious.

The sight of him had her heating inside and fire pooling in her belly.

He stretched and his grin was wicked as he caught her staring at his magnificent body, her eyes drifting over the honed muscles of his torso towards his hips.

His black loincloth appeared before she could reach them and she frowned at him.

He pushed himself up, yawned to reveal short canines instead of fangs, and rubbed the sleep from his eyes.

"I was resting." The deep raspy quality of his voice made her shiver. He sounded even more alluring and masculine than usual when roused from sleep.

The corner of his sensual mouth quirked.

Lysia blushed.

"You could have at least woken me with a proper kiss." He moved quicker than she could evade, sliding his hand around the nape of her neck and clutching it, pulling her into his arms and her lips against his.

She gasped into his mouth as he kissed her, throwing fuel onto the fire he had already ignited in her belly. She caught hold of his shoulders and kissed him back, her lips dancing desperately across his, hungry for more.

He broke away and smiled at her, one that had her heart fluttering in her chest. All the light in the world shone in his eyes and stole her troubles away. He seemed happy today. Because of what they had done or something else?

She felt at peace in this place, with him, as if the future didn't exist and they would always be like this. Together and happy. She wanted that more than anything, and the look in his eyes spoke to her soul and said she wasn't alone in her desire. He wanted it too. He was happy because he was here with her.

"Good morning," he husked and rubbed the back of her neck, sending shivers sweeping down it to her shoulders, keeping her hunger for him at a low boil. "Or it might be evening. Never can tell in this fucking place."

"It's morning."

He arched an eyebrow at that.

She glanced away and then back at him. "I can tell. I'm not sure how."

"I never thought this place had a morning or evening... I just figured it was always the same. Perpetual night. Like Heaven is perpetual day."

She hadn't known that. "I only know what I feel. It feels like morning. I sensed power awakening in the west."

"Power?" He frowned now. "You mean Asmodeus? We're south of him."

She shook her head. "No. Immense power. The Devil. He keeps hours based on the mortal realm. Even in my captivity I knew when he woke, signalled by a sharp rise in his power within the fortress, and I sensed when he moved away from the area, and when he slept."

"That I definitely didn't know. He sleeps?" The look on Nevar's face told her that it had come as a shock to him.

"Of course he sleeps." She couldn't understand why that seemed like such a strange concept to him.

Nevar rested his back against the cave wall and stared out of the wide arched entrance off to his right. "But he's an angel of Hell. Hell's angels don't need to sleep or eat in this realm."

She could see why he would have presumed such a thing. "He isn't a Hell's angel... or an angel of Hell. He's a true fallen angel."

"True fallen?" Nevar looked back at her. "Isn't that just a Hell's angel?"

"No." She didn't think it was anyway. "A Hell's angel is pledged to the Devil, a minion under his control. No one controls the Devil. He is a power in this realm... I mean... he was cast out but not stripped of his corrupted powers or pledged to another master."

"Like Asmodeus."

She shook her head again. "Asmodeus is the Devil's servant. You are Asmodeus's servant. The Devil has no master."

"I get that," Nevar said as his frown lifted. "So the bastard has to sleep... does he have to eat too?"

She shrugged. "That I do not know. But I heard rumours once, many millennia ago, that—"

A shiver bolted down her spine and the hairs on the back of her neck stood on end.

Nevar shot to his feet and his armour appeared, covering his shins, forearms, hips and chest. A black curved blade with a violet grip materialised in his right hand and he snagged her wrist with the other and pulled her up to him. Her shorts, top and sandals appeared on her body.

"We're not alone," she whispered and her claws extended.

He nodded. "Four of them."

The angels.

She would know their signature anywhere after encountering them on the island and feeling their power encompassing her.

"Stay here." He dropped a kiss on her brow. "I will see what they want."

He released her and strode out of the cave. Lysia huffed and followed him, ignoring his order. She wasn't going to let him face these four angels alone. He was stronger now because he had fed a little, but he hadn't taken enough from her to restore all of his power.

She looked off to her left, beyond Nevar to the small flat clearing beside the cave. The hill rose above it and on the peak stood the four angels, all staring down at her and Nevar.

How had they found them?

The one with the long white hair worn with the top half tied back from his face and the rest left to hang down his back stepped forwards. He unfurled his wings of purest snow and beat them, lifting off the mound. He spread them wide and glided down to the plain, landing a few metres away from Nevar.

Nevar backed off a step, coming to shield her, and his black wings grew from his back. He was preparing for a battle.

"What do you want?" Nevar growled and called another black blade to his free hand.

The angel raised an eyebrow at it and then his ice blue eyes lifted back to Nevar's face. He casually raised his left hand and the three other angels left their posts on the hill, coming to flank the male.

Mihail.

Was he acting as their leader?

The largest of the warriors, with his overlong pale hair and green eyes, landed off to the left of Mihail. The one with short red hair and golden eyes ringed with crimson landed at Mihail's side, furling his scarlet wings against his back. The last one didn't land. He hovered above the three, his black wings beating the hot air at her and his grey eyes locked on Nevar.

Each wore a grim look that held darkness in it, a shadow of menace that she found strange in angels of Heaven.

This close, with only a few metres separating them, she could make out that their black leather armour wasn't identical. The engravings each angel bore were different, and inlaid with a colour that matched their wings and hair. She dragged her focus away from Mihail's and the images of demons being defeated by men that were inlaid with dull white on it. This wasn't the time to take her eyes off her enemy. These four angels had come here with a purpose and she wanted to know what it was, just as Nevar did.

"I will not ask again. What do you want?" Nevar eyed each male in turn and she did the same, calculating their strengths and searching for any weaknesses.

Mihail stepped forwards.

Nevar stepped backwards, keeping the distance between them steady.

The angel smiled. "I do not mean you harm."

Nevar laughed at that and Mihail's eyes darkened.

"Excuse me if I find that difficult to believe after our last encounter." Nevar shifted his grip on his two blades and shuffled his feet further apart. "Where's Lysander?"

Lysia hadn't failed to notice that he wasn't present. Had the four angels not made it out of Hell after all? Asmodeus and Apollyon had said they were taken by the light, just as Lysander had been. What reason could they have for being here without him though? He had announced himself as their leader. What sort of leader allowed his men to go off on a mission without him?

"Lysander is busy making preparations," Mihail said.

"Preparations for what?" Nevar's question hung in the acrid heavy air between them.

The angel didn't look inclined to answer it.

She frowned at the four angels, studying them hard while they gave Nevar their full attention.

What sort of angels had such tattoos? Some of them were of dragons and beasts, and unholy things. Others were of skeletons. Some were angelic symbols. Others written in the demon tongue. Some were glyphs, protective charms that were ancient and beautiful, from all different lands of the mortal world.

And others still were in a language she now recognised as English.

She stared hard at the letters that curved beneath the navel of the angel with the short red hair, spanning hip to hip, trying to understand them. Just as she deciphered the word they spelled, she felt his golden gaze slide her way. Her eyes darted up to meet his.

His full lips tilted into a wicked smile and he stroked the letters that declared 'VICTORY', a suggestive glint in his eyes.

Lysia looked away from him.

These were not angels as she knew them.

They had a wickedness about them, a shadow in their aura that spoke of a darker edge to their souls.

"It has been decided that you will come with us," Mihail said and, for a heartbeat, Lysia thought he was talking to her but his gaze was firmly fixed on Nevar. "Heaven desires to speak with you. It has an offer to lay on the table."

Nevar laughed again. "I do not think so. Heaven has nothing it can offer me."

The angel shifted a step closer, towering taller than Nevar. "It has much to offer you. Do you not desire things which only Heaven can give to you?"

Mihail raked his cold gaze over Nevar's black armour and then his body. It lingered on Nevar's hands and he shook his head.

"So much darkness," Mihail said, his eyes on the black skin that covered Nevar's arms to his elbows, and she felt Nevar falter, sensed his momentary slip in strength through their link before his grip on his swords tightened again and he stood a little straighter, tilting his chin up.

The angel meant to play on his weaknesses, just as she had wanted to seek out and play on theirs. They were wicked indeed.

"Do you long for it to be gone?" Mihail canted his head and smiled. "It can be gone. Heaven will grant that if you come with us. They only desire to speak with you as the creature's master and find a way to avert the apocalypse she will bring about."

Nevar stared at the angel in silence, his jade gaze never leaving his, and Lysia could feel that he wanted to take the angel's offer. She pressed her hand to her heart, to the mark beneath her skin. Heaven was offering Nevar a chance to purge some of the evil that lived inside him and part of her wanted him to take that offer, to seize that which he desired above all else, while another part silently begged him to refuse and stay with her.

"I see." Mihail's deep voice gained an edge as sharp as the white sword that appeared in his left hand. His eyes brightened, white swirling among the pale blue like a snow storm, and he brought his other hand up and pointed at her. "Then we shall take the creature and perhaps you will be more cooperative."

The angel with wild short black hair and silvery eyes swooped from his position above them, a long black spear materialising in his grasp.

Nevar spread his obsidian wings wide to shield her and kicked upwards, coming to meet the angel and blocking his blow with his two blades. The metallic ring of their weapons clashing reverberated in the hot air and Nevar pushed both of his swords upwards, cutting in twin arcs that drove the angel away from him.

Nevar growled, beat his wings and launched himself at Mihail, his shoulder barrelling into the angel's exposed stomach and knocking him backwards. Nevar didn't stop. He kept sprinting forwards, heading for the hill. He slammed Mihail into it, the force of the impact shaking rocks loose and sending them tumbling down the slope.

Lysia extended her claws and snarled through her fangs as the biggest of the angels turned his attention on her and the other two went after Nevar. The angel's pale green eyes swirled darker as his power rose and twin blades shaped like sickles appeared in his hands.

He spread his pale jade wings.

He meant to launch himself at her.

Lysia flicked her left hand forwards and sent him flying through the air with a blast of telekinetic power. He shot towards the hill and crashed into it close to Nevar and Mihail where they fought, creating a deep impact crater. Basalt showered down on the immense pale-haired angel, burying him in the mountain.

The black-haired one turned cold silver eyes on her and beat his wings, shooting towards her.

She held her right hand out, her palm facing him, and halted him in mid-air with her power. He snarled in frustration and fought her hold, edging his spear around to point towards her. Sweat broke out across his brow, the exertion etched on his dark face. His power rose, coming to press against hers, and she focused harder, forming a stronger grip on him with her own power.

The smaller rocks strewn across the plain and down the hill began to rise, drawn upwards by the force of her telekinesis as she battled the angel, struggling to maintain her hold on him.

A strained grin curved his lips.

Lysia's eyes widened as she felt the presence beside her and turned towards the scarlet-haired angel just as he slammed into her side, sending her flying towards the cave. She struck the edge of the entrance and grunted as pain exploded across her side, searing her bones. Her hold on the black-haired angel shattered and she breathed hard as she tried to push herself up and shut down her pain at the same time.

"Lysia," Nevar roared and was before her in an instant, shielding her from the wrath of the angels.

He was a blur of movement as he took them both on, his black blades swiftly moving to block the spear of the darker angel and the twin swords of the lighter one. She couldn't let him fight alone. She pushed herself up and grabbed hold of the cragged wall of the cave, digging her fingers into the stone to haul herself onto her feet.

She mustered her strength, fighting to focus through the pain, and threw her hand forwards, knocking both angels away from Nevar. He looked back at her, a flicker of gratitude in his violet eyes, and then quickly brought his two blades up to block the flaming white sword that struck at him, catching it in the V they formed.

The blow drove him to his knees and he growled, baring emerging fangs, and his arms shook as he tried to force the sword away from his blades.

Mihail loomed above him and pressed harder, keeping Nevar on his knees.

"Surrender," he sneered.

Nevar growled through his clenched fangs. "Never."

The white blade pressed closer to him, the sharp edge nearing his forehead as his arms rippled, every muscle shaking from the exertion. His pain and fear ran through her and she rushed forwards, unwilling to stand by and allow the angel to harm him.

A silver arc cut across her vision and she stopped dead, her wide eyes locked downwards on the blade held against her throat.

"No!" Nevar beat his wings, kicking backwards at the same time, breaking free from under Mihail's blade.

The white sword struck the basalt ground hard, showering sparks across it and leaving a deep crack in the rock.

Nevar flicked a glance at her and then settled his gaze back on Mihail.

He lowered his black blades, set them down on the ground beside his boots, and raised his hands as he straightened.

"I will go with you. I will speak with Heaven." He swallowed hard, his violet eyes leaping back to her. "Just don't hurt her."

Mihail looked to the black-haired angel. The man nodded, grabbed Nevar's shoulder, and twisted him, forcing him face down on the ground. He shoved his knee into Nevar's back, pinning him, and her warrior unleashed a feral snarl and tried to fight his hold.

She shook her head, silently begging him not to because she could see the angel's face and there was only darkness in his eyes, a vicious intent to harm Nevar if he attempted to break free.

"Do not touch her," Nevar growled and clawed at the dirt. "She is not to be touched. Swear it."

Mihail waved his hand and the pale-haired angel released her, shifting away to stand beside his crimson-haired companion.

"She will not be touched. I give you my word." Mihail lowered his hand and the white blade in his other one disappeared. "Take him."

The three other angels grouped together and the black-haired one hauled Nevar off the ground, bringing him onto his knees.

Nevar stared into her eyes, his pleading her and speaking to her heart. She nodded, letting him know she wouldn't leave this place. She would wait for him to return to her.

He would return to her.

She stepped forwards, obeying the pressing urge to kiss him and hold him, to have him hold her and give her the strength to wait for him without succumbing to the fear growing in her heart, a fear that she would never see him again.

Bright blue-white light burst across her eyes, blinding her. When her vision came back, Nevar and three of the angels were gone.

Mihail remained.

He towered off to her left, a glowering dangerous male who radiated darkness at a level that had her shrinking back a step. No angel should possess such unholy power. It crawled over her skin and set her on edge.

"What will happen to Nevar?" She couldn't contain that question. It left her lips before she could consider the consequences of asking it. She didn't want to hear the answer he gave her but she found she could only stare at him and eagerly await it.

He looked up at the cavernous black ceiling of Hell, his handsome face giving nothing away, no flicker of emotion or hint of what he would say.

His ice-blue eyes fell to her, his head remaining tilted back, giving him an evil edge to his appearance.

"He will have his wish. He will become an angel again as payment for all he has done for Heaven."

She swallowed to wet her dry throat and mouth and told herself that the angel spoke true and it was what Nevar wanted, and deserved. He craved it. He wanted to be rid of the evil within him and she wanted that for him too, even though her heart hurt at the thought of it happening. She pressed her hand to it, unsure why the idea of Nevar becoming an angel again saddened her.

"Will they return Nevar when they have spoken to him about me and have restored him as an angel?" Her voice shook and the pain in her heart increased as she waited to hear what he would say. Nevar had longed to purge the evil and darkness and be good again. She had to be happy for him, she wanted to be happy for him, but for some reason, the tears burning the backs of her eyes and stinging her nose weren't ones of happiness.

Mihail dropped his chin and smiled, and she saw everything she despised in angels in him. He was vicious and cruel, and deceitful.

He deserved to die.

Her fingers twitched at her sides, her power rising and coming to defend her, fear driving it.

"No." That word dropped on her shoulders like a thousand tonnes and they sank lower, her insides pulled down under the incredible weight of that single word. "You can never see each other again."

Her heart squeezed in her chest and her blood ran cold, freezing in her veins. "Why not?"

Mihail took a step towards her, towering above her, an immense and formidable foe whose strength she had felt and knew she couldn't defend against. He had vowed not to hurt her but she knew better than to believe him. He was an angel after all. All angels meant her harm.

"The safety of all the realms rests on you and Nevar. You must remain separate."

She didn't believe that. She tipped her chin up and stood her ground, unwilling to waver in the presence of this angel. He was nothing to her. If he dared to raise a hand against her, she wouldn't hold back. She would unleash all the fires of Hell upon him. This was not his realm. He was weaker here than he was in the mortal realm or in Heaven.

This was her realm.

This land fed her power and gave her strength, just as Nevar's blood flowing in her veins did.

Blood that connected them.

"Nevar will return to me. He is my master. He is my male." She spoke the words with all the confidence she could muster, but inside she didn't feel as certain.

Perhaps the angel was right and Nevar wouldn't want to see her, such a lowly creature born of Hell. She would remind him of the evil he had purged, the darkness he had freed himself from.

"Nevar will not." Mihail's firm unwavering tone crushed the last of her confidence. "He will return to his duties. He will be happy."

Something in his icy cold eyes made that difficult to believe. She wanted to say that Nevar could be happy with her. He had been happy with her.

The angel didn't give her a chance to tell him that.

Blue-white light flashed across her eyes and he was gone.

Lysia stared at the place where Nevar had been before he had disappeared, returned to Heaven for her sake. She wished she had given him that kiss now. She wished she had been able to hold him one last time and feel his arms around her. She scrubbed her palms across her eyes.

Nevar would finally have what he craved and desired. He would become an angel again, the darkness he hated purged from him, and she would never see him again.

She was glad for him.

A tear raced down her cheek and the ground beneath her feet trembled. Her heart ached in her chest, the pain stealing her breath. She fought it and fought for calm, for thoughts that would soothe the hurt tearing her apart inside.

She was glad he finally had everything he desired.

The trembling worsened and the black basalt in the plain far below her cracked, lava bubbling up from below and spewing over the edge.

She really was glad.

Her claws grew into long black talons and her fangs dropped.

A huge section of the plain exploded, showering rock and lava across the land and pelting the hill with burning missiles. Massive cracks splintered down the slope, sending chunks of it dropping into the lava-filled abysses. Her gaze narrowed.

The ground around her fell away, thundering into the plain, leaving her standing on a pinnacle of black rock.

As far as her eyes could see, lava consumed the land, burning everything away, an echo of the pain laying waste to everything she had dared to feel, to hope for, and to desire.

Nevar was gone.

She threw her head back, flung her arms out at her sides and roared out her fury.

Lava shot from a thousand fissures around her, blasting high into the air.

He would be an angel now. Angels were deceitful.

He would not uphold the promise his eyes had given to her, an oath that he would return. He would not uphold the vow he had spoken, swearing that he would always be with her now.

She pressed her hand to her chest, to the mark pulsing across her skin like fire. A mark she wished no longer connected them. A mark that only brought her pain now, a terrible reminder of the broken promises that would forever haunt her.

She was alone.

No. She couldn't give up on Nevar so easily. She couldn't believe Mihail over him. She collapsed onto her knees on the spire of rock and stared off into the distance. Purging the evil within him hadn't been everything to Nevar. It hadn't been all that he had desired.

He had desired her too. He had whispered to her in the demon tongue that she was his everything.

She closed her eyes and focused on the mark, on their connection, feeling him through it.

He would keep his promises.

He would never leave her alone.

Because he loved her, just as she loved him.

CHAPTER 22

Asmodeus beat his wings and flew harder, the sense of urgency growing inside him in time with the pain that beat in his heart and flowed through his veins. He pressed his palm to his chest, his black feathered wings working furiously as he pushed past his limit and fought to fly faster.

The black landscape of the wastelands shot by below him, a featureless terrain that rarely changed, but the area ahead of him glowed as if all the fires of Hell had gathered there. The bright golden aura reached the very ceiling of Hell, chasing back the constant shadows that encased it and revealing enormous stalactites that speared downwards, each hundreds of feet long.

Lysia.

Her agony beat in his chest, driving him to find her. Something had happened. Something terrible.

The heat rose as he approached the boiling lake of lava that filled a vast expanse of land within a crater. Everything had crumbled into it, succumbing to the wrath that had exploded from the land.

Everything except a single spire of rock that stood over fifty metres from the curved wall of the crater where it had devoured a section of hill.

Upon that treacherous tower of basalt knelt a tiny figure, her long black hair fluttering and whipping around her slender shoulders.

Lysia.

She lifted her head as he approached, flying high above the crater where the heat from the lava couldn't singe his feathers. The area directly above the spire on which she knelt was cool, as if shielded from the raging fire all around it. He dropped down and landed beside her on the narrow wedge of land and she looked up at him, fathomless sorrow in her violet eyes.

"Where is Nevar?" He looked around him, at the destruction that had taken place. "What happened here? I sensed your pain and came as fast as I could."

She continued to stare up at him and the sight of her tore at his heart. Tear tracks cut through the dark dust on her cheek. She bore a large black bruise on her side. It covered the dip of her waist, ending just above her black shorts, and disappeared under the band of her silver bikini top.

"Tell me what happened, Lysia," he murmured softly, hoping to encourage her to speak this time, because he needed to know.

"The angels came," she whispered and tried to stand. Her knees gave out, sending her crashing back onto the rocky black ground and the spire wobbled beneath him. He flapped his wings, reassuring himself that they were there if the ground gave way, and caught her arm, helping her onto her bare feet. She trembled beneath his grip. "They came for him and he refused to go with them."

His jaw tensed and he frowned down at her, darkness rising within him as he pieced together what had happened.

"They threatened you." He lightly stroked his finger across a thin red line on her throat, a mark made by a sword. "They threatened you and he went with them."

She nodded and tears filled her eyes before she blinked them away and straightened, raising her chin.

"They said Heaven would make him an angel again and I would never see him again. We have to remain separated." Her voice hitched on the last few words and he spat out a curse in the demon tongue, his claws emerging as he thought about using them to tear into the angels who had taken Nevar from her and had driven her to unleash her fury and despair upon Hell.

What had they been thinking?

Had they been trying to awaken her?

He focused his power on calling Nevar to him, trying to issue a command that he couldn't deny. *Come to me, Nevar.*

Nothing. He couldn't feel him. Nevar's spell dampened his ability to control him, but normally if Asmodeus willed it hard enough, he could command him.

Nevar? Where are you?

Silence greeted him. He couldn't feel Nevar at all. The male had a tendency to shut him out, but this felt different. This felt as if the connection between them had been severed somehow. Their bond was intact. He felt sure of that. Someone had cut their line of communication.

It was possible that imprisonment in Heaven would make it impossible for him to contact Nevar.

"He will return," she whispered and the resolve and belief in her steady gaze faltered, making her statement sound more like a question to him, a plea for reassurance that he couldn't give to her.

Asmodeus solemnly shook his head. "He will not return to you."

Her violet gaze fell to his chest and she stared straight through him, the power she was constantly emitting growing at the same time as the pain in his chest.

"The angel Mihail said such a thing too." She swallowed and slowly lifted her gaze back to his face. "Because Nevar will be happy to be an angel again and would not want to see a creature of Hell like me?"

Asmodeus cursed her now for believing such a ridiculous thing. He had seen the way Nevar acted around her, how different he was since meeting her. The angel had fallen for her and was deep under her spell. Now that he knew love, Asmodeus could easily recognise the signs of it in others. Nevar had sacrificed himself to keep her safe.

Idiot.

He would have to teach the wretch a lesson when he next saw him. Nevar should have called for him. He should have cast a portal and brought Lysia back to the fortress. They could have fought the angels together.

He huffed and brushed his knuckles across Lysia's dirty cheek, wiping a stray tear away, and wished he had something better to tell her, something that would give her hope.

"Nevar would never turn his back on you like that, Lysia. He loves you."

He cursed again when more tears lined her lashes. He hadn't meant to make her cry and he knew those tears of happiness would become tears of sorrow and possibly rage when he told her why Nevar wouldn't return to her. He cursed himself for good measure, because he felt like a bastard as he weighed up his words and realised there was no way of breaking it gently to her.

"Nevar will not return because it is not possible to just make him an angel again, Lysia." He dropped his hand to her shoulder and squeezed it as he felt the rage beginning to lace her power and the lava around them churned, throwing great streams of it high into the air. "He will not return because he will not remember you."

Her face paled.

Her eyes darkened.

The ground shook beneath his feet and massive boulders cracked and tumbled down the slopes of the crater surrounding them.

"They mean to kill him."

The pain he could feel inside his chest changed, becoming one born of anger.

She stared up into his eyes and her dark leathery wings appeared, growing rapidly from her back, and her nails became deadly talons.

"I will not let them do such a vile thing to him when all he desired was to be one of their angels again. They will pay for taking him from me and tricking him into going with them. Deceitful creatures… I will pull him from their clutches before they can harm my male."

Asmodeus's eyes burned crimson and his claws emerged, black talons that were almost as formidable as hers were.

"We will save him," he said and she clenched her jaw and nodded. "But we will need help."

He threw his hand out and black ribbons of smoke swirled before it, growing outwards and forming a portal. He took Lysia's hand and looked down at her as she came to stand beside him.

"Be prepared. I do not expect a warm welcome." He waited for her to nod before stepping into the portal.

The bright sunlight stung his eyes as he stepped out on the other side, the soft sand cushioning his steps and the heat of Hell giving way to the cool salty breeze of morning.

"What the hell is she doing back here?" Veiron snarled and charged towards them. Asmodeus called one of his golden blades to his free hand and shifted sideways with her, keeping her away from the Hell's angel as he began to change, the skin around his eyes turning as black as night as they blazed red and turned gold in their centres. The immense male's step faltered as he looked from Asmodeus to Lysia, and then to the closing portal. "Where is Nevar?"

"The angels have taken him." Lysia stumbled through the English words and bravely stepped out from behind Asmodeus. He tried to pull her back again, unwilling to let her place herself in danger. He had to protect her in Nevar's stead and keep her safe until they were reunited.

"What?" Erin's voice boomed across the island and she appeared before them, materialising out of a swirl of black smoke. "Those angels took him?"

It appeared the Devil's daughter wasn't as upset about their presence on her island again as he had feared she would be.

The rest of the group raced across the sand to them, Apollyon leading the charge with Marcus and Amelia hot on his heels.

"What is happening?" Apollyon said and looked between him and Lysia. "Where is Nevar?"

"Those bloody sons of bitches took him," Erin snapped, her eyes golden fire and shadows beginning to flutter from her back. "This is my fault. I shouldn't have asked him to leave. I drove him away and now Heaven has him."

"Shh, Sweetheart, it's not your fault." Veiron gathered her into his arms and rubbed her back. "You didn't know this would happen."

"Veiron is right. It was more important that you protected your son," Asmodeus said and sent his golden blade away as Liora approached him, her hazel gaze overflowing with concern. "We know where he is and they have not had him long. I went to Lysia as soon as I felt the fight and her pain. I am going to take him back from them."

"I will go with you," Apollyon said and Asmodeus nodded, glad that his twin had done as he had hoped and offered his assistance. "I am sick of them interfering and toying with our lives. I will not let them kill Nevar. They will pay for this."

"Count me in." Marcus's blue shorts disappeared, replaced by the pieces of his blue-edged chrome armour, and his flinty grey-blue eyes swirled silver. "I warned them to leave us alone. I won't let them get away with forcing Nevar back to Heaven and stealing away his life."

Amelia stepped forwards and Asmodeus waited for her to refuse and order Marcus to stay with her on the island.

She slipped her hand into Marcus's and the dark-haired male looked down at her. She tugged on his hand, luring him down for a brief kiss, and spoke against his lips.

"Be careful. Give them hell. I'll watch over Erin with the others."

He nodded and kissed her again. Lysia looked away, closing her eyes, and Asmodeus felt a sliver of her pain.

"We will bring him back to you," Asmodeus said in a low voice, wanting to reassure her without everyone hearing him and storing up his kind words for use against him at a later date, making him out to be a sweet man.

It was becoming a habit of all of them. They found it amusing to tease him whenever he was nice, until he offered to unleash his darker side and all that was evil within him upon their heads.

Lysia's dark eyebrows dipped low and she flicked her eyes open and glared at him. "I am coming too."

He shook his head and signalled for Liora to come to him. His beautiful little witch halted beside Lysia and took hold of her hand, slipping it out of his.

"I cannot allow you to come with us. Nevar went to protect you. I will not be the one who delivers you to Heaven. He would never forgive me that sin." Asmodeus wouldn't relent on the matter either. If she refused to comply with his orders, he would have Liora create a cage to hold her here on the island, or ask Taylor to send Lysia to sleep with her demonic powers.

Finally, Lysia nodded and he stepped back from her and beat his wings to bring his flight feathers back into line.

"Liora will take you back to Hell." Asmodeus held his hand out to cast a portal and Erin was suddenly there, both of her hands wrapped around his wrist.

She looked down at her feet as she held him, drew in a deep breath, and raised her head to meet his gaze.

"That won't be necessary." Erin released his wrist and brushed her black fringe away from her golden eyes. Those eyes searched his, an edge to them that echoed the feelings he held hidden inside him, out of sight. "Bring him back, okay? Give them hell... for me. You always wanted to go to Heaven and teach them all a lesson... well... here's your chance. Make sure it's one they won't forget, and be careful."

She stepped to one side and looked past him, to Apollyon and Marcus.

"All of you... be careful."

Asmodeus nodded at the same time as Apollyon and Marcus. Liora came to him, the concern that had already been in her eyes growing into fear.

For him.

He slipped his hand along the curve of her jaw, tilted her head back, and softly kissed her, silently telling her that he would return to her and hushing her fears. He was no fool. He would work with Marcus and Apollyon as a team to ensure they all made it out alive, including Nevar.

He swept his lips across hers one last time, savouring her softness and sweet taste, and then forced himself to take a step back.

Marcus spread his silvery half-feather half-leather wings and beat them, slowly lifting off the beach. Apollyon followed him, the span of his black feathered wings as great as Asmodeus's, each beat of them shifting the white grains of sand.

Asmodeus lingered, absorbing the beauty of his wicked little witch as she looked upon him with endless love in her eyes. A male could battle a dragon for the sake of such a beauty and having her look at him like this.

He already had.

He smiled, turned and kicked off the sand, launching upwards with one powerful beat of his wings.

Apollyon took the lead as they shot upwards, Marcus bringing up the rear a short distance to Asmodeus's left side.

"They will be expecting us. We will have to break through the ranks quickly." Apollyon's voice caught the wind and rushed past Asmodeus.

He nodded and flew harder, picking up speed as they approached the first layer of cloud. He had never been to Heaven, but he knew he was capable of reaching that place because he had been born of Apollyon's blood, and Apollyon had been an angel of that realm.

The next bank of cloud approached, coming at them fast as they flew with haste, speeding upwards as quickly as their wings could take them. Marcus closed ranks and swept his left arm out at his side, extending the silver engraved handle of his curved sword into a long shaft and transforming the weapon into a spear.

"Next one," Marcus shouted and Asmodeus nodded, his heart lodging in his throat and anticipation pouring through his veins.

Soon he would see Heaven for the first time.

And soon Heaven would know his wrath and all of it would tremble before him.

He called his golden blades to his hands at the same time as Apollyon materialised his and readied them, preparing himself as they headed into the final bank of cloud between them and Heaven.

How many angels would be awaiting their arrival on the other side?

He had heard tales of Hell's angels battling them beyond the white walls of the fortress of Heaven. That realm had sent their angels out in the thousands.

The thought of battling so many sent a thrill through his blood and he flew harder, eager to reach the other side of the thick misty cloud and see what awaited him, the King of Demons.

Apollyon broke through ahead of him and Asmodeus readied his blades. The final wisps of cloud gave way and the brilliant glowing white fortress of Heaven hovered before him, the gateless walls stretching as far as he could see in both directions and the mighty castle spearing the blue sky in the centre of the grounds.

Between him and the fortress there was nothing.

No angels.

Marcus halted beside him. "You think it's a trick?"

Apollyon looked uncertain. Asmodeus wanted to agree with the whelp. It was a trick. It had to be one. Why wouldn't Heaven defend itself against intruders they knew would be coming?

He frowned as it dawned on him.

Heaven would never leave itself exposed. It would never risk intruders penetrating the walls. Not even to trick them into flying into a trap. It had sent thousands of angels to deal with a measly force of Hell's angels. It would unleash the entire army to deal with three powerful enemies such as themselves.

There was only one explanation.

"They did not know we were coming."

Apollyon looked across at him, his blue eyes shimmering with paler flecks. "Something isn't right."

Asmodeus didn't care. He was going in regardless. Nevar was in there and he would bring him back safely to the island and Lysia.

He beat his wings and shot towards the fortress. Apollyon cursed him in the black tongue of Hell and his power rose, swirling around Asmodeus. He flew harder, intending to be first beyond the wall, refusing to give his twin the pleasure of beating him there.

He looked back over his shoulder to see Apollyon closing in and Marcus just beyond him.

He didn't care if Heaven didn't want to defend itself. He was going to shake it to the ground regardless. They were going to pay for taking Nevar.

The wall passed by below him and the guardian angels patrolling it in their blue armour all raised their heads, stunned expressions on their faces as they watched him fly straight into the fortress. There was a moment of silence and stillness, and then horns blared and angels along the wall burst into action, combining their powers to form a protective shield over the entirety of Heaven.

Too late.

Apollyon and Marcus were through with him, barely feet behind him now.

His golden gaze scanned the angels rushing around below him, searching for the ones who had taken Nevar.

Several warrior angels with their tawny wings and dull brown armour flew in to attack him. Marcus intervened, handling all of them at once with ease as he unleashed a bright blue orb of energy, the same power that his master, Amelia could use.

Apollyon pointed towards something and then shot backwards, beating his wings and gaining height. A stream of angels from the guardian corps flew after him and Asmodeus tucked his wings back and rolled to avoid them. He spread his wings once he was below them and levelled out, scanning the fray in the white grounds for what Apollyon had wanted to show him.

His gaze zeroed in on a blond male.

Lysander.

Asmodeus snarled, his lips peeling back off his fangs, and sent his right sword away. Shadows swirled around his fingers as they began to turn black and leaped up his arm, twining around it and caressing him. He commanded them forwards, unleashing them in one long stream at Lysander, catching the male unawares.

The ribbons of shadows wrapped around the male's arms and stomach, and bound his golden wings.

Lysander's cold blue eyes shot up to him and narrowed. "What is the meaning of this?"

Asmodeus smirked and couldn't stop himself from responding in a manner reminiscent of his little wicked witch.

"You have some balls to ask me that question after what Heaven has done." He landed in front of Lysander and curled his fingers into a fist, causing the shadows that contained the angel to tighten, digging into his skin.

The angel grunted and wavered, but refused to fall to his knees as Asmodeus had wanted.

"Heaven has done nothing," Lysander spat and a darkness crossed his face, a shadow of something sinister. This one held evil in his heart or in his power. Asmodeus couldn't tell which it was. "Release me."

Asmodeus laughed.

Several angels tried to rush him and Apollyon landed beside him with Marcus, driving them back.

"You took Nevar," Asmodeus said with a grin. "And I think I shall take your head."

The shadows looped around Lysander's neck, twisting ever tighter, and his face turned red as he struggled to breathe, veins popping out across his forehead.

"Apollyon." A deep male voice cut through the noise of battle and his twin foolishly halted his fight.

Asmodeus snarled at him and the newcomer, a dishevelled sandy-haired angel dressed in the gold-edged white armour of the mediator division.

"Come to negotiate?" Asmodeus growled and sent his left blade away. He flicked his left hand towards the mediator and had his shadows wrapped around him before the male could even begin to defend himself.

"Asmodeus, no." Apollyon grabbed his arm and hissed as the shadows snapped and lashed out at him, striking blows at his vambraces and his bare upper arm. He withdrew and his power pressed down on Asmodeus, a warning he heeded because he wasn't in the mood to fight his twin today. "He is with us."

Asmodeus relented, releasing the mediator, and eyed him. "This... fuzzy warm thing is with us?"

The mediator's green eyes darkened and a spear with a golden blade and gold inlaid into the engravings on the staff appeared in his hand.

Asmodeus waved him away, not interested in battling such a puny enemy.

There was a blur of movement and he quickly shifted his hand, blocking the staff of the spear before the blade could reach his throat.

Perhaps the male was not as puny as he had first believed.

He pushed the weapon away from him and slid his gaze towards the male. "Name yourself."

The scruffy blond lowered his spear and the staff shortened, turning it into a sword. "Lukas."

A name he was familiar with.

"We have a problem, Lukas... care to mediate for us?" He curled the fingers of his right hand again and Lysander cried out as the shadows obeyed his command, snapping at the male, slicing into his stomach and legs and drawing blood. "This one has taken something of mine... something precious to me and to another... and I want it back."

Lukas looked between him and Lysander.

"Does he speak true?" Lukas said and Lysander tried to shake his head but Asmodeus throttled him with the shadows wrapped around his neck. Lukas's eyes darkened further and he approached Asmodeus. "Release him so he can speak and defend himself."

Asmodeus considered it and then shook his head. "I will allow him to speak though, since you asked nicely."

He flexed his fingers and the shadows around Lysander's neck loosened. The blond gasped at air, his eyes watering, and Asmodeus sighed, admitting to himself that it felt good to see the wretched angel suffering and he had missed punishing creatures who were beneath him. Not that he would tell Liora what he had done. She would be mad at him and would put him back in the doghouse, and he spent far too much time in that fictional place as it was.

Marcus moved beside him, shifting in time with a group of guardian angels now lined up in front of him. They were surrounded on all sides, but the numbers Heaven had sent were still too small to be of interest to Asmodeus.

When the angels numbered one thousand, he would have fun with them. Until then, Lysander had the whole of his attention.

"I have not taken Nevar," Lysander rasped and Asmodeus checked Apollyon to see if the male believed him.

He didn't seem convinced either.

"Lysia witnessed your angels in Hell. Those angels." He pointed beyond Lysander to the four males standing at his back, watching events unfold with cold eyes that held only fury as they stared at him. He had hoped to draw them out by attacking their leader and he had succeeded. Shadows swirled around his left hand and rose to curl around his legs as he called upon them, preparing himself to fight them all. "You took Nevar. You told him Heaven wished to speak with him and you brought him here."

"Not on my orders." Lysander edged his eyes to his left, to where Mihail stood. "When did this happen?"

Mihail's stony face gave nothing away. "It has not happened. The abomination speaks lies."

"It has happened," Asmodeus snarled. "You four came to Hell and took Nevar from Lysia."

"How long ago?" Lukas said and Asmodeus shifted his red gaze to him.

"Two hours... not more." Time moved strangely in Heaven and Hell, but it was in harmony. Two hours in Hell was two hours in Heaven. It was anyone's guess how long it would be in the mortal realm. Probably days.

Lukas shook his head, his expression grave. "Then I am afraid you are wrong. It isn't possible these angels took Nevar from Hell because they have been in a meeting for the past day, ever since they returned from first discovering her on the island. I know because I was there with them to discuss how to stop the Great Destroyer from awakening."

Apollyon looked as if he believed him. So did Marcus.

Asmodeus stared at him and then at Lysander and the four angels accused of taking Nevar.

He pressed his hand to his chest and focused on his bond with Nevar, placing all of his power into calling him, willing to weaken himself if it meant reaching Nevar.

I command you to return to me.

The tug in his belly came this time, faint but there.

Leading him downwards.

Asmodeus released Lysander, his shadows shrinking back into his hands and settling around his feet. He looked from the blond angel to the four flanking him, a cold weight pressing down on his chest.

Heaven hadn't been expecting them because it had been unaware of what had happened to Nevar. These four angels had had nothing to do with it, but Lysia wouldn't lie about who had taken Nevar. She had seen four angels who looked like the ones standing before him.

"If you did not take Nevar, who did?"

Their blank faces said they didn't have the answer to that question.

His every instinct told him that he knew who did.

His master.

The Devil.

CHAPTER 23

Erin placed her hand on Veiron's armoured forearm and closed her eyes as darkness engulfed them. The others could follow at their own pace. She had a bone to pick with her father and she was damned if she was going to wait while they all discussed plans of action and other factors.

The inky black dissipated and she stared at the landscape stretching below the plateau. Heat rose from the great lava river hundreds of feet below them. In the distance, the cragged black spires that formed the curved wall around the courtyard of the Devil's fortress spewed golden magma as they continued to repair the damage done to them by Asmodeus's battle with a dragon and Amelia's fight against the army of Hell several months ago.

That had been the last time Erin had set foot in Hell.

"We don't have to do this," Veiron rumbled beside her, his gravelly voice a sign that he was on the verge of losing his cool and turning demonic. "You don't have to do this."

She knew that. "I have to speak with him, Veiron."

Dante wriggled in Veiron's arms and she stroked his soft pink cheek until he settled again. His first visit to Hell.

His first meeting with his grandfather.

Her stomach somersaulted and she breathed slowly to calm the doubts that began to surface at the back of her mind and the fears lurking in her heart. She wouldn't let the Devil near her son. He would never be a vessel for her father.

"It doesn't look good though." She stared off at the obsidian fortress that rose in jagged spires into the dark cavern of Hell, each taller than the last, until the very tops of them blended into the shadows, too high for her eyes to make out.

Veiron grunted in agreement.

There was a new moat of boiling lava surrounding the curved walls of the courtyard, the churning golden liquid belching fire in places and launching blobs of magma high into the air in others.

Her father was in a bad mood.

A very bad mood.

"Never seen it like this before." Veiron shifted Dante in his thickly muscled arms, cradling their son closer to his black breastplate.

The boy squirmed again and Erin cooed at him, stroking his cheek and keeping her fingers constantly against his skin so he would know she was here with him too. Nothing was going to happen to him. Veiron had ensured that in his own charming way. He had used his angelic powers to materialise tiny armour for their son, a near replica of his own red-edged black armour. It covered his chest and stomach, and his hips, shielding his most vulnerable parts over his black romper suit.

With her other hand, she caressed Veiron's arm to soothe herself, reassuring herself that he was here with her and he wouldn't let anything happen to her. She traced the black and red tribal tattoos that curled around his biceps and over his shoulders, losing herself in following the ink and using it to give herself a moment to push all her fears to the back of her mind.

"Shall we?" Veiron murmured and she nodded, wrapped her fingers around his arm and teleported them into the courtyard of the Devil's fortress.

He was waiting for them.

Her father sat upon his black throne on the raised curved platform at the base of his castle, his legs crossed at the knee, revealing crimson socks that matched his shirt beneath his crisp black tailored suit. He leaned his left elbow on the arm of the throne, his cheek propped up on his knuckles and a faraway look in his red eyes.

Something had pissed him off.

Something had pissed her off too.

"Did you take Nevar?" she snapped and stormed towards him, shadows beginning to stream from her back, fluttering around the straps of her short black dress.

His crimson gaze slid to her, narrowed briefly, and then he sat up, bringing his leg down beside the other one and placing both hands on the arms of his throne.

"No."

"Someone has." She didn't slow her approach. Veiron kept pace behind her, staying in line with her, so her body blocked her father's view of him. He was protecting Dante, keeping him hidden from the Devil.

She sensed the others appear, Asmodeus coming out of the portal first with Lysia beside him, followed by Apollyon, Amelia and Marcus. It seemed Apollyon had managed to convince the others to remain on the island and wait for their return, but it had been a risk to bring the Great Destroyer to this place.

The Devil's gaze began to shift towards Lysia and froze on Veiron. His eyes widened. His face paled. His lips parted to reveal a hint of fangs.

He was on his feet in an instant and moving to the steps down to the courtyard where Erin stood with Veiron now beside her.

His gaze didn't leave her husband, or more precisely, the precious cargo he carried.

A maelstrom of emotions flickered through her father's eyes, tangled together and impossible for her to decipher. He was shocked though, taken aback by the sight of Dante. Not the reaction she had expected from him. She had thought he would take the sight of Dante in his stride and merely demand she hand the boy over to him now.

His mouth moved but no words came out as he stared at her son, unblinking.

She had never seen him so awash with feelings, things he would call a weakness if it was another exhibiting them, and she knew it wasn't because he wanted the baby as his vessel.

Dante's presence was affecting him.

He was as weak as the rest of them, caught off guard by the sight of a baby, left open to his emotions. They were wreaking havoc on him. His fingers flexed at his sides, his black claws shortening into nails, and he took the first step to the courtyard and then the second. His gaze remained locked on Dante, abject fascination in it as his irises melted back to golden, their normal colour.

He took the final step down and she couldn't believe her eyes.

Her father had lowered himself to stand at the same level as those he viewed as beneath him.

He ran a hand over his black hair, sweeping it back from his face, and she swore it had been trembling.

"May I hold him?" the Devil said without the usual commanding and confident edge to his voice.

Veiron growled and twisted with Dante, shifting him away from his grandfather. "Bugger off. Hell will freeze before that happens."

The Devil snarled, flashing white daggers as his eyes briefly blazed red and his nails became long claws. He recovered a split-second later, smoothing his hair again as he fought for composure. She had only ever seen him react in such a manner when someone had mentioned the G-word. He hated it whenever she said God. Sometimes she did it just to make him lose his shit whenever he was bugging her via their telepathic link.

"He is my grandchild." There was the smooth tone she had come to associate with her father and the charming edge to his expression and air. Charisma and silky persuasiveness that she felt sure he had been born with rather than honed through practice.

Unfortunately, she knew it wouldn't work on Veiron.

"He's my kid," Veiron shot back and tucked the bundle closer to him.

Dante wriggled and kicked, evidently not impressed by his father squashing him against a hard metal breastplate.

Erin waited, sensing that her father was edging towards losing his shit again.

He surprised her by sidestepping closer to Veiron and cooing at the baby from a distance, making all manner of soft noises and murmuring what she supposed he thought were sweet things to him. Erin had been on the receiving end of her father's clumsy attempts to pet and soothe before. It didn't come as a shock that he hadn't improved much in that department and thought that speaking in a soft voice about making his father pay for his insolence was the right thing to do.

"I could calm him." The Devil held his hands out, his claws shrinking back into nails, and smiled winsomely.

"Fuck off." Veiron stepped back and her father snarled at him and raised his hand.

Erin stepped between them. "You be nice. No trying to squash my husband like a bug. Anyway, Dante protects him. He can withstand your power just like I can."

She could almost feel Veiron poking his tongue out at her father from behind her.

The Devil's eyes burned crimson and he bared his fangs, and for a moment Erin felt sure he was going to attempt to crush her husband anyway, just for kicks.

He huffed, folded his arms across his chest, and stomped back up the steps.

Throwing a hissy fit now?

What was with her father today?

He slumped onto his black throne and glared at Veiron. She could almost hear him slowly dissecting Veiron piece by piece in his head.

"If you didn't take Nevar, who did?" she said and he turned his cheek to her.

Erin closed her eyes, inhaled slowly, and prayed for a modicum of patience. Just a sliver would do. She sighed and did the only thing she could to make her father help them, hoping she wouldn't regret it.

She bargained.

"You can get a closer look at your grandson, but not touch him, if you help us."

The Devil deigned her with his attention again and leaned back in his throne, crossed his legs at the knee and settled his hands in his lap.

"What do you desire to know, Daughter?"

It was a start. She just hoped he played nice and didn't send them around in circles or speak in riddles. He had a tendency to make things drawn out and difficult for others in order to amuse himself.

"No," Veiron snapped from behind her and she shot him a glare over her shoulder.

"We're in a pinch and we need help. Nevar needs us, remember? I'll let him look at Dante a little closer if it means we get Nevar back in one piece."

Veiron muttered dark things beneath his breath and rocked Dante in his arms, settling the squirming bundle. The poor thing was probably too hot in all his layers of romper suit and armour. She would let him laze around butt booty naked later when they were back on the island. He loved that. Which made him just like his daddy.

"Now where were we?" She turned back to her father.

He was staring at her son again. "Dante? You named him Dante?"

She shrugged. "It started out as a joke name because he's probably going to grow up traveling to and from Hell and he lives in paradise... on the island. It sort of stuck. We think it suits him."

"Dante." The Devil smiled, as charming and handsome as ever. "I approve of it. It is a strong name. It means enduring... and he will endure. I will be sure of that."

"He'll endure without your bloody interference," Veiron snarled.

The Devil flicked him a bored glare. "Quiet, Maggot. I'm speaking with my daughter."

"My wife," Veiron countered.

"I will overlook the fact that you married her without my consent, and you will be quiet for the next few minutes and tend to my grandson's needs... but in this instance, daughter trumps wife. She is born of my loins—"

"Whoa," Erin interjected. "I really don't want to get into that. The thought of coming out of you repulses me. I still like to think of myself as a test-tube baby, okay? Back on topic now... who took Nevar?"

"Some angels I do not want you near." The Devil sobered, his expression gaining a grim edge that sent a shiver down her spine.

"Who were they? Lysia said they looked like the angels of the apocalypse we met, but when Asmodeus went to Heaven—"

"Heaven?" the Devil barked and turned red eyes on Asmodeus. "Who gave you leave to venture to that realm?"

"We thought Nevar was there." The dark angel stepped forwards, coming to stand in front of Lysia with Apollyon.

Erin was never getting used to them looking like each other. If it weren't for the fact that Asmodeus had shorter hair and golden eyes like her father, rather than the long black hair and blue eyes of Apollyon, she would probably have spent her entire life muddling them up and pissing them off.

The Devil huffed. "Of course he is not there, Maggot. The ones who took him were not the angels you met before, but their predecessors. The original versions... those who are now fallen."

"Hell's angels?" Erin said. "Command them to hand Nevar back and stop whatever they're up to then."

"I cannot." Her father inspected his black nails. "They are not my angels."

"What the hell is that meant to mean?" She stepped forwards, regaining his attention, and he sighed theatrically.

"None have dominion over them, just as none have dominion over me."

"They are true fallen... like you." Lysia moved out from Asmodeus's shadow and her black eyebrows met above violet-edged hazel eyes. "You are wasting our time. Tell us what you know of these fallen. I wish to take their heads."

The Devil's lips quirked into a smile. "I like you. You have verve. I do not think you capable of taking their heads as you are though. Perhaps you can as you will be."

Lysia glared at him. "Speak and tell us of these fallen so we might take back Nevar. You desire it too, do you not?"

He pulled a face of mock consideration. "Do not. I do, however, desire to make the acquaintance of my grandson, so I will help my daughter, but not you. If you interrupt again, I will personally hand you over to these princes of Hell."

"Princes of Hell?" Erin didn't like the sound of that.

He nodded. "You would think them a victim of Heaven and Hell's cruel games if I told you of their origins and how they came to be in my realm. Do not make the mistake of feeling sympathy for them, Daughter. This time it might just get you killed."

She didn't feel sympathy for anything that came out of this realm, not anymore. Just as her father had wished for her, she had become hardened to everything and everyone except those she held within her inner circle. It took a lot for her to allow people inside now. He had made sure of that.

"Pay attention, Little Lambs, and I will tell you the story of Astaroth, Leviathan, Samael and Ramiel, the original four angels of the apocalypse." The Devil stood and cast one hand out behind him and a flickering image appeared, a rectangle of light that spanned the width of the courtyard and rose high into the sky.

Upon the light rectangle, images began to morph into focus. The four angels she had met on the island, but they were different. They had no ink and their hair was different styles, and these ones smiled.

Laughed.

The movie of them flickered and leaped at times, jolting forwards to illustrate her father's words, a replay of everything he told them had happened.

"In a time of darkness, when mankind seemed bent on violence and destruction, Heaven created these four to rule the apocalypse and carry out the end of days and cast judgement upon the mortal realm should it ever lose its way. That pathetic realm refused to listen to my advice—that angels were driven to fulfil their purpose, even to the point of making it happen."

The scene shifted, revealing the four angels raining hell down on the mortal realm. It lay in ruins, an ancient city levelled and burning because of their might.

"Not long after their creation, these four angels grew restless. They stirred trouble in the mortal realm, driving men to war, unleashing divine judgement upon them, and spreading famine and plagues that ravaged the land." The Devil smirked as the image behind him zoomed out to show the vast devastation caused by the angels in question. "Or, as they put it when Heaven finally reined them in and subdued them, they had done what they had been created to do."

Erin could easily believe that. The four had been given the task of bringing about the apocalypse and they had.

"What happened to them?" she said.

"They were returned to Heaven, but were the source of so much discord in the mortal realm that they proved a constant pain to that realm. When they again created a war that destroyed many lives, both beast and man, they were judged for their sins and cast out of Heaven and into Hell." The Devil grinned and the scene that flickered across the screen was so grotesque and horrific that she had to look away. "I stripped them of much of their powers, but it was not enough. They couldn't have their true divine power and purpose taken from them. Heaven counteracted it by creating the angels you met on the island—Mihail, Gabriel, Rafael and Aryel."

"Doppelgangers," Asmodeus growled.

The Devil nodded. "I helped create them."

Asmodeus's face darkened and his power rose, growing stronger and pressing against hers. She could see in his sharp red gaze that her father's words had hit a sore spot and she could understand why. The Devil and Heaven had scrapped the first angels because they hadn't come out as planned. As a doppelganger of Apollyon, a creation of the Devil, Asmodeus no doubt feared such a thing happening to him.

"The new four angels serving Heaven had a slightly amended purpose though. The power of the original four was funnelled through a conduit to the new four, transformed along the way into a new divine purpose. They were built to save, not destroy."

"So, Lysander hadn't lied and these angels of the apocalypse are there to stop it?" Erin hadn't quite believed him but her father nodded, confirming that Lysander had told the truth about the angels.

"The original four were unaware of this turn of events and settled far from this fortress. I let them be and they behaved themselves until you," the Devil pointed at Apollyon, "rained divine fury down on Sodom and Gomorrah with the assistance of a young angel you probably don't even remember, an angel who is now Gabriel."

Apollyon's blue eyes swirled brighter and he frowned, his gaze distant. "I remember him, but he did not appear as he does now."

"No. The tattoos are new. A slight rebellious flair that Heaven evidently didn't quite iron out in the new versions. It does somewhat irritate the originals, since I may have linked them via the conduit and now all that ink is appearing on their bodies too." Her father's golden eyes gained a satisfied glimmer. She couldn't quite see how it was a good idea to irritate already irate angels who held immense power. He sighed. "I am digressing... where was I?"

"Apollyon blew the shit out of Sodom and Gomorrah," she offered and he tsked.

"Should you be swearing in front of your infant son?"

Erin shrugged. "His daddy is Veiron. The kid will grow up swearing whether he learns it from us or not. It's in his blood. Now, if you don't mind, time is precious... tick tock... tick tock."

He shook his head, a flicker of something like despair in his eyes, and sighed. As if he could do a better job raising a kid? He hadn't even known she had existed until she was thirty, and then he had killed the man she loved in order to awaken her powers. He was hardly Father of the Year material.

"Astaroth grew restless and the others with him. They realised their divine purpose had been taken from them and they sought to set themselves up in positions of power within Hell, declaring themselves princes." The scene behind the Devil changed to show a replay of a battle in Hell. "They tried and failed to seize power in an area of my realm. I personally defeated them, showing them just how powerless they were now."

Erin called that rubbing salt in their wounds.

He sneered, as if he had heard her thoughts. He might have. Sometimes the telepathic link sort of popped open at the worst times, and it went both ways. She shuddered, still scarred by finding herself suddenly linked to her father at extremely disturbing moments. The glee he took from torturing demons and mortals she could handle. The times she got a headful of dirty thoughts while he was making out with a woman, that she could not handle.

"I sealed them in another crystal chamber far beneath my fortress. I discovered they were gone shortly after the Great Destroyer had awoken." The Devil preened his black hair back and pinned Lysia with red-edged golden eyes.

Asmodeus shifted in front of her again. "They took Nevar. What do they want with him?"

The Devil smiled. "The same thing I want. To get out of Hell. Only, their methods may be a touch more destructive than mine."

Lysia snarled and moved around Asmodeus. The dark angel caught her wrist and held her back.

"Say it straight and stop dancing around the subject," Erin snapped, losing patience fast. "None of your cryptic shit today. Tell me what these four bastards are planning."

"Very well." The screen behind him disappeared and he adopted a dull flat tone, as if he was reciting something inconsequential. "They will seek to awaken her in order to set her on a rampage that will cause the apocalypse, at which point the gates of Hell will be destroyed as she attempts to escape this place and the princes of Hell will be set free."

"How?" Erin didn't like the sound of that.

He sighed and waved his hands around. "There are many gates in Hell. Each gate is part of the seal between this realm and the mortal one. They are each a barrier that allows passage of certain species only, fallen angels not included."

Meaning, he couldn't use the gates and neither could the four angels who had taken Nevar.

"Only creatures sanctioned by Heaven, who controls the seals if the original angel's blood was last spilled in that realm, which it was, can pass through. The seals stop me from leaving, and therefore stop every other fallen angel too."

Erin had passed through a gate herself when escaping Hell and it had been a strange experience, like passing through a wall of burning liquid that hadn't quite wanted her to escape from it. Maybe it had been her father's blood in her veins that had made the barrier cling to her, briefly mistaking her for him.

"How will destroying the gates help these fallen angels leave Hell?" she said and looked at the others to see if they were following. Her sister and Marcus had moved closer to Veiron, coming to flank him and Dante, leaving Asmodeus and Apollyon to protect Lysia.

"Each gate is part of the seal between this realm and the mortal one. You *were* following that part, were you not?" the Devil snapped and she huffed and folded her arms across her chest.

"Don't make me want to slap you. You make me want to slap you and I won't let you meet Dante properly."

His expression soured and he glanced at Dante. "Fine. The gates form a circle around Hell that stops all fallen angels from leaving. With them all intact, the princes cannot leave Hell. Whenever I defeat Apollyon or I spill the original angel's blood in my realm, the gates are altered and I am granted passage. The princes can also pass through too. Why else would I have lost so many battles against Apollyon... a whole string of them over the last few millennia leading up to this point?"

Apollyon stood a little taller and pinned the Devil with blue swirling eyes filled with a burning desire to attack him. Erin hoped he managed to hold that urge in check. If her father was telling the truth, and for once he appeared to be, then they couldn't risk her father accidentally defeating Apollyon and releasing the four princes.

"You lost because you can't risk these princes going free," Erin offered when her father looked as if he required an answer to his question and wouldn't continue without one.

He clapped. She gave him the finger.

"We really must improve your manners, Daughter."

Erin shrugged that one off. "I get them from you."

He looked as if he wanted to bite her for that one, but settled for smoothing his black jacket down instead and sighing. "I had a duty to contain them, and they were contained until Nevar awakened the destroyer."

His golden gaze slowly edged back to Lysia. "They will use you to destroy the gates. You are the only thing powerful enough to do such a thing. Once four gates fall, they will be able to use a fifth to leave this place and head out into the mortal realm. I would suggest you all do something about them before that happens."

Erin mulled over everything he had said, frowning at him the whole time. He was powerful enough to fight the princes, but he couldn't leave the bottomless pit, which was a reasonable excuse for him kicking back and letting her and her friends handle the situation that he could easily deal with.

What set her on edge and had alarm bells ringing in her head was his tone and how he sounded a little too much like he actually believed they could save Nevar, stop Lysia from awakening, and keep the princes trapped in Hell.

"What gives? You want us to fail so the gates will be opened and you can go free?" she said and couldn't help adding, "Why haven't you destroyed the gates before now and left? You disobeyed and left the pit to see me in the prison, so you can wander away from it now that you're drawing close to fighting Apollyon again. You could just go around destroying the gates and set yourself free."

The Devil shook his head. "It is not so easy. I would not be freed by the fall of only four gates. I would need to destroy all six hundred and sixty-six seals in order to free myself. Not just the gates, but the smaller seals buried in the ceiling and the ground and the walls. In doing so, I would destroy the world, so it seemed rather pointless to me, as my intention is not to end my existence and the existence of everything else with me."

"Heaven would stop you before you could break them all anyway," Apollyon said.

Her father nodded this time. "True. Hell is my prison, but I have made it my home, and I have no intention of allowing four self-proclaimed princes destroy it. I will tell you where they are hiding and you will put a stop to their plans."

Erin smiled at that and the bite in his tone. "You're getting soft in your old age."

He returned her smile with a warm one of his own and approached her, taking the steps down to the paved area of the courtyard where she stood. "I think you have infected me with your sentimentalism. Now, I believe I am owed a moment with my grandson?"

She nodded, took Dante from Veiron, who reluctantly gave him up to her, and brought the boy to his grandfather.

The look on his face had her going against her better judgement, and he hadn't been an almighty pain in her arse for once and had actually helped them.

She ignored Veiron's warning scowl and held Dante out to the Devil.

Her father's golden eyes widened and leaped up to meet hers, a touch of uncertainty in them.

"Try anything funny and I'll kill you," she said sweetly.

He nodded and carefully took Dante from her, cradling him gently in his arms and canting his head so they were face to face.

Dante opened his eyes and smiled up at the Devil.

Erin swore her father melted a little.

He tickled Dante's nose and the boy wriggled and laughed, drawing a wide smile from her father.

"They mean to use Nevar to awaken the Great Destroyer," he cooed down at her son in a singsong voice. "They can kill him but it won't give them what they desire."

What did he mean by it wouldn't give them what they wanted? They wanted to leave Hell and if Lysia destroyed the gates, they would achieve that desire. Or wasn't that what they truly desired?

It was on the tip of her tongue to ask when the Devil slid his golden gaze her way and the coldness in it stopped her dead.

"Go home, Daughter, and take Dante with you. Do not set foot in this realm again until I allow it. Remain with your family. Only Asmodeus and the Great Destroyer will face the princes."

A chill went through her and her heart raced as her vision swirled in gory Technicolor through her mind.

Her father hadn't only sensed her pain and heard her thoughts after she had awoken from that terrible vision. He had seen it too. Her power to dream the future came from him.

It dawned on her that it hadn't been the angels she had met on the island in that vision. It had been the four fallen angels. They were the ones who would kill her and Dante.

"Sweet dreams, little Prince of Darkness. Until we meet again. I will not allow anything to happen to you or your mother. You have my word on that." He closed his eyes, pressed a soft kiss to Dante's forehead, and his power rose swiftly, driving everyone else to their knees.

Shadow wings tore through the Devil's suit jacket and streamed from his back as his obsidian horns curled from above his ears, parting his black hair, and his ears grew pointed. His black nails transformed into long claws, but he held them away from her son, cradling him gently in his demonic hands. His skin paled and lips darkened, and fangs flashed between them as he spoke, each word shaking the ground and hurting even her ears.

"I will personally kill them for their insolence this time."

CHAPTER 24

Nevar knelt on the sharp pebbly black ground on the small flat strip of plateau high above a valley. Black charred tree trunks spotted the landscape far below him and a bright golden streak snaked across the bottom of the slope that plunged down into the basin.

He breathed hard, fighting to shut down the agony tearing through him, burning in the lacerations on his arms and thighs, and across his stomach. The three angels who had transported him to this bleaker-than-usual patch of Hell had ensured he was too weak to be a bother to them, taking to the task with glee.

Correction. Not angels. Whatever these fiends were, they weren't angels.

They only wore the mask of an angel.

Their leader, the one with long white hair who had remained with Lysia when the others had taken him, stood at the edge of the plateau with his back to Nevar, his crisp white wings furled against his back.

The black-haired one sat on a boulder off to Nevar's left, holding the end of the length of silver chain that wrapped around Nevar's arms, pinning them behind him. Nevar hated him most out of the four. He reminded Nevar of Asmodeus and what that angel had done to him, trussing him up like a piece of meat with a similar chain and rendering him immobile and vulnerable. This chain drained his power and the cuts littering his body added to its effect. Combined with the fact he hadn't fed properly in over a month, it left him useless and weak, unable to fight them.

Something about this land negated his ability to cast a portal too. He had tried several times to call one the moment he had realised that the angels had taken him to another part of Hell, not to Heaven, and had concluded they were not the same angels he had met on the island. The vortex had refused to appear, much to the amusement of his foes. It hadn't taken them long to beat him into submission and get the chains on him. These angels were as powerful as the ones he had met on the island, if not more so.

He slid his gaze to the other two angels. They loitered together a short distance off to the right of him, discussing something in low whispered words.

In the demon tongue.

The scarlet-haired one seemed upset about something. Nevar had caught the pale-haired one, the largest of the group, calling him Leviathan. He wasn't familiar with the name.

He had heard of one of them though. When the white-haired one had arrived in a bright pale burst of light, the sort that Heaven used to transport angels, the black-haired angel had called him Lord Astaroth.

Nevar had thought that name had been little more than mortal folklore, but then he had thought the same thing about other angelic names too. If the Astaroth standing before him, his head held high and an air of arrogance seeping from his every pore, was the same Astaroth from legend, then he was an extremely powerful foe.

And by the looks of him and his band of men, and the things Nevar had managed to catch when they had been deep in discussion after Astaroth had returned, he had a bone to pick with Heaven, and possibly Hell too.

"Samael." Astaroth's deep voice swept across the land like darkness and he turned on the black-haired angel, his pale blue eyes cold but simmering with fire in their depths. "I asked you to keep our guest in check."

"He is in check." Samael tugged hard on the chain looped around Nevar's arms and he struggled to stop himself from falling on his side.

"If he is in check, why do I feel him glaring at me?" Astaroth curled his lip at Nevar, revealing the pointed tip of a canine. "Turn him around or something. He irritates me."

Nevar growled, the feral sound rumbling up his throat before he could stop it, and Astaroth's cold blue eyes narrowed on him.

"Threatening me?" Astaroth laughed and turned fully to face him. He stalked towards Nevar, an imposing figure in his jet-black tooled leather armour, and spread his white wings.

The angel came to tower over him, forcing Nevar to tip his head back and look up at the bastard to keep an eye on him.

"No," Nevar rasped, forcing each word past his bruised and battered throat. "Just wondering if you stole Mihail's face or he stole yours."

Astaroth lunged, slipped his fingers down the neck of Nevar's black breastplate and hauled him off the ground, bringing them face-to-face.

"Do not speak that name in my presence." Astaroth snarled, flashing sharp fangs, and hurled Nevar aside.

He crashed hard into the ground near Samael, who levelled a kick at his stomach and sent him tumbling across the sharp black rocks. Nevar grunted and gasped for air, his lungs burning with each strained inhalation. The son of a bitch laughed, stood and stepped onto his back, pinning him face down on the pebbles. They cut into him and he refused to give the angel the satisfaction of seeing his pain.

Nevar schooled his features, concealing both the physical agony caused by having his battered body shoved against the sharp stones and crushed beneath the angel's weight, and the emotional pain caused by finding himself at the feet of a stronger power again.

"What do you want with me?" Nevar slid his gaze to his left, towards Astaroth where he approached him, his icy eyes filled with sadistic pleasure. Nevar bit his tongue to hold back his growl, unwilling to allow these angels to hear his anger or his agony. They wanted him to react. They wanted to see him suffer. He wanted them to go to hell.

Astaroth paused by his head, looming over him, and smiled coldly. "You are a weakness we mean to exploit."

Nevar couldn't miss the irony in that one. He had done the very same thing to Asmodeus, seeking his weakness and discovering it in Liora in order to punish him. He was as bad as these four males, and he could see the error of his ways now that it was too late to correct his mistakes.

Part of his heart refused to regret what he had done, because it had brought him Lysia, a woman he would do anything to protect.

"What do you want with Lysia?" he spat out, unable to keep the dark edge from his voice as he glared up at Astaroth. "Why do you need a weakness of hers?"

Astaroth shifted his right foot and Nevar refused to flinch away. This male could do whatever he wanted to him and he wouldn't give the bastard the satisfaction of seeing his pain or his fear. The only thing he cared about now was Lysia and stopping their plans for her.

Astaroth furled his white wings against his back and ran his hands down their lengths, preening them. He took pride in those wings. They would be the first thing Nevar tore from him.

"We mean to awaken her."

A chill went through Nevar and he looked from Astaroth to the other two who had come to stand behind him, flanking him.

They meant to kill him in front of her.

"Why lure her here?" Darkness stirred within him, trickling through his veins right now but he knew it would soon become a flood that surged, obliterating everything in its path, and he would welcome it when it came. He would do whatever it took to protect Lysia from these fiends. "Why didn't you just kill me when you came to take me away?"

He cursed himself for falling for that one, but each of the four were a perfect replica of the angels he had met on the island. Or perhaps those angels were a perfect replica of these ones. Nevar's gut said that the Devil hadn't created these angels, not as he had Asmodeus. These had been made by Heaven and cast out by that realm, and replaced by better versions.

It would explain Astaroth's problem with hearing the name Mihail, and why these four seemed bent on awakening the destroyer. They wanted Heaven and Hell to pay for what it had done. He could understand that, could even sympathise a little, but he wasn't about to step back and let them carry out their plans.

Astaroth's eyes turned as frigid as the coldest depths of Antarctica and the combined power of all four angels pressed down on Nevar, turning his stomach and crushing his bones, reminding him that he was no match for them and wouldn't be even if he was at full strength.

"There is another part to the plan." Astaroth's lips curved into a wicked smile. "We required your friends to attempt to take you back, drawing the attention of our brethren."

Brethren?

The four angels he had met on the island?

"Why?" he said.

"It is none of your concern." Astaroth signalled to Samael and the black-haired angel stepped off Nevar's back and hauled him back onto his knees. "You will be dead soon and returned to Heaven, as we promised. You will forget everything and you will awaken to a different world, one where Heaven and Hell are no longer the only controlling powers."

Nevar barked out a laugh.

Astaroth's face darkened.

"It has been a while since Heaven and Hell were the only controlling powers." Nevar tipped his head back and narrowed his green gaze on Astaroth. "It has long been acknowledged by both realms that the group I have become a part of are a third power, and one neither realm dares to underestimate."

The white-haired angel glared down at him, fire beginning to break through the ice in his eyes, turning them bright gold.

Nevar held his gaze. "Lysia will not come alone… and those who come with her have enough power to defeat you."

The big pale-haired one smirked. "You did not mention your fate."

Nevar shifted his focus to him, feeling the edges of his irises beginning to turn violet with the darkness rising within him, pouring through his muscles now, crushing the pain and leaving him numb to it.

"My fate is what it is." Nevar twisted his arms, slowly flexing his muscles to see whether he was strong enough to break the chains that bound him yet and trying not to draw attention to what he was doing. "I cannot change that. As I am now, I'm not powerful enough to defeat you alone, and you will not give me a chance to fight you fairly."

All four of them shook their heads.

Nevar smiled.

"Do you mind if I try anyway?"

Darkness exploded over his skin, turning it inky midnight, and his black claws thickened and lengthened into talons. His black wings burst from his back, tearing through the chains that bound his arms. The silver links scattered, filling the shocked silence as they bounced across the basalt.

Nevar beat his broad wings and shot into the air. The light from the lava river below caught their feathers, reflecting back as a purple sheen. His horns curled, his skull aching as they emerged, flaring back from behind his ears and darkening to black. He snarled, his lips peeling back off his teeth as they all sharpened and his lower canines lengthened to match his fangs.

Astaroth was the first to regain his composure, calling a white blade to his right hand.

Nevar materialised both of his black curved swords in his hands and beat his wings, holding himself in the acrid hot air above the four angels.

He canted his head, narrowing his swirling violet gaze on Astaroth.

"What are you?" The white-haired angel growled that question through clenched teeth and signalled to the other three.

"You would have to ask my master that, but I do not think the King of Demons would grant you an audience, let alone an answer." Nevar pinned his wings back and swooped down on Astaroth.

"King of Demons? There is no king here. Only us princes." The male swung the glowing white blade at him but he was too slow, his actions sluggish compared with the speed at which Nevar could move when he was in this state.

Nevar landed his right boot on Astaroth's shoulder and grasped his left wing, sinking his talons deep through the white feathers and into muscle and bone.

Astaroth roared.

Nevar grinned. "I do not think such an impure being should have such pure wings."

He pressed down with his foot and pulled back with his hands at the same time, yanking on the offending wing.

There was another roar and Samael was coming at him, his twin black spears a blur as they shot towards Nevar. Nevar flashed his fangs and kicked off Astaroth, driving the angel into the path of his comrade's blow.

Samael's left spear nicked the angel's white wing where Nevar had gripped it and Astaroth turned on him with an unholy growl, his face twisted in dark lines as his power rose, all of it directed at Samael.

The black-haired angel grunted and stumbled backwards, his grey eyes blazing silver as he struggled to get his twin spears up in front of him to block the assault.

So easy to taunt and drive them against each other.

Nevar laughed.

It was short-lived.

Leviathan barrelled into him like a bullet, sending them both careening upwards. Nevar sent his blades away and wrestled with him, fighting for dominance as the angel beat his crimson wings, taking them higher. The red-haired angel slammed his left fist into Nevar's kidney, sending pain splintering across his stomach and ricocheting down his thigh. The male growled and struck again, harder this time, and Nevar grunted and doubled over in the air, barely managing to keep beating his wings to combat Leviathan as he drove them upwards.

He sucked down a hard, painful breath and grappled with the angel, managing to catch his fist as he tried to land another blow.

Nevar twisted it hard, contorting Leviathan's arm. The male let out a roar of pain and grabbed hold of Nevar's hair, bunching it into his fist and yanking on it. Nevar grinned and kept twisting, intent on breaking the male's arm.

His eyes widened as he sensed the power behind him.

He snarled and slammed his fist into Leviathan's jaw, driving it hard enough to crack the bone and loosen the angel's grip on him. Nevar brought his legs up between them, pressed them into Leviathan's stomach, and kicked hard, propelling him back to the ground at tremendous speed.

Nevar twisted in the air a split-second later, barely evading the sickle-shaped blades of the pale-haired angel, and beat his wings, shooting beneath him.

The big angel grunted and pursued him. Nevar used his speed to his advantage, slowly gaining distance between them, and called his black swords back to his hands.

"Ramiel," Leviathan hollered and the pale-haired angel broke away.

Nevar looked over his shoulder and watched him go, his gaze narrowing.

And flew straight into Astaroth.

The blow came out of nowhere, connecting hard with the underside of Nevar's jaw and snapping his head back, rattling his brain in his skull. Nevar flew upwards, trying to shake it off and stop his mind from spinning. He growled as his vision finally stopped splintering and found himself face-to-face with Astaroth.

The angel hovered a few metres above Nevar, looking down on him.

Nevar clutched his blades.

Astaroth spread his bloodstained wings and swept his white sword in a swift arc. A curve of light hung in the air, forming the path of the blade, and then it shot towards Nevar at sonic speed.

He tried to dodge it, furiously beating his black wings, but it grew as it approached, spanning more than a hundred feet. It caught his ankles and sent him spinning through the air, and knocked his swords from his hands. They tumbled through the air, plummeting towards the black valley, and disappeared as he sent them away. He spread his wings, stopping his descent, and unleashed more of his power, calling on all of it. His blades materialised in his hands. His talons grew longer, curved around their violet grips, and he turned dark purple eyes on Astaroth.

If he could defeat the angel, the others were bound to fall back. He could be with Lysia again.

Impossible.

He was no match for these angels.

There was only one thing he could do.

He could die here, before she could arrive and witness his execution. He had promised to return to her, and he wanted to keep that promise, but he wouldn't do it at the cost of her seeing him die and awakening as the Great Destroyer. She wanted a normal life, one without pain and suffering, and he wanted to give that to her.

Even if he couldn't share it with her.

It was time he took responsibility and corrected his mistakes.

He beat his wings and shot towards Astaroth, his swords at the ready. The angel sent another arc of light at him and he rolled to avoid it and flapped his wings again, gaining speed.

He sent one blade away and clutched the remaining one with both hands, and lowered it to his side. The distance between him and the white-haired angel closed.

Nevar roared and swept his blade up in an arc, pouring every ounce of his strength into the blow so it would deal damage even if Astaroth blocked it.

The angel did as he predicted, his white blade clashing with the black of Nevar's, and Nevar kept beating his wings, driving the angel back through the air with him. He snarled and clashed with Astaroth again, slowly increasing the distance between him and the others, separating them.

Astaroth was the most predictable out of the four. Unlike the others, he preferred to face his enemies alone rather than as part of a team, and it would be his undoing. One-on-one, Nevar was strong enough to deal damage to the angel. Not kill him. No. He was weakening with every second, his strength slipping as the wounds he had already sustained began to drain him again.

But he could provoke Astaroth into killing him.

He could drive the male into a rage where he would deal the final blow that would send Nevar back to Heaven before Lysia arrived, sparing her the pain of witnessing his death.

He would find a way to remember her, just as Veiron had remembered Erin.

He pressed his hand to his chest and swore it on the mark beneath his black armour.

Astaroth lashed out at him, cutting across Nevar's black wings. Pain tore through him, the agony so intense that it blinded him for a few seconds, sending him plummeting towards the ground. He ground his teeth and fought through the pain as he beat his wings, each flap sending fresh agony blazing through their bones.

He growled and barrelled into Astaroth, his shoulder striking the angel hard in his stomach between the pieces of his armour.

Nevar sank his talons into the male's side and tore through his flesh. The angel roared and smacked him on the side of his head with the hilt of his sword, sending his head spinning violently again. Nevar repaid him by sinking his fangs into the wound he had created above his hip and taking a great gulp of his blood before the male managed to knock him away.

Power flowed through him, a hazy warmth that left him feeling numb again, immune to the pain of his injuries.

Astaroth growled at him, baring his own fangs, and clutched his side. "You will pay for that."

Nevar wiped his mouth on the back of his hand and grinned. "Make me."

Astaroth's blade glowed brighter and white flames licked along the length of it. He beat his white wings and shot towards Nevar, diving through the hot thick air at him.

Nevar remained where he was, waiting. Welcoming.

Fury blazed in Astaroth's gold-edged-blue eyes, anger that was etched on his face as he sneered and laced his power. The angel drew his blade upwards, holding it in both hands above his head, and roared as he brought it down, aimed directly at Nevar's head.

Nevar closed his eyes.

He would find a way back to Lysia.

He swore it.

She would never be alone again.

"Astaroth." Samael's deep voice boomed from below them. "She comes."

Nevar's eyes shot open and Astaroth stopped above him, his blade mere millimetres from dealing the killing blow he had desired.

The white-haired angel's lips twisted into a cruel smile.

Despair went through Nevar and he turned, afraid of what he would see.

His eyes locked with Lysia's where she flew towards him beside Asmodeus, her leathery wings desperately beating the air as she reached for him.

Nevar reached for her, his heart slamming against his ribs.

His violet eyes widened.

White-hot pain blazed through his chest.

CHAPTER 25

"No!" Lysia reached for Nevar as the white blade sank into his chest and punched through his black armour, a stream of light beaming from its tip and cutting through the darkness of Hell.

Asmodeus roared beside her, his pain palpable, beating within his power as it rose and his horns emerged, his black hair fluttering back to reveal them. His golden eyes swirled into purple and shadows streamed over his hands as his nails became long deadly talons.

Her own claws underwent a similar transformation as she raced to reach Nevar, determined to prove to herself that it wasn't too late to save him.

The white-haired angel slowly turned his head towards her, his cold smile stoking the fury blazing in her heart.

She screamed and threw her hands towards him, blasting him away from Nevar with her telekinesis. The sword pulled free of Nevar's chest and blood burst from the wound, falling in a thick tangled ribbon from beneath his black breastplate as he hung in the air.

His head fell back and he dropped, his black wings fluttering upwards as the air battered him.

Lysia dove after him, tears blurring her vision briefly before they flowed across her temples, the speed of her flight driving them into her black hair.

The red-haired and black-haired angels flew into her path, blocking her way to Nevar.

She growled at them through her fangs and threw both of her hands forwards, slamming telekinetic blasts into both of them and thrusting them out of her way.

Her Avenging Angel

Asmodeus's black hand snapped around her wrist and he yanked her sideways just as a gleaming white blade slashed through the air where she had been.

The white-haired angel sneered at her, his gold-rimmed icy eyes filled with all the darkness of Hell.

She cursed him in her tongue, damning him, and left him to Asmodeus as she broke away from the angel and flew towards Nevar.

He was gone.

Pain burned like an ember in her chest that sparked an inferno.

She threw her head back and cried out her agony as the mark on her chest emerged, blazing bright purple and searing her. Her entire body shook as violent waves of pain pulsed through her, flowing outwards from the mark, and she pressed both hands to it.

Nevar.

The pain suddenly disappeared.

Her connection to him disappeared with it, leaving a void behind, a cold empty abyss within her that he had filled. She screamed and darkness poured in to fill the void he had left behind, a swirling black maelstrom of hatred and rage, a deep hunger for vengeance.

A world that would take him from her so cruelly was not a world worth saving.

She turned on the angels where they fought Asmodeus. He wore the same form as Nevar had done, his skin the colour of midnight and his vicious talons long and beautiful as he battled the angels, fury and sorrow shining in his violet eyes and radiating through his power.

She beat her wings as they began to grow, stretching wider. Her black hair fluttered against the breeze from her leathery wings and swept upwards, streaming back from her head and twisting into six long ribbons. A swirling black mist of rage and pain consumed her, threatening to take her over and devour her.

Her heart ached, briefly chasing back the change coming over her and halting it.

Asmodeus.

She didn't want to destroy this world or the people she had come to see as her friends.

Beneath her hands, the violet mark stuttered and faded.

Disappeared.

Shattered.

Rage swallowed her again, the surge of darkness too strong for her to contain as the seal broke.

Asmodeus paused and looked back at her, and she reached for him, tears blurring her vision.

"Tell them I am sorry... I never wanted this."

He beat his black wings and flew towards her, shaking his head as his violet eyes implored her to fight. She couldn't stop the change coming over her. She didn't have a choice.

She had to save him though, before it was too late and the darkness consumed the part of her that knew him, obliterating all that was good in her.

She held her hand out as her claws lengthened and darkness bled from them and into her skin. Her fingers thickened, her knuckles enlarging as her hand began to transform. She focused all of her will on Asmodeus and hit him with a telekinetic blast that sent him shooting into the shadowy distance, back the way they had come.

The darkness reached her elbows and she cried out as her wrist cracked and her hand stretched longer, flaring wider at the same time. White light shot across her sensitive vision and she roared as she realised the four angels had teleported.

She crashed onto the plateau and dug her hands into the black basalt, fighting her transformation. She didn't want this. She didn't want to destroy everything. Everyone. Their faces flickered through her mind and she kept picturing them and saying their names as pain tore her apart and pieced her back together.

Her leg bones snapped and distorted, her bare toes becoming talons as a tail grew from the base of her spine, ripping through her shorts. She screamed as her wings grew larger and black spikes burst down her spine as it stretched and her ribcage expanded beneath her black skin. Her cheekbones and jaw cracked as they reformed themselves, elongating into a long beaked reptilian jaw.

Black scales rippled over her skin and she roared as she grew, her paws crushing the rocks beneath her and becoming so large that she could barely stand on the plateau. Her tail whipped, the massive pointed barb smashing a section of the hill and sending it thundering down into the valley.

Her hair twisted tighter and hardened, becoming six curved horns.

Nevar.

She rose onto her powerful hind legs and beat her wings, holding herself steady. Smoke billowed from the lava below as each beat sent wind blasting across the valley.

The world would pay for what it had taken from her.

The faces in her mind winked out of existence one by one. She clung fiercest to Nevar's, determined not to surrender it and her knowledge of him, but the darkness was too strong, the rage too fierce. It burned away everything she knew and all that she felt, leaving only fury behind.

A dark urge to destroy everything.

She curled her talons into fists and bright orange glowed in the cracks between her scales. Heat burned in her chest, an inferno she would unleash upon this land. She would destroy everything.

She roared and released a devastating stream of fire that blasted the land below her, igniting the dead trees and melting the basalt, turning it back into lava.

The hill crumbled beneath her as she kicked off, lifting into the air with each heavy hard beat of her black wings.

Her violet gaze scanned the land, seeking her first target. The gate stood on the far side of the valley, carved into a sheer cliff face. She bared all her razor-sharp fangs and flew towards it. She would destroy everything.

Why?

She did not know.

She knew only infinite rage and an endless hunger for violence.

A hunger she felt sure would never be assuaged.

A patch of blood stained the ground below her. Spilled from an angel. She looked at it for a moment, feeling nothing, and then flew onwards.

Ahead of her, a legion of Hell's angels emerged from a swirling black vortex that stretched more than two hundred metres across.

She grinned and flew harder, the thought of destroying the puny army of the Devil too tempting to resist.

All who stood between her and the gates would die.

She would lay waste to this realm and gain her freedom.

And then she would lay waste to the mortal realm.

And after that, she would destroy Heaven.

She gathered all of the fire that burned in her veins, drawing it to her chest, and opened her mouth and unleashed it in a stream at the first wave of Hell's angels. They screamed as it incinerated them and she roared in victory.

The first of many.

There was no future for this world.

She would burn it all to ashes.

All would die.

CHAPTER 26

Pain echoed in his chest like a deep throbbing heartbeat, slow but steady, a heavy drumming that he found soothing for some reason, as if something else lived within him, encased behind his ribs, safe and secure there. A constant part of him. Forever.

Time unravelled behind his closed lids, twisting into reverse, filling his mind with images that flowed backwards. Darkness gave way to blinding light and that gave way to a vision of fear painted across the beautiful face of a woman. She flew backwards, distancing herself from him, and he looked down at his chest, seeing black armour and a white blade penetrating it. Agony joined the pain in his chest, a fiercer roar that overshadowed the quiet constant beat.

His heart shattered, not physically as the sword slid free of it, repairing the organ and then the point emerged from his armour, sealing the hole in it. It shattered because of an emotional blow, a wound so severe that nothing could heal it, a devastating fracture brought about by nothing more than knowledge.

Awareness that the beauty who had looked upon him with fear in her striking violet eyes would no longer be a part of him when he woke from the slumber of death that awaited him.

Awareness that she would witness that death and be torn from him, transformed by it into something she feared and thrust into a state that terrified her.

A state of loneliness.

The organ in his chest ruptured because of that knowledge alone.

And it shattered because he knew he would never see her again.

He had failed her.

Time continued to run backwards, reaching a point when he had been filled with a desire to spare her pain but clung to hope that he could still have forever with her, the future they both wanted with a hunger that consumed them.

The passing of seconds slowed to a crawl, the white-haired angel before him beginning to lose his smile before it came back and he moved forwards rather than in reverse.

Time sped now and he could only watch as the white sword punched into his chest, slicing clean through his heart, and could only look at the beauty as she raced towards him, her leathery wings beating furiously as she reached for him.

He reached for her.

He didn't want to die.

He wanted to live with her.

He stretched his hand out as his vision dimmed, the light fading as darkness encroached, coming to devour him with sharp teeth and swallow him whole.

Light burst back across his eyelids and he shot awake, his hand stretched above him.

Not towards the beauty but towards a black ceiling.

He frowned and gasped at air, sucking great mouthfuls down into his burning lungs. The pain in his chest continued its steady throb in the background of a fiercer ache, an agony that burned him to ashes.

He lowered his hand to his bare chest, pressed his fingertips to the material covering it, and curled his fingers into it, clutching the spot above his heart.

Where was he?

This wasn't Heaven.

This was Hell.

Wasn't he dead?

His head swam and the room spun violently with it, the black blurring together. A streak of bronze, crimson and cream appeared in the haze and he tried to focus on it. It shimmered and distorted, together with the noise in his ears that began to hush the constant drumming of pain in his chest.

"Nevar?"

The soft feminine voice curled around him, warming his bones but not easing the ache in his heart. This was not the beauty he had wanted to see on waking, yet he felt glad to see her as she slowly came into focus. Her hazel eyes brightened but the concern in them didn't fade as she approached him. She sat beside him, smoothing her scarlet short-sleeved top over the waist of her black jeans and fidgeting a little with it, as if she wasn't sure what to do.

Or she was nervous. Why?

His chest heaved with each laboured breath beneath his hand and he struggled to comprehend his surroundings. While the female had come into focus for him, they refused to do the same, remaining a black swirling blur.

She lightly pressed a hand to his forehead and drowsiness ran through him, a warm sedation that made his limbs feel heavy. His hand fell from his chest and struck his thighs, resting on the material covering him.

"Asmodeus," she called and he frowned.

He knew that name. The name of his master.

He shook his head in an attempt to clear it and she caught his cheeks, murmuring softly to him.

"Try to keep still. We weren't sure how you would be when you came around. You look a little groggy." She leaned in closer, peering into his eyes one at a time. "How are you feeling?"

Numb.

Confused.

Asmodeus entered, a hazy blur of cream and black and gold. He came into focus as he moved closer and the grim edge to his expression awakened a barrage of memories. He had been there. He had been with the beauty.

Lysia.

His female.

Nevar. His name was Nevar. He had died. Hadn't he?

"He does not look good," Asmodeus said, a glimmer of concern in his golden gaze. "Do you remember us?"

Nevar nodded.

"Master." He shifted his gaze from Asmodeus to the woman. "Witch. Liora."

He forced his hand up to his chest and splayed his fingers across it. "Nevar. In Hell."

He looked down at his body and it came rushing back. Black skin covered him, not just up to his forearms as it normally did. It covered all of him. His claws pressed into the bandages around his chest. Blood stained the cream material, crusty and near black. Old.

How long had he been sleeping?

Dead.

He managed to lift his gaze back to Asmodeus.

His master read the silent question in his eyes. "Almost three days. We were not sure what would happen or if you would ever wake up."

"I died." He needed to put that one out there, because he had felt the blade pierce his heart and burn it away with some sort of light. He had felt death's cold embrace.

He had expected to wake in Heaven.

Asmodeus nodded. "You did not disappear on dying though. When... when Lysia hurled me away from her, and was... in the midst of... her transformation, I returned unnoticed and retrieved your body."

"Wait... no. Lysia." Nevar shook his head, unable to bring himself to believe what Asmodeus was saying.

His master cast him a solemn look before dropping his gaze to his feet. "She witnessed your death as the fallen angels desired, Nevar. She is... not as she was."

Meaning she had awoken to her true purpose. She had become the creature he had often studied on the door panel, an immense dragon with six horns.

"How did I come back?" Nevar looked from Asmodeus to Liora, and then down at himself. He still wore his other form but it slowly began to fade as he focused on himself, seeking control over it. The shadows swept outwards from the spot above his heart, leaving pale skin behind, and didn't stop until they had reached just above his elbows.

"We all discussed that and we think it has something to do with your contract with Asmodeus and how it came about. You have his blood in your body, connecting you to him and this realm. You did die, and you were reborn, but as his servant and within this realm." Liora reached across and placed her hand over his on his chest. "I'm glad you came back to us."

He was too. He shifted his black hand, capturing hers, and gently held it. He still remembered everything and still had the strength his contract with Asmodeus gave to him, power beyond that which he had ever had when serving Heaven. He was grateful for that. For once, he was glad that he had made a contract with Asmodeus. He had feared death and forgetting everyone, and being reborn in Heaven with no recollection of his friends, and Lysia.

The bed beneath him shook and dust rained down from the ceiling.

"What is happening?" He looked to Asmodeus for the answer.

"Lysia," Asmodeus said, the grimness not leaving his expression. "She has already destroyed three gates. Every gate she destroys has an impact on the mortal realm, causing great devastation around the area where that gate to Hell exists. An earthquake has levelled much of the area around Chennai in India, causing a tidal wave that has wreaked destruction across many countries. The forces of Heaven and Hell are trying to stop her before she can bring down the next gate, both to end the devastation in the mortal realm, and to contain the four angels who planned all of this. If the fourth gate falls, they will fly free of Hell."

All turned against her. No one was on her side.

She was alone.

"No." Nevar swung his legs over the edge of the bed. "I have to go to her. She will be scared and confused… hurting… and now they want to kill her or sentence her to a fate worse than death by imprisoning her with nightmares of her defeat? I will not let that happen."

He stood and his knees gave out. Asmodeus was before him in a flash, catching him before he hit the floor and carefully settling him back on the bed.

"You are in no condition to fight." Liora took hold of his arm, as if that would stop him from attempting to rise again.

She could unleash every spell at her disposal on him and he wouldn't stop. He would reach Lysia.

"I do not care. I have to see her," Nevar snapped and tried to stand again but Asmodeus planted his hands on his shoulders and pinned his backside to the bed. He didn't have the strength to force Asmodeus to release him, and his master wasn't even using much of his strength to hold him in place. Despair went through him, twisting his insides and pulling a snarl from his lips. "She has to see me… she needs to see me."

"She will see you," Asmodeus whispered and loosened his grip on Nevar's shoulders. "But she does not remember any of us. There is no recognition in her eyes when she looks upon us. We tried… but you might succeed where we have failed."

Nevar clutched his chest and knew that the mark that had been on it was gone now. How could he make her remember him? When he had come around, he hadn't remembered who he was or who anyone else was. He had merely existed.

His memories had been all that he had together with tangled emotions that had felt distant and unreal, not really a part of him.

Was that how Lysia felt?

He didn't believe how he had felt in those moments when he had been unconscious and witnessing a replay of his death had anything to do with that process of death and rebirth. The loss of his sense of self and his knowledge of those he set eyes on had stemmed from his connection with Lysia. She suffered as he had and that was why she hadn't recognised Asmodeus and the others. She had forgotten them.

Or those memories had been locked away, trapped beyond her reach.

Nevar had to hope that was the case and that somehow he could get through to her and restore those memories for her.

"I will find a way," he whispered and then spoke with more conviction. "I swear I will get through to her and I will stop this."

Asmodeus nodded. "You will need your strength if you are going to survive until you can get through to her."

He offered his arm and Nevar realised that there was something different about his master. Asmodeus wore vambraces with a rampant dragon on them and had chest armour. The pointed slats of armour around his hips were shiny and new too.

He stared up at his master, knowing there was only one explanation for what he was witnessing.

Asmodeus lifted his broad shoulders in an easy shrug that didn't hide the discomfort in his eyes. "My master decided I needed full armour again."

It must have grated on Asmodeus's pride to have the Devil restore it so easily when he had been without it for so long, left vulnerable at the whim of his master. It had taken the end of days for the Devil to care enough to restore the pieces Asmodeus had lost throughout the centuries in his service.

Asmodeus tugged at the round edge of the collar and pulled a face. "It is more stifling and restrictive than I remember."

Nevar nodded in agreement. He had often found armour to be a hindrance, especially when not in combat. He never had fathomed how some angels managed to sleep in it.

"Now you look even more like Apollyon." Nevar couldn't resist slipping that one out quietly.

Asmodeus bared his fangs on a growl. "I can kill you again, if you wish? We know you will come back now."

Liora stood and stepped between them.

"Now, now, boys. Lysia needs us." She looked over her shoulder at Asmodeus. "If you kill him now, it will be days until he wakes up again. Kill him for it later."

Nevar stared at her, unable to believe she had just said such a thing to Asmodeus, practically condoning his killing him. She knew that her lover would take it as permission.

"I am joking," Liora said and when his expression didn't change from one of horror, she looked back at Asmodeus, and adopted a firm tone. "It was a joke. Don't you even think about killing him. I'm banning all attempts to kill Nevar. You were doing so well at getting along."

Asmodeus huffed and placed his hands on Liora's shoulders, over her crimson gypsy-style top. "Very well. I will not kill him. May I maim him a little?"

"No," she snapped and her dark angel's face fell and he sighed again. "Now be nice and give him something to eat."

The gold-edged black vambrace around Asmodeus's right forearm disappeared.

Saliva pooled in Nevar's mouth and he stared at the smooth flesh on the inside of Asmodeus's forearm, his hunger rising as his fangs slowly descended. He needed blood and wouldn't deny himself this time. It would give him the strength to fight for Lysia and protect her.

"I took blood from Lysia." Those words slipped like a confession from his lips as his gaze darted to Liora, his green eyes meeting her hazel ones. She smiled softly and he lowered his focus to his bare knees, realising he wore only his black loincloth. His gaze sought his armour. It rested on a chair near the foot of the bed in the black-walled room. "Only a little... I was afraid to take more. I just wanted to feel the connection between me and Lysia strengthen again."

"What?" Liora said and he felt sure she was angry with him for breaking his programme and taking blood, but she had looked as if she had been fine with it. She crouched in front of him, her hazel eyes locking with his. "What do you mean, again?"

"She took blood from me on the island. I fed her and it made the link between us stronger. We could feel each other more clearly. I wanted to feel that again, and we exchanged blood here in Hell, before the four angels came and took me away."

He had barely finished explaining before she was on her feet and rushing from the room.

Asmodeus watched her go, a frown marrying the black slashes of his eyebrows, and then looked back at him, desire for an explanation written in every line of his face.

Nevar shrugged. "I thought perhaps you would know why she ran away. Is she angry with me?"

His master shook his head and offered his arm. "Feed properly now and regain your strength, because you will need it in the fight to come."

Nevar was swift to take it, capturing Asmodeus's arm in both of his hands and drawing it to him, and sinking his fangs into it before his master could change his mind. Asmodeus's blood flooded his mouth and flowed down his throat, instantly absorbing into his body. Power rushed through him, strength he had forgotten he possessed, as he fed deeply, drawing everything that Asmodeus was offering him into himself.

Hope filled his heart, given life by the renewed strength flowing in his veins.

Hope that he now had the power to save Lysia.

The ground shook again, more violently this time, and Asmodeus withdrew his arm and ran his tongue over the puncture wounds. Nevar licked his lips, relishing every last molecule of blood, unwilling to waste any of them.

"I will help you reach Lysia and so will the others." Asmodeus lowered his arm and the vambrace appeared around it again.

"The others?" Nevar flexed his fingers and wriggled his bare toes, testing his body. It felt stronger now, more capable of holding his weight, but he didn't want to risk rising from the bed until he felt sure he wouldn't fall.

Asmodeus nodded and Nevar listened hard. The voices were distant but they were there. Everyone was in the castle with him and they were all willing to fight on his side for the sake of Lysia. They were going to fight on her side.

He wasn't sure what to say.

Until he realised with dread that if everyone was present, it meant his ward was too.

"Erin," he said and Asmodeus shook his head and pressed one hand to Nevar's left shoulder.

"She could not come. The Devil is forbidding her from entering this realm and has sent his men to guard her. Veiron is there with her."

He was glad of that. Her incredible power would have been of use and an advantage to them in the battle to protect Lysia, but her presence would have been a disadvantage too. Everyone would have been worrying about her and Dante.

For once, he didn't think the Devil was a complete bastard. He was doing the right thing by keeping Erin away from the battle and Nevar hoped it meant she would be safe and so would Dante. He wouldn't let the future she had seen happen. He would fight to protect her too.

"Come." Asmodeus took hold of him and helped him onto his feet.

Nevar walked with his assistance to the door of the bedroom and then made his own way from there, following Asmodeus down the black corridor towards the voices.

They had gathered in the main living space of what remained of the fortress and all stopped to look at him as he entered.

"The dead walks," Taylor drawled with a wicked smile from where she sat on the huge table, a book balancing on her lap. In her black combat gear of knee-high boots, jeans and t-shirt, and with her sleek black hair, she almost blended into the furniture and walls beyond her. Her blue eyes sparkled at him. "Welcome back to the land of the living… what's left of it anyway."

He stumbled into the long expansive black room and over to the obsidian rectangular table that occupied most of the space in the centre of it. He pressed his left hand against it for support and rested there, slowly beginning to feel stronger as his body used the blood Asmodeus had given him to nourish and restore itself.

He scanned the occupants of the room.

Liora stood at the far end, frantically scanning one of the massive bookshelves that lined the walls at the end and to the right of Nevar. Serenity was working with her, looking extremely out of place in her cream summer dress and with her long bright golden hair.

Marcus and Amelia stood off to his left, besides the large fireplace, both of them dressed in their silver armour but neither with their wings out. Amelia bore several wounds on her bare arms and legs, and one on her face that darted across her forehead and into her silver hair. Marcus was busy wrapping a bandage around a deeper wound on her upper left arm, his silver-blue gaze locked on his work and his dark hair falling down to brush his forehead.

"Where is Einar and Apollyon?" Nevar looked around the room again and added, "Where are the mutts?"

Asmodeus growled from behind him and then crossed the room to his black throne and sprawled himself out on it. "They are guarding the fortress outside and will come if they spot anything."

"The mutts, or Einar and Apollyon?" Nevar frowned.

"Romulus and Remus."

Serenity brought a book to the table and set it down. "Mon ange is… ah… scouting?"

Asmodeus nodded when she looked uncertain. "Einar and Apollyon agreed to head out to see the progress of Lysia. Heaven and Hell are trying to drive her to within the reach of the Devil."

Nevar growled at that. "No. We cannot let that happen. He will kill her… or send her back to sleep. I have to reach her before then."

He paused and ran back over what Asmodeus had said.

"Is Apollyon carrying Einar?" Because the angel was in a state of limbo due to his romantic relationship with a half-demon, stripped of his wings but still listed as an angel of Heaven.

Taylor's smile brightened. "Don't be silly."

"But he does not have wings." Nevar wasn't sure why she thought him silly for pointing out the obvious. Apollyon would be at a disadvantage carrying Einar around with him.

"Who says I do not have wings?" Einar entered with Apollyon in tow and Nevar could only stare at the tawny-haired male. Dusky brown wings arched behind him, their long feathers brushing the floor and the greaves of his dull-gold-edged earthy armour as he walked. Einar shot him a smile. "I was one of Heaven's best hunter angels… and it would appear that my case was heard and judged just in time for them to reinstate me and use me in this fight. Strange that, don't you think?"

Nevar shook his head. "Very odd."

Apollyon slapped Einar on the back and the hunter angel lurched forwards.

"You would almost think they were going to leave you wingless for the rest of your years, but had a sudden change of heart when they realised they were running low on experienced angels," Apollyon said with a smile that fell away as he sobered and turned to face the rest of them. "It is not good. Lysia is close to the area of the Devil's prison. She is heading for the plateau, driven there by the First Battalion of Hell's angels. She will be within reach of the Devil soon."

"We have to reach her before that happens." Nevar called his armour. The violet-edged black breastplate formed over his chest first and the back plate appeared and linked with it over his shoulders and under his arms. His vambraces followed, the rampant dragons on them matching the ones on Asmodeus's armour. The slats around his hips materialised and his boots came after them, shortly before the plates of his greaves completed his armour.

He released his black wings and flapped them to bring his feathers into line, and held out his hand, preparing to call a portal that would take him to the plateau.

"Wait." Liora rushed over to him with a thick tome opened and pressed to her chest. She slammed it down onto the black table, drawing everyone's focus to her. "You need to get through to Lysia somehow."

"I know that," Nevar snapped. What did she think he had intended to do?

Asmodeus snarled at him and stood, a towering wall of muscle and dark menace. "Tone, Nevar. Mind how you speak to my witch."

"I am sorry," Nevar said to Liora and she just smiled. "Please continue."

She spun the book to face him and pointed at a lot of gibberish on it. "If you can calm her and bring her back, I think I can restore the seals on your chests. Blood. It's all about blood. You said it yourself. When you shared blood, the connection grew stronger. It might still exist. Only the marks are gone… but the link is still there, buried in your blood… like your contract with Asmodeus."

His hand came up to his chest and he didn't dare hope she was speaking the truth and was actually able to do what she was saying.

Serenity came around her and peered down at the book, her hazel eyes scanning the pages. "This is a big spell. You will need help. I will help."

Liora nodded and clutched her hand. "Thank you. We can do this. Blood magic… it will be dangerous but we can do it."

Nevar caught the concern in Asmodeus's eyes as he looked at Liora as she excitedly discussed everything with her cousin in French.

He pressed his palm to his master's shoulder, drawing his focus to him. "If it looks as if it might hurt her, I will not let her do it."

Asmodeus swallowed and nodded, and then the emotions in his golden eyes cleared and he straightened, rising to his full height. "Liora, Serenity and Taylor will all remain here. The rest of us will head to the plateau and intercept Lysia before she can reach the sphere of the Devil's power."

Everyone nodded in agreement.

Nevar drew a deep breath. In for five. Out for five. He fought for calm among the raging storm of his emotions, a violent clash between hope and fear. No matter what he saw, no matter how she appeared, she was his Lysia inside.

He pulled in another slow breath, filling his lungs up from the bottom, and exhaled.

Cast his hand out before him, forming a swirling black maelstrom that would take him to the plateau.

Stepped into the void with confidence in his heart.

Vowed to never give up.

Not to save the world.

No.

He wouldn't fight for the world.

He would fight for his whole world.

He would fight for her.

He would save her.

CHAPTER 27

Nevar stepped out of the portal and onto the wide plateau that stood above the bottomless pit. The distant ring of screams instantly snapped his attention off to his right, away from the Devil's fortress where it rose into the inky sky of Hell ahead of him, surrounded by a ring of boiling lava.

At the very edge of his vision, a battle raged. Fire blazed a trail across the darkness, shuttering everything else with its brightness. More screams came, flashes of white light flickering like the most violent of lightning storms as Heaven recalled the masses of the fallen. Pandemonium.

The apocalypse.

Fire reigned all across the furthest reaches that he could see. Hell was burning to ashes before his eyes. With each swathe of flames that burned the sky came more bright flashes, the dead angels disappearing at an alarming rate.

A fierce shiver went through him like a bolt of electricity and he pressed his hand to the breastplate of his black armour.

Lysia.

She was aware of him.

In the midst of the distant darkness, twin violet spots glowed, directed at him. Horizontal bands of orange rushed up from below towards those purple eyes and another burst of fire erupted from between jagged teeth, each larger than he was tall.

More white flashes punctured the darkness as screams echoed around the cavern of Hell and the ground shook as the beast advanced, emerging from the shadows as it approached a wide snaking river of lava.

His heart launched into his throat, the sight of her stealing his breath.

He hadn't been prepared for her appearance after all.

She stood taller than he had anticipated, the clawed tips of her enormous black leathery wings almost scraping the ceiling of Hell in places. Her great talons ploughed the basalt with each hard step forwards, shaking the realm and causing cracks to splinter outwards from beneath her paws. She swiped with her long tail, cutting a path through the angels and Hell's angels swarming around her, the barbed tip skewering several of them in the process and sending them back to Heaven.

Her crocodilian jaws opened again and her roar shook the hot air as she unleashed another devastating stream of fire, decimating her foes and taking out an entire legion of hunter angels with one blast.

She threw her head back and the six black curved horns that grew from above her eyes and her ears on either side of her head shone in the light of the fire as she directed it upwards, towards a contingent of Hell's angels who had been coming down at her. They screamed as one as her flames tore through them, incinerating their wings and leaving them plummeting towards the ground.

Several angels made it through and attacked her, their blades bright arcs as they hacked at her scaly black body. She whimpered and veered right, trying to evade them as she snapped at them with her teeth and swung her right paw at them. He looked in the direction she was heading and growled through his fangs. The prison.

Within the sphere of the Devil's power.

Nevar had seen enough.

He ran towards the edge of the plateau, beating his black wings as he picked up speed, and sensed the others following him, bringing up the rear.

Nevar launched from the edge of the plateau and dropped into the valley, his wings pinned against his back until the last moment, when the ground came up at him and he spread them and shot across the terrain. He had to keep low. If he could fly beneath the angels attacking her, she might not see him until he was close enough to reach her.

He beat his wings and swung up at an angle on his right, avoiding an outcrop of rocks, and levelled off again, flying so low he could reach down and drag his claws across the ground if he wanted to.

Those claws altered as he unleashed his other form, calling all of his strength to the fore. He would need it if he was going to save her.

The inky darkness swept over his skin, turning it all the colour of night, and he ground his teeth as his horns pushed, cracking through his skull to flare back from behind his ears. His claws became thick talons and his wings gained a violet shimmer as he flew over patches of lava, swaying left and right to remain over solid ground and avoid the intense heat of the pools.

Asmodeus caught up with him, in the midst of his own transformation, his skin already obsidian and his horns curving through his black hair. His eyes flashed violet and the golden edge of his armour darkened to black before shining purple. Asmodeus looked across at him, nodded, and banked left, heading away from him and towards the prison.

Apollyon followed him, his broad black wings beating the air and his dark ponytail streaming behind him as he gained speed to keep up with Asmodeus as he shot towards the prison.

Amelia and Marcus remained behind Nevar with Einar.

The great beast unleashed another ear-splitting roar and swatted a group of angels from the division of death away from her left side, sending them flying through the air and crashing into the ground, throwing a long streak of black dust up into the air.

She turned towards them and Nevar gave a growl of his own when he saw the blood streaming down her front and leaking from deep wounds on her hindquarters.

He beat his wings and shot beneath a legion of Hell's angels hovering at a safe distance, all of them in their black demonic forms, their glowing red eyes locked on Lysia.

Waiting to attack her.

Nevar wouldn't let it happen. He was here now. No one would touch her.

He brought his right leg down, swiftly kicked off the ground to change direction without losing speed and shot upwards. He flapped his wings and stared up at her head over a hundred feet above him. She was far bigger than he had ever dreamed possible but it wasn't going to deter him. He would reach her.

Her violet gaze swung his way, the elliptical pupil flaring for a moment before thinning again.

"Lysia," he called above the noise of a thousand wing beats, the sound of angels preparing another wave of attack. "Look at me, Lysia. I am here. I am alive."

She reared back and swung her left paw at him. He pinned his wings back and dropped beneath her blow and unfurled them again, giving one hard flap to bring him shooting higher on her defenceless side. She snarled and snapped at him, and he beat his wings and shot backwards, beyond the reach of her fangs.

"Lysia!" He stopped right in front of her, at eyelevel to her, and held his hands out. "Recognise me."

She stilled.

His hope soared.

Fiery cracks appeared between the broad black plates across her chest, a dull glow at first but rapidly becoming fierce white. She arched her head back on her long neck and the light rushed up her throat. Not good.

The moment she opened her jaws, Nevar dropped, his wings tucked hard against his back to streamline himself. Heat chased him downwards. He wouldn't make it.

He desperately threw a portal beneath him and fell into it, reappearing in the air above her.

She shrieked and the spikes down her back shimmered violet.

He had the distinct impression he had just pissed her off even more.

"Lysia. Listen to—"

He grunted as six guardian angels barrelled into him and quickly called his black blades to his hands. A bright blue orb exploded below him and his breath hitched until he saw it was Amelia defending Lysia, driving back the wave of angels coming at her from all directions. More blinding bursts of blue light lit the darkness, coming faster as Marcus joined the fight.

Nevar wrestled with the angels, trying to break free so he could gain enough distance to take them down.

Pain exploded across his back and he shot downwards with the angels. He crashed into the basalt and tumbled across it, his wings twisting beneath him, taking the brunt of the damage from Lysia's blow.

The moment he stopped rolling, he pressed his hands into the dirt and shoved himself up, his blades at the ready to deal with the guardian angels.

Einar beat him to them, taking on all six with a single silver sword, his tawny wings tucked against his back as he fought with skill that awed Nevar. He would thank him later, when Lysia was back in his arms and safe again. He wasn't sure how he was meant to get her to transform back, but he would find a way. He kicked off and grunted with each beat of his wings that sent fire arcing along his bones.

Lysia swung a meaty paw at the Hell's angels now attacking her. Nevar snarled and flew harder, setting his sights on them. He had to drive them away before he could try to get through to her again.

Golden light shone in the left side of his vision and he briefly looked there. It lit the area around the prison and screams rent the air from that direction. Apollyon. He could feel his master there too.

Her Avenging Angel

Focus on Lysia, not me. Reach her. We will hold back the reinforcements.

Nevar was tempted to snap back at Asmodeus that he was focused on Lysia but he did as his master instructed and turned his gaze back to her. Apollyon and Asmodeus were fighting to hold back Heaven and Hell's reinforcements. Amelia, Marcus, and Einar were taking down the current wave of several legions from both sides. They were all fighting to give him this chance, risking their lives for Lysia. He hoped he could make her see that.

She wasn't alone.

The world wasn't against her.

They were with her.

He swung his black blade at the first Hell's angel, catching him across the patch of exposed skin between his obsidian back plate and the strips protecting his hips. The immense black-skinned demonic angel turned on him, his eyes glowing crimson, and bared his sharp red teeth.

Nevar swung again and the male blocked him with one red blade and drove the other one he held at him. Nevar shoved with his first blade, knocking the angel off balance, and slashed with his second one, clashing with the red one aimed at him. Sparks showered as they struck each other and Nevar pressed forwards, beating his wings to drive the demonic angel backwards.

His senses pricked and he twisted towards the demonic angel behind him, swinging wildly with his left blade to block the sneak attack. His sword struck the red blade of the black spear the demonic angel wielded but didn't block it completely. It bounced off his blade, scraped over his vambrace and sliced into his biceps.

Lysia roared and turned furious violet eyes on him and the Hell's angels. She launched her right paw at them, her huge black talons cutting through the air. It struck the first angel and she curled her talons around him and crushed him in her fist. Blood rained down from her closed paw.

The nostrils on her beak flared and she bared her black fangs as she dropped the first dead angel and swung again.

Nevar dodged her blow and her paw slammed into the angel who had cut him, sending the male careening like a rocket to the ground and crashing into a low black hill.

"Lysia," Nevar shouted and turned towards her as she reared again, rising up onto her hind legs and beating her wings.

Wind blasted against him and he furiously flapped his wings to keep from being thrown away from her as he called a portal. He let a gust send him into it and reappeared behind her, safe from the gale.

The Hell's angels didn't fare so well. They tumbled through the air and slammed into other angels, creating a swirling mass of them as they collided and struggled to maintain flight. His side didn't fare much better. Amelia and Marcus made an awkward landing and Einar ended up hurled into a group of five hunter angels, who all glared at him, evidently unimpressed that their kin was fighting against them.

More bursts of golden light exploded in the distance, followed by bright flashes of paler light as Heaven reclaimed the dead.

Lysia kept beating her wings, driving the angels away from her. When they were almost as distant as the immense grim long building of the prison, she slammed back down onto all fours and lumbered onwards.

No.

Nevar flew in front of her and she pulled her head back, snarling at him.

"Lysia... you cannot go that way. I will not let you." He spread his arms and his wings, uncertain whether she even understood him as she was now. He could feel the fury in her, the deep rage, and the hunger for violence.

Smoke curled from between her fangs.

Nevar prepared to teleport, his heart thundering against his chest and his hands shaking against the hilts of his blades. If she unleashed her fire on him at this distance, he wasn't sure he would be able to escape it, but he had to stand his ground. He wouldn't run from her.

Her huge violet eyes darkened and she swung her head to her left, away from him. She stared into the distance there, beyond the plateau. What had she seen?

He squinted and tried to make it out, and his stomach dropped when he saw it.

A gate, carved into a sheer wall of rock.

In front of it stood the four angels who had taken him.

They drew their weapons and Lysia roared, turned and thundered towards them.

He cursed the vile bastards for goading her into attacking a gate, but thanked them at the same time for luring her away from the area around the Devil's fortress, beyond the sphere of his power.

He wouldn't let the four angels get what they wanted. He wouldn't let Lysia destroy a fourth gate and set them free.

"We need to stop those angels," Nevar hollered at Amelia and Marcus where they stood below him to his right. He pointed towards the gate and they swung their heads in that direction.

They both nodded and spread their half-feather half-leather silver wings. Einar cut down the last of the hunter angels and rushed over to them, blood covering the front of his armour. Nevar hoped it belonged to his enemies. The male was a valuable asset and they couldn't afford to lose him.

A scruffy blond mediator angel flew towards the group and Nevar flexed his black clawed fingers around his blades and switched direction, heading towards them instead of the gate. The male approached from behind the group, unseen by them, wielding a long white and gold spear that matched his armour.

He landed and Nevar hit the ground between him and his allies, blocking the male's path to them.

Someone placed a hand on his shoulder and he tensed, swinging his gaze towards them. Einar.

"It is okay. This is Lukas, another friend."

Nevar looked back at the sandy-haired angel as he furled white wings against his back. The male nodded.

"I take it you are Nevar?" Lukas's green gaze ran over him. "An interesting appearance. Like your master's."

"How long have you been here?" Einar moved around Nevar, placing himself between him and Lukas.

The staff of Lukas's spear shortened, transforming it back into a sword. "I was assigned to the area around the prison. When I saw Apollyon arrive with Asmodeus, I knew I would find you all closer to the beast."

"She is not a beast," Nevar snapped and narrowed his violet eyes on the newcomer. "She has a name. Lysia. I will not let you and your kind harm her anymore."

Lukas's green eyes darkened. "I am not here to harm her. I am here to assist you. Lysander and the others are with me."

The angels of the apocalypse.

Nevar didn't believe they would be on Lysia's side. Their mission was to stop the apocalypse from occurring. He had no doubt that they would employ any method that would bring them success in that mission, including killing Lysia.

"Where are they?" Nevar said and stumbled when the ground bucked beneath his feet.

He swiftly turned to face Lysia and growled when he saw she had reached the gate and there was a swarm of angels heading towards her.

"If you meant to delay me, I will have your head," Nevar growled at Lukas and kicked off, beating his black wings hard as he tried to gain enough speed to reach her before the angels could.

"A touch distrustful, isn't he?" Lukas's voice drifted into the distance and Nevar had half a mind to shout that it wasn't that he had no faith in anyone; it was that he knew Heaven and he knew their tactics. That realm wasn't above forcing Lukas to delay them without him realising it.

Nevar flew harder, staying low and using the thermals coming off the cracks of lava that formed a web across the basalt to boost his speed and conserve his strength.

Lysia unleashed an enormous fireball at the gate, her focus seemingly turned to it now rather than Astaroth and his band of fallen angels. They fought the army of Heaven and Hell, keeping the angels away from her as she wreaked havoc on the gate.

Nevar shot beneath their radar and came up below them, his sights set on them.

He grunted as someone slammed into him and sent him tumbling through the air. He spread his black wings to stabilise himself and growled when he saw the blond angel hovering in the air between him and Astaroth, his blue eyes filled with cold fire.

"Stay out of this," Lysander said, his golden wings beating the air, shimmering in the light from the fires raging below them, devouring the black land. "I will deal with them."

The blond angel turned, gave one hard beat of his wings and shot towards the four angels.

Samael turned flinty silver eyes on Lysander and said something. Leviathan looked down, his golden gaze flickering with something akin to amusement, and beat his crimson wings. He took off and the others followed him, leaving their assault on the angels. Astaroth was the last to leave, fending off four angels with only one hand and half of his attention on them. The rest was pinned on Lysander as he approached.

Astaroth's mouth quirked into a cold smile and he crooked his finger.

Lysander flew harder, giving chase.

Fool.

He was strong, but not powerful enough to defeat the four angels if they fought together.

Unless he only meant to fight them long enough for Nevar to calm Lysia and stop her from destroying another gate.

Nevar snapped his gaze to her as she raked at the gate with her talons, screeching at it and stopping from time to time to attack the angels swarming around her.

He readied his blades and flew at the angels, determined to force them away from her so he could try to reach her again and stop her from taking down the fourth gate.

Twin blinding blue spherical explosions swallowed the angels ahead of him, leaving holes in the swarm. The angels closest to him turned their focus away from Lysia and towards Amelia and Marcus as they approached with Einar. In the distance beyond them, the golden bursts of Apollyon's power were growing closer. He and Asmodeus were coming to join the main fight to protect Lysia.

Nevar veered left, towards her, leaving the others to deal with the angels and hold them back for him. He had to stop her.

Lukas broke away from Einar, gaining his attention for a heartbeat.

"If you had given me a moment earlier, I would have told you this then," Lukas said, his green eyes swirling as he extended his spear again and halted just a short distance from Nevar. "She is different now. I was watching from the plateau. I saw you injured. I saw her react to it."

A cold chill skated down Nevar's spine and arms.

Lukas was right.

When the Hell's angel had cut him, she had turned her wrath on them, aiming specifically for the two he had been fighting and not launching an attack that would swat at the whole group of them, including him, as she had been before that moment.

He nodded his thanks to Lukas and the angel returned it and joined the fight beside Einar.

Nevar looked across at Lysia as she clawed at the air, battering the angels who dared to fly in front of her and attack her head on.

He could reach her.

He flew towards her and over her great black form. He maintained a few metres between him and the spikes along her tail and then her back, flying between her furled enormous wings and up towards her head.

She swatted the final group of angels between her and the gate away and stilled.

Her immense head turned, her violet eye swivelling towards him, and smoke curled from the nostrils in her beak.

"Lysia," Nevar whispered and sent one blade away. He pressed his left hand to his chest, wishing he still bore the mark that had connected them. He missed feeling her emotions in his heart, but felt sure that she was afraid somewhere deep beyond her rage.

He flew above her head and she tracked him, keeping her eyes locked on him but not attacking him.

Nevar moved his hand to his injured arm and palmed it, squeezing more blood from the healing wound.

Her nostrils flared again.

Her elliptical pupils widened.

"Recognise me," he said and breathed through his fear, not wanting her to sense it. It wasn't a fear of her. It was fear of losing her. "Follow me."

He flew sideways, heading off to his right, intending to lure her away from the gate and the battle raging behind her. Apollyon and Asmodeus were fighting together, cutting a path through the forces of Heaven and Hell, but the two realms had sent reinforcements.

The angels of the apocalypse had joined the fight.

Lysia snorted and stomped towards him, her chest beginning to glow behind the wide plates of her armour that spanned it.

She still wanted to attack him.

He drew in a deep breath, making it last five seconds, and then exhaled it just as slowly.

When the last of his breath had left his lungs, he stilled, beating his wings to hold himself steady in the air ahead of her.

Her huge violet eyes narrowed on him and she snarled.

She didn't trust him.

"Look at me. Am I not like you?" He looked down at his black form and then back at her. "You told me that once. We share more than a similar form, with similar eyes, Lysia. We share a need and we share a desire, and we came to share a heart."

He drew his hand away from his bleeding arm.

"And we share blood."

Her nostrils flared as he held his hand out to her, his palm facing her, coated in his blood.

"Remember me." His violet gaze flickered to the fight beyond her. He was running out of time. The others were struggling to hold back the angels of the apocalypse and the other angels.

He swallowed his thundering heart and gave a single soft flap of his black wings to propel him slowly forwards, towards her huge sharp black beak.

It would be easy for her to capture him now and snap him in half with the crushing force of her beak.

"I am here with you," he whispered and kept staring into her violet eyes as he slowly approached her. "I will never leave you alone again."

Her pupils narrowed into thin vertical lines and he swore her eyes had widened.

Nevar carefully placed his bloodied hand against her hard beak.

She exhaled, her breath hot and fierce, threatening to blast him away from her. He beat his wings to counter the wind and stroked her, feeling her warmth beneath his palm and sensing her fear as it went through him.

He closed his eyes and focused on her, on his blood and hers, searching for a connection to her. Heat travelled through his limbs, spreading outwards from his heart, as he savoured the feel of her and that she allowed him to come this close to her.

She huffed again and he soothed her, running his hand down her beak between her nostrils, and looked at her.

"Come back to me, Lysia. We have a way to restore the bond between us. We can be together again, and I swear to you, I will *never* leave you... because... I love you."

Something shone in her eyes, something that reached deep inside him, right down to his heart, and he swore she was looking at him. Not as a beast who didn't know him, but as the woman he had fallen in love with. That emotion reflected back at him, warming the cold violet of her irises.

"Lysia," he whispered with a smile.

She threw her head back and shrieked, the sound deafening, and stumbled backwards, her wings beating furiously. Her pain shot through him, lancing his chest, and his eyes widened as he searched for what was wrong with her.

His heart stopped.

A glowing white spear penetrated her chest.

The black-haired angel holding it pressed his booted feet against her body and thrust it deeper, ripping another agonized cry from her.

Nevar roared and shot downwards. The male didn't have time to block him. He barely had time to turn towards him before Nevar was on him and had slashed his black blade across the angel's chest. It swept down in a diagonal arc, slicing a line down his black leather-covered armour and cutting into his stomach and side.

The angel beat his black wings and kicked off Lysia's chest, coming at him.

Nevar had hated this angel's twin, Samael, but he despised this angel even more. He didn't care that the angel of the apocalypse was only following orders, doing his duty as dictated by his master. He had dared to hurt Lysia and he would pay with his life for that sin.

A black blur shot between them before the angel could reach him, shadowy tendrils wrapping around his body and sinking deep into his flesh.

Asmodeus.

The dark angel stood off to Nevar's right, his violet eyes bright with fury and his sharp teeth bared at the black-haired angel he held with his shadows.

Asmodeus curled his fingers into a fist and the shadows attached to them tightened around his foe, and he tugged hard, yanking the male through the air to him.

Lysia stumbled sideways, her pain increasing as it flowed through Nevar, and he flew to her. He grabbed hold of the spear and screamed as it burned him, blistering his hands. He refused to let go. He planted his feet against her broad chest and pulled on it with all of his strength.

The spear glowed bright white and he hissed as it sank deeper into her chest and he couldn't hold on to it.

She pushed him back with her enormous right paw and he shook his head and tried to fly closer again, determined to remove the spear for her and end her pain.

She stopped him with one huge black claw, pressing the tip of it to his chest, and he looked up into her eyes.

A wild look filled them and gave way to fear, and Nevar growled as he pushed past her and flew towards the spear.

Bright light exploded from the spear, the shockwave sending him flying through the air. He straightened and flew back towards her, battling through the wind and reaching for her as she looked up at him with terrified eyes and reached for him, her talons stretching towards him.

"Lysia!"

He stretched for her, his wings aching as he tried to fly harder.

The white light reversed, funnelling back into the spear and then died, leaving the weapon black. The armoured plates of her chest that surrounded it rapidly turned dull black and it swept over her body, everywhere it ran turning solid and grainy, like basalt.

Her talons twitched and stilled like a statue.

The violet in her eyes faded, becoming dark grey.

Nevar halted in the air, threw his head back and roared his agony at the ceiling of Hell.

No. He refused to believe what he was seeing. She couldn't be gone. He couldn't have failed her. Not again.

He screamed until he was hoarse and dizzy, his fury blasting through him, mingling with grief and turning him numb before it transformed into something else. Something darker.

Rage.

He breathed hard, his talons and fangs elongating, and his black blades reappeared in his burned hands. He gripped them, not feeling the pain. Physical trauma was nothing, inconsequential.

Eclipsed by the agony tearing apart his heart.

She stood as a statue, cold and motionless.

His beautiful Lysia.

She had only wanted to live, just as he had.

She had wanted to be free and to share that freedom with someone.

With him.

Now, she was gone.

The one good thing in his life, the one thing that had given it purpose and meaning, was gone.

He turned cold violet eyes on the black-haired angel below him.

Rage blazed through him, fiery and hot, driving him to lay waste to the angel and those who had assisted him in killing his beautiful Lysia, stealing her away from him and stealing her future away from her.

He obeyed that dark desire and need, surrendering to it and the release it promised him.

The angel would pay. All would pay.

He would avenge her.

CHAPTER 28

Nevar roared and shot down towards the black-haired angel with one powerful beat of his obsidian wings.

"Stop." Asmodeus held his hand out but Nevar refused to heed his command, ignoring the deep tug behind his breastbone and pushing through the compulsion to halt his attack.

He bared his fangs and slammed into the black-haired angel, knocking him out of the grip of the shadows under Asmodeus's command. The inky ribbons snapped at Nevar, sinking into his calves and thighs, and he snarled at them and slashed with his sword, severing their tips. They shrank back, going to swirl around Asmodeus's hands and feet.

Nevar pushed off the angel beneath him, sent his blade away, and hit him hard with a right hook, and then hit him again, pounding his face as he grasped his throat and pinned him to the ground. A hand closed around his right arm as he went to hurl another blow at his foe, twisted it, and tossed him through the air.

He spread his wings and set his sights on the newcomer. The white-haired one.

"Mihail," Nevar sneered and beat his wings, zooming down towards the bastard as he sought to help the black-haired one onto his feet.

He was as irritating as Astaroth.

Nevar called both of his curved black swords back to him and roared as he brought them above his head, tucked his right knee against his stomach with his left leg pointed below him, and swung hard as he dropped out of the air above Mihail, his swords aimed directly at his back.

The pale-haired one appeared between them, his twin sickle-shaped blades deflecting Nevar's blow, and thrust forwards with both swords, cutting at him.

Nevar beat his wings and shot backwards, beyond the angel's reach. He growled through his fangs at the interfering angel and then set his violet eyes back on the black-haired one.

"Mihail, take Rafael and drop back. Gabriel and I can handle this," the pale-haired one said, his green eyes locked on Nevar, an edge to them that relayed his belief that Nevar was little more than a bug to be trampled out of existence under his heel.

Never.

He bowed to no man, angel or demon.

Never again.

"You will pay for what you took from me." Nevar pointed his sword at the black-haired one, the one called Rafael. "I will bathe this land in your entrails."

Rafael shrugged free of Mihail's grip and smirked at him. "I would like to see you try."

"Rafael," Mihail snapped but his subordinate paid him no heed as he drew a black spear from the air with one hand and wiped the back of the other across his face, cleaning the blood off his chin and mouth.

Nevar breathed hard, lost to the darkness and welcoming it as strength flowed through him and the shadows covering his skin began to bleed from his fingertips, twining around his talons.

He looked down at them and smiled.

It seemed he shared other abilities with his master.

His smile stretched, becoming a grin that flashed his fangs as the shadows fluttered, awaiting his command.

Rafael stared at his hands and his smirk faded.

"Our duty is not done here," Mihail said and Nevar frowned at him. What did he mean by that? "Finish him quickly."

Rafael nodded.

Asmodeus roared and unleashed his shadows, sending them shooting towards Mihail like javelins. The angel was quick to defend with his white sword, cutting through the black spears and beating his white wings to gain ground to evade the rest. Asmodeus flapped his black wings and went after him.

Amelia and Marcus went after the red-haired one, Gabriel.

Apollyon and Einar targeted the nameless pale-haired one, the largest of the four.

Nevar grinned.

Divide and conquer.

Rafael suddenly looked less certain about the outcome of the fight and less inclined to attack him. Never mind. Nevar was happy to make the first move.

He thrust his hand forwards and sent his shadows streaming towards the black-haired angel. The male cut through some with his black spear and dodged the rest. Nevar huffed and twisted his hand, commanding the shadows to pursue his foe.

The angel bared his teeth as one struck his ankle and wrapped around it, swiftly snaking upwards to cover him up to his knee. Nevar yanked his hand back to him, sending Rafael face-first into the sharp basalt pebbles that covered the ground and then lifting him into the air upside down.

Rafael grunted and hung for a moment before hauling himself upwards and slashing through the shadow. It severed and he dropped, hitting the ground on his back.

Nevar sent more shadows after him and pursued them, his one blade at the ready to cut the bastard down when he reached him and his shadows had captured him.

The first shadow struck hard, puncturing the angel's black wing and pinning it to the ground. The rest of the shadows hit in rapid succession, each punching a hole in the angel's wings, leaving him spread out like an insect in a display case.

Nevar raised his sword and roared as he hurtled towards the angel.

A huge explosion rocked the air and shook the ground and he barely had time to look towards the source of it, the gate beyond Lysia's black stone form, before the shockwave hit him. The inky blast slammed into his side, tearing him away from the angel and sending him flying through the air with the others, hurling him far from the rest of his side.

He fought to level off and froze when he managed it, numbed to his core by the crater where the gate had been and the swirling black liquid that spun and twisted above it.

Angels rushed in to contain the liquid that formed the barrier between Hell and the mortal realm as it struck out at the land like a living being. Wherever it touched, things disappeared. Teleported to the other side?

It took out a whole section of the angels.

More raced to replace them, light glowing from their hands as they held them facing the mass of black liquid.

Nevar looked for the others, scanning the angels scattered around the black land. Asmodeus was picking himself up off the ground a short distance away, nursing his left arm, back in his normal form again. Blood covered most of his arm, leaving only a few patches of pale skin visible. Beyond him, Amelia and

Marcus were huddled together, Marcus having taken the brunt of the blast, holding her tucked in his arms with his back to the epicentre.

Einar had been hurled the furthest. Nevar spotted him with Lukas over five hundred feet from where he had last seen them.

Rafael spat blood out onto the black ground a short distance from Nevar and pushed back onto his feet, swaying a little as he leaned on his spear, using it for support.

Nevar called his black blades back to him.

He would finish this while the angel was still recovering from the blow the explosion had dealt.

He beat his wings and advanced a few metres until the ground below shook again and his gaze shot off to his left, towards the fallen gate.

Lysia.

Her charred form broke apart, falling to pieces before his eyes, and he couldn't take it. He clenched his fists around the hilts of his blades and tried to look away and spare himself the pain of seeing the final thing he had to remember her by splintering and crashing down into a pile of rubble, but he couldn't take his eyes off her.

A shiver ran down his limbs and his spine.

Amidst the black pieces of basalt lay a pale hand.

He blinked, sure he was seeing things, was imagining what he wanted to see, but it didn't disappear. It was real.

Rafael spread his wings and took flight, heading towards her broken form and the pale hand sticking out of it. Nevar looked around and his heart hitched as he saw the other three angels were racing in the same direction.

Their mission wasn't over.

Nevar roared and flew after them, determined to reach her before they did.

Lysia was still alive.

Mihail reached her first, grabbed her hand, and pulled her upwards, out of the rubble. Black dust covered her bare body and her head drooped forwards, her dark hair a tangled mess. Nevar focused on her and flew harder when he heard the steady, slow thump of her heart.

"Lysia." Nevar sent one blade away and hurled his right hand forwards, sending his shadows shooting towards her.

They blasted past Rafael and the angel swerved and shot a glare over his shoulder at him.

He ignored him and kept reaching for Lysia.

Mihail looked down at her unconscious form and then back at him, a flicker of emotion crossing his eyes, one that Nevar couldn't bring himself to believe was real. He looked remorseful.

The white-haired angel closed his eyes and lowered his head. "I am sorry, but it must be this way."

Bright golden light shot down, the beam blinding Nevar for a moment until his eyes adjusted to it. In the centre of the column, Mihail lifted Lysia into his arms and tipped his face upwards, towards Heaven.

The light stuttered and disappeared, taking Mihail and Lysia with it.

Three more beams shot down, reclaiming the other angels of the apocalypse.

"No," Nevar roared and hit the ground hard, stumbling a few steps before crashing to his knees.

Asmodeus appeared beside him with Amelia and Marcus but Nevar didn't take his eyes off the pile of black rubble.

"She isn't dead," he whispered.

Asmodeus crouched beside him and placed his hand on Nevar's shoulder. "I know. I sensed it too."

He slid his gaze across to Asmodeus, meeting his golden eyes, and sagged, every bone aching and muscle screaming in agony now that he had stopped fighting and the flood of adrenaline was leaving him, despair flowing in its wake to fill him.

His black form faded away, the shadows slipping from his chest and stomach and running down his arms and legs, stopping just above his elbows and knees. His talons shortened back into normal black claws and his horns shrank.

Lukas and Einar landed in front of him.

Nevar lifted his eyes to the blond mediator. An angel of Heaven.

"What will they do with her?" He wasn't sure he wanted to know the answer to that question, but part of him needed to know it.

Lukas sent his spear away and closed his eyes, his chin dipping as he sighed. "They will incarcerate her."

"I cannot let that happen." Nevar pressed his left hand into the dirt and pushed himself up, slowly rising onto his feet. His legs wobbled beneath his weight. "I cannot. I do not want her to wake alone in Heaven without me… she will be frightened."

A worse situation crossed his mind.

They might keep her unconscious, trapped within her own body, a prisoner subjected to the torture of seeing horrific endless replays of her past deaths.

It was her worst nightmare.

He couldn't let that happen to her again. He wouldn't.

"What will you do?" Lukas said.

Nevar mustered his strength and called his blades to his hands.

"I will take her back. I will set her free." Nevar flexed his fingers around the hilts of his blades. "I will tear down Heaven if that is what it takes."

Asmodeus rose to his feet. A golden blade appeared in his right hand and he placed his left hand on Nevar's shoulder as Amelia and Marcus came to flank him. His golden gaze simmered with red fire as he squeezed Nevar's shoulder.

"And you will not be alone."

CHAPTER 29

The plan was simple.

Nevar just hoped it would be effective.

He sat on the sand in the shadow of the swaying palm trees, a warm breeze stroking his bare chest and his gaze fixed on the bright turquoise water of the shallow lagoon.

When all this was over, he would bring Lysia here, back to the island she had been fond of, and he would teach her how to swim. He would give her that moment of normalcy she had wanted with him, a carefree moment, the sort that lovers should share.

He rested his forearms on his bent knees and studied each small wave that rolled and lapped against the shore, using the serenity of the scene and the steady sound of the ocean to find a sense of peace.

Calm amongst the storm raging within him, darkness that even now threatened to boil out of control.

He pressed his left hand to his chest. He would give it the freedom it desired and the blood and violence it hungered for. All in good time.

Einar and Veiron were busy healing the others, preparing them for the battle that lay ahead.

He had to be patient.

Nevar lifted his jade gaze to the blue vault above him and closed his eyes, pressed his fingers into his chest, and sought Lysia. She was far beyond his reach, but he would tear down the sky to seize hold of her and bring her back to him.

A Hell's angel stalked past him, grunting and dipping his head as Nevar dropped his gaze to the brunet male.

The Devil hadn't called back his guards. Erin had attempted to shoo them away when everyone had returned, but the Hell's angels had refused to leave, stating that their duty wasn't done.

Her father meant to protect her still.

Because the world was burning?

They were far from the devastation, but it was out there, mass destruction caused by the falling of the four gates.

Four gates.

He watched the angel go and then shifted his gaze back to the ocean.

The Devil had left them here not because the world was still in danger from the falling gates. That danger had ended when Lysia had been defeated by Rafael's divine spear, a destiny that had been written in Rafael's genetic code, given to him by his power over beasts.

No, the world was not in danger from Lysia now.

Four gates had fallen.

The world was in danger from the angels who had orchestrated the downfall of those gates and had won.

Nevar had no doubts in his mind. The four who had taken him captive and had killed him were now free in the mortal world.

Free to fulfil their divine purpose.

Asmodeus had explained it all to him, relaying all the information they had gleaned from the Devil.

The four princes would seek to destroy this world.

Nevar wouldn't let that happen. None on this island would. There had been a moment of silence following the revelation that the four princes of Hell were free, a stillness in which everyone had looked at each other and formed a pact without words. They would deal with the four princes together and protect the mortal realm from their wrath.

But first they needed to take back one of their own from Heaven's clutches.

He pushed onto his feet, brushed the backs of his black shorts down, and took one last look at the ocean.

He would return here with her and he would teach her to swim.

He would see her laugh again.

Would see her smile.

He would feel her beneath his fingers.

In his heart.

Right down in his soul.

And he would never let her go again.

He wanted to spread his wings and fly back to the other side of the island, or call a portal to take him there, but he walked instead, conserving every drop of his energy and wasting none. He would need it all if he was to survive what lay ahead.

The soft sand crushed beneath his bare feet as he strode past the Hell's angel meandering along the shoreline, keeping to the shadows as much as he could. The sun cursed him, blinding him as he turned the corner and there were no shadows to be found. He bore the wretched touch of the light and hurried towards the others.

Ahead of him, Asmodeus lay beneath a broad dark green canopy that they had set up on the island as a sort of infirmary after Nevar had insisted on being treated in the shade. He made a beeline for it and breathed a sigh of sweet relief when he ducked beneath the shadow of it, out of the sunlight.

"We need to introduce some therapy about that aversion into your programme," Liora said as she looked up from healing the wound on Asmodeus's left arm.

Nevar raised an eyebrow at that suggestion and stood over Asmodeus, giving his master all of his attention and ignoring how Liora huffed. He knew she was only trying to help him, but the thought of having to spend increasing amounts of time in the sunlight disturbed him. He was fine with living in the shadows.

"Are you close?" Nevar said to Asmodeus and he nodded.

"Liora will be done soon and we can be on our way. The others are ready." Asmodeus grimaced as Liora's purple ribbons of magic burrowed into his skin.

"Sorry," she whispered and frowned at her hands where they hovered bare millimetres from Asmodeus's arm. "It's a tricky one."

Nevar wasn't sure that her magic had caused his master pain because it had been attempting to heal a nasty wound. He felt sure it had been caused by a momentary slip in her concentration, a slip brought about by hearing her male say that he was about to head off to Heaven with only a handful of allies against the entire army of that realm.

Erin had called it a suicide mission when he had wanted to go there before.

Perhaps she would be proven right about that, but he still had to go. He couldn't leave Lysia there.

"I will not let anything happen to him, Liora," Nevar said and she looked up at him, her hazel eyes brimming with the fear he could feel in her. "I swear it. If it is not going well, I will go on alone and send everyone back. Nothing will happen to Asmodeus."

The dark angel huffed. "You speak like I need your protection. Remember who you're talking about. I am your master and more powerful than you are, and I have been to Heaven now. I know I can hold my own against the strongest of their angels."

Nevar almost smiled. "You are right, but I was attempting to reassure your female, not belittle you. I was being noble."

"I appreciate it." Liora withdrew her hands from Asmodeus's arm and sat back. "But I already made him swear that he will come back."

Asmodeus sat up and flexed his fingers, twisting his arm this way and that as he inspected her work.

"I will come back, Little Witch. You have my word on that." Asmodeus leaned over and kissed her.

Nevar turned his back and stepped out into the light again, giving them a moment alone. He crossed the beach to the others where they had gathered by the fire pit and were deep in discussion. As he approached, Veiron broke away from Erin and Dante and came to him.

"I'm going with you," Veiron said and held his hand up when Nevar went to speak. "You don't get a choice. I'm going and that's final. It's even sanctioned by the missus. I can heal and you're bloody well going to need someone with that ability."

Nevar couldn't argue with that. There was no way they would make it across the entire containment facility in Heaven without sustaining some injuries. Having Veiron there might just give them the edge they needed to succeed in their mission.

He walked with Veiron to the others and looked to Lukas, who was deep in conversation with the redhead he had brought to the island with the help of Veiron's ability to cast portals. She smiled, her brown eyes shining at Lukas, revealing all of her feelings for the angel of Heaven. Einar had filled Nevar in about her, calling her Annelie and informing him that she was immortal now as she had gone through the trials together with Serenity so they could be with their angels forever. Lukas had brought her to the island to keep her safe.

The scruffy blond angel had been the one to come up with the plan they were about to execute. Apparently, he and Marcus had done it before.

"When I send you all up there, Marcus will have to move quickly to get the cell open and then free you." Lukas looked from him to the others who would be accompanying him. Marcus and Veiron. Asmodeus joined them too, falling into line with the other two males. "I haven't used this technique to send more than one demon up to Heaven in a single go before, so I'm not sure whether you're going to end up in the same cell or not."

Marcus shrugged, lifting the blue-edged silver breastplate of his armour. "It makes no odds. I will use what remains of my angelic powers to force my way out of the cell and find the others and free them. It might work to our advantage if we do end up in separate cells. I will probably end up releasing some nasty demons in the process of finding them and it'll keep the angels busy."

Apollyon glanced up at the sky. "I will help keep them busy too. My team will provide the distraction and give you a chance to take her back."

It was a risk. Heaven would be expecting them and would shield the fortress, setting up the dome over it that would stop Apollyon and the others from entering but wouldn't stop Heaven from sending out masses of angels to fight them.

Apollyon would need to lead the others into the main fortress, beyond the protective shield, if they were to create a big enough distraction to draw most of the angels in Heaven to them and away from the containment facility.

The male had reassured Nevar that he had an ace up his vambrace that would allow them to make it through the barrier. Serenity had looked nervous then. It seemed Apollyon had used that ace before and had ended up plummeting to earth, unconscious and depleted of power.

Amelia had weighed in at that point and announced that she would be the one breaking into Heaven because her technique, blasting the crap out of the wall with her power until it collapsed, used less energy and had proven effective before. Nevar and the others had agreed with her plan, much to the chagrin of Apollyon. Nevar had reassured him then by telling him that they needed his power in the battle and in what would come after it. He was no use to them unconscious and out of the fight.

Einar and Lukas would go with Amelia and Apollyon. Those four would draw the eyes of their enemy to them, while Nevar's team freed Lysia. Once they had her, they would join forces and then it got complicated.

They had to convince Heaven to leave her alone.

Marcus and Apollyon had convinced that realm to leave Amelia alone. He only hoped that the eight of them could convince them to leave Lysia in their care.

Nevar wasn't going to hold his breath.

And he wasn't going to back down either. If Heaven refused, then he would do exactly what Asmodeus had sent him there to do all those months ago after they had formed their contract.

He would tear that realm down.

"Ready?" Lukas said.

Nevar nodded and stepped away from the others, placing adequate distance between them so they didn't get caught in the blast.

Asmodeus and Marcus joined him.

Veiron bent and dropped a kiss on his son's head. "Be a good boy for your mother now, understood?"

Dante wriggled and reached for him, pressing chubby fingers to his cheeks and then gently slapping them. Veiron smiled, took Dante's arms and pressed another kiss to each of his hands.

"He'll give me hell and you know it. He hates it when you're away." Erin looked as if she was putting on a brave face as she smiled at Veiron. It wobbled on her lips.

"Come here, Sweetheart." He pulled her against him and kissed her hard.

Asmodeus rolled his eyes. Nevar shot him a you're-one-to-talk look. Hadn't his master just done the same thing with Liora, stealing a moment with her that would reassure them both, strengthening their bond before he went off into battle?

Nevar called his armour, replacing his shorts with the violet-edged black pieces, and pressed his hand to his chest.

Lysia.

They would be together again and as soon as they returned to the island, Serenity and Liora would work the spell that would restore their blood bond. He hoped that bond would be the key to showing Lysia that she wasn't alone. He was with her again and he would never part from her. Never.

The bond Liora would restore with her magic would be permanent. Unbreakable even by death.

Lysia would never lose control again.

Veiron finally joined them and Lukas drew in a deep breath and held his hands out in front of him.

"This might sting a little."

Veiron looked on the verge of making a quip when the golden beam of light shot down and covered them. The big Hell's angel threw his head back and roared as his body transformed, growing three feet taller and turning black all over as his demonic side emerged. The red feathers fell away from his wings, revealing the dark leathery membrane beneath, and his eyes glowed golden as his teeth all sharpened and turned crimson.

He wasn't alone in his reaction to the light. It burned through Nevar like an inferno and he gritted his teeth against it, fighting a losing battle to contain the roar of agony that blazed up his throat. He unleashed it as his body followed Veiron's lead, changing against his will, the black shadows sweeping over his skin as his claws became deadly talons and his horns shattered his skull and emerged.

Asmodeus growled beside him, his head thrown back and lips peeling off his enormous fangs as the inky darkness consumed him too, unleashing his other appearance.

Marcus raised an eyebrow at all of them, seemingly unaffected by the burning violent light.

It pulled them upwards and Nevar twisted and writhed as he tried to get his body back under control and shut down the pain. Another reminder that he was no longer an angel.

When he had travelled in the light as an angel, it had felt warm and comforting.

Now it felt as if it was tearing him apart.

Fuck. How many times had he sent a demon to Heaven via this method?

Maybe karma was paying him back for it, condensing the pain of all those demons into one soul-destroying burst aimed at him.

Asmodeus grabbed his arm as white light surrounded them and tugged him into his embrace. Nevar tried to push away, not interested in getting that close to his master, but Asmodeus refused to release him.

Darkness swallowed them.

The fire subsided.

Nevar shoved Asmodeus off him and lost his footing in the pitch black, landing on his backside.

Asmodeus snorted. "You can thank me later."

Nevar reached out with his senses and realised that only he and Asmodeus occupied the cell. His master had grabbed him to ensure they ended up together. Their similar forms and the contract between them must have made them feel like one entity to the light, confusing it.

He heard Asmodeus shuffling around and muttering beneath his breath. Nevar got onto his hands and knees and crawled towards the sound of his voice. He loosed a muffled grunt when he hit something solid, pressed his hands against it and used it to aid him onto his feet. A wall?

He followed the sides around until he bumped into Asmodeus.

"No door?" Nevar said.

"Marcus warned me we would not be able to sense it." Asmodeus's voice sounded even deeper within the dark chamber, edged with steel. "I do not like this."

Nevar didn't like it either, but they were stuck here, voluntary prisoners of Heaven until Marcus freed them. He hoped it wouldn't take long. He leaned his back against the wall, feeling his powers already draining. The detention block had safeties built into it, and one of those was that the cells drained the powers of the demons they contained, until they were barely conscious and only able to answer the questions the angels posed to them.

Not a threat.

They needed to get out of the cells before they were completely stripped of their powers.

Dull light illuminated the cell, revealing grimy white walls that enclosed them in a hexagon. There were thousands of these cells, split into clusters. Each small cluster of around fourteen cells formed a circle with a central area and a path that intersected it. That path curved with each block of cells, forming a ring. There were hundreds of rings of cells, with more cells in each ring as they expanded outwards from the centre of the detention block.

Which ring were they in?

Nevar hoped Lukas had some ability with the light and had been able to place them in cells close to the central white tower.

Lysia would be there.

Brighter light flooded into the room and stung his eyes. He squinted against it and the rectangle came into focus, fading to reveal the centre of the courtyard and Marcus. The former angel stood with his left hand facing towards them, his silver half-feather half-leather wings furled against his back.

The dark-haired male smiled. "I thought you would be in the one with a special blocker. You both must be high on Heaven's interest list since you had a gold door."

Nevar followed Asmodeus out of the cell and looked around him, taking in the other cells that formed the rest of the circle. Some of the doors were black, meaning they were occupied by demons. Some were blue, meaning they were empty. Across from them was a red door.

Another special blocker.

"You think we should let him out to play?" Marcus's smile widened as he eyed the door.

Something banged around inside the cell.

"Erin would never forgive us if we left him here." Nevar headed towards the cell and Marcus followed him with Asmodeus.

It wouldn't be long before Heaven realised they were here and they were free.

Marcus held his hand out again and the door faded. Veiron snarled and stooped as he squeezed through the narrow entryway, his demonic form far too large for the small cell. He beat his leathery wings and rose to his full height, towering over all of them.

"Middle," he grunted, his voice deeper and rougher than normal.

Middle?

Nevar realised he was talking about their position within the containment facility. He beat his black wings to lift himself up to Veiron's eyelevel and scanned the rings of cells. They were dead centre in the rings, still a long way from the bleak featureless white tower that rose in the middle of them.

They had to move quickly if they were going to make it there before they were spotted. The angels who guarded the detention block were some of the strongest in Heaven, and rarely left their posts.

Marcus set about releasing demons from the cells that were occupied. They didn't stick around to thank him. Several rushed off together on foot, sprinting around the ring. The remaining two took flight, rising high above the facility.

Alarms blared.

CHAPTER 30

Nevar took the shrieking wail of the alarm as their cue to get moving. He beat his wings and shot over the first ring of hexagonal white cells, heading towards the central tower in the middle. Lysia. He was coming.

Asmodeus caught up with him, falling in beside him, still in his black form like Nevar. His broad obsidian wings beat the air as he flew, the breeze tousling his black hair and sweeping it back from his horns. His master's violet eyes fixed on the tower too and narrowed.

Veiron grunted as he flew past them, his larger leathery wings beating the air and easily carrying his extra weight in his black demonic form. He pointed off to their left.

Luck was not with them.

Six guardian angels approached, their silver-edged royal blue armour bright in the white light of Heaven and their pale-blue-silver wings steadily beating the cool air, bringing them swiftly towards them.

Marcus shot up into the air high above them, glared at the cells below and swept his hand out in a wide arc.

Every black door that Nevar could see opened and demons piled out, roaring and snarling as they rushed the angels on the ground.

Veiron broke away from them and Marcus joined him, heading towards the six guardian angels still pursuing them. Nevar let them go and set his sights on the twelve who had appeared ahead of him, blocking his path to the tower.

He called his curved obsidian blades and gripped them tightly in his black, clawed hands as he flew hard towards them, refusing to slow. Asmodeus beat him to them, easily cutting down three in one fluid movement, disabling their wings and sending them dropping to the ground. How the hell had he done that?

His master looked as surprised as Nevar felt before turning his black blades on the other angels and attacking them.

Nevar barrelled into the group and slashed at one of the angels. The guardian clumsily blocked his sword and fumbled an attack, and Nevar had his answer.

They were newly reborn.

He smiled wickedly.

Victoriously.

Heaven had sent angels into Hell to stop Lysia and she had decimated most of its forces with the aid of his side. All of those angels had been reborn in Heaven, stripped of their memories, including their knowledge of fighting. Meaning most of the angels in Heaven were now weak and near defenceless.

Nevar roared and cut down two more angels, turned in the air and dealt a heavy blow to a third. Asmodeus had already handled the rest, and Veiron and Marcus were heading back towards them.

This was going to be easy.

Nevar's eyes shot wide as he sensed the swift rise in power off to his left and quickly turned towards the guardian angel there, staring blankly at the silver blade of the spear shooting straight towards him.

Asmodeus barrelled into Nevar, sending him flying away from the path of the blow, and grunted.

Nevar twisted in the air to face Asmodeus and his eyes widened further. His master clutched the staff of the spear the angel had aimed at Nevar, breathing hard and frowning at the guardian at the other end of it. The blond male stared coldly at Asmodeus and shoved forwards, driving the spear's blade deeper into Asmodeus's chest through his black breastplate.

Asmodeus growled through his fangs as he pushed back against the angel, slowly tugging the spear from his chest, pain etched in every line of his face. His shadows twined around the spear, shattering the staff, and slipped from his skin, leaving him.

He paled and dropped to the ground, striking it hard.

Nevar roared and attacked the angel. The male tried to block with the remains of his spear but Nevar knocked it aside with one blade and thrust with his other, driving it deep into his side. Blood rolled down the black blade and Nevar pulled it free of his flesh and turned, bringing his other sword around in a swift arc.

The guardian angel produced another spear and braced it with both hands. Nevar's blade struck the blue and silver staff, the clash ringing loudly across the facility and vibrating down through Nevar's hands. This wasn't a weak newly reborn angel. This one was strong.

He swept his second blade upwards, catching the angel across his right thigh. The male grunted and beat his silver-blue wings, shooting backwards and placing some distance between them. Nevar pursued him and spun his swords in his hands so the guards rested against his little fingers and the dull edge of the curved blades ran along his forearms.

The blond male attacked, shooting towards him and bringing his spear up in a swift diagonal arc.

Nevar raised his left arm, blocking the strike with his vambrace, and brought his right one around, slashing at the angel's chest. The point of his blade cut across the male's blue armour and caught his extended right arm, slicing through his biceps. The angel grasped his spear in both hands and hefted it, breaking past Nevar's defences and knocking him sideways.

He didn't give the angel a chance to land a blow on him. He dropped his left blade, threw that hand towards the blond male and sent shadows rocketing towards him. They struck deep, puncturing his stomach and chest and shooting out of his back.

The angel swallowed hard and then coughed up blood, his blue eyes turning dull as his arms dropped to his side and his spear slipped from his grip.

Nevar recalled his shadows and the male fell, his silvery wings streaming upwards as he dropped towards the cells. Bright light burst from him and he disappeared.

Nevar turned and flew downwards as quickly as he could, heading for Asmodeus where he lay in a pool of blood.

Veiron reached him first, back in his normal more human form, his broad crimson-feathered wings furling against his red-edged black armour as he landed. Marcus joined him and helped him remove the blade from Asmodeus's chest. The dark angel gritted his teeth as it pulled free and collapsed against the white ground, fighting for breath. Nevar slowed his descent, unable to believe what Asmodeus had done. He had taken a blow for him, one that probably would have killed him.

The angel he had plotted to murder so many times had saved him.

He landed at Asmodeus's feet and his golden eyes slowly opened, fixing on him.

"Don't give me that look," he croaked and grimaced, grunting as his face contorted and pain rippled through his power.

Nevar wiped the confused expression from his face and the concern from his eyes and crouched beside him.

Asmodeus struggled to swallow and opened his eyes again. Blood flowed from beneath his black breastplate, covering his pale skin, and he looked down at it, frowning at the wide slash in the metal just to the left of his heart.

"I have only had it back for a few days and look at it now." His master's lips tugged into a humourless smile as he looked back at Nevar. "Go. Leave me. You have to reach Lysia."

Nevar shook his head, causing the strands of his white hair to slip down and caress his forehead. "No. I'm not leaving."

"Insubordinate wretch," Asmodeus muttered and closed his eyes and swallowed again. The pool of blood beneath him spread outwards across the white ground, creeping towards Nevar's boots.

"I don't take orders from you... get used to it." Nevar looked from him to Veiron. "Can you heal him?"

Veiron scrubbed a hand over his scarlet hair and nodded. "It will take time."

Marcus rose to his feet. "I'll hold them off."

The dark-haired angel launched into the air before Nevar could offer to help. Asmodeus grabbed Nevar's ankle.

"Go. Leave me. All of you. You are wasting time." His master shoved his leg, almost knocking him off balance.

Nevar removed his hand from his leg and clutched it. "Liora would kill me if I returned without you and, besides, you cannot leave her, remember? You made a vow that you would be with her and you definitely can't break it now that you're about to become a father."

Veiron paused at his work, his crimson-edged golden eyes darting to Asmodeus. "You're gonna be a dad?"

Asmodeus nodded and paled further.

Veiron's red eyebrows rose and he shook his head, a look of consolation on his face. "It happens to the best of us. Hey, our kids can be playmates."

Nevar could well imagine the hell they would cause together but didn't mention it. He focused on Asmodeus, holding his hand and bearing the pain whenever his master squeezed it so tightly that his bones ached beneath his black skin.

Marcus returned, bloodied and beaten, out of breath, just as Veiron finished closing the wound in Asmodeus's chest and sank back onto his heels.

The Hell's angel looked up at Marcus and sighed. "You couldn't take a few less hits?"

Veiron lumbered onto his feet and held his hand over the worst of Marcus's injuries, a deep gash across his left side. The laceration closed before Nevar's eyes and Nevar was glad that they had brought Veiron along. Without him, they probably wouldn't have made it further than this.

Nevar helped Asmodeus onto his feet and the black-haired angel grumbled in the demon tongue as he fingered the slash in his breastplate.

"I will help you repair it later," Nevar said and his master lifted his golden eyes to meet his. "Are you able to fight?"

Asmodeus nodded and shirked his grip. "Who do you think you are speaking to? Of course I am ready… and now I am angry. These angels will pay for damaging my new armour."

He spread his black wings, beat them hard and lifted off. Nevar followed him, materialising his blades back in his hands, and flew over the rings of cells.

The white tower called to him, almost within reach now.

All that stood between him and Lysia were two dozen angels.

A huge winged demon crashed through the left side of the wall of angels, taking several down with him, tearing into them as they fell.

Twenty angels.

Four against twenty sounded reasonable to Nevar. He liked those odds.

Asmodeus transformed again, his skin turning inky black and his horns emerging, and the gold edges of his obsidian armour shimmering violet.

Nevar followed him into the thick of the angels as Marcus and Veiron flew into them a few metres away, splitting the group in half.

He grunted as the first angel he encountered landed a swift blow on his jaw, snapping his head to one side, and slashed across his chest with a short blade. Nevar shoved his hand into the male's face and pushed him back, and thrust with his sword, repaying the angel by slicing across his hip armour, leaving a deep groove in the blue slats.

A second angel attacked from behind and Nevar arched forwards as the blade cut down his back plate and to the right of his spine. He turned, throwing his weight into the strike, and the angel blocked with the vambrace around his forearm, pushed forwards with that arm to knock Nevar's sword aside, and thrust at him with his blade.

He beat his wings and dodged the blow, and pinned them back to drop when the first angel tried to hit him from behind, ending up beneath both of them.

Nevar unleashed his shadows. They streamed from his outstretched hand, snagged the first angel by his ankle, and he yanked his arm downwards. The angel shot past him and he released him, not waiting to see him crash into the ground. He flapped his wings and shot upwards, towards the second angel, gripping one blade with both hands as he flew. He brought it down by his side and roared as he swept it upwards in a devastating arc, slicing through the stomach of the angel. A flash of light claimed him.

Asmodeus dispatched two angels with one single thrust of his sword, skewering both of them, and a third with his shadows, wrapping them around the male's neck and squeezing the life out of him.

Nevar attacked the next angel who stood between him and Lysia, a younger-looking fair-haired male who was gripping the hilt of his sword so tightly that it shook and his knuckles blazed white.

He sighed and put all of his strength into a swift right uppercut as he reached the male, landing a hard blow on his jaw and cheek and snapping his head backwards. The sword fell from the angel's grip and he dropped, landing hard on top of a cell below Nevar, sprawled out but alive.

He really didn't have the heart to kill newly reborn angels. It seemed cruel of Heaven to send them out to face him and his friends with zero training and experience. Lambs to the slaughter.

Nevar knocked another angel out with the hilt of his sword to the temple as the male dared to attempt an attack on him.

Asmodeus cut down three more of the angels and eyed the two unconscious ones below them. His right eyebrow lifted and he looked at Nevar.

Nevar turned his back on him. Asmodeus could point out that he had lost his mind later. He knew that an enemy was an enemy, but he preferred his enemies to at least know how to wield a sword.

He beat his black wings and sped over the remaining rings of cells. The door at the base of the tower came into view and he swooped towards it, Asmodeus following close behind him. The nearer he came to reaching the immense round white tower, the clearer he could feel Lysia.

He sent his weapons away, pressed his hand to his chest and landed in front of the black door.

"I am here." He reached towards the door with his other hand, his palm facing it, but held back from touching it.

He needed to reach her. He needed to have her back in his arms and know that she was safe.

Was this how Asmodeus had felt when he had come to save Liora from the crystal chamber?

He looked across at the male in question as he allowed the darkness to recede from his body, leaving only his forearms and lower legs black. Asmodeus transformed back too, the inky shadows draining from his bloodstained skin.

When Asmodeus looked his way, he dropped his gaze, unable to look him in the eye when guilt churned his stomach, eating away at him like acid. He had made so many mistakes, and he wasn't sure whether he could ever make amends, or if he would ever deserve the forgiveness of those he had hurt.

Asmodeus placed his hand on Nevar's right shoulder and Nevar briefly closed his eyes, absorbing the silent comfort and forgiveness that his master offered him, and offering the same forgiveness to Asmodeus. They had both done terrible things to each other, but now they could move past those things and work together to create a better future.

The one they both wanted.

Veiron landed on Nevar's other side and Marcus touched down shortly after him and strolled towards the black door.

The former guardian angel held his left hand out to it and the black slowly faded, revealing a dark interior.

Nevar slipped free of Asmodeus's grip and entered the cell, wary of his surroundings in case someone attempted to kill him in the same manner he had tried to kill Asmodeus when he had been on the verge of rescuing Liora.

Lysia lay in the middle of the cold room, her black hair spilling like ribbons of ink across the white floor and her arms wrapped around her knees, tucking them against her stomach and chest. She looked too small and frail like that. Vulnerable.

He growled and held his hand out, focusing on her as he called a black robe. The soft material appeared on her bare body, covering her, stitched with silver embroidery of dragons around the lower third. A garment worthy of his beautiful destroyer.

Asmodeus entered behind him.

"We must move."

Nevar nodded, stooped and scooped Lysia up into his arms. She settled against him, her weight in his arms, her warmth and her scent all a comfort to him, one that brought the reality of everything he had been through over the past few days crashing down on his shoulders. He trembled and tucked her closer to him, telling himself that she was safe now and they would never be apart again. He had no reason to fear.

He had fought for her and he had won her back.

No one would take her from him.

He turned and found himself facing a line of seven angels from different divisions. Not newly reborn. Not even from the normal ranks. These angels were the superior officers of Heaven.

Their power rose, buffeting him, but he held his ground, refusing to fall under the pressing weight of it. Marcus, Veiron and Asmodeus stood their ground outside the cell. Nevar moved to join them, each step draining him as he fought the incredible power of the angels.

He stopped in line with Asmodeus and Veiron, and stared at the seven angels. Marcus glared at one of them, a guardian angel with short sandy hair and cold dark eyes. Did they know each other?

The power they emitted weakened, the pressure on Nevar lessening.

Or was he growing stronger?

He looked down at Lysia where she lay unconscious in his arms. Shadows crawled up his biceps and under his armour, and spread over his thighs. His darker side. As it rose within him, the pressing weight of the seven angels grew weaker, until it no longer bothered him at all.

Asmodeus stepped forwards and tipped his head back, glaring down at the seven angels. Sweat dotted the brow of the one under Marcus's scrutiny. Two more looked ready to fall to their knees.

Even in their injured and weakened states, seven of the strongest angels in Heaven were no match for them.

That knowledge filled him with strength and his power rose with it as his fear fell away. These angels were in no position to take Lysia from him. They would die if they dared to attempt it and they knew it. An angel from the division of death, in his black armour edged with gold, crashed to his knees and the man Marcus targeted with his power followed him. Pain etched deep lines on their faces as they pressed their hands into their knees and breathed hard.

Behind the seven angels, Apollyon landed on the flat top of the white hexagonal cells, his long black hair loose and flowing over his shoulders and his eyes swirling vivid blue. He furled his great obsidian wings against his back.

Amelia landed beside him, frowned at Marcus, and her eyes shone bright silver. She kicked off again, flying to him and slowly descending towards him. He turned his glare away from the single guardian angel he had targeted and raised his left hand to her. She slipped hers into it and drifted down into his arms.

Einar and Lukas hit the roof behind Apollyon hard and huffed as they walked to the edge of it behind the seven angels.

"I am so out of practice," Einar grumbled and pressed his right hand to his bleeding side. "Who knew you could forget the tricks of fighting while flying in only a few years?"

Lukas shot him a smile and raised his hand. "I did. You'll get the knack of it again."

"Are these angels in your way?" Apollyon turned cold blue eyes on the seven.

Two more dropped to their knees and curled over to press their hands into the white ground as Apollyon's power rose, pressing against them from behind.

"I do not think so, but we could ask them, Brother." Asmodeus grinned wickedly, a cruel edge to his golden gaze as he raked it over the angels. "I feel I have not had enough exercise yet today."

Apollyon looked inclined to agree to Asmodeus's suggestion that they take on the seven angels. Nevar stepped forwards to capture their attention and remind them why they had come to Heaven, and that attacking the angels would only lead to more bad blood between their group and this realm. As much as he desired to deal more pain to Heaven, he didn't want to provoke this realm into coming after Lysia.

He hoped to do the opposite.

"You have no right to take her." The sandy-haired guardian angel tried to stand.

Marcus glared at him again and he grunted as he collapsed back onto his knees.

"You are mistaken." Nevar stared down at the male. "You are the one who had no right to take her. She is not yours to keep. She is not Hell's to keep. She is mine to keep. I am her master."

The angel narrowed his dark eyes on Nevar. "You are not her master anymore. You cannot control her. She must be held here."

Nevar dropped his gaze to Lysia's soft face. "I will be her master again. We have a way to restore the bond. With it restored, and with the pledge of Heaven and Hell that they will not seek to provoke her into awakening again, she will no longer be a threat to this world. She will no longer be a pawn in your games."

He slid his focus back to the angel and held Lysia closer to his chest.

"Heaven and Hell are the reason she was created and the reason she awakened... it was because of the war you waged with the demons that she awakened last time." He stepped forwards to tower over the angel and held his gaze, forcing the male to look up at him. "And it was because of the four angels you created, princes of Hell who are now free in the mortal world, that she awakened this time. Heaven and Hell will no longer play with her life and torment her with her death."

Nevar narrowed his eyes on the angel, his irises swirling violet as he unleashed more of his power, using it to warn the seven present that he would crush them if they tried to come after Lysia.

"It is time someone else was responsible for her, someone who loves her and will do all in their power to keep her safe from harm. I will ensure she never awakens again." He reined in his power and the others followed suit, allowing the seven angels to regain their feet and smooth their ruffled feathers.

"In exchange for your compliance in this matter," Apollyon said, drawing the attention of the seven around to him. He stood over them still, atop the cell opposite Nevar, his blue eyes swirling but his power gradually lessening back to the usual level he emitted. "We shall assist you in any way we can in capturing the four fallen angels. We will protect the mortal realm from them."

Asmodeus nodded. "You have our word that we will aid your five angels in seeking out the four fallen and sending them back to Hell and my master before they can carry out their plans. He will put an end to them."

The sandy-haired guardian angel bowed his head. "We will accept your terms. Our four angels have already gone in search of them."

"Four?" Nevar frowned.

The male looked over his shoulder at him. "Lysander has been captured by the fallen. Our four will be able to sense him and may discover his location before anything happens, but the fallen will attempt to destroy his conduit in order to release his power and weaken his brothers."

That didn't sound good.

"What conduit?" Apollyon said, the fire in his blue eyes dying as he looked down at the seven angels. Their expressions turned grave and Apollyon's followed them, his black eyebrows drawing down into a frown.

The guardian angel closed his eyes and lowered his head.

"The female linked to his soul."

CHAPTER 31

Black. It was everywhere.

A slash of red. Small at first. Growing. It flowed like a river, a stream running downwards.

Silence, and then a roar.

The sound startled her, so loud and vicious, and flooded with pain.

Agony that beat inside her.

Inside the river of blood that flowed over deepest black.

White. It pierced the red and severed the black. It glowed so brightly that it blinded her and she tried to reach out to touch it, but it shrank, sinking into the river of blood.

Into her.

She threw her head back and screamed out her agony as white flames ripped through her chest.

"Did it work?"

That voice swam around her in the darkness, a light ethereal sound that she tried to grasp but it slipped through her fingers and sank into the black. A second voice answered it, as soft and warm as the first, appearing as a delicate ribbon of purple that danced across the obsidian sky.

"I don't know… I hope so."

Silence. With more confidence.

"I think so."

She reached for that voice too and the violet ribbon. It curled around her fingers, turned crimson, and dripped from them like blood, fat drops that shone and fell into the endless dark below her.

The pain lessened, drifted away with each drop that fell.

Colours emerged, startling orange and deepest red, splattered across black. Blue and gold followed them, and dusky earthen tones. White streaked across her vision and she reared back, fearing it.

Violet.

It shimmered before her, twin spots on an inky canvas, crowned with silver-white.

The distorted figure came into view, slowly gaining form and sharpness.

"Did it work?"

A male this time, the deep timbre of his voice familiar and comforting.

Come back to me, Lysia.

The words echoed in her mind, shimmering brightly in flashes of violet as she stared at the figure forming before her. He stood with his hand outstretched towards her. Red with blood.

We have a way to restore the bond between us.

Great black wings beat the air, holding him before her, and black covered parts of him. Edged with violet.

We can be together again, and I swear to you, I will never leave you…

His form sharpened. Black horns. Silver-white hair. A flash of an image of her hand running through that hair. A sensation of savouring the silken feel of it beneath her fingers. A brief flood of warmth that poured into her weary soul.

Because…

His violet eyes held her transfixed, his heart shining in them, every emotion that his words relayed straight to hers.

I love you.

Love. A thousand flashes of images careened through her mind. All of this angel who hovered before her, his hand stained with his own blood, pressed against her beak. Not an enemy to be destroyed. An ally.

She pushed and reached for him too, fighting her body, willing it to move. She battled for a voice, a way of telling him the words that beat in her heart.

I love you too.

Sharp fiery pain lanced that heart and she looked down. White. Red. Black. Death.

She threw her head back and screamed.

Warm arms wrapped her in a tender embrace, holding her as she wrestled and lashed out, clutching her chest.

"It is over now. I am here." The deep voice curled around her, coaxing her into calming, soothing away the pain. "Open your eyes and see, Lysia."

She didn't want to. She was too afraid of what she would see. The spear. The white spear. The red river of blood. Her black scales drenched with it.

Death.

But the arms wrapped around her felt like life. It beat through her. Drummed in her heart.

Life. Love.

The scent of salt filled her senses as she gasped down another deep breath. The ocean.

"Come back to me, Lysia."

She would.

She slowly opened her eyes and all she saw was bare skin. The bump of an Adam's apple. The sensual curve of a strong shoulder. The powerful bulge of a tensed biceps.

The delicate form of inked violet wings.

How was it possible?

She breathed through her fear, forcing herself to believe what she was seeing. She was back with Nevar, in his arms, in her mortal form, and the mark that linked them was back too.

She could feel their bond and it was strong. It ran deeper than ever, so all of his emotions flowed into her together with all of his incredible strength.

"That's right, breathe, in and out." His deep voice soothed away the last of her fear and she settled against him, listening to the steady hard beat of his heart against her ear. Tears lined her eyes, burning them. "I've got you."

He did.

She wasn't sure how he had come to have her, but she knew he had fought for her. What she could see of his arm and chest bore more than one set of healing dark pink marks made by weapons.

"Let's give them a moment." Erin's voice held a commanding note, one that drew a smile from Lysia.

She was coming to like the Devil's daughter.

When everyone had drifted far away on her senses, Lysia slowly emerged from Nevar's arms and looked up at him, meeting his soft jade eyes. There was love in them again, deep and endless, and she wasn't sure how to react to it. So she kissed him.

He was quick to respond, gathering her against him, and she waited for him to unleash his passion and master her mouth, dominating her as he always did. He did the opposite, keeping the kiss light, mere brushes of his lips across hers that left her hazy and feeling as if she was floating. When he drew back, she didn't fight him. She looked at him, taking in the fact that he was real. He had kept his promise and had come back to her.

He raised his hand and swept his knuckles across her cheek. "What is that look for?"

"You kept your promise."

He smiled, as beautiful as she remembered him, stealing her breath away. "I always keep my promises."

She should have believed in him. She should have had faith that he would return to her, but instead she had allowed despair into her heart.

Lysia lifted her fingers and stroked the mark on his chest. "I thought our bond broke."

"It did." He caught her hand, the pad of his thumb against her palm and his fingers against the back of hers, and brought it up to his lips and kissed her fingers one by one. "Liora and Serenity went into action when I came around in Asmodeus's fortress and said our bond had strengthened when we exchanged blood. Liora found a spell. We think it worked."

She touched the mark shining on her chest between the two sides of her beautiful black robe, one that she knew Nevar had made for her. "It did work. I can feel you. It's stronger than before."

"I know." He dropped another kiss on her fingers.

"What happened after I..." she trailed off when pain flickered in his green eyes, not wanting to hurt him by mentioning her death, just as she didn't want him to talk about his.

"Heaven took you and we took you back."

"We?" She looked beyond his right shoulder, to the group of angels all milling around by the fire pit, pretending they weren't using their superior hearing to snoop on her and Nevar.

Nevar looked there too. "Yeah. We. I had some help. They fought to protect you in Hell too, and Erin has said you can live here."

She stared at the group of angels and then at Nevar, unsure how to respond to the knowledge that they had all come to her aid. They had fought on her side.

"I wasn't aware," she said and frowned. "In Hell... I wasn't aware anyone was on my side... until you..." She held her hand up, her palm facing him. "You reached me."

She stared at the back of her hand and swallowed hard, unable to get the words out while he was looking at her with such intense eyes.

"You recognised me?" he said.

She nodded. Hesitated. A blush climbed her cheeks. "You told me... you love me."

His hand tensed against hers. Her gaze shot up to meet his. She caught the brief heat that flared on his face before he cleared his throat and sat a little taller, adopting a hard expression that made him even more masculine and alluring. Behind him, Asmodeus nudged Veiron and the two of them grinned in Nevar's direction and began mocking him, pressing their palms together and holding their hands against their cheeks as they fluttered their eyelashes at each other.

Lysia glared at them. Nevar looked back over his shoulder.

The two of them broke apart and went in opposite directions, acting nonchalant.

Just as he began to turn back to face her, Lysia blurted.

"I love you too."

His eyes widened and he tugged her into his arms, dipped his head and kissed her hard, as fiercely as she had craved it before. She clutched his bare shoulders and the mark on her chest hummed as they came into contact. He moaned as if he had felt it too.

He drew back again and stroked his fingers over the mark on her chest, tracing the dragon that curled around the pentagram.

"I won't leave you again… I swear it."

She looked down at his hand and the mark that linked them. "But Heaven—"

He lifted his hand and pressed his finger to her lips, silencing her. "I took care of that. *We* took care of that. Heaven will leave you in my care, where you belong. Nothing will happen to you. I'll keep you safe."

"And I'll keep you safe." She wrapped her arms around his neck and pushed her fingers through the shorter hair at the back of his head.

She sighed as she looked at him and recalled everything that had happened after the fallen angels had taken him from her. Nevar seemed certain that Heaven would leave her alone, trusting him to take care of her, but she wasn't so sure. The only thing she felt certain about was that they blamed her for the destruction she had caused.

"I never wanted it," she whispered and Nevar's silver eyebrows dipped above his jade eyes. "I told Asmodeus when I lost control… I didn't want to become that thing and I didn't want to destroy everything. I wanted to live in this world… with everyone here… with you."

His frown faded and he took hold of her hand and helped her onto her feet. She squinted against the bright light as he led her out of the small hut and closed her eyes as she felt the warm softness of the sand beneath her feet.

"And you *will* live in this world," Nevar said and she opened her eyes, looking up into his. "With everyone here... with me. You weren't responsible for what happened. The four fallen angels behind this will pay for what they did."

He had that look again, the one edged with steel and as sharp as a blade.

It told her everything she needed to know.

He had struck a bargain with Heaven, pledging his sword to their cause if they left her alone and in his care.

He drew her against him, lowered his head and caught her lips in a soft kiss that sent heat radiating outwards from her heart, pulsing through her and filling her with light and hope that chased back the darkness and fear. He kept his promises.

He would never leave her side again.

They would be together now, inseparable, forever, just as both of them wanted and needed to be.

"Come on... everyone wants to see you're alright and then I think we'll see if you float or sink in water." He took hold of her hand, linking their fingers, and she looked down at them.

Her eyes drifted up the length of his arm as they walked towards the group, over the strong curve of his shoulder and to his profile. He had fought for her in Hell. He had fought for her in Heaven. He would never stop fighting for her. She could see that and it touched her, warming her heart and strengthening her love for him. That love would never die.

It was as eternal as the mark that now connected them.

A bond that had filled them both with a new purpose—to save not destroy.

A bond that had given them strength.

A bond that had given them hope for a future filled with light and not darkness.

Lysia clutched that future in her hand.

The hand of the man who had stood by her side and who would always be there, who had captured her heart and now held it within his grasp, forever.

The hand of a warrior who had fought for her and would now fight to avenge her.

The hand of an angel, one not of darkness nor of light, but a perfect blend of both.

He looked down at her, smiled, and twisted her into his arms for another long slow kiss. She surrendered to him, just as she always would, and vowed that nothing would part them.

Never again. Not even death could separate them now. It had tried and it had failed. It hadn't been an ending for them.

It had been the start of their forever.

The End

ABOUT THE AUTHOR

Felicity Heaton is a New York Times and USA Today best-selling author who writes passionate paranormal romance books. In her books she creates detailed worlds, twisting plots, mind-blowing action, intense emotion and heart-stopping romances with leading men that vary from dark deadly vampires to sexy shape-shifters and wicked werewolves, to sinful angels and hot demons!

If you're a fan of paranormal romance authors Lara Adrian, J R Ward, Sherrilyn Kenyon, Kresley Cole, Gena Showalter, Larissa Ione and Christine Feehan then you will enjoy her books too.

If you love your angels a little dark and wicked, her best-selling Her Angel romance series is for you. If you like strong, powerful, and dark vampires then try the Vampires Realm romance series or any of her stand alone vampire romance books. If you're looking for vampire romances that are sinful, passionate and erotic then try her London Vampires romance series. Or if you like hot-blooded alpha heroes who will let nothing stand in the way of them claiming their destined woman then try her Eternal Mates series. It's packed with sexy heroes in a world populated by elves, vampires, fae, demons, shifters, and more. If sexy Greek gods with incredible powers battling to save our world and their home in the Underworld are more your thing, then be sure to step into the world of Guardians of Hades.

If you have enjoyed this story, please take a moment to contact the author at author@felicityheaton.com or to post a review of the book online

Connect with Felicity:
Website – http://www.felicityheaton.com
Blog – http://www.felicityheaton.com/blog/
Twitter – http://twitter.com/felicityheaton
Facebook – http://www.facebook.com/felicityheaton
Goodreads – http://www.goodreads.com/felicityheaton
Mailing List – http://www.felicityheaton.com/newsletter.php

FIND OUT MORE ABOUT HER BOOKS AT:
http://www.felicityheaton.com

Printed in Great Britain
by Amazon